The Black Abbot of Cheng-tu

(annotated)

By G. H. Teed

First Published in the Union Jack magazine, issues 1236-1254, starting 25 June 1927.

Stillwoods Edition 2024

Stillwoods.Blogspot.Ca

Catalogue Information:
Title: The Black Abbot of Cheng-tu (annotated)
Author: G. H. Teed (1886-1938)
Edited by: Doug Frizzle (1949——
First published serially in the Union Jack magazine, issues 1236-1254, starting 25 June 1927.
This Edition by: Stillwoods, 2024
ISBN Canada: 978-1-998819-41-6
Blog: Stillwoods.Blogspot.Ca
Author Blog: http://ghteed.blogspot.com/
Storefront 1: http://www.lulu.com/spotlight/lulubook22

https://tinyurl.com/ve25d42s This link should go to a spreadsheet of all known Teed stories. The list is annotated with various information on the stories and my progress with recapturing the work. The library of Teed's stories increases almost weekly. /drf

Keywords: Sexton Blake, Tinker, Wu Ling, China

Cautionary Note: This series of books by Stillwoods are intended to make the stories of G. H. Teed, born in New Brunswick, Canada, available to collectors and researchers. The editor, or rather digitizer has not altered the original publication.

This story may contain language and racial terms that are not appropriate to today. I apologize for them; I know that the author was using his voice to excite and entertain an adventurous English audience. These works were published from 82 to 110 years ago. Most every work has characters of redeeming ethnicity within.

I hope you enjoy and share these stories; I have.
Doug Frizzle

**Special thanks to Mark Hodder for supplying all of the parts of this, and other stories. **

Contains racial slurs.

Introduction to the Annotated Edition

- Facsimile Reproduction
- Supplementary Information
- Historical Context
- Collectors' Commentary
- Author Biographical Notes

This Stillwoods collection is about the author G. H. Teed. The great majority of his 500+ stories were written anonymously. They also, at the time, were issued under copyright —under the Sexton Blake banner. Teed wrote from 1913 until his death at the end of 1938. Since most of these works were anonymous, no-one knew he was a Canadian —or at least I have never seen a mention.

Teed's novels appeared in 'pulps' mostly —magazines with cheap paper, and issued mostly on a weekly basis. In original format, they are difficult to obtain today in undamaged condition. And they can be expensive!

Included in the ancillary material is the usual advertising for the next weekly issue.

Digitized by Doug Frizzle. This story may have also been digitized by others. Often those copies revise offensive terminology; I have retained the original terms only to indicate acceptable language of the day. Again, I apologize to anyone that might be offended.

I have tried to ensure that this product is faithful to the Amalgamated serial as it was presented in 1927.

About 1920 Teed embarked on yet another of his globetrotting journeys. This was a long trip and there were no stories from him for more than four years.

Evidently he travelled extensively in China, including along the Yangtse River. He is known for his crafted descriptions of foreign lands and the customs of those lands.

Since this novel was published serially, I suspect that no-one had read the complete story for many decades —the issues are hard to find and a series, near impossible.

This story, as mentioned was made available by Mark Hodder, author of the Blakiana website.

The scanning, OCR, proofing and production was all done by me;

I have been unable to find local support for my hobby!

Wu Ling, the villain in this story, appears in a considerable number of the Sexton Blake stories. The 'formula' for the series includes recurring villains.

This novel includes some aspects which are unusual.

One quote caught my interest: "it is little wonder that their untutored, unopened minds are ripe fields for the preaching of any crazy doctrine that comes along." (speaking of the Chinese nearly 100 years ago.)

There are also elements of science fiction in this story. Cold fire —or light without heat is mentioned. There is the use of what we call television —one that did not require cameras to capture the images. Television is a sleuthing tool of Wu Ling —as it had been available in China for generations!

And the strange qualities of the 'People of the Pits' are certainly otherworldly.

Similarly otherworldly, there is a river under the Yangtse River, and it runs in the opposite direction; so that Blake and Tinker can speed up-river, so to speak.

This story appears to be very highly regarded by some readers of the time —'his best work'.

I had fun assembling the pieces, it was long work, and often read out of sequence, until the last read.

I hope you enjoy it.

Doug Frizzle
September 2024

Contents:

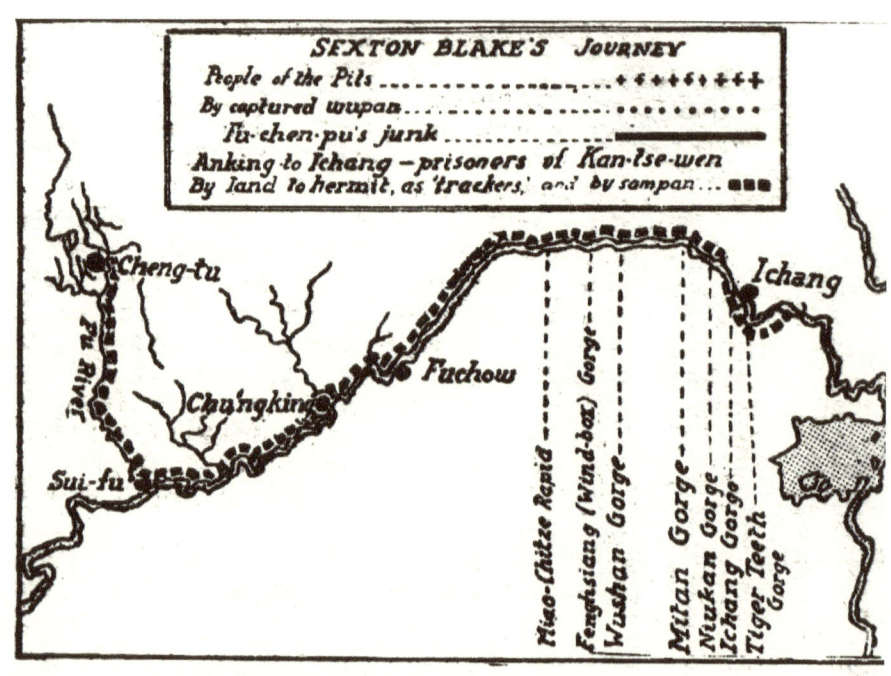

SEXTON BLAKE'S JOURNEY

People of the Pits .... +++++++++

By captured wupan .... •••••••••

Fu-chen-pu's junk ....

Anking to Ichang — prisoners of Kan-tse-wen

By land to hermit, as 'trackers,' and by sampan ... ■■■

Cheng-tu

Fu River

Chungking

Sui-fu

Fuchow

Ichang

Miao-Chitze Rapid ----

Fenghsiang (Wind-box) Gorge ----

Wushan Gorge ----

Mitan Gorge ----

Niukan Gorge ----

Ichang Gorge ----

Tiger Teeth Gorge ----

MAP of the River Yangtse, showing Sexton

See also Endplate for a modern map.   /drf

vi

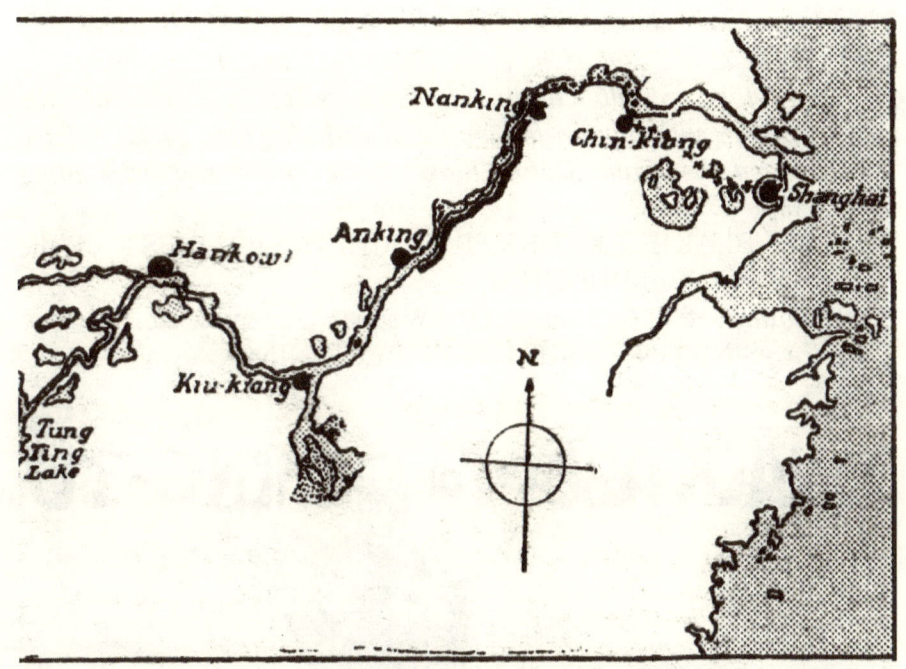

Blake's route from Shanghai to Cheng-tu,

Notes: This serial was later reprinted as a serial in THE BOYS' FRIEND LIBRARY starting second series issue 254 (1930) but with many revisions — the main one being the replacement of Sexton Blake with Ferrers Locke.

This cover adapted from 'The Terror of Tibet', the serial that started with issue 2/254 of the Boys' Friend Library, 4 Sept. 1930

(For this re-publication, I have selected little of the supplementary information for inclusion with this long serial. I have not included the main Sexton Blake stories from any originating issue....drf)

SEXTON BLAKE and TINKER in CHINA, in QUEST of the GOLDEN BOOK of BUDDHA.

By the Author of: "The House of the Wooden Lanterns," etc., etc.

THIS FASCINATING SERIAL NOW BEGINNING!

The Union Jack —No. 1,236.

THE BLACK ABBOT OF CHENG-TU

SEXTON BLAKE and TINKER in CHINA, in QUEST of the GOLDEN BOOK of BUDDHA.

By the Author of: "The House of the Wooden Lanterns," etc., etc.

THIS FASCINATING SERIAL NOW BEGINNING!

Part 1

The Creaking Darkness.

THROUGH the night mist that hung over the wide, muddy waters of the Yangtse crept a small river steamer, breasting the current with just sufficient movement of her propeller to make headway against it.

On either side were the banks, half a mile away to port and starboard —invisible through the wet blanket of mist. Hidden, too, were junks and sampans and wupans, all the myriad craft of the great river, but —they were there.

Eighty miles astern of the Che-sen lay Hankow; several hundred miles farther up was Ichang, the great walled city at the head of the first stretch of navigation on the way to the Upper Yangtse. Between were Yochow and Chungting, Changsha and Hsien Fu, and scores of other towns and villages which found their pulse of life in the flow of the great river which cuts China in half, and flows from the borders of Tibet in the west to the Yellow Sea in the remote east.

Slowly, stubbornly, the Che-sen pushed her nose against the mighty thrust of the river. In the wheelhouse the Chinese captain himself was at the wheel. On a night like this it needed a careful and knowing hand to get the "feel" of the river, and Fen-to had learned his first lessons in the whitewater gorges above Ichang.

Originally the Che-sen had been a harbour launch at Shanghai, in the service of Jardine's, the great European shipping firm. But now she belonged to the Hankow Navigation Guild —a Chinese organisation which had entered into competition with the foreign firms on the Yangtse. And on this occasion the Che-sen was on a very special and secret charter. She carried no passengers, but in addition to the crew of forty men there was a well-armed guard of sixty soldiers, every one of them a trained and trusted man from Peking. For the Che-sen carried in her safe that which was more precious than aught else in the whole vast expanse of the Middle Kingdom.

Outside the chart-room, the Chinese mate leant over the rail, peering ahead into the night. Not that he could see even as far as the stem of the ship; but it is more by "smell" and "feel" that the river men on the Yangtse sense the nearness of danger, and neither the mate nor the captain would relax vigilance for a single moment until the prize they carried had been safely handed over at Ichang.

Now and then the mate would creep to the side and, with head twisted round, listen to the murmur of the unseen life of the river. At regular intervals he would put his head through the open window of the chart-room and report all well. Then he would fade into the darkness (for the lights on the Che-sen had been doused) to listen and watch once more.

It was getting on for midnight, and a hundred miles had been logged since leaving Hankow, when from somewhere across the muddy bosom of the river a creaking sound reached the ears of the mate. He listened intently, his sloe-black eyes screwed into oblique slits in the effort of concentration. It was a steady, grinding sort of sound, which seemed to come from above, then from below, and again from directly opposite him. A second murmur of different timbre chimed in, and then a third. With the rising of this the mate waited for no more. Like a shadow he passed to the window of the chart-room and, putting in his head, he whispered:

"The sounds grow, honourable sir."

The captain, a short, wiry Celestial, dressed as a European, and with a broad, intelligent face, nodded slightly. He had learned the higher mysteries of navigation in a European ship running from Shanghai down the coast, and he knew his business.

"Pass the word below," he said curtly. "Each man to his post — and silence! The sign will be one stroke of the bell. I shall give the light if the attack comes."

"I go, honourable sir."

With that the mate stole away, and, swinging a leg over the rail, dropped to the deck below. Here were men crouching low on every side, men armed with short cutting swords and modern automatic pistols. A whisper travelled swiftly along the line, and in the shadows there was a stirring, accompanied by the faint scrape of metal as swords were loosened.

Now all ears were strained to listen. Across the water could be heard more plainly than ever the steady creak-creak of heavy sweeps as they ground in the hollows of their supports. Somewhere out there many craft were on the move —how many no one could know.

But their nocturnal, sinister business was bringing them nearer and nearer to the Che-sen, and —with the knowledge that not only the hordes of pirates of the river, but others as well, would sell their very ancestors for what the small river steamer carried on that secret journey —it behoved those on board to be on the *qui vive.*

Up in the chart-room the captain had just given the wheel to a man who had been standing by. He himself had moved to the open window, and with one hand resting on an electric switch was leaning out, listening. Presently the mate crept along and whispered what he had done; then the captain waved him back to the lower deck.

"Keep the foredeck, Li!" he ordered, in a low tone. "Leave the after deck to the captain of the guard. Every man at his post, and if they come give no quarter. At the word I shall give the light."

The mate disappeared, and for the next five minutes or so the Che-sen drove on, while the sound of many sweeps came closer and closer. Once, from the foredeck, a low voice came floating up, warning Fen-to that something was coming out of the blackness of the mist; then the voice sighed away as Fen-to gave vent to an imperative "chut" demanding silence.

From what source did Fen-to fear this attack would come? Was it from the hordes of river pirates who infest the Yangtse? Was it from the Cantonese forces who sprawled across the great river waiting their chance to break the line of the Northern allies close to Shanghai? Or was it from some other source? He was soon to know.

Silently he motioned to the quartermaster to take the wheel. This man had been standing by ready, and as his long, yellow fingers slid round the spokes, Fen-to muttered:

"Keep her as she goes, Wu."

Then he reached for the engine-room signal and jerked the handle once. Almost immediately the murmur of the engines increased as they were thrown into full speed ahead, and, with the quiver of that under his feet, Fen-to glided out on to the deck. He paused at the rail and listened. The creaking sound of the invisible sweeps seemed to be all about him, plainly audible above the noise of the engines. There was something terribly sinister about the menace of that sound. There were many craft there, Fen-to knew —junks and sampans and wupans and what-not. Like carrion they were collecting about the Che-sen, picking her up in that blanket of mist with uncanny precision, surrounding her like wolves round a dying moose.

Beneath the rail, half-shadows could be glimpsed moving restlessly as the pitch of waiting grew. Something appeared on the ladder leading to the upper deck where Fen-to stood, and a moment

3

later Li, the mate, was whispering:

"They are close, master. It is time for the bell."

Still Fen-to waited. His fingers were resting on the electric-light switch which would throw the whole vessel into a blaze of light. From the moment he had guided his craft out of Shanghai he had been on the qui vive for this that he sensed was coming. There were many of his race between Shanghai and the far borders of Tibet who would do much to gain possession of the sacred prize he carried. He had been well warned by those who had sent him. There was Chen and all the mob in control of the Cantonese. How they would lick their chops with glee could they but grasp that prize! How the deep-set eyes of the Chuen-to-yan of the Temple of Eternal Purity in Canton would glow at sight of the precious object which had been spirited out of Peking! There was Kan-tse-wen, the notorious chief of the river pirates —known as the Terror of the Yangtse, who would turn his thousands of rascals loose did he but guess that such a prize was within his grasp. And there was that mystery figure who loomed more sinister than all others —he who was spoken of in whispers as the Black Abbot of Cheng-tu.

So close did the sounds seem that he thought each moment would reveal the ghostly shape of the junks which were crowding in. Now there was imminent risk of a collision as the Che-sen raced against the flow of the river. But it were better to chance that than loiter along and make easy picking for the enemy. And still Fen-to waited until another urgent whisper came from Li. Then Fen-to gave utterance to one guttural command:

"The bell!"

Li dropped to the deck in a flash. The next instant there rang out a single, vibrant clatter as he struck the bell, and scarcely had the throbbing died away when Fen-to pressed the switch, and instantly the Che-sen became outlined with light from fore and aft.

For the space of five seconds or so she was a brilliant patch, alone in the mist; then there swept into the constricted area of light the clumsy form of a junk, followed by another and another, and then an appalling outburst of screaming.

Fen-to steadied himself against the rail and
lifted the pistol. Carefully he aimed, and pulled
the trigger. And, at the impact of the bullet,
the masked man in the black robe staggered
back.

The Coming of the Black Abbot.

THAT first outburst was but the forerunner of pandemonium.

There is no sound more terrible than the demoniacal yelling of a
Chinese mob bent on murder. In that fury which burst from hundreds
of throats the first impact of the Che-sen with the junks was scarcely

5

heard. The staunch little craft pressed and worried and panted against the wooden walls which enclosed her, but she was held securely. In the twinkling of an eye a score of bamboo hawsers were thrown on board; and after these came the rush.

Fiendish faces appeared as the human stream poured down upon her. Frightful demons, yelling with the blood lust, came in wave upon wave. Sampans and wupans crowded in beneath the high, angled sterns of the junks, and half-naked devils, knives gripped between yellow fangs, swarmed up, swinging with the agility of apes from hawser to hawser and rail to rail.

Came the crashing of weapons as the guard on the Che-sen steadied for the defence. Smoke and screams and the clashing of swords as the defenders met the first rush over the bows. Then the attacking mob was up the sides, and a more distant racket told that still another gang was at the stern.

Fen-to, standing alone on the upper deck, had watched the first onslaught with never a trace of emotion. He was worthy of a better command than that small river-boat —a brave, conscientious man, who would sell his trust and his life dearly. In one hand he was dangling an automatic pistol, but not during that first rush did he use it. He was watching and waiting for something —someone. He could not tell yet just what gang this was that had come upon him — Cantonese or pirate or the men of the mysterious Black Abbot of Cheng-tu.

He had stationed his forces in anticipation of a general attack. Half were at the bow defence, half were at the stern, and his own crew had been divided along the narrow side gangways. Li, the mate, was watching the stern. Even above the din that was now raging he could hear the peculiar, high-pitched scream of the mate, accompanied by the steady pop-pop of the shooting.

In the first clash there beneath him a full score of the enemy had gone down. Some of the guards were down, too, and within a few minutes the deck would be a shambles. Yet still Fen-to stood watching, as if his interest in the affair were purely detached; still fresh hordes swung over the rails, shooting, cutting, screaming, in a confusion of murderous fury that beggared description.

And then suddenly Fen-to saw that for which he had been seeking. Now he knew whence this attack had come.

Swung broadside on to the bow of the Che-sen was a great junk that effectually blocked any advance of the little steamer. It had been one of the first to close in, and it was from this that the chief onslaught had come. The bow lights of the steamer threw most of one side into sharp relief, although beyond that was abrupt shadow.

It was from this shadow that a figure appeared —a tall, black-robed figure topped by a demon's mask. Through the screaming devils who had come springing along from junks farther out, it moved slowly, until it stood close to the side, gazing down through that weird headpiece at the shambles beneath.

The Black Abbot of Cheng-tu!

Fen-to steadied himself against the rail and lifted his pistol. Carefully he aimed it, and pulled the trigger. That he had shot truly was certain, for at the impact of the bullet the masked man in the black robe staggered back. But only for a moment. Immediately he recovered, and straight at Fen-to peered those devil's eyes in the mask, as if the creature were mocking him —taunting him across that shambles at his inability to kill.

A throaty gurgle sounded in Fen-to's throat. This was black magic! Was the bullet of wool, that it had failed to pierce the other's heart? Or was this sinister and mysterious creature, about whom men whispered along the whole length of the Yangtse, immune from death at the hand of a human?

Fen-to possessed a full share of the superstition that is such an ingrained part of the Celestial mentality. He believed in all the gods and spirits of his race; he would as soon have flouted sacred Buddha as to sail in a craft that did not bear the two eyes painted on the bow to keep at bay the evil spirits of the waters. But he had mixed much with Europeans, and he had profound faith in the efficacy of a bullet when fired from an automatic pistol. He was as certain as he stood there that the leaden missile had struck that cloaked figure, and yet the other stood there unharmed, calmly watching the hell's fury he had let loose.

Again Fen-to pulled the trigger. And again the Black Abbot of Cheng-tu stood unscathed. A thrill of fear passed through Fen-to. This was magic, black magic. Who could fight against one from whom the bullets passed off as drops of rain? No river pirate was this thing of the leering mask; no Cantonese freebooter was it standing there, silent and watchful. It was the mysterious Black Abbot of Cheng-tu, none other.

And then Fen-to thought of the sacred treasure of which he was custodian. He had pledged his sacred oath on Buddha that he would guard that with his life. For some reason which he dared not ask, it had to be taken from China to Tibet, but the first part only of the journey concerned him. At Ichang his responsibility would be ended. But he must get it there.

A sudden onrush of the attacking party drove the guards back along the deck until the fight was raging just beneath Fen-to. The yells from the direction of the stern sounded more demoniacal than ever, and Fen-to guessed that Li was being hard pressed. Along the side gangways there was such confusion it was impossible to tell how things were going. But here in the bow under the masked eyes of the Black Abbot was the key to the situation. It was time for him to rally his men.

With a sudden yell that rose even above the screams beneath, he dropped among them. Through the scattered ranks of the guards he plunged, shooting as he went. This time there was no doubt about the effect. Man after man went down in the welter, and when the hammer came down with a click with no explosion Fen-to hurled the weapon into the face nearest him, and, snatching up a sword, swept forward like a madman.

A thousand Celestials such as Fen-to was in those ensuing minutes would have conquered China. Single-handed, he drove back those yellow fiends until they were crowding at the rail. Into them and about them he raged, striking, cutting, thrusting, hacking with a superhuman ferocity that carried all before it.

For the space it lasted he dominated the entire scene. Even the sinister, black-robed, and masked figure of the Black Abbot of Cheng-tu was forgotten under the terror of that dripping blade. And then, loud and clear above the din, a voice issued from beneath the grotesque headgear.

"Dogs of dogs! What doest thou?"

As if stung by a lash, the mob came out of the stupor into which Fen-to's fury had driven them. Half a hundred throats expanded in a fierce yell that hammered against the eardrums and beat across the mist-laden waters. With one accord they closed in about that gallant, lone figure —swords flashed, knives jabbed in and out, half-naked devils danced a fandango of death, and Fen-to was lost beneath a yellow wave.

To his knees they beat him, while the deck grew slippery with the crimson lifeblood. He staggered to his feet, and in a last supreme effort got the point of his sword against the very breast of the Black Abbot. Into that thrust there went the supreme effort of his spirit, and yet the point was stayed even as the bullet had been turned aside.

Again he was beaten to his knees. There was a squeal of rats as the sword dropped from his hand. Then his end came, under a score of blades.

The rest was slaughter. Fen-to had said "no quarter;" there was none. From stem to stern the Black Abbot's devils swept, cutting and thrusting until of all that company who had sailed out of Shanghai but one being escaped alive. That sole survivor was Li, the mate, who in the confusion managed to throw himself into the river, and under cover of the mist found a way out between the junks.

As for the precious treasure which Fen-to had carried, and which had cost him his life, it was carried in the safe which held it to the cabin of the Black Abbot's junk. Then the Che-sen was scuttled and the muddy waters of the Yangtse closed over another tragedy of the great river.

Eastward Bound.

TINKER was absent from Baker Street when Mr. Hong-Lo-Soo, the wealthy Chinese merchant of Packer's Court, in the East End of London, called on his master, Sexton Blake.

Consequently, he got something of a shock when he entered the consulting-room late in the afternoon to find his master turning out the drawers of his desk. This sort of thing almost invariably presaged a lengthy journey, and his eyes were full of interest as he inquired the reason.

"We leave for China to-morrow morning," was the crisp answer. "You will have your hands full to-night, young 'un, with the packing. We shall catch the eleven-twenty from Victoria and travel overland to Marseilles. We can just catch the Japanese boat there."

"China, guv'nor! My aunt! It isn't so long since we returned from there. What's the stunt this time?"

"I'll tell you later," grunted Blake. "I haven't time now, but you can take it from me that it is likely to be a long job."

It was true that Blake and Tinker had been in China not long before, during the most strenuous part of the revolution, but that did not mean that Tinker was averse to returning. On the contrary. China usually meant as much action as even Tinker desired.

"Was it a cable, guv'nor?"

"No —Hong-Lo-Soo. Now get busy; you will have your work cut out to get ready."

Tinker said no more then, but that evening, when the packing was well in hand, he again broached the subject to Blake. The detective, who was seated in one of the low saddle-bag chairs in front of the fire sunk in thought, roused himself.

"I'll give you a few particulars, young 'un. Hong-Lo-Soo came to see me this afternoon when you were out. Something has happened out in China that has created a nasty situation. We are going out to try and straighten things out."

"But just what is it, guv'nor?"

"I have told you enough about Chinese conditions —religious and social —for you to know that for several centuries there has been a strong rivalry throughout Asia between Tibetan Buddhism and the Buddhism of South China."

"Yes, guv'nor, I remember that. The Grand Llama at Tibet doesn't pull at all well with the Chuen-to-yan of the Temple of Eternal Purity in Canton."

" 'Doesn't pull' is right," remarked Blake dryly. "In other words, Tinker, despite the fact that the Grand Llama is the supreme head of western Buddhism and the Chuen-to-yan at Canton is the leader of the eastern Buddhists, they are deadly enemies. The Buddhist faith is a peculiar one. It is an extraordinary mixture of superstition, symbolism, and metaphysics. It is really beautiful in many ways — when it hasn't been debased. To my mind the Buddhism of Tibet is a fine and pure faith.

"Well, there is one thing that is the most treasured relic of Buddhism. This is a very ancient book known as the Golden Book of Buddha and, theoretically, it should be in the keeping of the supreme head of all Buddhists, just as certain relics are in the keeping of the Pope at Rome as the head of the Catholics.

"Until four or five hundred years ago —the exact date is rather vague —this Golden Book of Buddha was in the keeping of the Grand Llama at Tibet, and he was recognised without question as the supreme head of the religion. But in some way, probably by theft, this book was taken from Tibet and smuggled into China. Ever since then it has been under the care of the Chuen-to-yan (High Priest) of the Temple of Eternal Purity at Canton, and with that in his possession he has been a formidable rival of the Grand Llama.

"Needless to say, the Tibetan Buddhists have plotted and schemed all those years to get the Golden Book back in their possession, where it rightly belongs, but until very lately they did not succeed. Some months ago, however, it was spirited out of the Temple of Eternal Purity, and while no definite statement has been made to me, I have a feeling that Hong-Lo-Soo and our old friend Sir Gordon Saddler could tell a story about that.

"At any rate, it was got away and hidden in Peking until a favourable time should come for it to be taken through to Tibet. You must understand that Hong-Lo-Soo and millions of the northern Chinese are adherents of the Grand Llama of Tibet, and not of the Chuen-to-yan at Canton.

"About six weeks ago it was thought an attempt might be made, despite the confusion reigning throughout China. Every care was taken to ensure secrecy. A private river steamer was engaged in charge of a man who could be trusted to the death. His job was to get the Golden Book as far as Ichang on the Upper Yangtse, and there hand it over to another agent who would get it as far as Chungking, and so on it would go by stages until it was over the Tibetan border.

"Well disaster overtook the attempt. The river boat got safely through the Cantonese lines and past Hankow, but between Hankow and Ichang it was attacked one misty night."

"I can guess what that was like," put in Tinker when Blake paused.

"We've had some of that ourselves."

Blake nodded.

"Quite right, young 'un' and that is just what I was thinking of. Well the attack was a success. A clean sweep was made. With the exception of one individual every soul on board was slaughtered. That sole survivor was the mate, and it was he who managed to get back to Shanghai and tell what had happened.

"From what Hong-Lo-Soo told me I should say there is an extraordinary element of mystery about the whole affair. When we were last in China, do you recall hearing me speak of a mysterious person who was called the Black Abbot of Cheng-tu?"

"I heard you mention that name to Sir Gordon Saddler, guv'nor."

11

"Quite right! I don't know anything about this person and, in fact, I suspected he might be just a legend. But it would appear that such an individual really does exist and that it was he who led the attack on the river boat which was carrying the Golden Book of Buddha. The mate told a very wild story, according to Hong-Lo-Soo, but out of the confusion of it there would seem to emerge the indisputable fact that a mysterious black-robed figure, his features concealed under one of those fantastic masks such as religious actors in China wear, did lead the raiders. And the Golden Book of Buddha is now in his possession. It is our job to try and run that mysterious individual to earth and get possession of the Golden Book."

"Phew! It strikes me we are biting off a pretty good mouthful, guv'nor. It will be like looking for a needle in a haystack to find a single person among four hundred millions of Chinese."

"I do not think I should make the mistake of underestimating the difficulties, Tinker. At the same time, that Golden Book is too great a prize to be allowed to get back into the hands of the Cantonese Buddhists if we can prevent it. We know that the Cantonese are anti-British to a man; we know further that the Grand Llama at Tibet is very friendly to the British. For the sake of our own country it behoves us to do what we can."

"And the Black Abbot of Cheng-tu, guv'nor —what about him?"

"We cannot even make a guess about him until we run him to earth and unmask him. But I want to warn you that we have never embarked on a more dangerous mission than this promises to be. From the moment we leave Baker Street we shall need all our wits about us."

"I shall not forget it, guv'nor. We've diddled the Chinkies before, and we can do it again."

Blake frowned at Tinker's levity. He made as if to speak in reproof, but then he changed his mind and, rising, went back to his desk. But in proof of the need of Blake's warning was a pair of oblique eyes which lurked in the garden at the back of the house. Those same eyes had been keeping surveillance on Hong-Lo-Soo for many days past, and since the merchant's visit to Baker Street that afternoon their interest had been transferred to Blake's household.

BLAKE did not book passage by the Japanese liner past Hong Kong. His idea was to begin tentative inquiries there and, if possible, have a talk with Sir Gordon Saddler if that wise old gentleman was still on the China coast.

He realised that Sir Gordon (or, as he was known to the Chinese, who never suspected he was a European, Hsui Fsi), the Mystery Man of 'Frisco, might be able to give him valuable assistance.

Hong-Lo-Soo had not been able to tell Blake whether Sir Gordon would be in China or not, so Blake had sent a cautiously-worded cablegram to an address which he knew would find Sir Gordon if he were in China. But, in any event, Blake intended to break the thread of his existence as Sexton Blake at Hong Kong.

He did not lose sight of the possibility that his leaving London would be known. If it were known that Hong-Lo-Soo held a deep interest in the fate of the Golden Book of Buddha and that some weeks after its disappearance he had visited Sexton Blake, it was quite on the cards that Blake's movements would be watched, for no foreigner had played a more prominent part in China of recent years than Blake.

Hence his desire to drop from sight utterly as soon as he should reach the coast. Had it been feasible to do so before he would have tried to manage it, but that was out of the question.

From London to Marseilles nothing untoward was apparent. Neither Blake nor Tinker knew that a Celestial had lain in the garden at the back of the house all night, and had later witnessed their departure from Victoria. Nor could they guess that this same individual had left Croydon in an aeroplane, specially chartered for a straight run through to Marseilles, less than two hours after their train steamed out.

There were plenty of Orientals of all degrees on board the Kisu Maru, and it was impossible to know that among them was one who had left London after them. But from the moment they stepped on board they were once more under surveillance, and over them was an invisible cloud of menace that was due to break into a storm long before they reached Hong Kong.

It was when they had passed through Suez, had left Colombo behind, and were lying at Singapore that the first incident occurred which told them they were marked. All the way out Blake had not relaxed his caution. Even at Colombo he would only consent that they should go ashore together, and that in daylight. Tinker was of the opinion that Blake was rather overdoing it, but at Singapore he learned a lesson that very nearly cost him his life.

From Colombo Blake had sent a wireless message to Lung-Ying, Hong-Lo-Soo's agent in Singapore, advising him that they would be arriving in the Kisu Maru, and adding certain code words which told the Chinaman that if he had any secret word from Hong-Lo-Soo he was to bring the message to the ship.

On docking at Singapore, a young Celestial came aboard with a letter from Lung-Ying, making profuse apologies for not being in attendance, and explaining that he was laid up with fever. He informed Blake that he had received a message from Hong-Lo-Soo, and if Blake would forgive his non-attendance to the extent of coming to his house he would give it into his own hands.

In view of that, there was nothing else for Blake to do; so late in the afternoon, they got into rickshaws and drove to Lung-Ying's villa.

They found the merchant looking very ill indeed, and as soon as Blake had finished his business with him he made to depart, realising that the sick man should return to his bed with the least possible delay. Then, since they had come ashore, he thought it safe enough to go on to Raffles' Hotel for dinner. There would almost certainly be other passengers there, and it would be easy enough to arrange to return to the ship in a crowd. Blake knew his Singapore only too well, and was taking no chances.

Owing to this change of plan, it was past ten o'clock when they got away from the hotel. As Blake had anticipated, there were several fellow-passengers with whom they could return; but, even so, it was with an inward sigh of relief that Blake found himself once more on the promenade deck of the Kisu Maru. For some days past he had been suffering from a deep and unaccountable depression. A foreboding that evil hovered over him and the lad had seized upon him, and, try as he would, he had been unable to shake it off. Before another hour was past he was to discover just how well-founded it was.

Instead of night bringing relief from the heat, it seemed stickier than ever down by the docks. Even the harbour side of the promenade deck was like a furnace, and, on arriving back, both Blake and Tinker were glad to seek their large double-cabin, where the air, churned and re-churned by an electric fan, was more bearable.

"I think I'll get into pyjamas and read in my berth, young 'un," yawned Blake, as he slid out of his white coat. "This is a steam-bath to-night, and no mistake!"

"You've said it, guv'nor! I see wisdom in your suggestion. Thank goodness we get out of here to-morrow morning!"

He sat down on his own bunk, and, stripping off his coat and collar, began idly to examine a twisted Malay kris, which he had picked up in one of the small bazaars earlier in the evening. The blade and handle were orthodox enough, and exactly similar to the type that might have been picked up anywhere between Sourabaiya and Saigon; but it had been fitted with a wooden case, covered with shagreen of particularly fine quality, and this it was that had caught Tinker's eye.

"Was there anything from Hong-Lo-Soo, guv'nor?" he asked, when Blake had stretched out on his berth, with a sigh of relief.

"Nothing but a warning, young 'un. I shall be glad when we reach Hong Kong. We shall drop out of sight there."

Tinker was about to ask a further question, but Blake anticipated him.

"Not here," he said in a low tone. "I haven't got things quite worked out yet —and that port is open."

Blake settled back against double pillows, and, picking up a book, began to read —or, at least, he appeared to read. His eyes were taking in the words, but his mind was only absorbing the meaning in a mechanical way, for his thoughts were busy with the problem which was awaiting them when they should reach Hong Kong.

Overhead the low whir of the fan made a monotone of sound, and, outside the open port, they could hear the steady splashing of the bilge water as it was pumped out. Thus they sat, Blake in his bunk, with knees drawn up; and Tinker rubbing his thumb and finger up and down the surface of the shagreen casing.

Tinker, too, was thinking of the Golden Book of Buddha. Blake had told him a certain amount, but the lad knew there was still a lot which he should not learn until they reached the China Coast. He was trying to figure out just what Blake would do when they left the Kisu Maru at Hong Kong —how they would get to the Yangtse from there, and how Blake would plan on reaching the Upper Yangtse. Also he was thinking of the mysterious figure to whom Hong-Lo-Soo had referred as the Black Abbot of Cheng-tu.

A question came into his mind, and, looking up, he was about to speak, when the words froze in his throat, and his eyes widened in horror. For the space of, perhaps, twenty seconds Tinker sat there utterly unable to move hand or foot —paralysed at what he saw. Blake, his eyes fixed on his book, was all unconscious of the drama that was evolving in the narrow confines of that cabin. And Tinker dared not speak.

Slowly, stealthily, Tinker's fingers went round the handle of the kris. Not once did he remove his gaze from a spot a few inches below Blake's left ear. Then, inch by inch, his body tensed, his heels being drawn inward until they rested against the cabin trunk which had been thrust beneath the berth.

A moment thus he remained, while the muscles of his thighs and calves tautened; then he drove forward, with every bit of strength he possessed. The force of that effort drove him clean across the cabin. In the course of his flight his right arm went up, the blade of the kris flashing in the light. Then, even as Blake, startled by this sudden upheaval, jerked his head round, giving a sharp exclamation as he saw what he thought was a suddenly insane Tinker, the lad brought the kris down in a furious sweep.

The point of the blade whistled past Blake's ear, and struck just beneath. With his right hand still gripping the haft, Tinker began to jump and plunge, while the astonished Blake scrambled up.

"What the deuce?" he began.

But for answer Tinker straightened up, dragged the kris free, and, in another action, jerked something out from beneath the two pillows.

As he saw what it was, Blake landed on his feet, for what the lad was dangling before him was the three-foot length of a deadly swamp snake, the head of which he had severed clean in that one smashing blow with the kris. On the floor was the head, now crushed and impotent from the plunging of Tinker's feet.

"You have saved my life by a very narrow margin," said Blake, a little unsteadily. "Just what was happening?"

"I happened to look up, guv'nor, to ask you something, and saw this thing's head wavering about just beneath your ear. It had worked out from between the two pillows without you knowing it. There was no time to warn you, and I was afraid if I did speak you would turn and it would strike. I had to think quick, and I figured the only chance was to get it before it got you. It was lucky I had this kris in my hand. Gosh, I was scared, guv'nor!"

Blake bent and, with a gesture of disgust, took up the crushed head of the reptile. Handing it gingerly, he made certain that the fangs had not been removed, and then he flung it through the open port. Next he studied the leprous white body that was still twitching.

"It is a swamp snake, all right, young 'un," he remarked at last. "Just a little more deadly than a cobra. If it had reached me I should not have lived forty seconds. Fling it out!"

Tinker obeyed; then the two looked at each other.

"Isn't it kind of queer to find that thing under your pillow, guv'nor?"

"It is more than queer, Tinker. That is no accident. I am not even going to question the steward about it. It certainly could not have been there when he turned down the clothes to-night. Swamp snakes do not crawl all the way from the low land back of Singapore and entrench themselves under pillows on board ships in the harbour. That snake was placed there —deliberately."

"You mean by?" whispered the lad.

Blake nodded.

"There is no question in my mind. If we needed a warning we have had it to-night, young 'un. From this moment we must not relax our vigilance a single moment, day or night. Hung-Lo-Soo gave me a strong hint in his cable that we were under suspicion; but this is proof absolute that we are not intended to reach China alive if it can be prevented."

(Next week's great "Eclipse" issue will contain the second instalment of this remarkable story. "Remarkable" is the word, for it excels even the author's previous Chinese yarns —as you shall see from future instalments.)

THE BLACK ABBOT OF CHENG-TU

SEXTON BLAKE and TINKER in CHINA, in
QUEST of the GOLDEN BOOK of BUDDHA.

Part 2.

The Beginning of a Great Adventure.

(Last week's opening instalment summarised below.)

BUT for the fact that the Golden Book of Buddha —the cause of eternal enmity between the Chuen-to-yan at Canton and the Grand Llama of Tibet, and the most important religious treasure of Buddhism —had been stolen from the little river steamer, the Che-sen, by that mysterious figure, the Black Abbot of Cheng-tu, while on its way to Tibet as the result of the Grand Llama's plotting, Sexton Blake and Tinker would probably never have been aboard the Kisu-Maru, bound for the China coast.

At Baker Street, Hong-Lo-Soo, a wealthy merchant, had come to Blake and asked him to try and regain the stolen book, thus staving off the serious trouble which was bound to result from the theft of this treasured possession. And Blake, realising the seriousness of the situation, had accepted the mission, and accordingly set off with Tinker to China, where he knew it would be necessary to journey into the far interior in search for the sacred symbol —and the Black Abbot.

When aboard the ship, in dock at Singapore, Blake received a warning from one of Hong-Lo-Soo's agents, and that evening, while in his bunk, would have been murdered, but for Tinker's swift action in killing a deadly swamp-snake which had been placed under his pillow, with obviously murderous intent.

Our serial continues.

WHETHER it was by accident or design that the swamp snake was placed between Blake's pillows (and Blake had no doubt on that score), nothing else occurred between Singapore and Hong Kong. But at Hong Kong things began badly, and grew worse.

It was no part of Blake's plan to advertise his presence on the China coast. His aim was, if possible, to drop entirely out of sight at Hong Kong, and from there to find his way to the Yangtse in such a manner as to leave no possibility of connecting him up with the man who had travelled in the Kisu Maru from Marseilles.

Their landing at Hong Kong was open enough. They went ashore with the other passengers, and proceeded to the Hong Kong Hotel. They remained quietly at the hotel until the evening, and, late that night, Blake and the lad went out as if for a stroll. Half an hour later the two darted into a narrow lane in the western bazaar. Immediately, Blake grabbed Tinker's arm.

"Come on, young 'un, run for it!" he jerked.

They sped down the alley until they came to a narrow branching lane. Into this Blake wheeled, but almost immediately he drew the lad into the shadow of a building on the left. They stood there waiting, and well it was that Blake took the precaution, for a few seconds later two other figures came flying round the corner.

There was no need for Blake to tell Tinker what to do. As Blake threw himself forward, Tinker did likewise, and for the next five minutes they fought in silence. A sharp uppercut to the jaw sent Blake's man down with a grunt; a thud followed as he reached Tinker's antagonist just in time to catch a wrist before it descended. A knife rattled softly against the mat wall of the building, and then a squeal started in the Chink's throat as Blake's hands closed. It died in a faint whisper —there was another thud as Blake struck, hard and deliberately.

Then the two were once more racing down the lane.

They took a turning on the right, and again waited. A minute, two minutes, Blake gave it.

"Good enough!" he whispered. "There must have been only the two set to shadow us. We can get through from here."

The end of that lane brought them to a wider bazaar road, which was lighted by an occasional flare; but for the most it was in shadow. It was, Blake knew, a connecting link in one of the lowest and most disreputable parts of Hong Kong, and he knew it was safe betting that had it been suspected for a single moment that he and the lad would have ventured into that district alone at that hour of the night they never would have got through alive. But it was just that knowledge of the place that had determined Blake on the daring move.

For the next twenty minutes or so he guided the lad through a bewildering maze of streets and alleys. At last they emerged into a small square, from which they could see the lights of the ships riding in the harbour, beyond that was Kowloon, with its low-hanging glow.

They moved more slowly now, their heads bent so that their topees practically concealed their features. Off the square a wide, well-lighted street led into a decidedly better-class part of the Chinese quarter, and it was before a gate set in a high wall about a hundred yards along that Blake once more came to a pause. At one side was a handle, which he pulled vigorously. Inside, somewhere, they could hear the thrumming of a metal gong, and shortly after a small wicket opened in the gate. Blake thrust his face close.

"Your illustrious master is at home?"

"He is at his devotions, honourable sir," was the reply from the flat-eyed Celestial who peered out at them.

"You will say that one waits without who must see him this night. You will repeat the words: 'kai-lo.'"

"I go, honourable sir!"

The wicket closed, leaving them scuffling their feet impatiently until it swung open again some minutes later. But this time it was no servant who peered out at them. Framed in the aperture was the round, plump countenance of a Chinese mandarin. He took one look at Blake. Then a soft exclamation escaped his lips.

"My friend!"

There was a rattling of chains inside, then the door swung open admitting them into a large garden which lay before a wide-flung house. The stout mandarin took both Blake's hands in his.

"I did not expect you in this way, honourable one! I had heard from the illustrious Hong-Lo-Soo to expect you. Come with me and we shall talk."

He greeted Tinker, and led the way up the path to the house. The lower part was furnished like that of any European bungalow, for this Chinese gentleman, Wu-Fan-Sun, had many dealings with the English business houses of the place. He took his guests into a small room furnished partly as a lounge and partly as an office. Before speaking again he clapped his hands for a "boy" and ordered. Tea —the inevitable hospitality of a Chinese gentleman. But when the tray had been placed on a table and the boy had withdrawn, he looked from one to the other.

"You have not reached here unobserved, my friend!"

"We were followed, but we dealt with them. There were only two. I thought it best to come to you as soon as possible. It is not my intention to return. You guess why we are here?"

"I have heard of what happened some weeks ago on the Yangtse. The honourable Hong-Lo-Soo did not say much, but in our code there are words and phrases that one may read. Also I have heard from Hsui-fsi, who is in Hong Kong."

"Ah! I was hoping! He told you about the Golden Book?"

"He sent a messenger and —a warning. The Black Monk of Cheng-tu was there at the time. It is he, and Hsui-fsi is emphatic about the risk of your going up the river. Things are worse, much worse."

"Does he guess the identity of this hooded monk?"

"No; there are whispers. It was said that it was the chuen-to-yan of the Temple of Eternal Purity in Canton, but that is not so. I have been in Canton. The chuen-to-yan (high priest) is there and has not been out of the temple for many years."

"And the book?"

"It has disappeared utterly. Hsui-fsi cannot even guess where it has gone, except he is certain it has been taken up the river."

"To Cheng-tu, think you?"

"It is possible. The monastery there is very strong; it is under the jurisdiction of the chuen-to-yan of Canton. But it is up the river. They will not risk bringing it to Canton until things are more settled."

"Then we must go up the Yangtse!"

The Celestial was silent for a few minutes, studying Blake closely; then he spoke:

"Mr. Blake," he said slowly, "you realise just what you propose?"

"Surely; I have been up the river before."

"It is true. But the Golden Book of Buddha —there is nothing like it in Asia. There are millions whose lives counted in its service. And you, my friend, are of the West. It may mean your life —almost certainly will do so if you fail. And there are so few who can be of assistance to you after you once pass the barrier."

"I have considered; I go!"

"It seems strange that we have none of my race to whom we can turn. Hsui-fsi —but he is of yours. I need not tell you what the true world of Buddha will owe to you if you can recover the Golden Book. I can do so little. Have you any plan?"

"Yes, and for the immediate part of it I need your help, Wu-Fan-Sun."

"Everything I possess is at your service; and what I lack I can command in this great mission."

Blake bent forward and talked in low tones for some minutes.

22

From time to time the mandarin interrupted to ask a question. But when Blake had finished he nodded his head.

"If there is any plan that has a chance you have found it, my friend. I shall arrange what you wish. Also, I shall secure the passport papers and chits of discharge. You will not leave here until —"

"Not until we leave for good. What about your servants?"

"They are loyal, but I shall take precautions. You wish to begin this night?"

"There is no time to be lost."

"Then I shall send at once for the illustrious doctor."

For two days Blake and Tinker lay in a darkened upstairs room in that house. There were bandages over their eyes and bandages across the lower part of their faces. With the exception of narrow loin-cloths they were stripped to the skin, while a dark stain soaked into the pores of the skin. Four times a day was this stain put on afresh, and twice each day were the bandages removed from their eyes while a colourless pigment was poured in upon the pupils, staining them to the liquid brown of a Celestial. Certain facial changes with injected wax had been made by the skilled Chinese surgeon who was in the secret, and at the end of the second day he pronounced them as fit to move.

THAT night Wu-Fan-Sun, the merchant, left his house in a rickshaw. Between the shafts was a tall, ragged coolie, who ran with long, free strides; at the back, pushing to assist, was a Chinese lad —a most ordinary way for the merchant to leave, and therefore nothing about it to cause comment.

The coolie took his way along through the bazaar and along Queen's Road towards the section of the harbour where a maze of junks and sampans lay huddled. Apparently, the merchant's destination was one of these, for as they reached the line of jetties he spoke sharply several times to his coolie, berating him for going too fast.

The man would mumble something each time that sounded not a little like insubordination and, at last, so evident was it that he was not possessed of due respect for his master that Wu-Fan-Sun gave a bellow of rage and jumped out. He raised his umbrella and there was a swishing crash as he brought it down upon the bare back of the coolie.

"Pig, and son of a pig!" he stormed. "Thou wilt answer back to me! I will have your unwashed body broken on the press. Aie! Hold! Witness all, that this son of a pig has dared to lift his miserable voice to one of the heaven-born."

By this time the coolie had dropped the ends of the shafts to the road, while the stout mandarin, with surprising agility, had sprung out of the rickshaw. He was wielding the umbrella with vigour while a crowd that had gathered was muttering a screaming approval. The lad at the back had slunk away, standing near the edge of the road, watching fearfully.

And then, just as the mandarin would have struck for the twentieth time, there came a sound which grew and grew until, from a low, vibrating murmur it burst into the full howl of a Chinese mob. The next moment a human wave of yelling fiends swept upon them.

Wu-Fan-Sun gave a bellow of rage, and raised his umbrella. There was a swishing crash as he brought it down upon the bare back of the coolie.

According to Plan.

TWO thousand coolies of the Pi-Wen Tong were in that mob. They were shore coolies —waterfront labourers from the eastern bazaar. Their coming in force to this end of the settlement meant only one thing —a tong fight of the sort that Hong Kong has seen more than a few during the past few years.

Nor did they pause to choose their antagonists. Once inside the bazaar the human wave spread out, filling the side streets and narrow lanes, flowing up noisome backwaters until it lapped against the very fringe of the quarter.

The pandemonium was indescribable. Screams, deep-throated "aie's" from the down-coast portion, the flat high note of Cantonese, the pig-like squeals of the Kowloon section —blind rushings and the yells of the invaded as shop poles were jerked clear, allowing the top structures to come tumbling down into the dust.

The merchant, Wu-Fan-Sun, darted away like a very swollen lizard. From the moment that first roar had sounded he was oblivious of his rickshaw coolie. His one aim seemed to be to get clear before he was engulfed in the chaos that was descending upon him, and he moved to such good purpose that in less than a minute he was among the nearby sampans, springing from one to the other with an agility that would have done credit to a slip of a youth. Had there been any to take sufficient interest in his subsequent movements, they would have seen that he succeeded in reaching a small motor-boat which was moored on the outer edge of the line of sampans. No sooner did he spring into this than it went off with a rapid "phut-phut" of its engine, heading directly out into the harbour.

Once clear, Wu-Fan-Sun turned his head and gazed back towards the glare of the bazaar. He knew what a melee must be in progress there by now; but, curiously enough, he was not thinking of his own narrow escape. On the contrary. He was thinking of the half-naked rickshaw coolie whom he had been chastising and berating when the invasion came.

"It is on the lap of the good Buddha now," he muttered to himself. "It was timed well. But shall I ever know if he got clear or not? I have done what I could."

As for the two on whom his thoughts were dwelling just then, they had pushed into the surrounding press of humans as soon as the merchant fled. Nor did they wait for the onslaught. The taller of the pair wormed his way through, followed by the younger. By the time the collision came they were almost clear, and in the confusion no attention was paid to them. They were not the only ones anxious to get away from that promise of battle.

Soon they were running, and, following the line of jetties, kept on until they reached the lower section of the bazaar. They were now in a street of the brass workers —a thoroughfare which was fairly well lighted at night and a place of musical clangour during the day.

Into the open door of one of these shops they dashed. Behind a counter, listening in apparent anxiety to the sounds of the distant storm, was an elderly Chinaman who gave them quick scrutiny as they passed him. Then he faded from sight in a way that is typical of the East, and which must be seen to be believed. Like a phantom, he rose to view again at the back of the shop. A single word was uttered by the tall Coolie, there was a swift response, and a heavy curtain was lifted.

Blake, for the taller coolie was he, slipped through into darkness. Tinker followed, and the two stood behind the dropped curtain until a sudden draught of cool air reached them. Then a spark of light appeared, followed by a gnome-like countenance as a head was thrust through a hole in the floor.

"S-s-s-s."

They could not have told whence the sound came. But it was enough for Blake. He moved forward and pushed his legs over the edge of the hole. They touched the rung of a rickety bamboo ladder. He followed with his body, the Celestial with the masked light swinging aside as he did so. Down, rung by rung he worked his way, still followed by Tinker. At the bottom was water, and tied to the foot of the ladder was a small sampan. Blake slid aboard; Tinker did likewise. Then the Celestial landed beside them. The rope was thrown off, the light was completely obliterated, and a moment or two later they found themselves drifting out from beneath the shelter of the building into the suckway of the tide, while nearer and nearer came the roar of the battle that was now sweeping through the bazaar.

Neither spoke. They huddled under the curving mat shelter which spread from side to side of the sampan, breathing quietly, listening. Against the starlit sky they could see the silhouette of the Celestial.

He was wielding a heavy sweep, sculling easily and with scarce a sound. They slid past other sampans and out into full view of the bazaar front. Off to the left lay the bright lights of the Hong Kong front; a maze of riding-lights floated over the harbour. On the other side was Kowloon. It was towards this that the sampan was moving.

Slowly they progressed, until the man at the sweep paused in his labour to hoist a small mat sail. Then they were into the full pitch of the harbour, bobbing like a cork as the run of the tide came up against the night wind that was sweeping down from the Peak.

They skimmed the stern of a big Canadian Pacific liner by inches. Above them the decks and public saloons were brilliantly lighted; an orchestra was playing, and these two disguised Britishers could hear the light, trilling voices of women —their own kind of women —as they paced back and forth. How little did any of those light-hearted travellers dream that two ragged coolies in the sampan which swept past unseen were of the same race as themselves —famous in more than one continent, and yet had deliberately cut themselves off from all hope of succour in order to plunge into the dark interior of the Middle Kingdom in search of something which might, or might not, exist!

The music died away astern. A low squat destroyer loomed up. A voice was hurled in rough warning to the "benighted Chink" to keep clear. Then they were past, and the lips of the elder of the two coolies parted in a faint smile as the echo of that honest, blustering voice died away.

Then the lights of the Kowloon ferry as it lumbered across the harbour. A drifting sampan almost collided with them. A heavy junk, graceful none the less, loomed above them; cries in Cantonese obscenities, and again they were clear once more.

Then they came about, heading up towards Kowloon Creek, that haven of the junks when the monsoon sweeps across from the China Sea. But it needed another full hour before they found themselves among the myriad craft that were moored there.

At a big Chinese shipping company's wharf lay a dilapidated tug. The sampan was brought in against this, and they tumbled aboard. They found themselves at once in the midst of a gang of some hundred-odd coolies. From somewhere forward a stout comprador appeared. By the light of a lantern he scrutinised them closely, then he snarled an order for their papers.

From beneath his thin shirt Blake took a bit of folded leaf. Inside were two papers which he presented to the comprador. They were covered with Chinese characters, which apparently the man found in order, for he passed them back and ordered the pair to one side. For the next ten minutes or so the examination of papers went on, the confusion being added to by new arrivals. But at last it was finished, there was a bustle forward, a single hoot was sounded on the whistle, and the tug swung round.

Once more they found themselves pitching out on the harbour. This time their course took them eastwards. Again they passed the big liner, then another destroyer, and slowed down for another craft that lay riding at the next buoy.

They found this to be a small coasting steamer which Blake knew to belong to one of the big Shanghai shipping firms —Jordan, Skinner, & Co. When a rope had been flung to them they followed the mob on board, where another examination of papers took place —this time by an European mate. Then a serang took charge of them, and, after a sorting out that was accompanied by much profanity, they were pushed down several iron ladders into the bowels of the ship. Another engine-room serang took them in hand there, and before another quarter of an hour was past they each gripped the handle of a heavy shovel.

Stokers in the hold of a cargo tramp on the China coast! It was strenuous enough on that steaming night in that foul hole, but the time was not far distant when Sexton Blake and Tinker would regard it as a little bit of heaven compared to the horror of something far, far worse.

For four days Blake and Tinker stewed and shovelled and stewed in that pit.

On the morning of the fifth day, when they had a few moments breather on deck, they saw the yellow waters of the Whangpoo, with its flat mud-banks stretching away on either side. Shanghai! Never had the prospect seemed more enviable to them. Anything was better just then than a further spell below.

The sun was shining on the splendid buildings along the Bund when the Kei-Sang was warped in to the Jordan-Skinner wharf at the lower end of the British portion of the Bund, and within half an hour they, like the rest of the crew which had been scratched together in Hong Kong, were paid off.

Their passage along the Bund was in sharp contrast to that on their previous visit to the great port. Then they had been clad in spotless white and bound for the Shanghai Club; now they were as ragged and miserable-looking as any of the teeming hundreds of coolies who paddled beside them, bound not for the classic portals of the European Club, but for the squalid native city beyond.

They left the British settlement behind them, and, passing through the French concession, followed the course of the wall surrounding the native city until they came to the Sing-Poh-Mun. At that hour of the day the gate was packed with people passing in and out. And beyond was an even greater press, for the streets narrowed at once to passages which one could touch with outstretched arms on either side.

The streets —or passages —were running with filth; the stench was awful; the pandemonium of coolies and chair-men was deafening. It was exactly like stepping from the present into the historic past. And immediately they were lost in the yellow torrent which flowed about them.

(Another stage of Blake's great adventure safely passed! Keep in touch with him throughout. Place a standing order!)

30

Part 3

No. 1238 The Union Jack.
THE BLACK ABBOT OF CHENG-TU
SEXTON BLAKE AND TINKER IN CHINA!
OUR GREAT NEW SERIAL. BEGIN HERE.

The Red Streamer.

IT was the raiding and sinking of a small river-steamer eighty miles above Hankow, on the great Chinese waterway of the Yangtze, that was the direct cause of Sexton Blake's and Tinker's latest visit to China.

The boat was carrying a treasure which, to millions of Orientals, was holy —the Golden Book of Buddha. This sacred book had been in the possession of the Chuen-to-yan (high priest) of Canton until the emissaries of the Grand Llama of Thibet secured it; and it changed hands once again when the mysterious Black Abbot of the monastery of Cheng-tu stole it in turn from the river-steamer.

Sexton Blake, at the urging of Hong-Lo-Soo, a wealthy Chinese merchant of London and for patriotic reasons agreed to make a journey to China, and there follow the trail of the Golden Book wherever it should lead. He arrived in Hong Kong with Tinker, and there they were able to sink their European identities and become to all appearances Chinese coolies —a thing made possible only by the help of the agents of the Grand Llama, for whom they were seeking to regain the sacred relic.

Rumours had been heard of the Black Monk's retreat far up the river Yangtse, so Blake and Tinker made the first stage of their journey as stokers in a Chinese steamer to Shanghai, whence they hoped to work their passage up-river in a native junk.

Leaving the steamer, they passed along the Bund at Shanghai, ill-clad and dirty as the multitude of coolies who pressed about them, heading for the squalid native city beyond, which they entered by the gate of the Sing-Poh-Mun.

Once inside the gate, Sexton Blake and Tinker found the crush even more congested, for the evil-smelling streets narrowed into mere passages, and immediately they were lost in the yellow current which flowed about them.

They paused at a small, dirty tea-shop in the Street of the Paper

Makers, and here, for the price of a small silver slug, they procured a meal of rice and unleavened flat cakes. Scarcely a word had been spoken by the two since leaving the wharf. Now and then the taller had given utterance to some remark in the Cantonese dialect, but of conversation there had been none.

Outwardly they were completely oblivious to what was going on about them; but, in reality, both Blake and the lad were on the look-out for the slightest sign that they were being followed. Their attitude in the teashop was that of ordinary overworked and underfed coolies, grateful to have been paid off a job, thankful for a respite brief enough to secure food and drink.

An hour or more they remained there, then Blake paid the score, haggling vehemently over a few cash, and, like most of the Cantonese, gaining his point over the Northerner. Back in the street their footsteps took them in idle fashion through street after street, until they reached the western side of the native city. There, by the Si-Mun, they paused before a small temple, the front of which was decorated with a gigantic statue of the god of storms and war. Curiously enough, there were far more women devotees than men inside, for it is to this god that Chinese women look to receive strength and courage for their offspring.

Between the black pillars which held up the main roof of the temple hung hundreds upon hundreds of red and yellow paper streamers most of which bore characters laying forth texts from the philosophy of the blessed Confucius, or proverbs from ancient Chinese lore. The streamers were each a charm against evil spirits, and, in the Buddhist religion, might be said to answer the same purpose as candles in the churches of the Roman West.

They paid their devotions along with several other coolies, who were bowed before a massive statue of Great Buddha. But if one had been keenly observing the taller of the two, one might have seen that; before prostrating himself he took swift notice of a wide red paper streamer that was hanging close to a pillar that by actual count, would have been found to be the seventeenth in the second row. Again, as he rose, Blake allowed his gaze to sweep past the streamer; then he shuffled out, followed closely by his young companion.

They seemed to be very tired, very apathetic, as they moved in aimless fashion along through the streets towards the Si-Mun. Passing through this gate, they continued until they were near the western boundary of the French concession. Here there was an open piece of swampy ground where other coolies were gathered, some cooking, some cleaning, but most smoking opium. They squatted down some distance apart, and there they remained, heads bowed on knees, apparently oblivious to everything that was going on.

But from the corner of Blake's lips a slow monotone was issuing, to which Tinker listened eagerly.

"The streamer was there," the lad heard him say. "Hsui-fsi is on the alert. It bore the message; but I haven't quite solved it yet, I must drag out the meaning."

"What did it say, guv'nor?" whispered the lad.

The slow monotone began to quote:

"'The Kingfisher is over the river;

The Eagle is over the hills;

The Golden Glory of the Heavens

Shines down where the green rice Shoots Highest!'"

"What on earth can it mean, guv'nor?"

"Our secret is there, I can't tell yet, but those words convey what Hsui-fsi wants me to know. There is a meaning, it is the key of our next step. Now, no more; I want to think."

So they sat and apparently dozed all through that morning while the life of the city passed and repassed them. They were just two coolies —of less account in China than a measure of water-melon seeds. What mattered it if they remained there, or wandered on to some other place, where they might rest their tired bones?

But that keen, analytical mind of the great detective was tearing apart the age-old quotation from the classical section of Confucius. Sentence by sentence he was pondering it, for, against the seventeenth pillar in the second row of the colonnades at the temple by Si-Mun, in the native city at Shanghai, it had been whispered to him by the merchant in Hong Kong, he would find a message from Hsui-fsi; in that message would be the clue he sought.

"The Kingfisher is over the river —"

There was —there must be an initial key in that.

"The Kingfisher is over the river —"

The Kingfisher is, as Blake knew, plentiful along the Yangtse. "The river" —what else could be meant but the sacred river —the Great River—the Yangtse?

Now was the month of January. In Shanghai it might blow warm, or blow raw. One might find a blazing sun as lay above them that morning, or one might find heavy clothing a comfort. There was no telling. But one thing Sexton Blake could assert —there were precious few Kingfishers along the lower Yangtze at that time of year.

"The Kingfisher over the river —" He mentally marked the form of the verb "is." The quotation on that silly, flimsy bit of red paper used the present tense. "Is" —well, they were to be found at that time of the year, darting and diving along the waters of the Upper Yangtse. But that might be anything from a thousand to two thousand miles above Nanking.

"The Eagle is over the hills —"

Where did the king of birds wheel in China along the tortuous course of the Yangtse? "Is over the hills" —one must travel even beyond Ichang, at the foot of the stupendous gorges to find the eagle in his eyrie.

"The Eagle is over the hills" — What was next?

"The Golden Glory of the Heavens—" That in China, would mean the moon rather than the sun, and at the present time there was a waxing moon, nearing the full, riding in the night sky.

"The Golden Glory of Heavens shines down where the green rice shoots highest."

"Ah!"

The exclamation escaped from between Blake's lips in a faint sigh.

"Where the green rice shoots highest."

Did the key lie there?

Methodically his mind began to follow the course of that mighty river, which cradles a quarter of the population of China. Up, up, up he went from Nanking to Hankow, from Hankow to Ichang, and through the mighty gorges, beyond —through the Tiger's Tooth gorge, through Ichang gorge, through Mitan, and the lesser gorges until, in fancy, he climbed the mad tumbling rapids of Hsin-tan. Away along further vast reaches until he passed Chung-king; then he was gazing upon the turbulent waters of Min-yang —which some say is the true Yangtse —and at last, he found his eyes gazing upon a vast plain which he had traversed many many years before.

Cheng-tu!

More than a thousand years ago a local governor of benevolent nature, spent much time and money and employed many thousands of men to make that plain a blossoming paradise. Dykes and channels and revetments were built to endure. Within these man-made works was harnessed the rich, silt-bearing flood-water of the Great River, and even to this day, the rice shoots are greener and higher, more vigorous and more prolific than in any other part of China. It is, in truth, the blooming of the desert.

"Where the green rice shoots highest."

Cheng-tu!

And the hooded monk —that mysterious figure which had snatched the Golden Book of Buddha away from those who would have borne it safely along the first stage of its long journey to the Grand Llama at Tibet —had been dubbed the Black Abbot of Cheng-tu!

Over those wide, watered stretches the Kingfisher, even now, would be wheeling. In the rugged, gaunt crags of the mighty Baian Kara mountains that lift high in the centre of Sze Chuan, are the eyries of the royal eagles; and over those watered plains, the Golden Glory of the Heavens would shine, even that night, upon the green rice which lies thick and heavy as in no other part of China.

Tinker was in reality dozing when at last the faint whisper readied him.

"We return within the walls, as I have been instructed" he heard in the same flat monotone which Blake had used before. "I believe I have the key, young 'un. If I am right, then it means a long, long journey into the interior. But how we are to get there, or what we shall have to contend with when we arrive —if we do —heaven above only knows."

Then they rose and, shuffling aimlessly, wended their way back info the native city through the Si-Mun.

The Water-melon Seeds

THEY were once more in the midst of the screaming confusion of the quarter. From in front of the statue of the god of storms and war, led two streets, diverging fan-like until each was swallowed in the maze beyond. One of these —the Street of the Beggars —led through the lowest and most depraved section of the native city. In that welter of filth and gloom, existed horrors unspeakable. Within this tangle were the lairs of the deformed, sore-laden creatures who roamed like night vermin in search of offal. A teeming world of its own, was this district, where no mandarin would insult his august senses by breathing the pollution of its reeking stench.

Into it turned the two shuffling coolies who had entered by the Si-Mun gate.

In the hours of early afternoon there was less life here than in any other parts of the native city. No chairs or rickshaws forged through the narrow passages miscalled streets. No bearers with shoulder poles jogged along calling their mechanical cry of warning. No open shops displaying wares of silks and brass and copper and Ning-po lacquer; no teashops, no drug shops, no displays of cotton. Only an occasional rice stall and the dark labyrinths where the beggars could buy "water," tobacco and opium. A foul, noisome, mephitic hole.

Few persons there were to witness or obstruct the passage of the two travellers. Shuttered hovels with hanging mats and flapping strips of wood lined the way. In the filth of the dark corridors, pigs and dogs and children played, pawing and quarrelling over the few scraps of offal that might be found. Here and there a deformed wretch muttering in the first throes of the "black smoke" dreams; or a sleeping monstrosity lying face down in the muck. From behind the lowered mats, moans, curses, animal-like mouthings —an inferno.

Blake and Tinker proceeded with slow paces. Ragged as was their clothing, they were dressed in kingly fashion compared to the terrible strips which flapped about the loins of the lost creatures who dwelt in that lost world. They passed, unheedful of the curses which followed them.

At one moment a cur, flea-bitten and covered with sores, lowered his nose to Blake's heels. Though the disguise which Blake had assumed was otherwise perfect, there had been nothing to obliterate the ineradicable scent of the white man. The cur was puzzled. To push the animal away would have been useless. A scuffle would attract the other four-footed vermin in the place. There was only one thing to do, and Blake did it. Reaching down he caught the cur back of the shoulders, then, with a swing, he flung it clean over a near-by row of rickety palings. Followed a confusion of yelpings and human cursings, but the cur was not flung back.

They reached a turning, coming into another gloomy corridor, which might have been the one they had just left, so like was it. But here, as they proceeded, the sound of someone singing in the flat monotone of China reached them. A thin, reedy wail it was, but there was that about it which made Blake give ear.

"Aie —aie —ola —aie
There is no rice but where the waters flow,
There is no rice but where the waters flow,
The great waters are bathed in the golden glory.
And they are far away.
Aie —aie —ola —aie!"

They came upon a singer, a decrepit ancient, wizened and as yellow as the shrivelled rind of a lemon. From somewhere he had secured the battered remnants of a single string instrument from which he was picking the flat monotone while he sang. At his feet was a small wooden bowl, and in the bottom of this bowl six water-melon seeds.

Now, in China, water-melon seeds are, with rice, the one great staple of rich and poor —of coolie and beggar and mandarin. But whereas rice is a necessity, water-melon seeds are, to the poor, a luxury. And here, in the midst of this infernal hole, was a ragged beggar, squatting in filth, playing and singing, and in the bowl at his feet, six water-melon seeds.

In Hong Kong the merchant had whispered in Blake's ear (among other cautions): "Watch for the water-melon seeds; heed their message."

At first sight it would seem that the seeds had been thrown into the bowl carelessly. But if one regarded them closely one might have seen that by drawing an imaginary line from one to the other one could form the double Chinese character "Phi-si." Like most words and characters in Chinese, which has more than two hundred separate symbols in the written tongue, the symbol "Phi-si" has many meanings. But one interpretation it has is direction. And, standing so that he might regard it from the lower side, Sexton Blake saw that he was facing the east.

The symbol phi-si is to be found in each section of the written divisions, but in that dealing with action it is followed by the symbol "da-tung." And the Da-Tung Mun is the eastern gate of the native city of Shanghai!

The tall coolie thrust his fingers beneath his poor cotton shirt. From a twisted rag which encircled his waist, he took out two water-melon seeds, and very deliberately, dropped them, one at a time, into the wooden bowl. Then he moved on, pointing his footsteps to the east, and as they turned another corner they heard only the distant wail of that thin voice:

"The great waters are bathed in the golden glory —"

"The Word Cometh."

HSUI-FSI, the wise old man of China, and known as the Eagle of the North, sat on the upper veranda of the House of Many Virtues in the Suchow Road, staring down into the luxuriant garden which stretched away to the high walls which shut it off from the Suchow Creek.

He had just finished his siesta, and now, clad in loose silken kimono, with soft Nanking slippers on his feet, he reclined on a great heap of cushions, snipping the husks from water-melon seeds, and mechanically working the kernels between his teeth.

Nearly ninety years had passed over the head of Hsui-fsi. For more than sixty of them he had been a power in China. Back in the days of long ago, when the Dowager-Empress ruled her terrible Court in the Sacred City at Peking, Hsui-fsi had been one of the elect. Now, of all those who had intrigued and fought for favour and power, only he was left to gaze with jaundiced eye upon the doings of new China.

Sixty years before he had been a slim, upright young Englishman. Sir Gordon Saddler, he had come out to China; Hsui-fsi he had left it when the revolution of nineteen-eleven broke out. And to-day not half a dozen living persons knew that Hsui-fsi was no Chinaman, but an English baronet. Those sixty years had put the stamp of the East upon him; the opium which impregnated his system had turned him as yellow and wizened as any Celestial ancient. Never again would he return to his own country, but for some years he had lived in the House of the Silver Moon in San Francisco, where he had been known as Hsui-fsi —the Mystery Man of 'Frisco.

But he had come back to China. What he had foreseen behind the curtain that had obscured the yellow dragon for so long, was now coming to pass. More than once he and Sexton Blake had worked together to drag from out the chaos something tangible for the good of Britain. And now Blake was again in China —just where not even Hsui-fsi knew.

He was still pondering while the afternoon shadows lengthened. A boy brought a tray of pale tea, and soon after a visitor was ushered in. A strangely Oriental figure was this, a thin individual who salaamed to Hsui-fsi. Clad in a gorgeous robe of grey silk embroidered with white and crimson peacocks, he was clearly alien to Shanghai. On his head was a high, pointed head dress of grey, and his shoes were not the shoes of China. But he was of the East.

Hsui-fsi showed him great ceremony, for this visitor was a high priest of the Buddha, and his garb was the priestly garb of Korea. It was in Korean that he spoke.

"I have sought you soon after my arrival, honourable friend." he said, in extraordinarily deep tones, "We of the north are in great anxiety for news."

Hsui-fsi nodded slowly.

"I watch, and I wait, and I listen to all whispers, reverend priest, but out of the winds nothing has come."

"Thou had learned nothing since the outrage on the river?"

"There have been faint whisperings, that is all. There is no doubt that it was the Black Monk of Cheng-tu who sank the vessel of Fen-to."

"Ah! Who is this monk who goes masked and robed in black, honourable one?"

Hsui-fsi made a faint gesture with one hand.

"Would that I could say," he responded. "He works on the upper river. They call him the Black Monk of Cheng-tu. There is the monastery at Cheng-tu. They in that monastery are no friends of his Holiness the Grand Llama at Tibet. Thou knowest as well as I, reverend priest, that it is under the direction of the Chuen-to-yan of Canton. Is it not great treasure that the Chuen-to-yan seeks?"

"Aie. And the Golden Book of Greet Buddha has disappeared. Honourable friend, we can look to no one but thee. Violence is forbidden by Great Buddha. But the soul of our temples has been ravished."

"Think not that I have been idle. There is one now in China who works as the mole. In that way, and in that way only, can one burrow to the place where the golden treasure lies hidden."

"This person —of whom dost thou speak?"

"He is one of another race."

"Of another race! And he seeks the golden treasure?"

"Even so. He works for the Dalai Llama."

The priest shook a puzzled countenance.

39

"I understand not, honourable friend. Is there nought else we can do?"

"There is the Great River. Thou knowest that the upper reaches are within the dominion of the priests of Cheng-tu; and the priests of Cheng-tu bend the knee to the Chuen-to-yan of Canton. Thinkest thou any ordinary mortal can probe the mystery of those upper reaches? Thinkest thou that thou or I could pass the guardians of the Black Monk?"

"And thou knowest not by what means this one of another race worketh?"

"I know not, but I wait for news."

"He is to be trusted?"

"As his Holiness himself."

"Then we can but watch and pray and leave all in the lap of Great Buddha."

"Even so. But he is somewhere among us. I have left my signs that he may read. I have blazoned the temples with streamers which hear my message. I have sent my beggars throughout the native city, each with his message sing, and his rice bowl holding the word I would have him know. Who knows what may follow? Some days ago he was in Hong Kong. To-day he may be in Shanghai or Nanking. It is beyond my ken. And the danger is great —so great that although my heart yearns solely to speak with him I must be sure —I must be sure. He is dear to me, and he carries his life in his hands each moment —has cut himself off utterly in order that he may serve an alien race and the cause of his Holiness at Tibet."

"Thou wilt tell us something when thou art able?"

"Of a surety, reverend priest! And thou wilt remain with me this night. It is possible —at any moment, at any hour, some sign may come. Until then I brood with a troubled heart, and in anxiety. So — but hold! What cometh?"

As he spoke Hsui-fsi leaned forward and gazed over the railing at a figure which was running up the garden. It was to all appearances, a coolie lad, who had entered the place by climbing the river wall. And as Hsui-fsi followed the course of those long, clean strides he sighed.

"The word cometh even now, reverend priest," he said.

40

Before the monk could dodge,
the heavy cutting sword had
struck him full on the mouth.

The Black Monk.

IT was a serious development that led to Tinker's unexpected appearance in Hsui-fsi's garden.

In accordance with the direction of the water-melon seeds in the bottom of the beggar's bowl, Blake and the lad had continued on their way towards the eastern gate of the native city —the Da-Tung Mun. As in the case of several other gates, there was, just within it, a temple, it being the custom for travellers to worship both on entering and leaving the city.

Here, as before, Blake looked for a sign. The paper banner at the other temple and the clue of the water-melon seeds had led him so far, only to retrace his footsteps. But Sexton Blake knew that behind all this lay a definite purpose in Hsui-fsi's brain. Knowing that shrewd old gentleman as he did, he knew now that Hsui-fsi would never have arranged such elaborate precautions unless he had strong suspicion that every move was being watched by the enemy —an unknown and even unguessed quantity so far as Blake was concerned.

At the temple by the Da-Tung Mun he might find another beggar, or, within the temple, another banner. Or, again, there might be an entirely different form of clue. It was, in one way, like a paper chase, with the exception that the trail was laid by means of which Blake had only an inkling.

At this time of the day the Da-Tung Mun was packed. Beyond the gate was a stretch of land running as far as the Whangpoo, where a vast array of junks, sampans, and wupans lay moored. From here there was direct access to the Bund along the front of the European settlement, and, to the south, another water connection with the canal which runs down to Hangchow some hundred miles or so distant. From that canal one could turn north along the "old" canal and reach Nanking, debouching into the Yangtse at that point.

It was this throng which Blake and Tinker joined. Though each kept a sharp look-out, there was no sign of a beggar who might be the bearer of a message from Hsui-fsi. That did not mean that there were no beggars at all. On the contrary, the place was swarming with them; but, as far as Blake could see, the clue of the water-melon seeds was ended.

They tried the temple. There, as in the other, they found an array of red paper streamers covered with verses and proverbs, but Blake saw nothing that indicated by the agreed secret mark that it contained the direction he sought. After that fruitless effort they emerged once more into the narrow street, allowing themselves to be carried along with the crowd, through the gate and into the more open space beyond. Between them the edge of the Whangpoo stretched a line of shacks and shops for about a hundred yards, and here they found several groups gathered about loud-voiced serangs, who were recruiting men for the up-river voyage of the junks.

Sexton Blake had already learned enough —or thought he had — from that red paper streamer in the temple by the Si-Mun gate to come to the decision that their trail would lead them to the Upper Yangtse. There, he felt, was the answer to the riddle, and there, in that vast stretch of tortuous valley and rugged gorges, was the hiding-place of the Golden Book of Buddha. At the same time, he felt that Hsui-fsi must have some further hint to give him than just to bring him and the lad as far as the Da-Tung Mun and leave them stranded there, as it were. But where was the sign?

Slowly the two shuffled along, their outward manner as blank as that of any other coolies whose lives were a hopeless purgatory of toil for the mere privilege of gaining a few grains of rice and the discarded ash of opium that had already had a double smoking. There were millions, yea, hundreds of millions, in that position in China, and they could not have chosen a disguise that would have drawn less attention to them.

But a clue —where was it?

One of the larger hiring groups was gathered near the bank of the river. Here, on an upturned oil-case, a burly Swatow serang was standing, exhorting of the moving crowd listening to join up without delay if they desired an easy passage up the Yangtse. It was all very much as it might have been in the West. Not one of those coolies but knew the terrible dangers of the Upper Yangtse; not one but had been up and down it a dozen times. And yet they were fooled now, as they had been again and again by the specious promises of the recruiting serang.

Blake and Tinker drew near. At sight of the tall coolie on the outskirts of the crowd the serang paused and eyed him. Then he shot out a stream of words that promised such pay and such fare as no coolie had ever had before. A strong-looking fellow like Blake was just the sort he needed on that trip.

Blake made no response of any sort. He was marking time, so to say, waiting for a sign. And even as he stood there it came. From somewhere in the press a hand slipped against his. As his fingers half curled he felt something drop into the hollow, and, feeling what it was, he knew that someone had given him three water-melon seeds.

He turned his head slowly and gazed about him. Which one of those scores of yellow men had been responsible for the act? It was utterly impossible to tell. By now he might be yards away. But it was a sign. Three water-melon seeds! What did it mean?

Blake turned back, apparently listening to the serang. But all the time his mind was working on this other matter. Three water-melon seeds! Was it a sign of direction? Or might it be a tong sign? A tong —there was the tong of the Three Feathers. Could it have any reference to that? The Three Feathers Tong was, Blake knew, affiliated to the Four Lakes Tong, of which he himself was a member. That tong also was Hsui-fsi's tong. Three water-melon seeds!

He started to edge his way out of the press, followed closely by Tinker. At this movement the serang turned back to him and held up a piece of red paper. It might have been a stray bit of stuff he had picked up from the ground. But as his eyes fell on it Blake saw that it had on it some gilt characters which indicated the symbol "three." Three water-melon seeds and now the gilt "three" on that bit of red paper.

It was too apt to be mere coincidence. Somehow he knew now that this message was the next clue which Sir Gordon had laid for him. It was a sign that he should sign on as one of the crew of the junk for which this Swatow serang was recruiting coolies. And then, as his eye once more met that of the serang, he gave the affirmative sign.

In response the serang waved his hand towards a line of coolies that straggled towards the river bank. On the outside of the line of craft was a large junk of close on a hundred and fifty tons. From the mast of this hung several strips of red paper. As these papers waved in the slight breeze Blake thought he could make out gilt characters on one of them which would correspond to the symbol he had just seen. That was the junk.

He did not look again at the serang, but pushed his way through, and started for the bank, it would be necessary to cross the inner lines of sampans and wupans before reaching the outer line of junks. To this end he picked his way through a heap of refuse towards a spot that was less crowded, he was almost in the act of putting out a foot to the nearest sampan, when suddenly a terrific uproar sounded behind him.

He and Tinker turned. They saw a mass of men surging about the upturned oil case where the Swatow serang had been standing. The man was no longer there, but they could see his head and shoulders above the rest of the crowd as he laid about him strenuously, the while he carried on a heated argument with another serang who had apparently, picked a quarrel with him.

Blake and Tinker could hear snatches of words and phrases, which gave them a clue. There was mention of Chen and others of the Cantonese; there were foul epithets hurled at the heads of Chang-tso-

44

lin and other Northern commanders. On the face of it it was nothing but a political upheaval such as is common enough in China at the present time.

But, somehow, Blake had a feeling there was something more behind it all —that the quarrel had been started to cloak something else. And a few moments later he knew he was right, for, on the outskirts of the crowd, his body concealed by a long black habit, his head covered with a capacious cowl, and his arms folded while he gazed at the swaying, fighting mass of men, was a monk, habited in sombre black. He could only be a monk from the Black Monastery of Cheng-tu!

Ferocity Let Loose!

THE battle spread with extraordinary rapidity.

At any time, in China, it is easy enough to start a riot, but there was a system about this one that revealed to the watching Blake a definite direction behind it. Outwardly, the Swatow serang was the centre of the disturbance. From the words one could distinguish it would seem that some of the Northerners had taken exception to this man from the south recruiting coolies for a Yangtse voyage.

It was puzzling, even to Blake, who knew a vast deal about the bewildering wheels within wheels of the China coast. Swatow was, nominally, under the influence of Canton. Canton was, nominally, at odds with Shanghai. Yet here was a southern serang in charge of a Yangtse junk, and, to judge from the epithets which were being hurled at him, he was being attacked by Cantonese.

But about one phase of it there could be no doubt. The attack was deliberate and vicious. If it continued as it had started there would be nothing but the bleeding and mutilated body of that serang left as evidence. And who cared in China about a stray body?

There was no question in Blake's mind about the message that had reached him. That serang, in some obscure way, must be one of Hsui-fsi's men. Despite his southern origin, he must be a member of either the Four Lakes Tong or the Three Feathers. Should Blake risk discovery by going to his assistance, or should he hold back?

The doubt was settled for him. With a swiftness that was amazing a fresh mob poured through the Do-Tung Mun. Hundreds and hundreds of Celestials, screaming and yelling and brandishing every handy sort of weapon, from bamboo staves to the short, wicked sword of the interior. There was going to be bloodshed in earnest before this riot was quelled.

An overflow of the crowd swept towards the bank of the Whangpoo. Before Blake and Tinker could spring out on to the sampans or escape along the bank they were in the thick of it. For them it was quite impossible to distinguish friend from foe —if friend existed. But it was essential that they took action, if only to save their own skins. So, snatching up a couple of bamboo staves, Blake pushed one into the lad's hand, and, taking care to keep to the Cantonese dialect, said:

"Defend yourself against these Northern dogs!"

His words reached the ears of the nearest participants. A dozen swung at the sound and made for them. Using his stave as he would have wielded a quarter-staff, Blake set about him. Tinker followed suit. All languor dropped from those two coolies in that moment. They turned into screaming devils, as irresponsible in their outlet of rage as any of those about them.

Thwack, thwack, thwack!

The crack of stave against stave, the ring of blade against blade, the squeals that always accompany a combat among Chinese, the flying tails of shirts and coats, the ancient craft moored in the river, the barbaric calls of rally from one section to another —it might all have been taking place in the Middle Ages. And yet it was in the present day, with modern Shanghai not a stone's throw away, and grey British destroyers, filled with complicated modern machinery, lying off the Bund.

Now and then Blake caught sight of the Swatow serang. His aim was, if possible, to reach the fellow's side and line up there. He had a feeling that his own presence somewhere in the neighbourhood of Shanghai was suspected and that the Swatow serang was definitely known to be one of Hsui-fsi's men.

In that case the whole thing would have been planned with a definite object —to try and discover through the serang if he knew anything of Blake's whereabouts. Blake did not believe that Sir Gordon would allow any of his men to guess why they should do this or do that —why they should go there or come here. But he knew equally well that there was a very cunning brain at work away up the river at Cheng-tu.

The unmasked monk who had planned the raid that had secured

the Golden Book of Buddha had not been able to carry out such a coup without having first made use of a marvellous system of espionage. And it was more plain than ever to Blake that every action of either side was being watched by the other.

These thoughts were passing through his mind as he laid about him lustily. All the time fresh combatants were pouring out through the Da-Tung Mun, and, from what he could see the forces which were lining up against the Swatow serang were greatly outnumbering the handful of men who surrounded him.

Every now and then Blake caught sight of the black robed monk as he moved about on the edge of the mob. His very presence seemed to act as a spur to those screaming madmen. He had no need to speak a gesture here and there was all he used.

Blake wondered if he could be the mysterious black monk, the man who lurked behind half the sinister and mysterious doings that had created chaos in China for several years past. No one had spread greater ruin about him than that strange being who was spoken of only as the Black Monk, and sometimes as the Black Abbot of Cheng-tu. Not even Blake's old enemy, Prince Wu Ling, had left a wider swathe of wreckage behind him than the Black Monk.

By now there were fully a thousand coolies engaged in the struggle. Unless something occurred to stop it, the affair promised to spread through the Da-Tung Mun into the native city, and once it got going in those narrow streets it would bring in the whole population, not one percent of which would know why they were fighting.

Together they advanced step by step until they struck the full pressure of the mob. Behind them others had closed in, and now they were as isolated as the Swatow serang himself, and with not a hope of getting through to him. Twenty men could not have forced a passage against that human wall.

It became necessary to think only of themselves, to keep on their feet and try to work a way to the edge of the mob and thus escape. But each way they turned the mob seemed denser, and suddenly, as Blake's eyes caught those of the black monk, he knew that the latter was definitely suspicious of him.

Despite his native courage, a cold shiver ran down Blake's spine. There was something in those slit eyes that rested on his that held an overpowering menace. There was telegraphed to him the threat of unmentionable tortures if he should be the man the black monk suspected him of being. The thought drove him to a fresh access of frantic effort.

Tinker sensed that something had occurred, but could not guess what it was. It was sufficient for him, however, that Blake was making a special drive for some reason, and, playing up to his master, he broke into a perfect fury of cutting, stabbing, hacking.

The very force of their combined efforts carried them through the press. On and on for a good twenty feet or so they plunged until the edge looked within measurable distance. Then as the mob closed in once more, they saw just ahead of them the black monk. He was still standing with the folded arms, his head bent and his eyes regarding the battle in a detached manner as if it touched him not at all, as if he were profoundly interested in an abstract contemplation of this outburst of men's passions. But, as his eyes came round to Blake's and he saw how near the edge Blake had fought his way, there came suddenly into those sloe-colored orbs a sudden flame. It glowed but for a moment before giving way to a sinister narrowing of the lids.

Then for the first time since the riot had started (so far as Blake knew) he spoke. One word only he muttered —a guttural command that seemed to change those on the outer rim into demons. Their yells grew wilder than ever. For some reason they gazed as one man towards Blake, then they came plunging in towards him and the lad who was with him.

They did not seem to connect the lad with the tall coolie, but before they reached Blake they felt the force of Tinker's sword. There was no room now for easy work; no time to strike with flat blade; it was a case of defence or death as they stood, and, snatching a sword from the hand of the man who was trying to thrust the point in under his arm, Blake caught the lad by the shoulder, jerked him back and dived into the fray.

Never in all his long career had Sexton Blake fought more fiercely than during those next few minutes. Those flat, slit eyes that mocked him from the edge of the mob drove him to an insane fury. He was completely berserk. There, within that black robe, was one of the creatures who had come out of that layer in Cheng-tu. There, by the permission of high heaven, was one who knew the secret of the Golden Book. There was one who had been sent to the coast to discover him, Sexton Blake, and mete out to him horrors that were unholy and unthinkable.

48

Every drop of blood in Blake's body was a-surge. Within him was a flame that gave him the strength of three men. And he needed it.

Despite the added flurry of the attack he stemmed it —he and the lad. Not even that crazed fury of the mob could carry it against those two flashing blades. Man after man went down, and still those two stood unscathed. It was a miracle that some thrusting weapon did not reach them from low down, for there seemed to be dozens of the Yellow Devils crawling about beneath the ones who stood upright.

At one moment, so furious was their assault, that they carried their weapons almost to the edge of the crowd. Two yards more then they would have a clear run for. The black monk now watching closely, saw the danger, and called out another command. Instantly those to the right and left wheeled and made a fresh wall between Blake and the lad and freedom. For a moment Blake's control snapped, and with a cry he hurled his weapon full at the face beneath that black cowl. His aim was good. Before the monk could dodge the heavy, cutting sword had struck him full in the mouth.

(Blake is now well in the enemy's country, menaced by the sinister hordes of the Black Abbott. This fine story goes from strength to strength. Don't miss even one future installment!)

Part 4.

The Black Abbot of Cheng-tu
The Most Stirring Action-Serial we have Yet Published!

How it Began

IT was the raiding and sinking of a small river-steamer eighty miles above Hankow, on the great Chinese waterway of the Yangtse, that was the direct cause of Sexton Blake's and Tinker's latest visit to China.

The boat was carrying a treasure which, to millions of Orientals, was holy the Golden Book of Buddha. This sacred book had been in the possession of the Chuen-to-yan (high priest) of Canton until the emissaries of the Grand Lima of Thibet secured it; and it changed hands once again when the mysterious Black Abbot of the monastery of Cheng-tu stole it in turn from the river-steamer.

Sexton Blake, at the urging of Hong-lo-soo, a wealthy Chinese merchant of London, and for patriotic reasons, agreed to make a journey to China, and there follow the trail of the Golden Book, and recover it, if possible, on behalf of the Grand Lama.

Rumours had been heard of the Black Monk's retreat far up the River Yangtse, so Blake and Tinker made the first stage of their journey, disguised as Chinese coolies, to Shanghai in the stokehold of a native steamer, intending to work his passage up-river on a sailing junk.

Various clues as to the whereabouts of the Black Monk are given Blake by his friend Hsui-fsi, otherwise Sir Gordon Saddler, an Englishman. These lead him to the riverside, where he becomes involved in a fierce mob fight.

During the fight there appears on the scene the figure of a black garbed monk, who appears to be directing the attackers, but in sinister silence.

Blake and Tinker are hemmed in, trying to cut their way through the mob which set upon them, when the disguised detective flings the sharp cutting sword which he has been using direct at the Black Monk's face.

His aim was good. Before the monk could move the weapon had struck him full in the mouth.

50

Our story Continues.

It dropped to the ground at his feet, and a hand flew up, covering his mouth. There was a spurt of crimson as the blood poured between his fingers. He stood rocking on his heels, a look of terrible threat in his sloe-coloured eyes as his hot gaze held Blake's.

But the success of that chance throw had put new life into Blake. With a sudden twist and grab he possessed himself of a fresh weapon, and then, yelling the war-cry of the Four Lakes Tong, he drove forward once more. His arm rose and descended like a flail. Hacking, cutting, sweeping the long broadened blade in a great circle had cut a swathe before him as one mowing a field of grain.

Once more he almost succeeded in reaching the edge of the crowd, when he became aware that Tinker was no longer close to him. He paused, even allowing himself to be driven back as he sought desperately to locate the lad. He was no longer on his feet, that was certain. Had one of those weapons found his heart?

All oblivious now to freedom or anything but Tinker, Blake started back. He was deliberately turning his shoulder on the promise of escape; but what mattered that if the lad had fallen to the mercy of these yellow fiends?

Then he saw the lad.

Down in the dust and filth of the ground he lay, huddled up in a way that sent a chill to Blake's heart. If before he had fought furiously, now he cleaved a way through that press as if his arm were the flail of a giant. Right and left he swept the steel until he had a circle cleared about him. Another effort and he would be at the lad's side.

But that moment was not to come for Sexton Blake. Before he could achieve his purpose there came a terrific drive of hundreds of coolies, who seemed to be driving a human wedge straight through to the bank of the river.

Blake was caught up in it.

He had one last agonised sight of Tinker, then the lad's form was blotted from view and Blake was lifted clean off his feet, and the wedge swept on —lifted clear of the ground and carried out over the maze of sampans, where a score of hands caught him and bore him to the outer line of junks.

Tinker Tells His Tale.

TINKER was severely bruised, but by no means as badly wounded as his huddled attitude had led Blake to believe.

When he felt himself going down, after being separated from Blake, Tinker knew that unless he protected his head from those plunging feet, and stabbing sticks he would be trampled to death without a chance of saving himself, even if the feet of the mob were bare or clad only in slippers. Therefore he rolled over into a crouch, as he would have done had he gone down in the middle of a football scrum, and while the battle raged overhead he played doggo.

When a lessening of the pressure came he essayed to rise, with the idea in his mind of fighting away through to Blake; but he soon found that to be out of the question, so, praying that his master would get clear of the press and away without discovering how he had been cut off, he cowered lower, waiting patiently for an opportunity to slide out.

He was aware when the great back-rush came as Blake drove furiously back into the press. He tried again then to rise, but was smothered down. From then on he could not tell what was happening until, for a reason he did not know, the press above him suddenly thinned. No one seemed to pay any attention to him as he staggered to his feet. He was dizzy, and at first, could not make out anything except to see in a hazy way that the greater part of the mob had surged down the bank of the Whangpoo and was now tossing about on the sampans and the wupans.

Among the few who still remained on the scene of the recent battle he saw a group over to the right, and thought he could distinguish among them the Swatow serang. But it was Blake for whom he was now concerned, and when his gaze came back to the river he uttered a sudden, sharp cry. For there, in the very centre of that tossing throng, he caught sight of his master, and, gliding about like some sinister wraith, was the Black Monk.

Horrified, Tinker watched the progress of the mob as they bore Blake outwards towards the line of junks. To go after him would be sheer madness, as he well knew. Single-handed he could do nothing against that horde, now that Blake's mighty arm was quiet. But he could watch and then seek aid.

He saw Blake lifted high and swung over the side of a great junk which lay stern to stem with the one from which dangled the red paper streamers. There was one brief moment during which Blake was flung high in the air, then he disappeared from view and the human wave rolled on over. He was gone.

Tinker turned and gazed once more towards where the Swatow serang was lying. That individual was now on his feet, being supported by a dozen of his adherents, his gaze rested on Tinker for a moment, but there was no sign of recognition, no fleeting message in that regard. It was this lack of recognition that determined Tinker on seeking aid elsewhere. Where could he go?

Hsui-fsi!

He knew well enough that Blake had been deeply anxious that there should be no personal contact between them and Sir Gordon. So careful had Blake been that he had cut even that thread. But surely he had not counted on such a disastrous occurrence as this? Tinker did not know just what was causing the hostile demonstration against them, but, he had seen enough since they arrived in Shanghai to know that already the strength of the mysterious Black Monk of Cheng-tu was pitted against them. And this Black Monk who had hovered about during the battle like some loathsome vulture could only be one of the creatures from that evil hole.

Was this not sufficient reason for him to disregard Blake's caution and seek the wise council of Hsui-fsi? To whom else could he turn? Certainly not the British authorities. Even if they knew that Blake was in China, they could give no official countenance to his presence. His mission was one upon which the British Government would probably have frowned.

From the moment he had discarded his own identity in Hong Kong he had cut himself off from all succour in that direction. He was there, not on behalf of either the southern faction or the north allies. Sometime before that he had played a political hand in China; but this time he was there on a private mission which had to do with the obscure battle waging between the Chuen-to-yan of Canton and his Holiness the Dalai Lama of Tibet. Therefore a lone hand it must be.

Tinker hung about the bank for some time longer. It was torture to him to drag himself away from the spot. There, so near, was Blake, in the foul hold of that junk he had been cast, and Heaven alone knew what devilry was in store for him. The desire to remain near, and the urge to seek aid, warred within the lad until he knew not what to do. Then, as he once more caught sight of the Black Monk, he came to a decision. He would seek Hsui-fsi, come what might.

Once clear of the place he broke into a shambling trot. He made straight along the river bank, past the Da-Tung Mun, keeping away from the curve of the wall of the native city until he came to the edge of the French concession. He entered this, but instead of continuing through to the British concession, which lay just beyond, he turned to the left.

A direct north-westerly line brought him to the edge of the racecourse that lies in a corner between the French and British settlements, and skirting that, Tinker passed through the flat, dusty, central district until he came to the Suchow Creek. On the other side of that along the Suchow Road, was Sir Gordon's estate, a place of extensive grounds shut in by a high wall.

Tinker did not disguise from himself the risk of approaching the place by road. He was quite aware that eyes may have followed his course all the way from the Da-Tung Mun, although if he had been shadowed he had been unable to pick up the person who might be trailing him, though he had tried again and again.

He determined, therefore, to approach the place by the Suchow Creek. That would run along the rear wall of Sir Gordon's place, and, from the creek, he might be able to gain the grounds without attracting attention. But to attempt to hire a sampan would be too risky, so, despite his impatience to see the old man and his anxiety over Blake, he forced himself to walk slowly along the bank of the creek as if he had nothing whatsoever to do.

There were, as usual, packed lines of sampans in the creek. The lad's objective was an empty craft —not an easy thing to find when one remembers that the great majority of the river people live, eat, and spend most of their lives aboard the sampan which happens to house them. But at last he saw a small one swinging by itself on the outer fringe of the line. It was necessary to cross several in order to reach it, but little attention was paid to him as he made his way outwards. He stepped aboard as if the boat was his own property, and, picking up the sweep, cast off.

He was on the qui vive for a shout at any moment. It did not come. Not a voice hailed him as he slid along the sluggish surface of the creek, moving slowly until he should get away from the immediate vicinity of where the sampan had been moored.

Once he was under the arch of a bridge, however, he laid to with a will, and in something under a quarter of an hour he saw ahead of him the old grey lichened walls that separated Hsui-fsi's garden from the water.

Tinker brought the sampan into the bank, and sprang out at the water-steps. He allowed the craft to drift away, careless now of where it should fetch up. He knew the waterside gate would be closed, and he found the wall high. But that was not an impassible barrier to Tinker.

Springing up, he grasped the top, and, despite the crossed spikes on it, managed to squirm his way over. He dropped to a soft earth bed on the other side, finding as he straightened up that he could just see the house in the distance through the trees. Then, weak and shaky though he was, he started on a staggering trot through the garden, to appear a few moments later to the astonished eyes of Hsui-fsi and the Korean priest.

For a man who had weathered eighty-eight years, most of which had been stormy, Sir Gordon Saddler revealed an extraordinary activity at sight of the lad who came lurching up through the garden. He knew it was Tinker, despite the perfection of the lad's disguise. He knew his coming meant that disaster of some kind had overtaken Blake.

He hastened in from the balcony to the upper hall, clapping his hands as he went. By the time he reached the lower floor half a dozen servants had appeared, and, gazing fearfully at their master —for they knew only something very exceptional could inspire him to this activity —they followed him outside.

Almost at the edge of the lower veranda Tinker went down. His spirit was still fighting, for he struggled to rise; but not even his gallant effort was sufficient to overcome the wave of unconsciousness that swept over him.

Hsui-fsi made a clicking sound with his tongue. It acted as a spur to his servants. Half a dozen pairs of hands picked up the lad and carried him in. A word from Sir Gordon sent them up the stairs, and, after visiting a room on the right of the lower hall, Sir Gordon emerged with a small green phial in his hand.

Tinker had been laid on a chaise long on the upper veranda. He was lying back with closed eyes, quite relaxed, while the Celestials clustered about, wondering why their august master —one of the most unapproachable in all China, should waste his time over this carrion coolie. But they did not get a chance to discover. Hsui-fsi drove them away and bent over the lad. A few whiffs of the pungent liquid in the green phial soon brought him round, and as his lids lifted Sir Gordon laid a hand on his wrist.

"It is you?" he whispered, in English.

Tinker made an effort to nod.

"Yes, sir," was the hoarse response. "The —the guv'nor!"

"I know —I know. You will feel better in a few moments, my lad. This spirit is powerful. As soon as you can tell me just what has happened."

The thought of Blake's present danger was a more powerful tonic to Tinker than the spirit in that flask. As full realisation returned to him he struggled into a sitting posture. Then, beginning in halting fashion, but getting his voice more and more under control as he proceeded, he told Hsui-fsi what had happened from the moment they reached Shanghai that morning.

At mention of the red paper streamers in the temple by the Si-Mun, Sir Gordon nodded understandingly. Again when Tinker spoke of the message of the water-melon seeds he made a gesture. Those were part of the trail he had said. And once more when Tinker mentioned the Swatow serang he showed that he knew.

But when the lad came to the riot that had broken out, the attack on the Swatow serang, and the appearance of the Black Monk, Hsui-fsi gave a startled exclamation.

"And Blake," he urged quickly— "what of him?"

"I went down, sir, and they got the guv'nor —carried him across to one of the junks. I saw them pour over the side like a horde of rats. And the Black Monk was there, too."

"The junk —would you know it again?"

"Yes, sir, I marked it well."

"Then there is no time to be lost. Unless we can cut out that junk this night and rescue your master we shall be too late. How it is to be done, Heaven only knows!"

Bad Tidings.

BEFORE Hsui-fsi could speak further, there was the sound of a commotion somewhere below. The old gentleman lifted his head and listened; then he made a swift gesture for the Korean priest to step in through one of the open windows near at hand.

The voices of several servants were now plainly to be heard, and Tinker was wondering if he, too, should make himself scarce when, through the wide-open door that led to the central upstairs hall, he caught sight of the Swatow serang. Sir Gordon saw the fellow at the same moment, and laid a hand on Tinker's arm, signing to him to remain as he was.

The serang presented a grievous sight. His clothes —what few he had been wearing —were in rags, his nakedness being covered now by little more than a loin cloth. One arm was in an improvised sling, his face was scarred and caked with dried blood in half a dozen places, one ear was almost severed from his head, and a dirty, blood-stained bandage was tied round his head. Yet, with it all, he carried himself erect, and the fire of battle still shone in his eye.

He had brushed aside the servants who would have restrained him, and now, as he reached the veranda, he made a deep salaam to Hsui-fsi. He, like nearly everyone else in China, had no suspicion that Hsui-fsi was other than a very rich and powerful mandarin.

"Well?"

Sir Gordon shot the word out curtly in the man's own language.

"August One, I have dragged my unworthy person here to submit to the punishment, it may please thee to name. I have failed, and my unspeakable carcass is filled with shame."

"But thou didst as I commanded?"

"Excellency, I went to the Da-Tung-Mun even as thou didst graciously command me. There I took up my stand and spoke to the river recruits as thou didst plan. And there came one who seemed to my unworthy gaze to be he whom thou hadst bid me watch for. I gave him the sign —he seemed to respond —but before aught else could be done a fight broke out. And the Black Monk was there."

"Aie. Look you at this lad, Kan-Wo. Hast seen him before?"

The serang turned bloodshot eyes in Tinker's direction, he did not show surprise, but he must have been amazed to see the same lad sitting there whom he had seen wielding a cutting sword back by the Da-Tung-Mun. Up to this moment Tinker had been partially concealed by Sir Gordon's long tunic and, of course, out of respect for his master, the serang had not dared to allow his eyes to stray about him.

"Hoo-la, August One, I have seen him before, and to-day!"

"He, too, was there during the fight; and he, too, saw the Black

Monk. Knowest thou, Kan-Wo, what became of the other?"

"Hoo-la, Excellency. He was taken aboard a junk."

"Speak, for time is short"

"Excellency, the tall one was carried aboard a coffin junk."

Sir Gordon Saddler started up and, in his excitement, almost gave vent to a round English exclamation. This was worse, far worse than he had looked for.

"A coffin junk! Art thou sure, Kan-Wo? Mark you, if thou be mistaken I shall take from thee the few things which the Black Monk has left you!"

"Excellency, these unworthy eyes have seen. It is the junk of Len-tse-fo —the coffin man of Ichang. The mark was on the bow beneath the eye which charms away the river spirits."

"The circle and line?"

"Even so, Excellency."

Hsui-fsi turned to Tinker. Their eyes met, and Tinker gave a slight nod. He remembered perfectly seeing a rough circle drawn on the bow of the junk aboard which Blake had been carried. Like every other junk, there was, of course, an eye painted on the bow in order to pacify the river spirits, and guard those aboard from their attack. But beneath this had been the other mark, and while Tinker had not known what it might indicate, he had identified the junk by it, for he had seen nothing of the sort on any other craft. But a coffin junk — what did it mean? Why should Hsui-fsi show such perturbation at the news?

"Aie, Kan-Wo. This is indeed bad tidings you bring! The junk of Len-tse-fo, the coffin man of Ichang."

Sir Gordon walked away to the other end of the veranda and stood in deep thought. Tinker would have given much to know just what this all meant; but not even before the serang, whose loyalty had been proved, dared he to reveal the fact that he was no coolie lad. But a wave of deep uneasiness overwhelmed him as he saw Hsui-fsi strike his hand again and again on the rail of the veranda. Never before had Tinker observed Sir Gordon upset like this.

A coffin junk! What could it mean?

Presently Hsui-fsi came back, walking slowly now, showing to the full the burden of his years. He stood before the serang and spoke deliberately in Cantonese —a dialect with which he knew Tinker was well acquainted.

"This coffin junk —it is still there?"

"No, Excellency. I waited at the Da-Tung-Mun until I saw it moving off down the Whangpoo. Even now it will be working along past the Bund of the British to the lower waters of the Great River."

"It will go up the river?"

"Where else, Excellency? It is the junk of Len-tse-fo. It is loaded with coffins. It must go to Ichang and, perhaps, through the gorges beyond. It is on the lap of Great Buddha."

"Aie! Speak not of Great Buddha, thou who hast permitted this!" snapped Hsui-fsi.

The serang flinched under his words, but his eyes did not waver. There could be no doubt that the man was speaking the truth as he knew it.

"The lower waters of the Yangtze," repeated Sir Gordon. "If it enters the river to-night, it will go up with the flotilla to Chinkiang. Perhaps it may reach Nanking by to-morrow. Once it gets beyond Nanking it is all hopeless. It must be overtaken. Go below, Kan-Wo. Hold thyself in readiness, I shall send for thee later. Thou hast thy men?"

"Hoo-la. Excellency —I have what are left."

"I shall provide others. But hold! Go now to the Da-Tung-Mun. Collect men and bring thy junk along the Bund which lies in front of the British concession. Cast thy cables beyond Suchow Creek —be ready for the river this night. Return here as soon as thou has done this."

"I go. Excellency."

With another deep salaam the battered and wounded serang took himself off. The moment he was gone Tinker asked the question that had been torturing him.

"A coffin junk, Hsui-fsi," he said, in low, eager tones, "what does it mean?"

"It is bad news, Tinker, bad news. It could scarcely be worse. The coffin junk and the Black Monk —a devilish combination. Len-tse-fo, the coffin man of Ichang, has several junks. He carries but one cargo —coffins, with human remains.

"You know that death among the Chinese is a peculiar thing, Tinker. It is all part and parcel of their ancestor worship. If a Chinaman lives abroad, he tries in every way to leave enough behind him so that his body may be brought back to China, and buried with

59

his ancestors. There is an enormous traffic in this, and Len-tse-fo, of Ichang, handles most of the coffins going to the Upper Yangtse. This junk with the circle and line is one of his craft, and Kan-Wo says it is loaded with coffins. A coffin junk is sacred from interference. Not even the river pirates would interfere with such a cargo. As for the bodies, they may be kept for weeks or months, or even years, until the elders of the village where the man was born pronounce an auspicious day for the burial.

"So don't you see what it means if your master is being spirited away in one of these junks? He may be thrust into one of the coffins, to die by slow suffocation? He may be kept alive for further torture. But, whatever fate is in store for him, that junk will not be interfered with. They are safe in taking him out of Shanghai that way, as if they were able to spirit him away. And unless we can locate that junk, cut it out from the rest of the flotilla going up the river to-night —unless we can capture every man jack on board so that no word of the truth may go up river, then it means a horrible doom for your master as surely as the sun will rise over the China Sea to morrow."

Tinker's lip was quivering as he staggered to his feet.

"But —but it must not be, Sir Gordon!" he cried hoarsely. "The guv'nor must be rescued before it is too late!"

Hsui-fsi held up one hand.

"My lad, you may depend that I shall employ every resource I control in order to effect his release. But to pick out that junk in the darkness —boldly to attack a coffin junk and cut it out of the flotilla . . . I must think, Tinker, I must think! This is such a thing as I never anticipated!"

The Coffin Ship.

ONCE Blake found himself being overwhelmed he was helpless to resist, more particularly because his sword had been twisted from his grasp. The moment this menace was removed scores of hands reached out for him, and he was literally lifted across the line of sampans and wupans to the outer junks, as Tinker and the Swatow serang had seen.

They had seen, too, how Blake had been heaved into the air by his captors; then that sinister disappearance with the Black Monk hovering on the outskirts of the gang, apparently a mere observer but in reality directing everything.

60

But both Tinker and Kan-Wo were mistaken in thinking that Blake was immediately hurled into the hold of the junk. It was, as Kan-Wo had maintained a coffin junk from Ichang, and, at that moment the hold was packed with Chinese coffins —rough contraptions hollowed mostly from trees, their covers sealed over the contents with heavy Ning-po lac or varnish.

It was a gruesome cargo, and in saying that it would pass through even the river pirates without being molested Hsui-fsi had been right. There is nothing held in greater respect in China than the dead, and, indeed, there is considerable ground for maintaining that the terrible Boxer outrages of a quarter of a century ago were inspired because a railway was carried through a Chinese graveyard.

But it was into the cabin in the high stern that Blake was taken. For himself he was now quiescent, waiting to see what the next move would be. He was perfectly well aware that the Black Monk was behind it all, and he was not a little anxious to discover if the latter had any suspicion that he was not what he seemed.

From the words and actions of those who held him he knew that they looked upon him simply as a crazy coolie from the south, who, for some reason or other, had incurred the enmity of the Black Monk. Not half a dozen among them knew just what the Black Monk was doing there. They only knew that the word had gone out from several tongues that any Black Monk was to be obeyed in whatsoever he should demand. And from Shanghai to the Somo country on the far western borders of China every coolie, be he never so ignorant, knew of the Black Monk of Cheng-tu, and of the power of the sable robe.

The interior of the cabin was rough indeed. It filled most of the high stern of the junk, and, at the back, were two windows, having no glass as we know it but being filled in with translucent oyster-shell plaques. The dim light that was admitted was rather pleasing than otherwise; but for Sexton Blake, the effect was considerably modified as he saw several crimson paper streamers, bearing certain gilt verses, which told him for the first time that he was aboard a coffin junk.

Blake's mind worked swiftly. A coffin junk! What did this mean? Only the most highly educated Chinese were as conversant with the history, mythology, art, religion, and classics of their own country as Sexton Blake. For many years Blake had studied China and things Chinese. More than any other private investigator he had handled cases in the vast expanse of the erstwhile yellow empire; more than any secret agent he had carried out delicate investigations for his own Government. He was steeped in the lore of the Middle Kingdom — and as he realised that now he was aboard a coffin junk a shiver ran down his spine.

In a flash he realised just how safe his captors would be to keep him on such a craft. He had no means of knowing if it carried a cargo at present, or if it was waiting for one. But he did know that he would have to be very, very wary if he were to outwit his present captors.

And then suddenly he found the Black Monk standing before him.

For a long time past Sexton Blake had heard vague rumours about the mysterious Black Monk of Cheng-tu. Where this gossip had had its genesis, in just what way it was spread throughout China, what it really portended, he did not know. But that there was a sinister figure of the sort he believed; and, after the events of that afternoon, was more certain than ever.

But this black-robed monk who stood before him —was he the supreme figure of mystery? Or was he but a unit in some widespread scheme which had burst out in one direction in the daring theft of the Golden Book of Buddha?

Time and again Blake had pondered on the possible identity of the Black Monk of Cheng-tu. From among all the various figures of importance in the land of the dragon he had tried to fit some one individual into the picture, so to speak. It was only natural that in his consideration should loom the shadow of Prince Wu Ling —the master mind in nearly all the intrigue in China which Blake had come up against for some years past.

But he had been able to get hold of nothing definite to point to Wu Ling as being the Black Monk of Cheng-tu. Even quite recently he had played a daring game against the Manchu, but not once then had he seen anything of the Black Monk. That mysterious figure seemed to have leaped into prime importance quite recently. And now he asked himself if this man who stood before him could be the master or just an underling.

One thing at least was plain —the riot which was started that afternoon by the Da-Tung-Mun had been inspired by this monk; it was, without doubt, a showing of the hand of the master mind behind the affair. It was plain warning that every loophole was being watched. So far Blake knew what that meant. But he could not know the full threat of it until he knew whether his identity were suspected or not. If it were guessed that he was no southern coolie, but the British detective, Sexton Blake, then all his efforts had gone for naught, and his death would be slow as it would be sure.

He eyed the monk with as little expression as any Celestial could have shown. The man had thrown back his cowl, revealing a shaven head. Flat eyes, protruding ears, a triangular-shaped face (disfigured now where Blake's sword had cut him), the fellow was no true Chinese, that was plain. He may have been a Tartar, or even Tibetan. And when he spoke, although he used the dialect of the Upper Yangtse, Blake could detect the accent which stamped him as coming from much farther west. But the thing that mattered most to Blake just then was the certainty borne in upon him that he had never seen the man before.

"You have given much trouble to my men, dog," came the words coldly, dispassionately. "Whence comest thou and what hast thou to do with him of the south who would recruit men in the north?"

There was a faint stirring within Blake. Those words contained no hint that his identity was suspected. They might be sheer camouflage, however, to draw him out. It was going to need wary treading.

"The quarrel was none of my beginning." he answered, deliberately choosing Cantonese as his vehicle of speech.

"You speak the tongue of the north, or you would not be here. We have no Cantonese here."

Blake switched into the dialect of Shantung and gave the same reply.

"But you were in the midst of the fight." persisted the monk. "You are no stray coolie from the south country. You were friend of the other dog from the south."

Blake was a little puzzled that the monk had not demanded greater respect in his answer. He had deliberately eschewed using the usual flowery adjectives, his pose being that of a rough character from the south who cared for no man of the north.

"Never before had my eyes rested on him." he responded. "I am, as thou hast said, a man of the south country. I know nothing and care nothing for the north. I came to this place in a ship. It matters not to me whether I return to the south or sail up the Great River. I am without bonds."

"Whence comest thou? Thou art no Cantonese."

"Yunnan."

The monk studied him closely. In naming the far south-western province of China, Blake had taken a chance. In all China there is no rougher element than the Yunnanese, and if this statement were accepted then it might account for much —that is, if the monk was not playing with him. But, in any case, Blake had made up his mind that the moment an opportunity occurred, he would make a dash for freedom. He knew only too well what would be his fate once he was imprisoned in the hold of this coffin junk. Little did he dream then what the real cargo of that craft was.

"Thou wilt have a chance to speak further to one who will know how to extract the truth!" snapped the monk suddenly. "You have been anxious to travel up the Great River. You shall do so."

He swung to the Celestials who were crowded behind him. Before giving his instructions he deliberately spat, then he made a gesture towards Blake.

"Take him. Place him safely. He shall travel with the other sacred bodies which we carry. But give him air. We shall deliver him alive."

Blake did not resist. As a dozen or more coolies rushed in on him he allowed them to seize his arms and legs and body. They half carried him out on to the deck, and then along the deck forward to the open hatch. As they paused at the edge Blake looked down. A sudden wave of nausea swept over him as he saw beneath tier upon tier of round, wooden coffins, each glistening with a coat of Ning-po varnish. It seemed to him that a breath of cold death rose from this charnel house, but the time was to come when Blake was to learn that this was pure imagination.

Still he did not resist. Just beneath him was an empty coffin with the cover drawn back. Already a couple of coolies were cutting slits in the cover so that air might enter. This was to be his "berth" during the long journey up the Yangtse. Thus was he to be "delivered," as the monk had said. And no one knew better than Sexton Blake that the moment the lid of that coffin closed on him he would be lost for ever to any chance of rescue.

So quiescent had he been that those who held him were lulled into a feeling that all the fight had gone out of him. Their hands loosened a little as they bent forward to watch the progress of the two who were cutting the holes. Still Blake waited until the work was almost done, and then, gathering every particle of strength to his aid, he turned into a human hurricane.

Right and left he flung them as if they were dolls. Before they could grasp what he was at he had ploughed a way through them, and was making for the side —the waterside, where the river ran past towards the Bund of the British concession.

Directly in his path stood the Black Monk. As during the progress of the fight on shore, his arms were folded and his head thrust forward as if viewing the whole business in a purely detached manner. Whether he expected his robe and cold eye to subdue this tall Yunnanese who was running amok, Blake didn't know. But if he did he learned differently when Blake struck him in full rush. The monk was flung against the side, a startled oath escaped him as he recovered, and, flinging out his hands, made to grasp the fugitive. But by this time Blake was on the gunwale, and, without waiting further, took the water in a clean header.

He swam under the surface as far as possible. When he was forced to break for air, he found himself some distance away from the coffin junk. He did not doubt that pursuit would follow immediately, and he would not have been surprised if coolies from other junks joined in. But he was determined to sell his freedom as dearly as possible. Beyond was the French concession, then the British, and for him the latter meant safety even without disclosing his identity. To attempt to swim the full distance with a horde of howling yellow devils after him was, of course, out of the question; but there was the chance that he might come upon a stray sampan, and he had no doubt about being able to get control of such should he once get aboard.

Yet, had he looked back he would have seen that no apparent pursuit was in progress. The mob of coolies on the coffin junk were crowded at the rail, watching his progress, but not one essayed to plunge in after him. Nevertheless, the Black Monk was not inactive.

After his clutching hands had missed Blake he had rushed into the stern cabin of the junk, and by the time Blake was ploughing along a good hundred yards or so from the spot where he had taken the water, the Black Monk broke through the coolies who had been gathered at the side, and who now made way for him at his approach.

In his hands he bore a long bow, an affair of mediaeval times, and thrust in the girdle of his robe was an arrow. No ordinary arrow was this, but a long shaft with a wide, slightly padded head. Away up on the Yangtse there are those who wield this antiquated weapon with extraordinary skill, and, in the hands of an expert, it can stun and bring down any beast up to the size of a cave tiger. It depends entirely on the nicety with which it is handled.

Standing at the side the Black Monk fitted the shaft.

Twang!

Away sped the arrow over the muddy waters of the Whangpoo. It rose and fell in a long curve towards the dark spot that marked the fugitive's head. And then, as he urged himself forward in a mighty stroke —as he was beginning to feel the first faint stirring of hope — something descended upon him with the force of a pole-axe.

Blake never knew what struck him. He plunged into oblivion in the fraction of a moment, rolling over like a drowned dog as the blunted arrow recoiled from his head and floated alongside him.

Back on the coffin junk the Black Monk made a curt gesture.

"Bring the pig back!" he snapped.

And a score of coolies sprang to obey.

(In the Black Monk's power —stunned and helpless! That is Blake's present plight. What startling events happened after Tinker's desperate attempt at rescue you have yet to learn. The next instalment will put you wise. Order in time!)

A Coffin Junk in China   /drf

Part 5.

First published in issue 1240 of the Union Jack magazine, 1927.

How it began.

ONE of China's most sacred possessions, "The Golden Book of Buddha" is stolen by the Black Abbot of Cheng-tu while on its way up the Yangtse from Canton to the Grand Lama of Tibet. Sexton Blake, having been implored to help trace it, is in China with Tinker, both disguised as coolies, for that purpose.

After many adventures, the pair become involved in a mob fight, inspired by a monk dressed in black. Blake is separated from Tinker, and carried on to a coffin-junk, where he is imprisoned by the Black Monk. Tinker, fearing for his guv'nor's safety, rushes to Hsui-fsi, otherwise Sir Gordon Sadler, an Englishman. The lad tells how he saw Blake taken to the junk, and Sir Gordon decides to try and capture it with another boat belonging to one of his men, Kan-Wo.

Blake, in the meanwhile, makes a desperate bid for liberty, but he is thwarted by the Black Monk, and brought back to the junk.

Our story continues.

THE muddy up rush of the lower estuary was sweeping up in full volume. Into that giant swirl came the waters of the Whangpoo, the Suchow Creek, the Hanchai, and all the other branch streams that had their life from the drainage of the Great River.

Between the low mud-banks hung a heavy mist, blanketing the face of the waters with suspended drops that was almost a rain. Not a light showed; scarcely was there the creak of a sweep to mark the passage of any junk. And yet the teeming life of the river went on under that curtain almost as industriously as if it had been day. The river folk of the Yangtse have an uncanny faculty of seeing through —or "smelling" through —the mists which have shrouded them from infancy.

It was a night when the river spirits would be abroad. Those craft which slid along through the shadows moved cautiously, not even a finger trailing in the water for fear that some evil demon would rise up and snatch at it. Farther down, along the great mooring lines, there would be much noise, shouting and beating of cymbals in order to scare away the demons of the mist. But higher up all was heavy and silent until . . . .

From out of the mist came the sound of distant pandemonium. Somewhere beneath that oppressive blanket moved a craft with full complement of "devil-chasers." Gradually the noise grew and grew until it seemed to reverberate from bank to bank —a full mile just there and it increased to a wild chaos of crashing discord, while the invisible craft slid along into the Chinkiang Channel.

Cymbals and brazen gongs clattered out harsh notes; hide drums and wooden tom-toms added to the horror of sound; short, sharp explosions of fire-crackers gave a more emphatic punctuation to the racket; and, mixing with it all, the hoarse voices of men as they chanted and howled and screamed to warn away the dread spires.

Such confusion of sound, such prodigality of burnt powder could only come from a vessel of some consequence. And those who know the Great River would have realised, as the medley smote them, that a coffin junk must be on the move. No silent passage was its, as would have been the carrying vehicle of the dead in the West; but an infernal upheaval of sound so that those who rode to their last abode should be well protected from the numerous demons which are so real to the Chinese mind.

On it came. Not another craft sliding through the murk but gave wide berth to this vessel of the dead. Its safe passage was secured. No man, not even the boldest of river pirates, would risk eternal perdition by interfering with the journey of the dead; for nothing is more sacred in all China.

Into the Chinkiang Channel it came, the men at the bow sweeps toiling mightily, even though the uprush of the water was in their favour, the lao pan (captain) hanging on the great stern steering sweep and the tai-kung (bow outlook man), most important of all, peering forth to detect the first sign of danger.

A journey in solitary state it was, until the great junk passed the unseen mouth of a muddy creek that drained out of the Tai Hu Marshes. A deep creek, and, by day, well-travelled, for by it one could reach the great canal that connected Nanking with Hangchow. But on this night only one vessel moved along its turgid current. And, as the clashing pandemonium signified the close approach of the coffin junk, a long, low wupan slid out of the mouth of the creek and headed into the Chinkiang Channel in such a way that it must run perilously close to the point where the coffin junk must pass.

Until that moment the wupan had revealed scarce a sign of life. In the stern, of course, was the lao-pan, and in the bow half a dozen rowers, with the tai-kung peering ahead. But all within the long mat covering which served as a cabin was silent —deathly still until the wupan struck the full force of the current.

But then a horde of shadowy forms crept out from beneath the mats. In an unceasing stream they crawled into bow and stern until fully a hundred men were gathered; and had there been light it would have been seen that each man carried either sword or fighting stave, or, in some eases, firearms. It was a sinister-looking crew, and at a well calculated moment, just before the gliding wupan slid in under the low counter of the coffin junk, a brilliant naphtha flare burst out in the bow, creating even in that blanket of mist a wide circle of illumination.

The terrific noise which had been beating upon the ears of those in the wupan —which had seemed above and below and all about them, now collapsed into scattered noises. Like magic that flare had arisen upon the surface of the river, and before the astounded crowd in the junk could guess what was at hand, two fearsome figures went bounding over the side, plunging among them with terrible cries and groans.

The figures were robed in long, trailing blue, with half-human, half-animal masks which completely concealed the features of those who wore them. In appearance they were exactly like the mythical river demons, Cho and Se, of whom every river coolie had heard dread whispers since childhood.

Not all their trailing white and red paper streamers —not that wild concatenation of sound had sufficed to keep them at bay. Heralded by that wild flare they had come out of the waters, and on their heels poured their creatures.

After one amazed breath those on the junk went into a mad panic. Utter abandon to the most awful terror that had ever gripped them drove them in a screaming mob along the deck, to the high stern. Followed the two masked demons and their yelling creatures, wielding weapons and showing stark bodies in the ghostly glare.

And then suddenly on the very crest of the high poop appeared a black-robed figure. No craven fear did he display at sight of those masked demons who had sprung out of the mist. On the contrary. He stood, calm and quiet, holding up one hand in a command to the press of terrified coolies who crowded at his feet.

What he would have said had he been given opportunity will never be known. But no matter what words had poured from his lips they would not have quelled the attack of those half-naked spirits of the night, who, had they been Buddhists, had committed the grossest piece of sacrilege in the whole calendar. But they were not Buddhists; nor were they Taoists. That mob consisted to a man of Mahommedans, of whom there are many thousands in China —and a Buddhist coffin junk meant nothing more than its name to them.

There was a settled procedure to their attack, for while a portion of them kept the crew of the junk herded at the stern the rest tore off the hatches, and, with torches which had sprung seemingly out of nowhere, jumped down among the tiers of rough, round coffins which glistened under the glare where the Ning-po varnish showed.

Among the first was a big serang with bandaged head. In his eyes was an expression that boded ill to any who might cross him, and in his hand a broad-bladed executioner's sword that could sever a man's head at a single blow.

It was he who pried out coffin after coffin, scrutinising each, while a coolie lad who attended him flung the discarded shells aside to the hands of those who waited. But at last the searching eye of the big serang came upon a big coffin in which slits had been cut. A guttural exclamation escaped him, and with half a dozen mighty prisings he ripped off half the cover. By this time the coolie lad was standing close to him, peering under his arm, and, at sight of the still face which was suddenly revealed, a sound, strangely like a sob, welled up in his throat.

A further ripping followed. They got the limp body out of the coffin —the form of the same tall coolie who had fought by the Da-Tung Mun that afternoon. Ready hands hoisted him to the deck. After him clambered the serang and the lad; then there came a chorus of shrill screams from the stern as the Black Monk rushed down among his men driving them with the flat of his hand to attack.

Anything might have happened during the next few minutes. There in the mist was the makings of a slaughter which might be lost in the same cloud which has hidden so many tragedies in China — might have happened, and would have run its course had it not been that the coolie who had been taken from the coffin opened his eyes.

His gaze was vague at first, but when one of the masked demons bent over him and spoke a few words, intelligence rushed into them. He made frantic efforts to get to his feet. At the first rush, half a dozen flaming torches had been knocked into the hold, and that seemed to drive him to greater frenzy.

Pawing, talking, gesticulating, he managed to convoy to the serang what he meant. There followed a sharp, shrill blast on a whistle.

It was well that those Mahommedan river dogs were well trained, for, all in ignorance, they were standing on the edge of annihilation.

The retreat was a confused tumbling over the side. So swiftly was the wupan cast off that some had to swim, but before the great naphtha flare was dowsed the last swimmer had been dragged aboard the wupan.

Came a sharp command:

"To your sweeps! Pull, you dogs; pull for the creek!"

Followed a rattle as the sweeps fell into the hollows, then a creaking as the wupan got under way, moving faster and faster under the urge of the lao-pan until it was out of the Chinkian Current and heading for the creek.

A couple of minutes passed —perhaps three —then, even as the wupan shot into the mouth of the creek, the whole world seemed to go up in a stupendous flash of crimson that shattered the night and tore asunder the curtain of fog as if it did not exist.

Then the awful bursting of sound, so soon after the flare that the human ear and human eye could not separate them —but it hammered down upon those aboard the wupan, flattening them physically to the deck, and thrumming on the eardrums to the point of unbearable vibration.

That upheaval —then darkness and the wild sweep of rushing water as a wave carried the wupan farther into the creek.

Danger Ahead.

FROM the creek the wupan slid into the channel which led to the Tai Hu Marshes. But it did not continue to that sodden stretch of country. There was, some two miles along, a narrow branching canal by which one could work along into the Suchow Creek, and, if one's craft was not too large, debouch into the Whangpoo near where it joined the outrush of the Yangtse.

Not a word was spoken during the passage except an occasional grunt of caution from the tai-kung or a low-voiced command from the lao-pan. Only those needed in the actual working of the wupan were on deck; the rest were once more concealed beneath the curved mat cabin that stretched along the whole centre part of the vessel.

In the very darkest corner were clustered three figures, quite invisible to each other in that stygian gloom. One was wrapped from head to foot in the long blue robe which, as a river demon, he had worn in boarding the coffin junk. But now his hideous mask was removed, and, had one been able to see his face, one would have discerned the wrinkled features of Hsui-fsi.

A second huddled figure was the coolie who had been rescued from the coffin in the hold; the third was the coolie lad who, in company with the Swatow serang, had taken a leading part in the attack. Needless to say, those two latter figures were Sexton Blake and Tinker.

There was much to be said between them. Blake, in a rough way, could put two and two together and understand how it had come that his rescue had been planned and so successfully carried out. The sight of the serang had given him the key to that. But Hsui-fsi was completely at a loss to understand why the coffin junk had been annihilated in that terrific explosion. He knew from Blake's agitation on regaining consciousness that he could explain the mystery, but not even among his trusted Mahommedans dared they discuss the matter. That must wait until they were safe inside the enclosure of the House of Many Virtues.

So they huddled together in silence while the wupan crept through the mist and stench of the almost stagnant canal into the narrow confines of the Suchow Creek. Here, an invisible but teeming population was all about them. On either side, they knew, lines of sampans would be moored, each containing its human quota —men and women and children. Even though they were now some four miles away from the spot where the coffin junk had gone up in flaming holocaust, the thunder of the explosion must have carried as far as the creek, and it was safe betting that all ears that heard it would have put it down to some terrible doings of the river spirits. The aim was to creep through and get the men dispersed while the river people still cowered in their craft under that blanket of mist.

It was some distance above where the high walls girdled the

House of Many Virtues, that the Wupan was drawn up. In uncanny fashion the tai-kung gave directions so that the craft was brought in close to a low stone revetment, which was quite empty of any moored sampans. So dense was the fog, that it was impossible for them to see anything else but the edge of the revetment, but each man knew that, less than a biscuit toss away, was a high-arched bridge by which one could reach the Suchow Road. Thence it was a straight way into Shanghai, where the men would scatter.

The Mahommedans crept out from beneath the mat shelter as stealthily as they had gone to the attack. One by one, they sprang from the side of the wupan to the revetment and disappeared in the mist. Not until the last was gone did Hsui-fsi stir himself, and then it was but to utter a command to the lao-pan. The man's silhouette was just visible against the dim outline of the curved end of the shelter.

"You can work the wupan back into the Tai Hu Canal from here?"

"Hoo-la, Excellency."

"Thou and the tai-kung?"

"Hoo-la, Excellency."

"Then let it be so. We shall proceed from here on foot. Kan-Wo, he is waiting?"

"Hoo-la, Excellency."

"Bid him attend me on the revetment. And mark thee well that no word of this journey shall be whispered by thee or thy men; the flame which thou saw and the noise which thou heard, did not exist. Remember this as the command of the Eagle of the North."

"Thy servant is deaf and blind, August One."

"Be it so. Thou wilt hear again when my commands are ready."

"Ho hang, Excellency."

With that, Hsui-fsi touched Blake's arm, and rose stiffly. The three crept out on to the deck where, at last, they were able to stand erect. As they stepped on to the revetment, they found the Swatow serang waiting for them, and he it was who acted as guide while they moved cautiously along the bank. They passed the end of the bridge, but did not cross. Keeping to the path along the revetment, they plodded on, coming once more to dense lines of moored sampans, which they sensed rather than saw.

Blake gave an arm to Sir Gordon on one side, while Tinker leant to his support on the other, and each of them grasped a loose end of

74

the serang's loincloth in order not to loose him.

It was indeed a strange procession that felt its way through that mist which lay over the whole basin of the Lower Yangtse —an aged man of nearly ninety years, a mystery man, indeed, who for more years than he cared to remember, had been mixed up in the whole gamut of intrigue that had riven China from end to end, and who, on this night, had been in the van of that attack on the coffin junk as if he had been less than half his age. That mystery man was known to the Chinese as Hsui-fsi, the Eagle of the North, and yet who was, in reality, an English baronet. Then the tall coolie who was on his right —a coolie who had passed muster under the searching gaze of the Black Monk, but who was no Celestial; and lastly, the coolie lad who was the exact counterpart of any dirty urchin that might have been picked up in any bazaar street from Peking to Canton. And yet all three were British!

How little that unseen river population dreamed that those ghostly figures creeping along, had been responsible for the dull booming sound that had swept over the low flatlands a couple hours before! How little they guessed that, close to them, were three individuals who were destined to play the leading part in one of the greatest mysteries that had ever shaken the Middle Kingdom!

The Swatow serang was like a bat.

Steadily, without any apparent hesitation, he strode on until it seemed to the confused senses of Blake and Tinker that they must have covered miles. But, at last, their guide came to a pause, and spoke in low tones to Hsui-fsi. The old gentleman fumbled under his robe for a few moments; then they could hear the faint tinkle of metal as he handed keys to the serang. A low, scraping sound followed, Hsui-fsi advanced, still supported by Blake and Tinker. They passed through an opening that made them press together, and the two detectives guessed they were in the garden of the House of Many Virtues. Like a shadow, the serang disappeared, leaving Hsui-fsi to guide them to the house.

Their first glimpse was a lantern hanging in the centre of a small aureole of illuminated mist. Next they stepped on to a veranda, and as they passed into the wide lower hall they recognised familiar surroundings.

Servants appeared, but Hsui-fsi paused only long enough to order refreshments to be served in his private room. And not until they had been seated some time —not until he had forced Blake to partake of both stimulant and nourishment, was any mention made of the startling denouement which had followed the attack on the coffin junk.

By now Hsui-fsi had discarded his long blue robe and, clad in loose tunic, was reclining on a divan, chain-smoking the yellow opium-impregnated cigarettes which he favoured. He had not sent for the Korean priest. He did not desire that even he should get a glimpse of Blake.

When Blake leant back at last, the old man nodded his head sagely.

"It is well that you recovered consciousness so soon to-night, my friend. Had you not done so, we should all have been in eternity now. And even yet, I do not understand it all."

Blake made a slight gesture with one hand.

"Nor did I guess the secret of the coffin junk, until I had been imprisoned in the hold," he answered. "It is well that I recovered consciousness there, if even for a few minutes, for it was there I heard certain words which told me the truth. If my attempt to escape had succeeded, then that sinister craft would still have been afloat."

"Your attempt to escape? When was that?"

Briefly Blake related to Hsui-fsi and Tinker how he had plunged through his captors just before being thrown into the hold, and how he had managed to get some distance away from the junk before something struck him into unconsciousness.

"I can't tell you what it was, for I don't know," he went on. "But whatever it was it acted like lightning. I only remember something striking me on the base of the skull with stunning force. After that I knew nothing more until I recovered consciousness in a very dark, confined space. I found myself unable to move, except to roll over, and it did not take me long to discover that I must be in an empty coffin. Holes had been cut in the wood, so I knew that it was not intended I should die just then.

"It was while I was in this sort of half state —half-conscious and yet on the verge of swooning again —that I heard muffled voices close to me. I listened and succeeded in gathering snatches of what was said. I recognised the voice of the Black Monk. The talk was of the coffin junk, of the cargo, and of the intention to make up the Yangtse to-night. I also was mentioned, only I could not hear what was said. But I knew then that the junk carried no cargo of corpses, even though the coffins were loaded."

"Not corpses? Then what?"

"Arms and ammunition."

"Great Heaven! That explains. But why was she disguised as a coffin junk?"

"Isn't it obvious? As such she would be immune from interference by any of the warring factions during the whole voyage up the river. Not even the river pirates would commit such 'sacrilege.' What better vehicle for the conveyance of arms and ammunition could be found? It does not concern us for whom the supplies were intended. In the present chaos in China the foes of to-day are the allies of tomorrow. Their political aims have no part in our present mission. It is the Golden Book of Buddha which we seek, and which has been lost somewhere among the little-known stretches of the upper Yangtse."

"You are right, Blake. It is the Golden Book. But if I had guessed what sort of cargo that junk carried. It was in my mind that not only must we rescue you, but that every man-jack on board the junk must be taken prisoner, and kept put away until your mission was completed. But now Fate has taken that duty from us. Those poor creatures —we can only regard them as ignorant tools of their masters —have been annihilated. They, at least, can send no whisper about you up the river."

Blake was thoughtful for a few moments.

"The explosion was terrific," he muttered at last. "It would seem that no creature on board could have survived that holocaust. And yet, the Black Monk, I am not so sure. When that burst of flame shattered the night I could have sworn I saw him going over the stern. If he had dived even a few moments before the explosion came he might have got clear. The greater force would be upwards not outwards."

"If that is so, then the danger is not lessened. He is as elusive as a shadow. Time and again I have been told of his presence, and again and again I have attempted to throw my net about him, but he has always slipped through. I had even begun to doubt his existence."

"He does exist. Both Tinker and I have seen him. He bears on his mouth the marks of the sword with which I struck him. He is no ghost."

"I believe now."

"Yet we cannot remain here even for the duration of this night," said Blake. "We must in no way be connected up with you. I wish it had not been necessary for us to have come into contact with you, even this evening. Nor would it have been necessary but for the disaster at the Da-Tung Mun. We must take up our pilgrimage again, Hsui-fsi. Our destination lies far up the Yangtse, and there is much dangerous ground to cover before we reach the place where 'the green rice-shoots are strongest.' Shanghai must know us no more. We must get past Chinkiang and Nanking before the truth of what happened to the coffin junk can be sent up the river."

Sir Gordon was sunk in deep silence for a long time. He knew that every work Blake spoke was true. Yet it grieved him sorely that these two lone Britons should plunge into the unknown, so ill-equipped for the dangers that lurked on every side. Even to get them to Chinkiang, to Nanking, and on the first stage of the long journey was, under the circumstances, a terrific problem. He could not go with them; he could only use what power he possessed to indicate where a friend might be found here, a helping hand there.

At last he spoke.

"Chinkiang it must be, Blake. And Nanking without delay. From that on there is the stretch to Hankow, and then Ichang. Ichang marks the halfway point, as it were. But if the stretch from here to Ichang is dangerous, those wild gorges above will prove doubly so. I must not hide from you the terrible menace of the upper basin. You will be there among the millions who give obeisance to none but the Chuen-to-yan, of Canton, and he is suzerain of the Black Monk of Cheng-tu."

"I have considered all that, dear friend. Can you think of anything to cover our way from here to Nanking?"

Hsui-fsi glanced round him slowly, then he bent forward, sinking his voice to a whisper.

"There is one way, Blake. It is pregnant with danger, but if you can get through, your passage will be won."

"You mean?"

"I mean the People of the Pits."

Sexton Blake's head lifted sharply, his stained eyes were fixed on those of the baronet.

"Sir Gordon, do you mean that?" he asked, in a hoarse whisper. "Do they really exist? I have heard weird tales —"

"They do exist, Blake. Years ago I went among them. I once did them a service. I hold a talisman, an obscene thing, but it may prove your salvation if you are prepared to take that plunge. I do not suggest it. I mention it as a desperate way."

Blake glanced at Tinker thoughtfully, then he looked back at Sir Gordon.

"No way can be too desperate in this case," he said slowly. "I was thinking of Tinker and not myself. If that is a way, then we will take it, he and I together. We shall become one with the People of the Pits."

Word of a Weird Race.

THE People of the Pits!

It was many years since Sexton Blake had heard that phrase. Back in the early part of his career, when he had determined to specialise on China, so as to become an authority on every possible phase of the country of the yellow dragon, he had heard a whisper. Was it in Peking, or in Shanghai, or in Canton? He could not recall. But he remembered it.

The People of the Pits!

He had made inquiries, but each time his mention of the subject had been met with horrified denials. Yet he had felt vaguely that some such thing —or things —did exist; that the phrase did refer to something —some unspeakable mystery of China. Yet never had he solved the riddle. And now, after all these years —here, in the House of Many Virtues, on the Suchow Creek —he heard the words again. To whatever mysterious thing they might refer, he and Tinker were to trust themselves; and Sir Gordon himself had shuddered when speaking of it.

The People of the Pits!

"Just what does it mean?" he asked at last.

Hsui-fsi touched the glowing end of his cigarette to a fresh weed. His eyes —oblique as those of any Celestial —were half closed as he peered back into the dim past. Sixty long years and more it had been since he had taken the plunge among the People of the Pits. Sheer chance had enabled him to do them a service —his power at the Court of the terrible Empress Dowager had saved them from annihilation. And mysteriously to him, even beyond the well-guarded walls of the Sacred City in Peking, had come a talisman. Would it be effective after all that time? Did the People of the Pits still exist? Or was it, after all, but the aftermath of some mad opium dream of his youth?

Without answering Blake's question, he rose, and, with a muttered excuse, left the room. When the matting panel had closed behind him Tinker pressed close to Blake.

"What does it mean, guv'nor?" he whispered.

Blake shook his head.

"I don't know, Tinker. I can't even guess. Wait until we hear what Sir Gordon has to say."

They sat in silence for nearly half an hour before Hsui-fsi returned. When he did so he seated himself once more on the divan, and then from the slit pocket in the inside of the loose sleeve of his tunic he took something, which he laid on the floor in front of where Blake and the lad squatted.

"The talisman," he said in a low tone, "Examine it, Blake, and tell me what you make of it."

Wonderingly Sexton Blake took up the object, which at first sight seemed to be a piece of very fine green jade about six inches long, fashioned in the form of an animal of some sort. Then, as he held it closer, a shiver of disgust shook him as he saw that it was indeed the representation of an animal —a rat in the attitude of a crouch —a grinning rat, but with the slit eyes of a Celestial in its head, instead of the beady orbs of a rodent. It was a grotesque creation, and all the more so for the fact that the carving was of the most exquisite fineness.

Blake handed it to Tinker and looked at Sir Gordon.

"It is horrible!" he said.

The old man nodded.

"Yes —you have used the word. Listen, Blake, while I tell you of the People of the Pits. Until I left this room I should not have been prepared to swear that they really existed. But that talisman is proof. If the same way to their lair exists now that I used more than sixty years ago, I can take you to them.

"Even as a youth I heard tales of the People of the Pits. At the court of the Empress Dowager everything was rotten. He who could provide the most repulsive tale of an evening was in high favour. That is how I heard of the People of the Pits. And, hearing, I resolved to find out for myself if it were true. I came to Shanghai; I searched and searched, and at last —it doesn't matter how —I stumbled upon them. Why they did not kill me I do not know. But they treated me well enough. I was taken into the inmost places, where they exist in a most horrible manner. They are not humans. I do not know their true history. They are, I should think, descendants of the indigenous race of Chinese who were along the lower reaches of the Yangtse many thousands of years ago. They do not live above the ground."

"Ah!"

Both Blake and Tinker uttered the exclamation.

"They are people of the depths —of the pits," went on Sir Gordon. "Those pits —underground burrows —have been dug during the passing of many, many centuries. No one knows how extensive they are, but I know for a fact that one can disappear underground in Shanghai and come to the surface in Chinkiang or Nanking! I cannot even guess at their population. There may be thousands of them. Ethnologically I cannot place them.

"But there is no doubt that they are fearful physical and mental degenerates. They are diseased —they are halt and lame and many are blind. They live as vermin on offal and roots and such. Their habits are those of vermin, and they worship vermin. The rat is their most sacred symbol; the crocodile is a god with them. You will find it hard to believe that among those vast pits they have warm lakes, where hundreds of crocodiles are kept in sacred captivity. You are surprised that crocodiles should exist so far to the north. So was I.

"Heaven alone knows when they were first brought to those underground warrens. They may have been there since prehistoric days. But this strange, degenerate caste does exist, and their existence is one of the great secrets of China. Not even among the most intimate gatherings are they mentioned, but terrible stories of them are known to every Celestial. And they never come to the surface. But woe betide any wandering coolie who plunges by accident into one of the pits connecting with their maze of warrens! He never reappears.

"That is little to tell you of the People of the Pits. It is not much; I cannot even tell you if the talisman will have effect after more than sixty years. I do not know how you are to get through them —to make use of them. I fear for you to go among them. But I feel it my duty to tell you that such a way exists."

Blake did not underestimate the weighty warning contained in Sir Gordon's words.

He knew that only the utmost stress of anxiety on his behalf could have caused him to speak of the People of the Pits. It seemed incredible that such creatures could actually exist so close to all the life and bustle of modern Shanghai. And yet —China —there were many secret things about that country which had never even been whispered within hearing of any foreigner.

"Do they speak a language that one can understand?" he asked slowly.

"A few words which I recognised as having some remote connection with the earliest form of spoken Chinese. Yet it is not even that. It is a brutalised system of gutturals. I got along with that and by signs."

"You went among them and you returned, Hsui-fsi. I do not say that we shall be equally successful, but we can but try. It is, as you say, a way. And since the explosion of the coffin junk the whole of the river will now be watched. If we can reach Nanking —"

"There is still Hankow."

"Ay. And the stretch to Ichang. But after Hankow we come to the waters where the Hawk of the River holds sway."

"You mean the pirate, Kan-tse-wen?"

"Who else?"

"He is your friend, Blake. He might give his aid. But this matter of the Golden Book is different from anything political. We do not know to whom Kan-tse-wen gives spiritual allegiance."

"I can but test him. He is my friend, as you say, and Kan-tse-wen is one whose word is safe, despite the fact that he is one of the most bloodthirsty villains in all China."

"Then —then you will try the People of the Pits?"

Blake gave him a level glance.

"Can you give us guidance to some spot where we can gain entry to their warrens?"

"If the old one still exists I can take you. Would that I could go with you!"

"Then we go within the hour, if Tinker chooses to come. But the lad must decide that for himself."

"I go where you go, guv'nor," said Tinker steadily.

Blake nodded.

"As soon as you are ready, Hsui-fsi," he said simply.

Into The Depths.

NEVER in all the strange situations they had faced together had

Sexton Blake and Tinker embarked on a more weird and, as was to be proved, more awful experience than the one which began for them that night.

Of equipment they possessed none except two small automatic pistols, which Hsui-fsi insisted they should take. A small parcel of nuts and dried meat was their only food; not even a strip of matting had they upon which to sleep.

Their first plunge into the native city at Shanghai had seemed then to be a complete cutting off from all their kind. But that, at least, had been above ground, while this new journey promised to take them into the unspeakable places of a quite different world. It seemed all too grotesque for belief —like some mad dream which Hsui-fsi had conjured up from his opium-soaked cigarettes.

And yet, there was that jade rat with its repulsive eyes of a human. There was no dream about that. It was concrete reality —the work of a mind that could only dwell in a pit.

It was just before dawn was due that they finally got away from the House of Many Virtues. So secret was their going that nobody knew of it, or that only Hsui-fsi accompanied them. They had not even caught a glimpse of the Korean priest, although Blake had given Sir Gordon a message for him.

They left the grounds by the water gate, and proceeded on foot along the bank of the Suchow Creek until they came to the racecourse. By now the night mist was dying away. A few stars were visible overhead, and from years of intimate knowledge of the place the way presented no difficulties. It was, in fact, much the same course which Tinker had followed from the Da-Tung-Mun. They traversed the French Settlement, keeping close to the outer boundary, and at last entered the native city by the Si-Mun.

For the second time within twenty-four hours Blake and Tinker found themselves traversing the reeking quarter of the beggars. At this hour the place was full of moving shadows, and ever and anon a face would materialise out of the gloom —a vile, bestial face, to peer at them with an evil leer.

But on each occasion Hsui-fsi uttered a single mysterious word, which caused the face to disappear with startling rapidity. Just what power it was which Sir Gordon wielded over the beggars' quarter of the native city Blake did not know. But he had known for a long time that Hsui-fsi's word was law with them, and already that day he had seen some proof of it. But now, in these dangerous hours of the night, that single mysterious word opened a passage for them as if they had been accompanied by a fully-armed guard.

Hsui-fsi took many turnings which confused even Blake. All the time they seemed to be getting more and more deeply into the heart of the district, and each moment their surroundings grew, if possible, more terrible. Description by words could not paint the noisome stench through which they waded —the mephitic breath of a decayed and dying human colony. And yet that old, old man ploughed his way through as if his nostrils were immune to it all.

Suddenly, when it seemed that they must have reached the very limit of what even that quarter could provide in the form of smells and filth, Sir Gordon drew up at the narrow entrance to an alley along which they could see for a matter of two or three yards.

"Wait here," he whispered. "At no time shall I be out of hearing if you call."

With that he was gone, disappearing in the gloom of the alley. Somewhere in the darkness they heard the sound of a low "tap-tapping," then came the guttural murmur of voices, and a few moments later, Hsui-fsi was back with them.

"It seems well —if anything can be so in this business," he said in a low tone. "Come, dear friends."

Both Blake and Tinker took a long breath, quite unconsciously, as if they would cling even to the foul air of that quarter. What horrors lay beyond they could not guess. But they had a feeling that before long they would crave the upper air, no matter how putrid its breath.

They walked only a score of steps until they came to an open door —a rickety bit of boarding that revealed the black mouth of an opening. Hsui-fsi guided them through, and in some mysterious fashion the portal closed after them. Followed the flare of an oil dip and they saw, weirdly in the leaping shadows, the yellow, wrinkled face of an old, old man. Beside him even Hsui-fsi looked almost young.

His thin lips were drawn back over blackened, toothless gums as he peered from one to the other. Blake had a feeling that no disguise would ever hide his identity from this probing orbs, and, indeed, he was right, for the ancient gave vent to a harsh chuckle, which conveyed to Sir Gordon that he had read their secret.

Hsui-fsi made a curt gesture.

"Time moves," he said curtly. "You know what thou hast to do, even as if thou didst the same for me. Guard these, my friends, during the time they are with you, or by the eyes of the blessed Confucius I will throw the bones of thy ancestors to the four winds."

He turned then to Blake and Tinker. Swiftly he embraced them. Then, in a broken voice, he muttered:

"Heaven go with you, dear friends. I shall be in torture until I hear word that you are safe."

He could trust himself to no more, and before either Blake or Tinker could make reply he was gone.

There was nothing to do but to trust themselves to the leering old wretch, who was still regarding them. He was bent almost double, and as he turned to move on they saw that he supported his infirm body with a short stick. No word was spoken as they moved along a narrow passage, the floor of which consisted only of hard-packed black mud. It may have been a hut of some sort which they had entered, but if so it speedily gave way to nothing but an earth passage, which, they noticed, descended at an easy angle as they went along.

What was to come next they hadn't an idea. If this was but the first stage on their way to the underground warrens where the People of the Pits roamed, they did not know it. But by the time they had traversed a good hundred yards of that descending passage, they knew they must be not less than sixty or seventy feet beneath the surface of the beggars' quarter. And still it went on and down. Now the walls changed from mud to a porous stone, from which water dripped ceaselessly.

Blake guessed that they might be directly under the Whangpoo. Lower still the porous stone gave way to sand, and now they found themselves wading at times through miniature lakes.

It seemed that they would never come to a stop. The old man was still going down, apparently entirely oblivious to their presence. The sight of a stream of considerable size made Blake think that they must be near the bottom of the way, and, in fact, it was at the edge of this that their guide came to a pause. Holding his oil dip high, he gestured with his stick along the course of the stream, which seemed to disappear through a black tunnel.

"I leave thee here," he mumbled. "Follow the stream through the passage. Turn neither to right nor to left, although you will see other passages. If the people ye seek are there they will appear."

With that he started to turn back as if their fate was of not the slightest interest to him. But Blake caught him by the arm.

"But the light?" he snapped, using the river dialect which the ancient had employed. "How are we to see?"

The old man turned his bleary eyes upwards.

"Foreign devil, canst thou not see in the dark?" he jeered. "Canst not thou see with the eyes of the babies thou has eaten?[1] If not, then wait and watch for the blue light."

He shook off Blake's hand and started back up the slope. For a moment Blake hesitated as if he would force him to return or give them the light. But he conquered that sudden wave of panic and, laying a hand on Tinker's arm, whispered:

"Stand steady, young 'un! Heaven knows what will come next, but we'll meet it in the dark if needs be."

And so they stood together while that winking oil dip grew smaller and smaller, and finally disappeared. Then they were alone in utter, impenetrable darkness, watching and listening for —what?

Fully a quarter of an hour must have passed, during which time they scarcely moved, and spoke only occasionally in whispers. Then all of a sudden Tinker gripped Blake's arm convulsively.

"Look, guv'nor, look! The blue light!"

"The People of the Pits."

NOTHING more weird could be imagined than the dancing, wavering globe of bluish light that came floating towards Sexton Blake and Tinker as they stood waiting in that eerie underground passage.

There was no definite central point of flame to the thing; it seemed to be just a phosphorescent glow about the size of a football, without contact with anything material. No controlling hand could be seen —absolutely nothing that might connect it with either human or mechanical agency. And yet it gleamed with sufficient illumination to create a halo about itself as it moved towards the two, who stood at the edge of the stream, with uncanny precision. Could any vagrant current of air be bringing it in their way? Or was there a directing mind behind it.

Once before, many years ago, Sexton Blake and Tinker had been

---

[1] It is a firm belief among the ignorant classes of China that foreigners eat children. —AUTHOR.

on a mission into the interior of French Indo-China. On that occasion they had come upon many of the unexplained mysteries of the East, and, away in the depths of the marshes which lie in the unexplored back country of Annam, they had seen a somewhat similar phenomenon. That had eventually been proved by Blake to have its genesis in natural marsh gas, but the production of the light in question had been the work of minds that were deeply versed in obscure scientific lore —minds that were even more advanced in physical law and the knowledge of dynamics than the most advanced of Western scientists.

But these People of the Pits —if they did exist —were, according to Sir Gordon Saddler, mentally on the level of the beasts of the field. Could there be among them a mind which could grasp the scientific laws that, so far, had eluded the best minds of the West? Or might it be that this phenomenon, as other unexplained phenomena, was a relic of those days of long, long ago when China had evolved an extraordinary civilisation when the peoples of Europe were living in caves?

Despite the menace of their surroundings and the uncertainty of what lay before them, Sexton Blake watched the approach of the globe of light with a critical eye. As it came nearer and nearer it was plain that it was borne by no human hand. It floated entirely unattached, and whether by some air current or not, it was floating directly towards them.

In an uncanny way it hovered directly over their heads, lighting up their features in ghostly fashion, and showing to them the surface of the stream at their feet. So close was it that Blake could reach up and touch it. Swiftly he took the risk of being burned, and thrust his hand full into the glow. It was absolutely cold!

(In what weird mysteries have Sexton Blake and Tinker become involved? Don't miss one instalment of this thrilling yarn.)

Part 6.

Sexton Blake and Tinker in China!

How it began.

ONE of China's most sacred possessions, "The Golden Book of Buddha," is stolen by the Black Abbot of Cheng-tu while on its way up the Yangtse from Canton to the Grand Lama of Tibet. Sexton Blake having been implored to help trace it, is in China with Tinker, both disguised as coolies, for that purpose.

Blake is captured by the Black Monk, but is rescued by Tinker and Hsui-fsi, an Englishman and their friend.

The journey into the interior being so perilous, Hsui-fsi decides that Blake and Tinker must seek the aid of the People of the Pits, a mysterious nation which lives underground, and of which very little is known. Having arrived at one of their entrances, the pair are led down a long passage. Their guide leaves them, and while standing in the darkness they see a blue light approaching. It does not seem to be connected with anything material, and as it hovers over their heads Blake reaches up to touch it, expecting it to burn his fingers. He is astounded, however, to find that it is quite cold.

A THRILLING SERIAL OF MYSTERY AND ADVENTURE.

The People of the Pits. (*Continued.*)

COLD fire! The dream of Western scientists for centuries! How had it been accomplished? Of what was it composed? Illumination without heat! Western science had never even approached that achievement, though scores of research workers were seeking the solution, for in illumination with heat some ninety per cent of combustion is required in order to produce ten per cent of light.

Straight into the glowing mass went his hand, and out again. And then both he and Tinker uttered an exclamation of amazement, for as Blake lowered his hand it was seen that it, too, now glowed like the ball of light. In some fashion it had been "clothed" with the cold flame, and for the time being, at least, was a living human torch.

But a ghastly vision jerked their thoughts away from this display of magic. The first warning came from Tinker, who, all of a sudden,

88

gave a jump that carried him a full two feet straight upwards. Almost on the same moment Blake felt a sharp pain in his ankle, and, he, too, gave a jump backwards. Then each looked down, and at the sight that met their eyes a deadly nausea overwhelmed them.

A few moments before the stream that seemed to run into the pits of the underground people had been only a sinister black rush of water; now it was literally alive with hundreds, thousands of huge rats.

Under that blue glow their eyes gleamed with an eager lust that was unnerving to the strongest soul. The long, front rodent teeth showed where the whiskered lips were drawn back; long tails floated out as they came on, rank after rank; and, above all, it was that pale greyish tint that made them more repulsive than all else.

The two gazed in horror. In that moment it came to Sexton Blake that he had embarked upon too much for a human being to attempt. Who could blame him if he retreated while there might yet be time? What other living person would deliberately plunge into such an obscene pit as had vomited forth this army of vermin?

Up that sloping passage they might rush; it was a long way, but at the top was daylight and safety. And was it fair that he should have allowed a lad like Tinker to accompany him into such an inferno, even though the lad's life was linked to his, and his loyalty and courage unquestioned?

For those few moments his mind quailed. It was not a lessening of courage. It was the natural upheaval of everything within the man that was civilised rebelling at this horror of the pits. As for Tinker, he was being frankly and violently ill. He could no more have suppressed his sickness than turn the course of the stream at his feet. The nausea had gripped him to the marrow, and Nature was doing the rest.

Yes, Blake quailed. But in the back-rush of his feeling came a dull anger that this thing should be. These beasts of the night —were they to drive him back, even though they came on in their thousands? Were he and Tinker to come to the end of everything there, in that foul tunnel a hundred feet beneath the beggars' quarter of Shanghai? Was it for this that they had lived and fought and worked?

A wild fury seized him. With a roar he threw himself among the ranks that were leaping over each other in their haste to reach the promised feast. Into them, with only thin sandals to guard his feet, went Blake, followed by Tinker. Squeals, scurryings, retreats, rushes —a medley of horrible stench and the touch of repulsive, silky fur. And yet the two kept springing about, finding that no sooner was one of the creatures killed than it disappeared into the maws of its fellows with sickening rapidity.

All this time the blue light hovered over their heads. During the first part of the attack Blake had used only his feet, but now, as fresh hordes of the creatures came on, he bent to use both hands as well. And now it was that he made a startling discovery. The blue flame that had clothed his hand still adhered to it, and he found to his amazement that at threat of this contact the rats closest to it fled with terrified squeals.

Obviously they feared that blue light. So, springing up, he thrust his other hand into the globe as well. He jerked out a word to Tinker to do the same, and when they bent once more to the attack, they found that by the simple expedient of keeping their glowing hands swinging in a circle about them they kept the hungry, savage vermin at bay. It was amazing.

But this weird procedure could not be kept up for ever. As long as that ferocious mass hung about —and they were being reinforced by newcomers each moment —any suggestion of going forward was out of the question. There was only the alternative of retreat, and that Blake was not ready to consider yet. Apparently the same thought was in Tinker's mind, for as they squatted on their heels, desperately sweeping their hands back and forth, back and forth with the regularity of pendulums, the lad said hoarsely:

"This is a queer game, guv'nor. What the dickens is this blue stuff, anyway?"

"It is beyond me, young 'un. I don't know, except that it is some sort of heatless phosphorescent matter —a diffused self-radiant vapour, I should say. But how it is formed, whence it comes from, or how it was directed towards us, is a mystery I can't attempt to solve. But at any rate, it has saved our lives."

"But we can't squat here for ever, fanning these brutes back."

"No."

"What will we do, then? If we don't go forward we shall have to go back, and, my aunt, but I am thirsty!"

Blake did not reply at once. He was engaged in watching a new sort of activity among the hordes of rats. By this time they were literally a living carpet right across the stream, keeping their places by swimming, and, when opportunity offered, scrambling over the backs of their fellows in order to get as close to Blake and Tinker as possible.

But what had attracted Blake's attention afresh was an indefinable something in the actions of those rats which were farthest away. All of a sudden they seemed to show frantic desire to reach either bank, and on their efforts a sort of lane in the centre of the stream was opened between the two sections.

This patch of water stretched away into the darkness towards which the ancient Celestial who had guided them to the spot had waved them if they desired to reach the People of the Pits. And now there suddenly appeared a second blue globe of light. At first it was in Blake's mind that the rats were striving to get away from this glow, but as it drew still nearer he thought he could make out some sort of a shadow in its thin halo, and, a few moments later, he knew he was right.

Someone was walking along the bed of the shallow stream, lighted by that globe of light!

Blake made a cautioning noise to Tinker, who, turning his head, saw what was holding Blake's attention. A soft exclamation escaped from between the lad's lips, but Blake silenced him with a soft hiss. Then they both sat and watched while that sinister shadow bulked larger and larger.

Wavering, dipping, and rising, the bluish light advanced in much the same fashion as the first. Its progress appeared aimless enough — as if it might be at the mercy of some vagrant current of air; but all the time it approached nearer and nearer to them, and each knew that in some way it was being directed by human intelligence.

Then the shadow beneath took more definite form —became lined out in blurred silhouette into the form of someone moving along slowly, with body bent grotesquely and arms swinging across in front much as an ape walks. Twenty feet, fifteen feet, ten feet, and by then the two who squatted at the edge of the stream were able to distinguish vague features. They scarcely noticed that the whole army of rats had now disappeared as if by magic; they were wholly concentrated in peering at this "Thing" that was coming to them out of the bowels of the earth.

Was it one of the People of the Pits? If not, what else could it be?

Closer still it came, until the bluish light hovered but a yard away from the first. And then the two watchers saw that it was a human form of some sort clad in nothing but the thick natural hair which covered the whole body.

Came a short, sharp sort of barking cough, a creeping closer of the Thing, the thrusting forward of a face —a terrible mask of degeneracy, with deep-set eyes, no forehead, wide-splayed nostrils, and an enormous loose-hanging mouth in which shone long, rodent-like tusks.

A rat eater! A rat worshipper! It was one of the unspeakable People of the Pits!

The Terror of the Tunnel.

SEXTON BLAKE and Tinker stood up.

This thing that was coming towards them was not to be faced sitting. As the creature paused not two feet in front of them and thrust his head forward, Blake touched the lad's arm ever so lightly, just as a cautionary measure. Then the thing began to laugh —or so it seemed, although scarcely any sound came from that gaping throat. From one to the other it kept peering, and presently a talon-like hand, also hair-covered, crept out and touched Blake. It needed all the detective's powers of self-control to stand quiescent under the pawing that followed. But he did not flinch, and at last the repulsive creature drew back a little.

It seemed incredible to Blake that this object could be even degenerate human. It seemed less man-like almost than a gorilla. And yet, if Hsui-fsi were to be credited, before them stood a descendant of the original race which had peopled and civilised Asia long before the present Chinese came on the scene, and more ages still before the first Manchu appeared.

Could it be that this hairy beast had declined to his present level from the peak of early human achievement? Was it possible that a retrograde motion could set in in the human family and take it down and back to the beginning? Was it the terrible price paid by in-breeding? Was there any light of the intellectual past still gleaming in that low-browed skull?

Strangely enough, it was this of which Blake was thinking; nor is it surprising considering the shock of seeing such a creature come to them out of that tunnel which led heaven only knew where —which was part of that amazing underground system.

Suddenly a voice issued from between the slavering jaws of the monster. It broke upon their ears harshly guttural and at first it seemed to be no more than a jumbled medley of throaty sounds, such as an ape might make. But when the same sounds were repeated again and again Blake's ear began to separate the vowels (if such could be said to exist), and he remembered then what Hsui-fsi had said.

"The only means of communicating with them is by word and a debased form of early Chinese," was what he had said.

"Ka-ee-nha-zhoo."

It sounded as much like that as may be expressed in ordinary written form.

Blake racked his brains. He had studied the first forms of attempts at a language in Chinese, and he knew that ka was one of the most frequent and most expressive syllables. It might mean more than a score of things, depending entirely on the inflexion with which it was expressed. And he began to think that this poor creature before them was indeed speaking to them in the primitive form of that ancient tongue. He might be, for all they knew, the most accomplished linguist among the People of the Pits.

"Ka-ee-nha-ee-zhoo."

"Ee." That, too, he had come upon shown by the very primitive symbol of a straight line with a slight hook at one end. Back in those early times the more complicated system of Chinese writing had not been developed.

If the fellow was using that language, it was safe betting that his words were a question, and that he was asking them who they were, what was their purpose in being there, or whither they were bound — something along those primitive lines. Never in all his life had Sexton Blake racked his brains to remember harder than in those following moments. Into his mind came the picture of the ancient tome in which he had studied in an old, old monastery on the boundaries of Tibet. Then there leaped to his eyes the vertical lines of simple symbols, and suddenly in the acute concentration of his mind that which he sought came to him.

"Ka-ee-po-ka-ee-nntu."

A queer, crazy jumble of sounds it made, and like nothing in any known tongue, no matter how primitive. Even the Australian black fellow's language possesses more distinction of syllabic division. But a sudden throb jerked Blake's heart as he saw that he was undoubtedly understood.

What had he said? Just what inflexion had he put in the double use of the "ka" and the "ee"? He had taken a shot in the dark, but it had, at least, been intelligible to the other. And even while the creature seemed to digest what had been said, Blake bethought him of the talisman which Sir Gordon had given him. Would it be remembered after more than sixty years? Would this creature, who may not have been born when Sir Gordon entered that foul hole, know what it signified?

With a swift motion Blake thrust his hand inside his ragged shirt and took out the bit of jade. Gripping it firmly lest it be snatched away from him, he held it before the other's eyes. At the moment the creature was gazing down as if pondering laboriously on Blake's words. But as he lifted his head his orbs encountered the jade rat. For a moment he gazed in fixed fashion, as if the thing was not real; then he flashed a wild glance at Blake, and the next moment was flat on his face at their feet mouthing unintelligible sounds.

"What does it mean, guv'nor?" whispered Tinker in urgent need to know what was passing. "That rat has knocked him cold."

"I don't know," responded Blake swiftly. "But it has certainly had an extraordinary effect on him. He recognises it as something very potent. It may be our Open Sesame. Watch carefully while I try and get him on his feet."

Blake bent down and laid a tentative hand on the shoulder of the prostrate one. That touch acted as if an electric shock had flashed through him. He came to his feet with startling agility, and for a moment Blake thought he would spring upon him. But again his eyes fell on the jade rat, and his whole manner became submissive.

His eyes searched Blake's as if he would read what was in the detective's mind. Next a perfectly unintelligible jumble of throaty sounds poured from between his lips, but Blake could make nothing of them. He gestured, however, towards the black tunnel from which the creature had emerged. The fellow turned and peered along it, looked back to Blake, and at last seemed to comprehend that Blake wanted to go that way.

Another rush of sounds came from him. Then, turning, he started along, keeping to the bed of the stream. Blake and Tinker followed immediately, and, to their amazement, the two bluish globes of light floated on ahead as if endowed with human intelligence. Later on Blake was to understand how it was those tenuous globes of illuminated molecules were controlled.

They saw no further signs of the rats just then. For some reason or other the vermin had fled, but ever and anon they passed the mouth of a dark passage from which came strange whispering, scuffling sounds. They might have emanated from hordes of rats, or, was it possible, that others of the creatures like their guide were lurking in the dark watching their passage?

It was distinctly uncanny that passage. They hadn't the remotest idea whither they were heading. It seemed a mad dream —a ghastly nightmare. To count on reaching Chinkiang or Nanking by means of this lost maze of underground passages seemed incredible of belief. And yet Hsui-fsi, the "wise old man of China," had led them to the starting-point. In those long ago days he had been one of the most adventurous Britons living. He had plunged into every form of intrigue and danger, and had even eloped with a princess of the royal blood from under the very nose of the terrible Empress Dowager. Was it possible that his visit to these vile passages had been a mere scraping of the surface which, as the years passed, had assumed exaggerated proportions in his mind? Blake was not forgetting that Sir Gordon had been for many years an addict to opium, and although it had not affected his wonderful mental faculties, there were periods when he hid himself away until the orgy was past. Had this, then, become merged in the dreams which he had when he was under the influence of the drug?

If so, what was the explanation of that jade symbol which had acted as such a potent charm on the creature who had appeared from the blackness of that foul hole?

As he plunged along Sexton Blake was pondering deeply on this. He knew that he must come to a decision of some sort before they got so deeply into the maze that they should never be able to find a way out. He had not only his own safety to think of, but what was of far more moment to him, the safety of the lad with him.

If nothing but annihilation lay beyond, he would go to his death with a scar on his soul that no purgatory would cleanse. He began to feel now that it had all been a terrible mistake. He knew that Sir Gordon had only disclosed his knowledge of the People of the Pits when he saw that it was hopeless for Blake to squeeze through any loophole to reach the Upper Yangtse.

So absorbed was he, indeed, that, plunging along through the stream, he was almost oblivious to the black openings on either side, which now grew more and more frequent. He kept his eyes fixed on the hairy back of the creature in front, following the lead of those two unwavering blue globes of ghostly light.

But as his anxiety regarding Tinker smote him, as his self-reproaches grew more emphatic, he turned his head to throw back a cheery word to the lad who had been silent ever since they started. At first he could not see him, and he came to a stop and revolved a full turn.

But still there was no sign of the lad, and as he peered back the way they had come, thinking Tinker had loitered behind, a cold chill of fear swept over him, causing his teeth to chatter as if a spasm of ague had gripped him.

He opened his lips to call, but before his voice could issue forth a faint echoing cry reached him —a far-away shout for help which was pregnant with urgent need, and in the echoes Blake recognised the tones of the lad's voice.

His heart almost stopped as he realised what must have happened. Forgetting the man ahead, thoughtless of light or rats, or anything but to get to Tinker, he started back, but before he had gone half a dozen steps the whole tunnel seemed suddenly to become alive with stinking, hairy creatures, who swarmed over him with the agility of apes and bore him, fighting, down into the black waters of the stream.

The Basket-Cell.

TINKER had been quite as preoccupied as Blake.

Ever since their arrival at the edge of the stream the lad had been doing a good deal of hard thinking. He had heard what Sir Gordon said to Blake about the People of the Pits, and from the moment he first set eyes on the unearthly creature who had come out of the tunnel, he had not entertained a doubt in his own mind about the existence of the lost beings of whom Hsui-fsi had spoken.

The globe of bluish light had intrigued him not a little; but that wonder had been obliterated from his mind when he saw the effect the jade rat had upon the creature that had confronted them.

Tinker was no coward, as his life had proved over and over again.

Nor did he contemplate for one moment making any suggestion that they should abandon their purpose. But he did experience such a feeling of acute nausea and actual physical sickness, such a wave of repulsion, when they had plunged among those hordes of attacking rats, that he would not have been sorry had Blake come to the decision to retreat. But as he hadn't, then Tinker was game to go ahead into even that unknown maze.

All the same, he didn't like it, and, like Blake, he heard those mysterious sounds of scrapings and scufflings and whisperings as they ploughed a way through the shallow waters of the stream.

Thus his preoccupation while he kept one eye on Blake's broad back, which was faintly silhouetted against the glow of the two spheres of light, and the other on the inky waters at his ankles. He did not fall behind, as Blake at first imagined when he missed him. On the contrary he kept pace for pace and length of stride with length of stride, being never more than six feet in the rear of his master.

But even that short space was sufficient for what was to happen in that hole of terror. So stealthily did the menace come upon the lad that he never even guessed its presence. Behind him, from either side, crept creatures of darkness who followed with footsteps that had trodden that way thousands of times. Where the two Europeans splashed noisily, those creeping shadows at the back waded with the silence of a flamingo. And it was not until a hot stench struck the back of Tinker's neck, sending a shiver of sharp disgust through him, that he suspected he was being dogged.

He wheeled sharply. His lips were open to speak to Blake, but before he could make a sound, ere he could lift a hand in self-defence, he was overwhelmed. A score of arms enwrapped him; heavy, sweating, foetid bodies smothered him; a vile, hairy hand covered his mouth, and he was swung bodily out of the water with so little noise that it was entirely lost in the sound of Blake's splashing. Perhaps the creature in the lead knew what was passing, but if he did, he gave no sign. As for Tinker, he was spirited into one of the side passages near at hand, and from that on, during what seemed to him like a long, long journey, he was able to discern absolutely nothing in a visual way. His other senses, however, told him enough. He knew the closeness of those foul bodies; he was conscious of the reek of foul breath and bestial sweat of body. He was as utterly at the mercy of something as unbelievably awful as ever danced through the nightmare of a madman.

The mephitic stench of it all, or else the lack of oxygen in the air of the passages, must have overpowered his consciousness, for after a time he was scarcely cognisant of what was happening. Now and then he would come to himself with a jerk, to realise that he was still being borne along through complete darkness. How his captors could see was a mystery to him. As a matter of fact they could see no more than could he. They were blind, each and every one of them. They were as much at home in those Stygian tunnels as full-sighted beings would have been had the way been strung with electric lights. They did not need to see along the road. It had been familiar to them from the time they were given life in that foul pit, and to the generations before them.

Each turning they took with utter certainty. It is impossible to say how that colossal maze of tunnels was formed. If the theory which Sir Gordon Saddler had formed was the right one (and if those strange People of the Pits were not a degenerate fragment of the earliest indigenous Chinese race, then whence did they come?), then it was possible that, whatever upheaval it was that drove the original inhabitants of the district to take refuge, disclosed to them in their need a natural series of caves or passages. These caves, during the thousands of years they had remained there, breeding among themselves and gradually descending the human scale until they became what Blake and Tinker saw, they had gradually enlarged until the whole vast system was evolved.

And what relics of their one-time high state of civilisation remained to them? Apart from that weird faculty of producing the globes of bluish light, what else did they possess? What had come down to them from their forefathers, if anything? And if anything at all remained of those ancient days, did this present half-bestial fragment understand any of it? Or had everything become brutalised, even as their ancient religion must have become brutalised to the worship of vermin?

Tinker was closer to some of the answers to these questions than he realised. All of a sudden his senses cleared as a current of comparatively fresh air struck him. Opening his eyes he saw, far in the distance, a faint bluish glow of light. His spirits, which had been in the most profound deeps, grew visibly lighter. Where there was light there was sight, and, as the old saying has it. In the country of the blind the one-eyed man is king. But being in complete darkness in the grasp of these stinking monsters was more than human nerves could stand.

As they drew nearer to the glow he could make out dimly that he was being carried through a very wide passage which seemed to be lined with smooth, shiny stone slabs. When he attempted to change his position, so that he might see better, no opposition was offered, and thus he could make out quite clearly a vast amphitheatre as they entered it. The lad could not suppress a gasp of amazement as his eyes made a sweeping turn about the place. It was, he thought, at least as large as Trafalgar Square, and that, he knew, was five or six acres in extent.

Trafalgar Square! What a comparison to come into one's mind in those surroundings! The thought filled him with an acute wave of home-sickness.

Now he could make out semi-human forms passing back and forth —scores and scores of them, none of whom seemed to pay the slightest attention to him or the party which bore him. Upwards the amphitheatre's roof seemed to go into a peak instead of into a dome, as was most usual in such cases; a little later Sexton Blake was to make a most startling discovery in this connection.

Near at hand Tinker could see low tiers of what appeared to be a black sort of stone, and on them scattered utensils which might have been cooking pots or some other equivalent domestic vessel. Then, towards the centre, the space became vast to his eyes until he made out a low stone parapet which formed an enclosure of some sort.

It was towards this that his captors were carrying him. At this moment his gaze went beyond the stone parapet to the opposite side of the place. His eyes bulged as he saw two gigantic images standing under twin globes of the same bluish light he had already noticed, but globes which were much larger in diameter. One of these statues was a monster likeness of the jade rat which Hsui-fsi had given Blake, fashioned in shining metal that might have been gold or brass. The second statue appeared to be in the likeness of a crocodile —a hideous thing.

Then, as Tinker jerked his eyes away, he saw what looked in the distance like nothing so much as a field of snow —a vast white blanket that stretched away until it was lost to view in the gloom beyond. What it was he couldn't even attempt to guess.

Then his mind was brought back to himself, for by now they had arrived at the low stone parapet. A stone slab was pushed aside and Tinker was carried through. Now he could see that with the exception of a narrow footway which encircled the area close to the wall, the enclosure was a vast pit of some description, but for what purpose he could not make out.

His enlightenment came with startling unpleasantness. A narrow footway ran across the pit, and hanging from the middle of this was a large wicker cage affair. He was borne along this narrow bridge, and then, before he could do a thing to resist, the lid of the basket was jerked open, he was thrust down feet foremost, and the cover pushed down over him.

All too late Tinker realised what had happened. What he had been jammed into was one of those prisoner's baskets of old China, in which the captive may only stand, and, no matter how fatigued he may become, it is quite impossible to lie down. As an instrument of refined torture it takes some beating, even in a country where there are one hundred and thirty-six varieties of torture in the first-class alone.

But five seconds later, as Tinker's gaze went downwards, the sharp wave of anger that had assailed him gave way to a wild upheaval of horror and sickness. For beneath him the water in the pit was alive with gigantic crocodiles, which were swimming lazily about or floating in bloated coma on the surface of the pool.

And they were leprous white!

The Ape Enthroned.

SEXTON BLAKE knew in his heart the inevitable end of that struggle.

Had it been possible to draw his automatic he would have been able to account for at least some of the brutes by shooting and, he had little doubt, would have been able to floor others by clubbing the weapon. But, eventually, he must go down, and while he fought with fists and, when he got the chance, with feet as well, he did not attempt to draw. Something whispered to him that not yet was the time to risk the few precious cartridges in the magazine.

Nevertheless he was creating havoc among his assailants. Thud, thud, and thud went his fists into those hairy bodies, the contact ringing out hollowly as his knuckles struck the rounded barrels of their chests. Man after man went down, for they possessed no guard to this form of fighting. Their one aim seemed to be to swarm over him like so many apes; like their physique and habits their methods of attack had become as primitive as those of man's simian ancestors. And, with numbers which kept increasing each moment, there could be only one result.

Blake was crushed to his knees, driven down by sheer weight of bestial bodies. Still he fought desperately, dragging one after another down beside him and smashing home fist or foot before tackling the next. But the end came when a combined rush drove him flat, driving his head completely under water and forcing him to battle for breath before they should drown him out of hand. Then, and then only, he surrendered.

He was dragged to his feet and stood quiescent while they gripped him from every side. His mind became suddenly detached from his own predicament. It went back to Tinker, and again he peered back along the tunnel, wondering with deep uneasiness what disaster could have overtaken the lad. That he had been cut off and spirited away while only a yard or so from him he now felt certain had been the case.

These sinister developments had upset all his calculations. From the attitude of the first of the pit people at sight of the jade rat —the undoubted awe which had been displayed —Blake had been encouraged to think that, after all, it would act as a potent talisman. But now that idea was shattered.

If it were a safeguard, why hadn't his guide informed the others that he was possessed of such a sacred passport?

Blake was more and more puzzled as he thought of this phase of it, and yet it would serve no purpose to make further resistance. What must come to him and Tinker in that lost pit of the underworld, must come and must be faced with the courage of the race that was theirs.

So he allowed himself to be pushed along through the shallow stream. The two globes of blue light began once more to dance on ahead of them, and by the tenuous light which they emitted he could see a close pack of forms both before and behind him. He was being well attended by guards at least.

He kept a sharp look-out as they went along, noting more carefully now the many side passages they passed. It was plain to his critical gaze that these branching tunnels had been artificially cut at some time in the past, but he believed the main tunnel which carried the stream had been originally hollowed out by Nature with additions made at some time or other by the People of the Pits.

He was asking himself if the whole warren was but a confusion of such passages, or if there would be some sort of central rallying point. Surely a people who could produce such a piece of exquisite carving as the jade rat must have some sort of working community where the work could be produced.

If the hairy nudity of those who surrounded him was any criterion, there could be no weaving industry among these lost people. But Sir Gordon had spoken of rat and crocodile worship. There must be a centre of worship, even though it might be but a caricature of what had existed among their forefathers thousands of years before. It was unthinkable that every shred of that civilised past could have disappeared into the limbo of these foul pits.

And their food —Hsui-fsi had said they were vermin eaters. Well, Blake remembered being once in the country that lies between the High Range and the Polnis in South India, where he had come upon the lowest of the four castes of the Toda tribes. These, too, had been eaters of vermin —forest rats and snakes. There were tribes in Africa and New Guinea as well who had sunk —or never risen, from the same level. But with it all there had always been a certain proportion of grain or seeds or berries in their diet.

Were these People of the Pits without even that? Or could it be possible that they produced some sort of grain of their own. The orthodox understanding about any plant was that it needed sunshine and air and the rains of high heaven to grow. What could be produced in these stretches of darkness except some leprous white root such as celery? Or, was it possible that they had retained a certain trading connection with the upperworld —that the go-between, so to say, was some ancient old beggar such as he who had guided them to the underground stream?

There were a hundred and one such questions revolving in Blake's acute mind as he splashed his way along, despite the peril of his position.

Then he noticed that the main passage began to grow much wider, revealing rude galleries at either side now and then. There seemed to be a series of upper passages leading off these galleries, and he thought this must indicate their approach to the central point of

102

the system. The light, too, began to increase. It was of the same bluish tinge as that produced by the globes, but from what source it came he could not see.

And then, all of a sudden, a turning brought him in full view of a great amphitheatre. It was the same vast space into which Tinker had been carried not ten minutes before Blake's eyes fell on it, but the lad had been brought in from the other side. Blake's entrance was on the left of the huge statues, and close to one side of the wide stretch of white which had looked to Tinker like a field of snow.

But, passing close to it, Blake was able to see what it was, and as he realised the truth a deep sense of amazement filled him. It was not snow, or anything like it. It was a species of grain which, just then, was heading into ear —a grain that was not unlike a stunted rice plant in appearance, but completely lacking in green colouring matter of stalk or leaf. What had appeared to him as something fantastic had been accomplished! Here in the bowels of the earth these degenerate people were producing a grain without the aid of sunlight.

How it could be done was a mystery to Blake. The only explanation he could think of was that in some way there had descended to this lost fragment a secret of Nature which had been discovered by the first fugitives who had sought safety underground —something that took the place of sunlight in the development of the plant. Was it electricity in some obscure form? Or what could it be? The answer was beyond him.

His interest in the "field" of grain gave way to keen interest in the amphitheatre. His natural instinct was to look upwards, where he expected to see a domed roof. Instead, he noticed that nothing of the sort existed, and then he was aware that the place seemed to be supported by four sloping lines of masonry which met in a point at the top. Suddenly a startling idea came to Sexton Blake, but before he could follow it up further he was dragged along to the two giant statues (which he scrutinised in disgust as he came in front of them), and then along another passage until he arrived at an inner sort of amphitheatre much smaller than the other.

This place was almost brilliant with light, so profuse was the bluish radiance which shone on every side. Here, too, were other smaller statues of the rat god and the crocodile god, and at one end a sort of throne, on which he suddenly realised a figure of some sort was sitting. It was towards this that Blake was dragged.

On getting closer, he saw that the throne was a chair, carved, he was certain, from an enormous block of pink jade. It was a magnificent bit of work, and, he felt sure, quite beyond the capacity of the present denizens of the pits to produce. If it had been wrought by the early refugees, then it must be thousands of years old —older than the earliest of any known Chinese work. Gazing at that exquisite piece of ancient artistry, Blake realised to the full how utter had been the plunge downwards of the descendants of those first people.

And what was this that squatted on the chair? Could it be human? Could this deformed, under-sized hairy thing be the offspring of anything that ever had been man?

Blake shivered unconsciously. It seemed almost indecent that this thing should sit there aping humanity.

It was only when Blake was within a yard or so of the throne that he could make out further details of the creature. He seemed to be of vast age —a wizened little ape of an old man who crouched there. His brows were completely hidden under thick, bushy grey hair. There was no more white to the forehead than a gorilla would have revealed. His eyes were deep, deep hollows beneath those beetling brows, and the nose was wide and splayed after the lowest human type. There seemed to be no chin, or what there was appeared only as a hairy slope which was lost in the wrinkled folds of a hirsute neck. His feet were drawn up ape fashion, and the soles turned inwards. His hands, black and hairy, lay on the arms of the beautiful chair, and they, too, were turned inwards, with the thumb straight. An absolute ape characteristic!

The swift thought came to Blake that Darwin might have been all wrong: that instead of man descending from a joint parent stock with the apes, the apes had degenerated from a pure parent stock of man. Was he witnessing here some such phase of evolution? In more thousands of years of such inbreeding and such conditions of living would these people of the pits, once an upright, cultured race, become nothing but pure ape in body and mind? They were perilously close to the edge of that chasm now, as witness the primitive way in which the thing on the throne held himself; and, too, even their speech was showing signs of becoming an unintelligible animal blur. How long would it take for that mark of the soul to die away into nothing but guttural grunts? The thought was appalling.

And then Blake became aware that the little wizened creature on the throne was stirring, was leaning forward peering at him closely, that certain sounds which began to emerge from his throat were speech!

The Menace of the Bridge.

IT would be but a wearisome repetition to give a detailed account of the verbal struggle that followed between Blake and the chief of the people of the pits.

As far as Blake could make out, the creature's first words were practically similar to those which had been used by the one who had first discovered them at the edge of the stream. At any rate, he took it for the same inquiry, and as well as he could muster his recollection of the primitive Chinese he had studied, he answered it.

But to Blake's mind it was essential that he should make another test of the efficacy of the jade rat. If it were received here with no sign of interest, then it would be plain that his position and that of the lad (little did he dream how close to him Tinker was even then) would be desperate indeed. On the other hand, if it should prove potent, then there was still a hope that they might get through, and after seeing the great amphitheatre, Blake was convinced that a way of some sort did exist as far along underground as Chinkiang, and perhaps to Nanking.

So when his words seemed to be received with a certain degree of intelligent understanding by his interlocutor, Blake lost no more time in producing his talisman.

The effect was all that could be desired. It was plain that his original guide had, so far, made no mention that this strange invader of the pits bore such an object. This puzzled Blake, but he did not know that so feeble was the intellectual process of the creature that long before they reached the presence of the chief he had entirely forgotten about it.

The sight of the rat caused the chief to spring up in the air, as if he intended leaping to the floor. But he sank back, and thrust out a trembling hand. Blake surrendered the jade rat freely enough, and waited while the other brought it close to his eyes and mouthed over it. So old did the chief look that Blake thought it quite possible he might have been alive in the place when Sir Gordon visited it more than sixty years before, though if he would remember such an incident was another matter.

Indeed, this old man had been there at the time, but until Blake produced the jade rat he had forgotten entirely that anyone from the upper world had ever visited the place. But now, as he held the talisman in his hand, some whisper seemed to come to him from the past —a faint, but distinct stirring of that empty mind took place. Almost desperate, he struggled to remember what it was.

What legend of the tribe was it that he was trying to resuscitate? For so many years there had been so little tribal inter-communication that even the old legends were repeated no more. It was even an effort now to remember to teach the youth of the tribe the secrets which still remained to them —the method of producing light (which they did not understand, but which they could bring about by following the rule of thumb instructions which had been handed down from generation to generation); the system which produced the grain for food; the ritual of rat worship.

Even the most simple laws of the tribe had fallen into almost complete abeyance. The position of chief was purely nominal. It was a matter of inheritance by birth which was accepted by the tribe apathetically. Half of them hardly understood what it meant, so close to the animal world were their minds functioning. To those it was no more than the leadership of the pack. It is almost impossible to portray the extent to which the mind of man had given way to the dull morass of animal intelligence among those people.

And it was this morass through which Sexton Blake was trying to find a mental way. Yet, it was not fated that it should be through his own acuteness of brain that he was to secure safety there. From time to time he noticed that his captors would draw away from him and sniff loudly —snort almost as if they found nearness to him unpleasant to their olfactory senses. Little did Blake guess that it was the natural body odour of the white man that offended them. Had he been Celestial, they would have noticed nothing; but to them he was a strange animal, despite his appearance. And gradually, he found the chief also sniffing in apparent disgust. Had the position not been so pregnant with danger it would have been almost funny.

More than once the little old creature on the throne leaned forward and wrinkled up his nose. Through his senses was working the association of ideas —a more powerful reviver of memory than anything else. Even the most highly tuned intellect will leap to the recollection of some far-away spot when the nostrils are assailed by an odour that was associated with that spot. It is the last of the strong attributes of the cave and jungle which has remained with man.

And then, suddenly, recollection poured in upon the chief. With the jade rat in one hand he reached forward the other and touched Blake's arm. A flood of sounds came from his lips, but all that Blake could gather was one single syllable which was being used over and over again. It sounded like "g'nu." He racked his brains to try and think what it could mean. Had he ever come across it? The orderly state of his mental equipment stood him in good stead then, for out of some dim corner he dragged what he wanted. It meant "the strange people" among the indigenous Chinese who had been lost to history and now, as he knew, rediscovered here among these pits by Hsui-fsi —that would mean the same as "fan-kai-lo" in modern Chinese. And "fan-kai-lo" meant foreign devil.

He made an affirmative gesture, repeating several times the syllable "ka," which had so many meanings. But he knew that he had made himself understood, for when he had finished the chief turned in obvious excitement to the others and jabbered at them for some minutes. He was telling them the legend of the visit which one of "the strange people" had paid to the pits long ago. And now they understood that Blake was of the people who lived on the surface above them —of whose existence they were aware through legend. Moreover, he carried the most sacred talisman of the tribe.

Blake began to feel that he was making headway. Just how all this was to get him through that subterranean maze to Chinkiang he couldn't figure out; but it was something to know that because he was one of "the strange people" —something they did not understand, and because he bore the sacred talisman he was safe. Next, to locate Tinker, if some ghastly fate had not overtaken the lad already, and then to make use of these people as guides. Could he convey that desire to their blunted intelligence?

He was debating what line he should take to do this when a faint cry reached him. It sounded like that urgent wail he had heard away back among the passages, and he knew the voice for Tinker's. The lad was near, and some devil's work must be afoot for the lad to cry out in that fashion.

Without waiting for permission, Blake turned and raced for the passage which led to the large amphitheatre. On bursting into the great space he gave a shout.

"Tinker! Tinker! Where are you?"

From the great pit in the centre came a faint reply.

"Here, guv'nor! Hurry!"

Blake raced for the low stone parapet. Hurdling it in a single bound, he landed on the narrow footway that ran round it. Now the lad's voice reached him more clearly, and, as he tore along the narrow bridge, where the sight of those leprous white reptiles broke upon his gaze, his blood ran cold on realising that somewhere down there was Tinker.

Again a faint cry came to him. Reaching the centre of the bridge, he dropped down and peered over. Then he was able to see the large basket-like cage which had been lowered to within a foot or so of the surface of the water. Inside the cage he could glimpse a human form, and round about were the eager noses of at least a score of the brutes.

(Tinker is in deadly peril. What will be the outcome of this strange adventure? Another thrilling instalment next week.)

Something for Nothing

at the seaside this year for you! Arrangements have been made for our representatives to visit practically all the coast resorts during this summer season, and distribute free packets of Wrigleys' Chewing Gum to everyone seen to be carrying the current issue of the Union Jack. *When you buy your U.J. at the seaside, remember this, and carry your copy where it can be seen!*

Part 7.

First Published in the Union Jack magazine, issue 1242

How it began.

ONE of China's most sacred possessions, "The Golden Book of Buddha," is stolen by the Black Abbot of Cheng-tu while on its way up the Yangtse from Canton to the Grand Lama of Tibet. Sexton Blake, having been implored to help trace it, is in China with Tinker, both disguised as coolies, for that purpose.

After many adventures, Blake and Tinker, on the advice of Hsui-fsi, an Englishman and their friend, penetrate into the mysterious underground kingdom where dwell the People of the Pits, of which little or nothing is known to the outside world.

Following the discovery of a peculiar heatless blue light and a strange adventure with thousands of rats, they encounter one of the People of the Pits, a degenerate, gorilla-like creature, who leads them farther into his kingdom,. They are attacked, and while Blake is taken before the king, to whom he shows a certain talisman given him by Hsui-fsi, at which he is at once treated as a friend, Tinker has been spirited away in the darkness. As Blake is trying to make the king understand him, he hears Tinker's cry, and dashing to help him, sees the boy suspended in a basket-like prison, over a pool full of crocodiles which are trying to reach him.

Start this enthralling serial right now!

A COARSE rope held the basket dangling. What hand had lowered it, Blake didn't know. He could not even tell whether the chief had been cognisant of this or not; he had nothing to tell him if the latter even knew of the existence of another captive. As a matter of fact, it may be stated here that he did not.

So lacking in co-ordination of action was the tribe that the blind mob which had spirited Tinker away had acted entirely on their own initiative. To them the captive had been just an extraordinarily lucky find —a toothsome offering for the sacred reptiles in the tank. And by now they had forgotten entirely how the prize had come into their possession.

But it was ghastly enough for Tinker, who had been helpless to resist when a hand had loosened the rope and had lowered him over the pool, so that the terrible creatures beneath could almost touch him with their snapping jaws. Had those crocodiles not been bloated with overfeeding, Sexton Blake would never have arrived in time, for the distance of the basket above them was so little that they could easily have reached it. But it was a usual thing for a tempting morsel to be hung close to them before being given, and they had assumed this to be just that.

Needless to say, Blake caught hold of the rope and began to pull desperately. The moment the basket began to swing and rise the reptiles revealed sudden excitement, and a dozen huge tails whipped the water as they rushed in, making a desperate effort to reach the prey which was being withdrawn from their reach.

One enormous mugger, fully twenty feet long, and a sickening shade of white, leaped high, the jaws coming together like a steel trap against the bottom of the basket. It tore the thick reeds clean out, and Blake's heart missed a beat as Tinker's feet dropped down. But the lad clung on desperately, while Blake made a superhuman effort with the rope.

In that violent pull he got the basket up a clean two feet, and then he was able to reach through the reeds and grasp the lad by the hands. Thus he heaved him on to the bridge, and a few minutes later he had torn the enclosing reeds to bits. Both the rope and the basket itself, he found, were made of the stems of the grain-plant he had already seen.

Tinker lay panting on the bridge. For the time being speech was beyond him. He had been so perilously near to terrible death that he was shaken to the depth of his soul. The reaction of finding himself safe —even the safety of that appalling place —was almost too much for his self-control.

Blake, with a hand on his shoulder, was talking to him in soothing tones, and thus he did not see that scores of People of the Pits had gathered round the pool and had watched the rescue. Unlike the blind ones who had captured them in the tunnels, they appeared to be possessed of sight.

He only knew that something was wrong when there came a sudden scurry of feet on the bridge, and, looking up, he saw a mass of hairy forms advancing from either end. Near the low stone parapet he caught sight of the tiny, wizened form of the chief. That was enough for Blake to realise that, whatever was afoot, he approved of the proceedings.

It came to Blake's mind that the purpose was to throw both him and Tinker into the pit among those vile reptiles. And, jumping up, he made to defend himself. But before the clash came he saw the chief pushing a way towards the low entrance to the inner footway.

In his hand was the jade rat, and at sight of that Blake decided to play his luck. With this decision still forming in his mind he helped Tinker to his feet, and then it was too late to resist, even if he would. For the gangs were upon them, and scores of hirsute hands were reaching out to grasp them.

A Staggering Surprise.

THEY were hustled across the bridge to the footway, and through one of the openings in the wall to where the chief stood. A dwarf he was beside the others, but now that he was among them there seemed to be a visible acceptance of his leadership.

He did not look at Blake, but kept his eyes on the jade rat as he gave vent to guttural commands. Those who held the two prisoners dragged them towards the great statues and then along a narrow passage between them. At one end of this there was a heavy stone slab which took the combined efforts of fully a dozen of the creatures to draw aside.

Without any further ceremony Blake and Tinker were thrust through the opening, finding themselves in a sort of stone-lined cell some ten feet long by nearly twenty feet wide. The roof was almost lost in the dimness above.

The closing of the stone did not leave them in darkness. They found the place illuminated by the same ghostly bluish light, and, as he gazed about him, Sexton Blake forgot the danger of their position in a startling discovery. On the floor, on stone benches, and on rude stone shelves he saw heaps of great mouldy tomes, bound in ragged bits of what had once been leather. There were, too, strange instruments of plain wrought iron, copper, and what seemed to be bronze.

An extraordinary collection of stuff to be found in those pits, and suddenly it came to Blake that he was looking at nothing less than the remnants of the treasures of those refugees of thousands of years ago. Would those tomes contain the secret of the lost people? Would they reveal in what condition China was —yea, how the world stood in those far-off days which had drifted into the mists of almost forgotten legend? Would he find the explanation of the strange bluish light?

Would he come upon some hint to reveal the extraordinary knowledge of physics possessed by those early peoples?

And, above all, would he discover if that great amphitheatre outside was, as it had appeared to him, the floor of a great pyramid such as that in Egypt? The amphitheatre was, so to speak, inside the pyramid, but, nevertheless, Blake had been immediately struck by the four great stone supports that were carried up in an angle to meet at the top. If that were so, then here in these lost pits was the first pyramid that had ever been built —the father of all the pyramids. Was this early people of China the genesis of the extraordinary wave of culture that had swept across the world before written history appeared?

For three days and three nights —during the time they were there —Sexton Blake scarcely lifted his head from those ancient tomes. Periodically food and water were brought to them, and at times he snatched a little sleep. But he was wrapped up in a wonderful voyage into the past such as he had never dreamed of making, and for the time being he hadn't a thought for the perilous journey on which they were bound, nor of the Golden Book of Buddha.

For these three days and three nights they were left strictly alone. Tinker, who had more time to ponder on their situation than Blake, came to the conclusion that, unless the chief had forgotten all about them he must be waiting for something, waiting for guidance from the rat god or the crocodile god, or, maybe, for something else. But that their presence was at least remembered by some of the tribe was evident from the regular appearance of food and water, the food consisting of soaked but uncooked grain, which was not half as unpleasant as one might have thought.

But on the fourth day Blake came back to the present. It was with a deep sigh of content that he laid aside the tome he had been studying and rubbed his tired eyes. Tinker, who had been almost bored to tears, was in no pleasant mood.

"This has been wonderful —wonderful, young un," was Blake's first coherent remark for days. "I've struck the most priceless records of the past. There can be nothing else like them in existence unless something of the sort is eventually found to have been buried in the Great Pyramid of Egypt. I've secured enough material here for half a dozen books."

"Huh! That sounds all right, guv'nor, but when do you expect to write them? It strikes me that this hole is a good distance from Baker Street, and there aren't many signs of our being let loose."

The acid in the lad's tone brought Blake to a full realisation of the position. He smiled wryly.

"I deserve your censure, my lad. It is a fact that I was completely absorbed in these records. But they are the most remarkable documents in existence. The British Museum would give anything to possess them. They must be the very earliest of any written records. Why, some of the stuff was written more than ten thousand years ago. But enough of that. I shall get my mind back to the problem in hand. How long have we been in here?"

Tinker looked at him sombrely.

"This is the fourth day on water and pasty-soaked grain," he grunted.

"I had lost count of time. However, we shall begin to-day to stir things up. I wonder how long that wizened little fellow intends to keep us cooped up here, if he hasn't forgotten our existence? What time do they bring us food?"

"If my count of time is right, someone ought to turn up soon."

"In that case, we shall wait, and when he comes we shall take the initiative."

Scarcely had Blake finished speaking when there came a scraping sound, and the stone in front of their cell was pushed aside. A second or so later one of the hairy people entered, bearing a kind of hollowed-out stone platter, in which was a heap of soaked grain; water was already in the cell. The platter was set down, and mechanically Blake and Tinker fell upon the uninteresting food. But they were hungry and it was necessary nourishment.

"Wonder why he's hanging, about?" mumbled Tinker, after a bit. "He usually slings his hook as soon as he's chucked the grub at us."

Blake was wondering the same thing, and no sooner did they finish scraping up the last few grains, than they received enlightenment. The fellow uttered some gibberish and made motions which they interpreted as meaning that they were to follow him. They were by no means averse to anything that meant a change and action, so they rose with alacrity.

Just outside the cell they found a dozen or so of the others in waiting. Their arms were seized, and in this fashion they were guided along to the smaller amphitheatre where Blake had had his first audience of the chief.

On entering the place they saw the little wizened bundle on the "throne," apparently waiting for them. They were pushed along towards him, and had almost reached a spot in front of the low dais, when suddenly they caught sight of another figure standing somewhat in the shadow behind the pink jade throne.

As their eyes were able to take in the details of the figure, there came a gasp of amazement from Tinker, and Blake's hands clenched hard. For there, without the slightest doubt, was the sinister figure of the Black Monk.

How he had got into the pits, Blake didn't know nor could he guess. But that he had possessed some knowledge of the people, and some means of establishing contact with them, was plain. It began to look as if their three days in the cell had been a period of waiting while the Black Monk had been communicated with. As a matter of fact, later on Blake was to learn that this surmise was correct, and was to discover just how it had come about.

But just then, the one thing that mattered was the actual presence of the Black Monk. Here was visible proof that he, at least, had not perished in the explosion of the coffin-junk. It was confirmation of Blake's fear that he had succeeded in diving over the side in time to escape. And, being here, it meant that, were his word to be their judgment, their lives wouldn't be worth five minutes' purchase. Indeed, even as their eyes met there flashed from those of the monk a threat of what was to come.

Blake knew that if they were ever to escape from that hole now, it would need resource and remarkably good luck. Every moment that passed would tighten the net about them. Somehow, some way, they must make a dash for it. And in the urgency of the moment, he snapped out his thoughts to the lad in English.

"This has got to be smashed," he jerked. "No time to waste —I'm going to tackle that man —lay into the first one that comes for you, Tinker —hold your weapon until the last need —all ready —take them on the jump, and don't worry about the chief unless he asks for it. Now!"

At the word, Blake threw aside the hands that held him. In one flying leap he was half-way across the dais and past the throne. In the same instant, Tinker broke loose, and with a yell, began to lay into those about him.

114

So utterly unexpected was the outbreak, that for the first few moments, every arm hung paralysed with astonishment. It was just this brief advantage that Blake had been counting on, and before any of them could recover, he felt his fingers against the rough black stuff of the monk's robe; a savage snarl broke from the scarred lip of the latter as he whirled to meet the attack, and the next moment he and Blake were at it with a fury that meant to yield no quarter.

Overthrown!

FOR one moment Blake thought that, at last, he was to come to physical grips with the Black Monk. Within him was a wild surge of rage against this sinister creature who, like an evil shadow, had appeared in those lost pits.

He did not pause to ask himself whence he had come; nor how he should be on visiting terms with these lost people. It was enough for Blake that he was there —that in some way he had come to know that the tall coolie who had precipitated the riot at the Da-Tung-Mun, and had been rescued from the coffin-junk, had chosen this underground way to steal through the cordon which had been thrown round Shanghai.

It was proof in full how closely every outlet was being watched. It indicated that every solitary traveller, coolie as well as mandarin, must be under scrutiny as he passed up the river.

But all Blake wanted now, was to get his hands on this black raven, scout of that greater raven who perched in his eerie in Cheng-tu, and crush him as one would vermin. It was a miracle, nothing less, that he had escaped from the holocaust which had devoured the coffin-junk and those on board.

But what Blake sought was not to be. Even as his fingers closed on the rough stuff of the black robe, the monk sprang back, tearing himself free. From his throat came a peculiar, guttural exclamation that sounded to Blake like a command in the primitive vocabulary of the People of the Pits. It had immediate effect, for it was taken up by the dwarf chief, and before either he or Tinker could get across to the back of the dais where the monk had throw himself behind some curtains, the whole mob came at them.

There followed one of the strangest struggles in which the pair from Baker Street had ever taken part. It was a mass demonstration of flabby resistance —a smothering pressure without a single violent blow being struck. Even though Blake and the lad, standing close together, kept hammering away with their fists against body after body, no hand was lifted against them. The strange blue lights faded to nothing, as before; then they glowed again from every direction. It was like some battle with ghostly gnomes. The whole thing was a wild nightmare, in which it seemed that they were pitted against scores upon scores of antagonists, who seethed about them like fantastic creatures of some crazy world.

Blake knew now that the power of the jade rat had saved them from violence, but the fear was even more sinister that once they succumbed to that silent deadly pressure of numbers they would never again emerge from those pits. If they failed to get clear now they were done, and not even Hsui-fsi would be able to save them. It called for a supreme effort. Somewhere, close at hand, was that black monk, watching, waiting, like the carrion he was, for their surrender. It was the thought of this, even more than the futile hammering of that surging mass of flesh, that gave Sexton Blake an inrush of supreme strength. The culmination of muscle and will, and mind and determination coincided in a single instant, and his voice rasped its purport to the lad.

"We've got to get through," he panted, as he smashed his fist into a puffy face. "No time to plan. Break through and reach the passage. Keep them back by shooting. When I give the word wheel and make for the opening. Now!"

On the word he swung round, Tinker following as if he were part of Blake. Between them and the passage which led into the great amphitheatre were massed fully two score of the creatures, spread out, and forming a solid wall of resistance. From his hidden point of vantage the Black Monk must have seen and guessed what the tall coolie intended, for his voice rang out again, mouthing that same guttural command. It was taken up by the chief, and hard on this the mob swayed back to cut off the retreat.

But Sexton Blake and Tinker used a means which those of the pits had never known in all their existence. Tinker got his arms round Blake's waist, and Blake, with head down, roaring like a bull, charged. The violence of impact drove them clean through the first press of the creatures. Like a flying wedge they cut a swathe through that mass, and for one breathless moment they were clear, not a soul between them and the passage, which was their immediate objective.

They did not pause. With the removal of the pressure they stumbled a little, and then, recovering, continued their rush, with the whole mob after them. They won the opening, and there Blake caught the lad, swinging him round so that he was in the passage. In the same sweep of movement he whipped out his precious weapon and sent two low shots into the mass that was coming towards them.

In those vaulted confines the double roar was terrific. So terrifying was it to ears that had never heard such a shattering crash of sound that, despite the renewed command of the hidden monk, they paused. In front of them lay the squirming figures, dragging each a shattered limb as they tried to crawl to safety. Blake would have spared them that had it been possible, but it was his freedom and Tinker's in the balance, and everything hung on the next few moments.

With this brief pause checking them, he and the lad raced along the passage into the amphitheatre. Back of them they could hear the soft pad, pad, pad of feet as the mob came on.

Within the great pyramid Blake cast about him desperately. On the left was one of those barbaric statues, on the right another. His harassed gaze sought first one, then the other. It lingered longest on the repulsive idol of the rat god. The thing was a gigantic affair, placed on a wide base, but for the first time Blake saw that the stone from which it had been carved was fashioned, where it rested on the base, into the form of a curled tail. In some extraordinary way the balance had been made perfect, much after the fashion of some of the enormous cromlechs of the ancient Druids, that have been balanced on a mere point.

With a smothered imprecation Blake caught the lad by the arm and pushed him away, so that he stood facing the entrance to the passage.

"Your pistol!" he jerked. "Hold them back. Shoot low, and not too fast, make every bullet count. I have a plan."

Tinker whipped out his weapon. He was just in time, for by now the foremost of their pursuers was almost at the end of the passage. Taking a careful, low aim, Tinker pulled the trigger once. The explosion was caught up in that place of which the acoustic properties were magnified in amazing fashion, making the roar repeat again and again. It was as if a dozen weapons had been discharged in rapid succession, and, remembering the strange and terrifying phenomenon which had brought two of their fellows down, frightened of this strange flame that could bite so terribly at a distance, the mob again paused, being jammed into a compact mass by those who crowded at the back.

In the meantime Sexton Blake had raced towards the base of the rat god. Leaping on to it, he had climbed the slope until he was standing close to the monstrous coils of the statue's tail. Then he leaned over, pressing both hands against the lower part of the statue, just above where the coils ended.

Seaton Blake was a powerful man, and in that moment he summoned to his aid every shred of strength he possessed. The sweat broke from his forehead in the strain of the effort he made. It seemed at first as if he might have pitted himself against the solid wall itself for all the impression he seemed to make on the balance of that giant statue. But when he eased back a little he felt the great rat move a little towards him. He waited until it stopped, then he gave another slow heave against it.

This time he could actually feel the mass draw away from him, and again the return pressure as, like an enormous pendulum, it started on the return.

To keep it going —to increase the sway from top to base until he should swing it beyond its pivot of control —could he do it? With the realisation that it might be done Sexton Blake jerked out a couple of frantic words to Tinker, telling him to hold the passage at any cost; then he gave himself and all his strength to the backward and forward sway of the statue, his hopes rising as the distance lengthened little by little. Once he gazed upwards. From the base where he stood to the top far above he could see the rocking of the whole mass, and from that angle it seemed as if the whole gigantic affair must topple at any moment. But by the "feel" of it at the base Blake knew that the ratio must be increased much more yet before he would be able to upset the pivot of gravity, and it was maddening to think that he must wait each time until the sway had reached the natural limit.

Tinker's voice warned him that the crisis was approaching.

"Only one more shot left, guv'nor," he heard the lad cry. "Can't keep them back after that."

At that moment the great stone rat was swaying towards Blake. He allowed himself to bend back with it, releasing his right hand long enough to claw out his weapon. This he sent slithering along the ground towards the lad's feet. He had no need for words; Tinker would understand.

Then Blake gave himself once more to the outward push of the statue, and this time his heart gave a jump as, on reaching the far point of its sway, the stone emitted a distinct cracking sound at the base. It returned to him slowly. But his hope was higher now, for he knew that it was not very far from breaking-point.

On the pause, he had laid his whole body against it, and strained frantically again on the outward push. Over and over it went, until there sounded again that ominous cracking at the base. But still it did not topple, and the shots from the second weapon which Tinker was using seemed to be sounding terrible rapid.

Towards him it swayed once more, and this time the cracking at the base could be heard again. If it toppled in this direction, all his efforts would have gone for nought. It was the other way it must fall if it was to save them, and on that return pressure Sexton Blake called forth the urge of every muscle and every sinew in his body. His heart and soul were behind it, too, and not the infinitesimal fraction of an ounce did he relax as the mass of stone swayed away from him — away and away and away, until the cracking at the base came in little short, sharp snaps that told of the uprooting of stone that had been settled for centuries.

Away and still away, until it was at the angle from which it had swung back the last time. But this swing did not stop there. Still the upper part of the statue kept swaying at a greater angle, and suddenly there came a terrific tearing sound as the whole base of the mass was torn loose from its foundations.

Crash!

Then an appalling cloud of dust and fine particles of stone as over and over the statue went, crashing into the great alligator god that stood on the other side of the passage —a roar as of a monster landslide, the breaking of thousands upon thousands of stone chips as the statue came to earth in an upheaval of dust that filled the whole amphitheatre with a cloud of litter that no current of air had disturbed in centuries.

It was done! The whole mass lay in a confusion of complete ruin, full in the mouth of that passage. Sexton Blake staggered back, to find Tinker, amazed beyond all expression, literally gibbering in his excitement. For a few moments Blake was as powerless to move as if he had become paralysed. That last supreme effort had shaken him to the very root of his being; but as his lungs filled with that dust-laden air he staggered back, choking and spluttering.

" Come!"

It was but a hoarse croak he gave, but Tinker understood. Mechanically Blake took the pistol which the lad thrust into his hand. Then they reeled through an opening into the passage outside the amphitheatre, and, hanging on to each other, there they saw before them the means by which the black monk had come to the People of the Pits.

Drawn up on the slightly shelving bank of the underground stream was a round, shallow skin coracle such as was used by prehistoric man. Sticking out from it were two paddles. At sight of that fragile craft, Blake gave a croak of renewed hope. He motioned the lad to get in. Tinker obeyed, and together they worked the little craft off the gravel. Next, Blake stepped in gingerly, almost capsizing the ticklish affair in doing so. He squatted down gingerly and seized a short paddle. Tinker did likewise, glancing at Blake as he did so.

"Back the way we came, guv'nor?" he jerked.

Sexton Blake shook his head, grinning like a yellow gargoyle as he replied hoarsely:

"No, we've come so far; we'll finish this job. Give her to the stream, lad."

And the next moment they were swirling and turning in that crazy craft on the run of a current that grew swifter and swifter as the seconds passed.

The Peril of the Pool.

WITHIN a few moments from the start of their desperate voyage in the coracle, the two voyagers were in pitch darkness. The legendary gloom of Tophet was as nothing to that heavy, velvety black which enveloped Blake and Tinker. It was as if they had been precipitated from the earth and become disembodied spirits in some cosmic vortex of roaring sound. There was for them nothing but the feel of the coracle, as it plunged along faster and faster, to give them definite connection with anything they had ever known.

Whither they were bound —what might be the depths into which that underground stream finally plunged —they couldn't even begin to guess. For all they knew, it might pour over the lip of some unfathomable deep and lose itself in the unknown bowels of the earth.

One thing, however, became more and more evident as they proceeded. The speed of the stream increased each moment, and, following that, the coracle began to revolve regularly, slowly at first, so that in the pitch dark it was almost impossible to be aware of it, but continuing to increase in rate until they could not but realise the effect of the circular motion.

Although the rush of the stream filled the air with its sound, it was not difficult to make each other heard, and when he grasped the fact that the frail craft had yielded to some centrifugal pull of the current, Blake shouted to Tinker to try and get his paddle against it as a brake. He did the same with his own paddle, and after several clumsy efforts, in which the coracle dipped dangerously in all directions, they managed to bring it to a slower rate of revolution.

But what caused Blake most uneasiness was the undoubted increase in the rate at which they were being drawn through the tunnel. There could be no doubt that the stream must strike sharply sloping ground soon after passing the caves of the People of the Pits. The sensation was an exaggerated one of tobogganing down a watery slope, and while they would have given much for even a faint gleam of light, it was well for them both just then that they could not see the precipitous decline down which they were plunging. The sight would have appalled the stoutest heart.

They must have been sweeping along at this terrific rate for the better part of half an hour when the rate of motion became perceptibly slower. Blake shouted an encouraging word to the lad as he grasped this fact, but nevertheless as they continued to travel on and on and on into that region of perpetual gloom, he could not help but ask himself if, after all, they should not have gone back the way they had come. There, at least, was a known connection with the world above. By this way they had come there was only the faint possibility of an opening somewhere beyond.

Blake had gambled entirely on what Hsui-fsi had told him about there being some means of communication from the underground pits with Chinkiang far up the river. But the current of this stream was rushing at such a rate that it did not seem possible it could be taking a course which would lead up the valley of the Yangtse. Going by the topographical lay of the delta of the Great River, the flow of water should make towards the mouth of the delta. The only chance that this natural course of flow might be reversed was in the possibility that the river had a subterranean source —that it came from some spring far down in the earth, and that the natural upheaval which had caused the formation of those caves and passages had thrown the slope higher at the lower end of the delta than farther up the basin of the Yangtse.

This was all just theory on Blake's part. The stream might end as suddenly as it had begun. It might, as he had already thought, plunge over some rocky lip into the bowels of the earth. In that case he and Tinker were on the last voyage they would ever make in this world. And, of course, in the Stygian gloom there was no chance of seeing whether they were passing other openings or not. They might have whirled past scores which should be the ones to take did they but know.

And then Blake's thoughts were brought back to the immediate present by a shout from Tinker. Looking up he saw ahead what seemed to be a faint glow of light of the same bluish tinge they had seen back in the amphitheatre. The flow of water was perceptibly slower now, and the mad spinning of the coracle had slackened. It was possible, therefore, to gaze ahead at intervals while they approached the faint suggestion of grey. They noticed that it grew slowly to what was undoubtedly a patch of irradiation, and a little later they could make out the dim outjuttings of stone walls and corners as they tore towards it.

Ahead of them there appeared a rough oblong which was silhouetted against the glow, and it was just beyond this opening that the patch of light seemed to be concentrated. The light was plainly the same sort of strange marsh light they had seen before, back in the caves. But this —was this just a chance illumination of some natural phenomena of the caves, or was it, too, under control of the People of the Pits?

If the latter were the case, it meant that they had some means of communication with this place, some miles from the amphitheatre which formed the central point of their life; and it meant, too, that there would be some means of reaching it on foot. But to Blake and Tinker it meant, just then, nothing but a promise that for the moment they were not to plunge into unknown deeps in the earth.

But immediately ahead of them lay a horror that could be little less than such a blind dive to death. They had no hint of it until the coracle swept through that jagged opening into a wide, vaulted space fully as large as the great amphitheatre they had left in such precipitate fashion.

The whole place was aglow with the bluish light, though they could not see whence it came, and the next moment they had no thought for it. It was Tinker who turned his head as an awful foetid stench filled their nostrils, but it was Blake who saw the cause.

Inured though he was to terrible sights, the detective's eyes widened in speechless horror and loathing as he espied several leprous white objects on the surface of the water, made more unnatural still by that weird bluish tint which the light cast.

When the coracle bumped into one of the mounds it moved, revealing the long, wicked snout of a crocodile. An exclamation of disgust and consternation broke from the lips of each. That feeling seemed for the moment to overpower everything else. They had plunged straight into the heart of the pool where the sacred crocodiles were bred for the tank in the amphitheatre. What was it Hsui-fsi had said? He had mentioned that these crocodiles must be fed on their own kind and on human sacrifice. He had said that they could only exist there as descendants of reptiles which had been brought from the swamps of the south when the world was still steaming. And these were the creatures of the People of the Pits, kept in sacred satiety, fed on human flesh and their own kind.

The monster into which the little coracle had bumped must have been half-asleep, for it moved sluggishly away, not offering to attack. Tinker, white-lipped but steady, essayed to move his paddle in an effort to guide their frail craft between two white mounds a little farther on, into which the current threatened to bump them, but Blake stopped him with a quick gesture. He bent forward so far that he needed to emit little more than a whisper for Tinker to hear.

"Steady! The current may take us through. I think I can see the opposite side of this ghastly pool. They may be sluggish enough to pay no attention unless we stir them up."

Tinker withdrew his paddle, and together the two sat, while the coracle drifted with maddening slowness out along a sort of lane that showed between those dozens of white mounds.

Sexton Blake sat with mask-like countenance gazing ahead, his eyes fixed like those of a sleep-walker. He was using every shred of will power to keep his self-control in this pit of horror, for he knew that did he show but the slightest weakening the lad would break.

Tinker was on the sheer edge of collapse just then, as his chalk-like face and drawn lips showed.

Still they continued to drift along. Now and then they would graze the side of one of those nauseating mounds, and once their hearts came into their mouths as one of the monsters, smaller than the others, flicked his tail in a show of temper. They gripped the edge of the coracle with whitened fingers while they passed beyond the range of that particular danger.

Blake figured that they must be almost half-way across now, and a faint hope was stirring in his breast. Foot by foot they were moving, and it was plain that the current was running true towards an opening of some sort on the opposite side of the cavern. Came a patch of more open water, where only an occasional crocodile could be seen. They passed this, and a few moments later the opposite opening became plainly visible. Hope was beating higher than ever in Blake's breast, but a terrible dread seized him the next moment as, without the slightest warning, one of the ghastly reptiles rose to the surface immediately in the path of the coracle.

Blake thrust out his paddle, and, with infinite precaution, tried to swing the coracle away from this menacing obstacle. The current, however, was too persistent just there, and before he could achieve his object they were upon the monster. This one, at least, was not sluggish. It had evidently just risen from the bottom of the pool, and at the touch of the coracle it went into a sudden frenzy of rage.

It threshed about like a mad thing, and in a moment the whole pool seemed to awake to the fact that something unusual was in progress. Blake made a vicious jab with the paddle to try and drive the thing off, while he yelled to Tinker to get his own blade to work. The sound of his voice came echoing back again and again, and the thunder of it seemed to drive every reptile in the pool into the same frenzy that had seized the one with which they had collided.

A hundred terrible snouts were raised, and each one was pointing towards that frail craft in the middle of the pool. A hundred tails swirled the water into as many foaming upheavals as the fleet got into motion.

It was the last degree of horror to watch that closing in with the little, frail craft in the centre, its thin skin covering all that lay between its two passengers and the agonies of a revolting death.

Dangers Past —and to Come!

THERE wasn't one chance of retreat in a million.

On either side the great natural cave came down in a jagged hemisphere right down to the edge of the water. There may have been foothold here and there, but of that Blake and Tinker could see nothing. The only possible way in which there seemed even the ghost of a chance of pushing the little coracle was straight ahead towards the opening which led, Heaven only knew where.

It was now some fifteen yards or so distant, and so engrossed were the two in the craft over the dire threat of the approaching crocodiles that neither had noticed a slight quickening in the current which would have carried them more speedily towards that exit from the place had it not been for the press of loathsome reptiles about them.

Sexton Blake's mind was working hard, trying to find some means of combating this impossible position. Tinker had got his paddle into action, and, so viciously did he jab the blade into a pair of open jaws, lined top and bottom with cruel teeth, that the rounded end went clean into the creature's throat. The resultant upheaval was appalling. The crocodile gave vent to a hoarse bellow, and, like some gigantic steel trap, the jagged rows of teeth clamped on to the paddle, crushing it like paper.

Nothing was left to Tinker but the broken shaft, and now, as the maddened creature came on, he poked desperately with his short weapon for one of the eyes. He knew that this was the most vital spot among that breed of reptile, and the next moment he got visible proof of the truth of it. The end of the shaft went stabbing into the nearest orb of the crocodile, and the next moment all pandemonium broke loose.

Blake had been thrusting at others of the reptiles on his side of the coracle, but at sound of this terrific commotion he turned to see one great monster rising out of the water in its efforts to get over the edge of the coracle. The little craft tilted to such a degree that it seemed as if it must capsize.

Blake's heart came into his throat as he saw the lad striving desperately to drive the creature back. Then, in one final effort to save the situation Blake dragged out his automatic. He did not know if it contained a live cartridge or not; he did not know whether Tinker had emptied it back in the amphitheatre, or whether one or two shots might still remain.

Leaning forward, he pushed his hand in front of Tinker and pulled the trigger. The explosion in that echoing space was ear-shattering. It roared upwards, and then hammered down about them in a hundred interlocked echoes. The bullet crashed into the nearest eyeball of the crocodile that had all but got its muzzle over the edge of the coracle, and as the thing fell back among its fellows the pool turned into a perfect maelstrom.

The cannibalistic proclivities of the creatures was revealed in sickening horror. Now, for the moment the coracle and its occupants were forgotten. The creatures, caught by the scent of blood, came swirling in upon the doomed monster with great jaws agape.

A terrible mass of slimy life, covered with warty nodules, they fought and scrambled for the feast; and, seizing this temporary advantage, Blake once more plied his paddle.

With the desperation born of the knowledge that what they were looking at was what would overtake them did they but once touch that water, he worked as rarely before in all his long career. Somehow he managed to work the coracle out from the press, and, feeling the pull of the current, allowed it to sweep them towards the opening which, despite their ignorance of what lay beyond, beckoned them now as the only way of hope. Better, far better to drown in the Stygian depths beyond than fall to the jaws of those slavering creatures in the pool!

Ten yards, and they could feel an even stronger sweep of the current. Five yards, and their hearts beat high with hope. Then Tinker, who was gazing back, gave a cry. Blake gave a swift look over his shoulder. It was enough. The whole mob of crocodiles, having finished the feast in one swift orgy, were coming after them, all sluggishness gone now.

Blake made one more grab at the automatic, which he had dropped into the bottom of the coracle. Again the place was roaring with the echoes of the explosion that followed; a second time Blake pulled the trigger, but only a dead "click" followed. By now the leaders of the pursuing monsters was almost within reach; the opening of the tunnel towards which they were striving was scarce a yard away. Who would win that race? Or would the crocodiles leave the lighted pool and follow in the darkness?

That question will never be answered, for all of a sudden a new commotion started a little way back, and Blake and Tinker could see that the last shot which had been fired had, after all, had its effect. It had only wounded, but it had brought blood, and now, the monsters were swirling once more about the doomed reptile that was trying to sink from view.

The feast was in progress once more, and even while the foremost of the pursuers swung with terrific flicks of the tail that almost tore the skin side of the coracle to shreds, the little craft shot into the opening of the tunnel. For a few moments the glow of the pool followed them, becoming fainter and fainter, and then, as they whirled round a bend, it died away. Once more they were sweeping through a region of impenetrable night.

During some considerable time while they progressed at the will of the current, neither spoke. The reaction from the immediate menace of that pool of horror had left them both in a state of semi-collapse. It was enough, just then, to crouch down and try to recover some portion of composure before casting about to deal with what might lay ahead.

And even if they would, they could do nothing. There was no return —there was no branching off that they could see. They could only let the coracle follow the course on which it was borne; but if they came again to such a place as they had just passed through, each knew that they would not again escape, though each kept this thought to himself.

(What fresh menace awaits the pair in this tunnel of horror? Make sure of future instalments!)

Part 8

First published in the Union Jack magazine, no. 1243.
Our Super Serial

How it began.

ONE of China's most sacred possessions, "The Golden Book of Buddha," is stolen by the Black Abbot of Cheng-tu while on its way up the Yangtse from Canton to the Grand Lama of Tibet. Sexton Blake, having been implored to help trace it, is in China with Tinker, both disguised as coolies, for that purpose.

After many adventures, Blake and Tinker, on the advice of Hsui-fsi, an Englishman and their friend, penetrate into the mysterious underground kingdom, where dwell the People of the Pits, of which little or nothing is known.

These strange folk are, however, in league with the Black Monk, but the pair escape in a frail boat down an underground stream. They encounter a pool full of crocodiles, and barely emerge with their lives, hurtling down the stream, caught in the current, to still another terrible menace which awaits them. ...

The Giant Chute.

SLOWLY, almost imperceptibly, the speed of the current increased. It was not until Sexton Blake and Tinker had been travelling from the pool for twenty minutes or so that they became conscious that they were flying along at a terrific rate, it was, indeed, the increasing sound of the swishing of the water that conveyed the knowledge to them, and as the realisation filtered into his numbed brain. Blake bent forward until his hand found Tinker's arm.

"Seems to be falling at a sharper angle," he yelled; and a dozen voices, caricatures of his own, mocked him from the roof and sides.

"Anything is better than that!" yelled Tinker. "But I think I felt a bump, guv'nor. Do you suppose there are any more of those along here?"

"No; crocodiles wouldn't lurk in a current of this rate. Must have been your imagination."

But a few moments later Blake found that it had not been imagination on Tinker's part, for once again the coracle bumped against something so acutely as to tip it at a startling angle. Blake crouched lower, trying to figure out what it could be. He thought of rocks, but it seemed unlikely they would find boulders strewn along this sort of stream. And yet it had been something.

They seemed then to swing into a quieter stretch, although the speed did not diminish. Blake figured —and rightly —that the lessening of noise was because the tunnel had grown much wider. In fact, could they but have glimpsed their surroundings they would have found that the sides were quite invisible, although the roof could have been reached had they thrust up their hands.

Through this they went whirling along for an hour, two hours, three —how could they tell? They had lost all count of time and distance. Their brains were too numb to make even a guess at the space of time that had elapsed since they had escaped from the pool, let alone since they had fled from the amphitheatre.

Then suddenly they felt another bump. This time it was so violent that each uttered an involuntary exclamation of alarm. Before the coracle, which had tilted acutely, could right itself, they struck another obstruction which sent them spinning rapidly. Blake shouted something which Tinker could not hear. The lad yelled in reply, but his voice was lost in a sudden torrent of sound that arose on every side.

Another bump, still another, and then they were in the midst of a boiling cauldron of objects from which they were literally thrown like a cork.

"Rapids!" yelled Blake.

That one word was the last he was to utter for a long time. Even as it passed his lips the coracle plunged down an acute slope that carried them with terrific speed into a roaring cataract in which they pitched and tossed helplessly. The speed was appalling, and Blake knew if it continued for even a few moments longer they could never remain above the water.

He was right. With one terrific plunge the coracle swept down faster than ever; there were several terrific bumps, then a sharp upheaval against which they were helpless, and, following that, a wild cry from Tinker as the coracle turned completely over, precipitating them into the unseen cauldron which boiled about them.

It was beyond human power to attempt to do aught but cling frantically to anything that one encountered in that mad rush of water.

Time and again Blake's fingers scraped over the sharp edge or round surface of what he now knew to be stone. But he could not cling. His nails were torn, and he knew the ends of his fingers were oozing blood.

He had lost the coracle entirely, and of Tinker he had had no sign since they capsized. As a matter of fact, Tinker had fared even worse. In the upheaval which had thrown the coracle upside down and had precipitated them into that maelstrom, Tinker's foot had caught on the upper rim of the little craft, and before he could jerk it free he had plunged down head foremost, striking his temple with terrific force against one of the stones, The coracle had fallen on top of him, and then he had been swept down on the rush, bounding and rebounding from boulder to boulder.

His progress was faster than Blake's, for the latter had begun a wild struggle to get handhold or foothold somewhere. Yet, bit by bit, he was forced to give in, and at last, with fingers raw, he yielded to the downrush.

It was hopeless to call out to Tinker. The roar of the cataract drowned everything. Blake knew that if he ever again encountered Tinker, or what might remain of the coracle, it would be sheer chance. A desperate sadness overwhelmed him even in his own physical stress. Now, as he pounded along from boulder to boulder, knowing not whither that lost stream was carrying him, he realised what desperate chances he had taken in trying to pass through by that underground way.

Even if they had met with friendly help on the part of the people of the pits, there had been such a slim chance of winning through. For a few moments there came into his mind a deep reproach against Sir Gordon for having suggested such a way; and then Blake knew that this was unworthy. Sir Gordon had bared his mind of his own secret knowledge; Blake had but chosen of his own will.

For himself, he would not have cared so much. He had lived a full life and a rich one. He had, in a way, achieved what he had set out to do, and if it were his fate to plunge to his death along the bosom of this lost stream in China, then let it be. But Tinker had but tasted the first breath of life, as it were. The lad, in his fine courage and utter loyalty, had said that he would fellow wherever Blake led. But had it been fair to permit the lad to come? Where was he now? Had he been thrown among those boulders, and did he now lie unconscious in some cleft? Or had he been swept on ahead into the Stygian unknown?

A terrific collision with the outjutting edge of a huge boulder, stopped Blake's thoughts. His senses reeled, and it was in purely mechanical fashion that his fingers sought once more for a hold. They did not cling —he was too nerveless to exert sufficient strength. Despite the urge of his will to overcome the lethargy which was threatening him, he could not make a hold. It was with a feeling that Fate was too much for him that he was forced once more to let go.

Again he went plunging along, beating against a boulder here, being hammered in the ribs by another as he bounced clear. Once a terrific whirlpool caught him, spinning him madly as he fought with arms and legs against it. The realisation that he was being sucked under brought his wits back to control, and he made a last desperate effort to break free.

His wild struggles drove him out of the whirl into the face of a large boulder. He rebounded from this, finding himself in a rush of the current which seemed to be dropping at an angle of fully thirty degrees. He could not tell; it was all guesswork. But he was descending now faster than ever.

Then came another spinning, followed by a region of comparative calm. Had he come to a pool at the bottom of the rapids?

He pulled himself together, and attempted to swim. He found that the current was not nearly so swift now, and it was while he was progressing slowly, feeling for some projection against which he could cling and rest that his hand encountered what he knew at once to be the upturned coracle. He grasped it, finding that it came towards him easily. He was about to throw the upper part of his body on it for support when his leg struck against some object.

His heart leapt at that touch. Quickly his hand went out. His fingers encountered saturated cloth. He gripped and held. A nameless dread filled his soul as he knew the limp object he dragged out from under the coracle was Tinker. He needed no light to realise that the lad was either unconscious or dead —battered and hammered into oblivion.

The touch of the lad acted on Blake more swiftly than the most potent stimulant. His brain cleared swiftly, and when he had succeeded in getting one arm under the lad's shoulders so that he could support his head above the surface, he set himself to face the ghastly peril which overturned them both.

His supreme care was Tinker. Again and again he called to the lad, his voice laden with the anxiety that filled him. But not the slightest response did Tinker give. He hung as limp as a sack against Blake's arm. The problem allowed of only one solution so far as action was concerned. That was to follow the stream.

It must end somewhere, if only in the bowels of the earth. To remain where they were was to lose strength, and that meant only one thing. It were better to move onwards, if it be but to death; and, indeed, Blake became aware, now that he gave his mind to this phase of the problem, that he was to have no choice. Their frail support — that fragile little coracle that had served them so well —was on the move. So be it —they would go whither it took them!

How long they drifted on a comparatively sluggish current Sexton Blake did not know. He made no effort to compute time or distance. His every faculty, was concentrated in trying to rouse the lad to consciousness; to conserve his own strength for the final struggle that must come.

Was it day or night above ground now? He did not know. Was there, indeed, any world at all beyond this watery pit? All of his life that had gone before seemed now but a filmy dream. It was as though his body was not his; as though the arm that gripped and the legs that kicked, gripped and kicked because of some will other than his own. He began to feel detached from himself.

That was the inevitable effect of the utter darkness, and was, Blake knew, a dangerous sign. He made a desperate effort to shake off the feeling. He cast his mind back to the world of sunlight and men.

It was bitter comparison, but it kept him sane. That world did exist, and this was but a foul nightmare that could only exist beneath the crust of sinister China.

Thus he whipped himself back to a sane outlook as they drifted along that approach to what might be the nether world. At any moment they might go plunging over the edge of an abyss which had no bottom. And, indeed, a little later, when there came a distinct quickening of speed, Blake felt that they were approaching some sort of definite crisis.

He tightened his hold on Tinker and shifted his grip a little on the coracle. As before, when they were approaching the rapids the current

132

began to slide down what seemed like an acute incline, and with terrible rapidity they were again rushing along with the speed of an express train.

So far there were no rocks. Up to now Blake had been almost unconscious of the temperature of the water. It had been neither so warm nor so chill as to have any perceptible effect upon him. But now he felt it to be growing distinctly warmer, and he began to wonder if this presaged a plunge into greater depths, for he knew that, up to a certain point, the crust of the earth grows warmer as one descends. But then reason told him that unless the surrounding stone and bed of the stream were very warm the water would not be affected by what lay below, for the simple reason that it was the same stream, so far as he knew, as that by which they had first entered the caves of the People of the Pits.

It seemed impossible that the angle of descent could become more acute, and yet it was so. The sensation in the darkness was one of shooting down a giant slide. A physical explanation of the phenomenon was beyond Blake; it was something entirely outside any experience he had ever undergone. All he could think was that they were bound on the final wild plunge into the depths of the earth.

It soon became apparent, however, that the natural chute was not without angles. Every now and then Blake felt his body touch an outjutting of the wall, but the contact was not heavy enough to bruise. It was all a confused race which may have been many miles in extent for all he could determine.

And then they seemed literally to go rushing down in a vast perpendicular stream of water that made Blake think they must have gone over the edge of a waterfall. Down and down they plunged, with water over them and about them. It might be some subterranean Niagara, which would carry them into some bottomless cauldron far, far beneath.

Blake could think of nothing else until, still clinging desperately to Tinker with one hand and to the coracle with the other, he found himself struggling in some sort of pool.

Before he could adjust himself to this new experience he was caught up again by the current and carried along at a terrific rate, until for the second time he felt himself shooting wildly out into space. This time there could be no doubt that he was as a chip in some giant's plunge, but above it there was a different quality which impinged upon his senses numb though they were.

There came a second terrific plunge into a pool, which carried him under and wrenched both Tinker and the coracle from his grasp. Fighting desperately Blake got back to the surface, and then, as he breathed deeply, he felt an entirely different tonic in the air which filled his lungs. It was cool and fresh —blessed relief from the chill, clammy atmosphere of what had gone before.

Then, even as he cast about desperately for Tinker, his eyes saw a myriad of twinkling points of light overhead. For a moment he trod water, overcome by the sight, which he thought must be some fantastic vision of his battered senses.

But a moment's pause and he knew they were real; they were the stars in high heaven! They had come into the open out of the depths of the very pit!

Peril —and Piracy.

THAT much and no more did Blake grasp before casting about in search of Tinker.

Subconsciously he knew he had left those foul caves and that evil stream behind. He was still in water, it is true, but it was an open stretch; in some wild, unbelievable way he had come back to the surface of the world! It was night —the blessed stars were there in proof. It didn't matter what part of China that broad, placid flow might wash, so long as he found Tinker. That thought, and that only, filled him just then.

Sweeping his arms about, he felt the wreck of the little coracle. Never did shipwrecked mariner give greater thanks for the succouring lifeboat than did Blake for that frail craft which had borne him and the lad through such a maze of incredible dangers. Gently he pushed it on its way, almost murmuring aloud his gratitude.

Then a thrill shot through him, as his groping fingers encountered again the touch of sodden cloth. It could only be Tinker. He got his arm once more about the lad and, steadying him, spoke softly. By the faint light of the stars he could see a great dark stain on the lad's temple, and his eyes closed against yellow-white cheeks that struck a fresh stab of fear to Blake's heart.

Now, holding his precious burden well clear of the water, he lifted his head to gaze about him. In one direction he could see nothing but the dark sweep of the water; in another there was the same black stretch. But as he twisted round to peer in a fresh direction he thought he could make out a dim, jagged silhouette against the lowest stars.

Was it land? Was it a shore? Were those irregular points the outline of a rocky shore, or were they the pagodalike structures of men? Where in all that yellow empire was he? Into what open flow of water had that lost stream flung him and the lad?

Desperately he began to swim in the direction which seemed to promise a possible point of landing, if nothing else. By now he was so stiff and chilled from long immersion in the water that he felt a dull numbness creeping up his limbs. From his shoulders and thighs it seemed that he had no more control over muscular action than if all four limbs had been amputated or belonged to someone else. It was the sort of deadly chill which no amount of swimming will counteract, and Blake realised that unless he made landing soon he would find it beyond his power to continue. That for himself; for Tinker a greater dread, because he knew the paralysing effect of the creeping cold in a body which had no conscious power of resistance. It was the same stealing death that overtakes the man who succumbs to the drowsy spell of the snow blizzard.

With only one arm free it was slow work but, using every atom of will power and buoyed up by the hope of that dim silhouette ahead, Blake persisted in his efforts. A renewed strength flowed through him as he saw that he was approaching perceptibly nearer. More and more the points began to assume the curved lines of up-pointing Chinese eaves and layered roof terraces of pagodas.

Had he ever seen that sky-line of buildings before, he kept asking himself; for now he was certain that they were buildings. He did not realise until some little time later that they were becoming more and more distinct because dawn was spreading in the eastern sky. He only knew that he was making headway; and then, all of a sudden, he saw a nearer line which he recognised as a mass of moored sampans, wupans, and junks.

It was Chinese water front all right, but which. He risked a slight pause and raised himself higher in the water. Now, beyond the irregular silhouette of the buildings —a considerable place it must be from the extent of the line —he saw a low rounded hill, and a deep awe overwhelmed him as it came to him that the sight was familiar. He knew that city. It was, it could be none other than Chinkiang!

He renewed his efforts with a fierce determination to make a landing, despite the chill which was becoming more deadly each moment. It was the knowledge that this place which loomed before him was no chimera of a tortured brain, but solid fact. There lay reality and he must reach it. Time enough then to plan the next step.

He used his free hand and both legs violently. Nearer and nearer came the dark mass of the moored craft. For a moment it came to him that he must shout to rouse some form of aid. Among those boats would be hundreds, perhaps thousands of sleeping river folk. Surely some would come to succour him. But then he remembered the fact that he was outlaw even thus.

He remembered, too, the deep superstition of the river folk, and something told him that instead of succouring him they would drive him off with poles and firecrackers. To them he would be some evil spirit of the river come to do them harm. If he were to survive it would have to be by his own efforts.

So that he, who had already passed through horrors and blows which would have killed many a man, struggled on gamely, fighting with his one free hand against the distance that separated him from safety, and against that deadly, creeping chill.

He almost gave in when he found himself in the shadow of the outer boats. It needed all his restraint to refrain from giving one cry for help. False counsel whispered to him that perhaps after all they would understand that it was a human being in distress. Then his sanity told him that there did not exist among the river Chinese that quality of mercy.

So he toiled on until it seemed that he could almost touch the low freeboard of a small wupan which hung on the outer line of craft. Unconsciously, Blake had been making this his objective. He knew that he must pull himself and his precious burden aboard the first boat his fingers touched, but now came the inward warning that he would probably have to endure physical encounter with the occupants.

If he could get over the side and dispose of Tinker in a safe spot until he could start the blood coursing once more through his numbed limbs he would be ready, he told himself, to tackle a dozen of the brutes. But if they rushed him before then —

His fingers scraped the side of the wupan and slid away. He made another desperate effort to catch hold, and. succeeded in holding himself against the drag of the current. It was the southern side of the

Yangtse as he knew now. Pausing for a few moments he listened. Not a sound came to him from beneath the curved mat structure which formed a shelter in the waist of the boat.

So far, it would seem, the occupants were wrapped in heavy slumber. If they had possessed sufficient "cash" the night before to buy the low-grade but very potent "second-smoke" opium, then it was possible that they would still be deep in the grip of the drug.

In that case there was a chance, and never did Sexton Blake pray that "cash" had been plentiful and opium available as in those few moments when he hung alongside that wupan.

It was perceptibly lighter in the east now. Blake could see the tumbled litter in the sloping stern of the wupan —poles and roughly-hewn oars, bits of sacking and wooden food-bowls. He fixed his eye on one of the shortest of the oars as a possible weapon then, summoning what remaining will-power and strength he had, he began to heave up Tinker's limp body in an effort to get the upper part over the low side. It was the first time in his life Sexton Blake had seen any advantage in building a craft with such a low freeboard as the average Yangtse wupan possesses.

Little by little he achieved his purpose. When he had worked his burden over so that the weight of the shoulders rested on the side he managed to get his hand down below the knees and, rough though the resultant roll must be, succeeded in pushing the lad over into the stern. Then, like some mechanical robot, he crawled over after.

Once aboard, Blake crouched listening. Now, from beneath the mat shelter the sound of heavy snores came to him. So far the occupants slept. He cast about him, reaching out for the short oar which he had already marked down. As he did so he thought he heard the low sound of voices coming from one of the nearby sampans. That was a danger he had forgotten for the time being, but now it came to him that those aboard the wupan were not the only difficulty he had to face. A sudden fracas would probably bring scores of other Celestials on the scene.

Just at his feet lay a broken-bladed knife. It gave him his next idea and, stiffly, he bent to retrieve it. Had he not been half-numbed with cold and privation, Blake's mind would have worked more freely. But slowly his wits were functioning as an object here and there carried suggestion to his mind. It was the most primitive example of the association of ideas.

A knife! A knife was made for cutting, and the wupan was held to the other moored craft by a thin bamboo rope, fore and aft! The next move was obvious. Cautiously Blake crept across the stern knowing that he must pass full in the line of vision of anyone under the mat shelter. Yet no voice challenged him as he pushed out the knife and sawed gently through the twisted rope.

Encouraged by this, he crept back and made his way along the narrow gunwale, actually scraping against the side of the mat shelter as he passed. But still no voice called out to know who was moving aboard the wupan, and again he essayed a crossing in front of the opposite opening of the carved mat shelter. This rope gave him more trouble, but he managed to sever it and then he paused, watching while the wupan, relieved of all restraint, drifted out on to the bosom of the river.

Yard by yard the water between it and the line of sampans widened. Well was this for Blake, for now he could plainly hear several voices coming from the other craft. He noticed a bit of sacking thrown back over the top of the shelter. This, by cautious work, he managed to drop down in front, thus leaving the stern end only open to the air. Next, he made his way back along the gunwale to the stern and, risking sudden discovery, managed to get Tinker pulled to one side where he would be out of the way.

Not yet did he rouse the sleeping inmates, although he knew that moment could not be much longer delayed. He wanted the wupan to drift still farther from the other craft, and tensely he watched while they slid past, leaving the city on their right —that city which had been such a welcome sight to Blake so short a while before.

When he judged that a good hundred yards separated them, he began to creep forward, On his way he caught up some tangled bits of rope, and now, as he bent forward still more, he felt the hard lump of the automatic which, mechanically, he must have thrust within his shirt after that last desperate shot at the pursuing crocodiles. It would be a better weapon for his work than the oar.

He worked it out, and gripped the barrel; then he continued his progress, seeing, as his eyes pierced the grey of the interior, that there were three prone forms within. Two seemed to be those of full-grown men; the other of a mere lad.

Blake did not pause to employ any finesse. This was a matter of life and death for him and Tinker, and if he were to strike at all it must be swiftly. Foot by foot he crept nearer, until he was close by the bent knees of one of the men. Another few inches and he paused while his right hand went up, holding the automatic by the barrel. A moment thus, then it came down with a dull thud on the skull of the sleeping man. The fellow passed from the dreams of opium into the deeper abyss of complete unconsciousness without ever knowing what hit him.

Blake moved a little to one side, and crawled on until he was close to the second man. Some instinct of danger must have crept into this one's dreams, for, of a sudden, his eyes opened and he started to rise, his gaze one of stupefied amazement at the sight of the menacing, wild figure which was bending over him.

Crack!

Before he could utter a sound the automatic had descended for the second time, sending the fellow back like a log. Next, Blake turned to the lad.

He would have given much to spare the youngster, but he knew that he dared not risk even that much hostile activity while he and Tinker depended for life on the wupan. So, more gently than before, he struck with just sufficient force to keep the lad quiet for the present.

His fingers trembled with the reaction of this complete victory as he untangled the rope, and bound his three victims securely. Next he had to cast about for stuff with which to gag them. But at last it was finished, and now, at last, he could devote himself to Tinker. Not yet did he know whether he had been succouring a corpse, or whether a faint beat of life still remained in the lad's limp body.

It was with a fervent prayer, utterly forgetful now of self, that he crawled back to the stern.

A Surprise at Nanking.

SEXTON BLAKE did not complete that journey as he had intended. While he was still but a yard or so from Tinker's huddled body a sharp wave of dizziness assailed him. He pitched forward on to his face with startling suddenness, and, for the matter of several minutes, lay in a dead faint. His iron will and matchless constitution had caved in under the terrific sequence of strain and drain to which he had subjected them.

But the will still struggled within him, for a sharp convulsion of the whole body brought him back to consciousness. He tried to rise, but fell forward again. He remained conscious, however, and slowly, ever so slowly, his determination that he would keep up while there was such dire need brought him back to his hands and knees.

It was then that the bloodshot eyes encountered a small stone jug that was lying almost within touch. He became aware that a terrible thirst was consuming him, and greedily he reached out for the promise of liquid. His fingers closed round the narrow neck, his chattering teeth managed to drag out the wooden plug; then, with trembling arm, he canted the jug so he could drink.

A sloshing sound followed as the contents poured into his mouth, over his lips and down his neck. He had looked for water; he found a fiery burning spirit that caused him to lower the jug suddenly and sink back coughing.

It was raw rice liquor, and while it did not assuage the thirst that was tormenting him, it served to send a stimulating warmth through his body and along the arteries that acted just then in magical manner. It was the best thing he could have encountered.

Clutching the precious receptacle, he crawled along to where Tinker lay. When he managed to turn the lad over a cold chill entered his soul afresh as he saw the chalky whiteness of the lad's countenance. Bending down, he laid his ear against his chest. A faint, faint throb seemed to be there, but he could not be sure. With hands that were foul with dirt and dried blood where the nails had been torn in that terrible struggle in the rapids, he lifted Tinker's head, and, forcing apart his clenched teeth, allowed a quantity of the strong rice liquor to slop over his lips and into his mouth.

It was impossible for him to induce swallowing by massage. All he could hope for was that some of the stimulant would trickle down the lad's throat and do its work.

And now he occupied himself with trying to induce circulation through the lad's body by chafing his cold limbs. For a solid half-hour Blake toiled, until the sweat was running in rivulets from his own body. Where he had been cold and stiff he was now burning like one in a fever. Forgotten entirely was the progress the unguided wupan might be making. It was not until he detected a definite relaxing in Tinker's limbs and a faint tinge of colour in the cheeks that he desisted even for a moment.

Gazing over the side, he saw that they had drifted out into the very centre of the broad river. Chinkiang was out of sight, but Blake could make out an occasional junk coming up on the early morning breeze and other smaller craft nearer each shore.

He knew he was running a big risk of being challenged, and he was troubled at the thought that each moment they drifted with the current was taking them back towards Shanghai, from which, to escape, they had endured such ghastly privations.

But Tinker must be attended to. And at the end of an hour Blake had his reward. The lad's lids fluttered and opened. For a moment or two his eyes rested blankly on Blake; then, to the latter's great relief, understanding showed. He seemed to comprehend perfectly, for he whispered:

"Guv'nor, what has happened? It is daylight. What is it?"

Blake bent over him swiftly.

"It's all right, young 'un. We are out of that ghastly hole. This is the Yangtse, and we are safe. Don't worry any more now. Take another drink of this spirit, it will warm you. Then lie still until you feel better. There is work I must do."

The youngster struggled gamely to rise, protesting that if there was work to do he must share it; but at a light pressure from Blake he fell back weakly.

"If you are to help when you are needed, you must do as I say now," urged Blake. "Lie still!"

Stern words, perhaps, but he needed to use them to make the lad obey, and to hide the vast feelings of tenderness which had welled up in him at the sound of the lad's voice

As he straightened up Blake felt the chill wind cut through his thin shirt. Overheated now, as he was, he knew the danger of getting one of the deadly doses of Yangtse fever. A bit of old sacking tied with a length of string served him for a jacket, and at the same time assisted his disguise, though Heaven knows he little needed anything now to make him a more bedraggled figure than he was. Then, picking up the long stern sweep, he eased it into the hollow, and began to scull.

Blake had a definite object in view. Mad as it all seemed, he knew without a doubt that he and Tinker had been spewed out into the Yangtse somewhere quite close to Chinkiang. Sir Gordon had been right in saying that a way probably led through the vast series of caves from beneath Shanghai, up the basin of the Yangtse to Chinkiang, and, possibly, on as far as Nanking.

The latter was the first stage of Blake's effort to get up the river, but not for all the gold in the world, much less the Golden Book of Buddha, would he have sought again the way of those foul passages.

Nor had it been anything but the chance will of that subterranean torrent that he and Tinker had reached Chinkiang. Now the current was rapidly carrying them downstream again, and Blake would not rest until he had passed Chinkiang and had worked the wupan into Nanking, another fifteen miles higher up. If they succeeded in reaching that point, time enough then to plan the next step.

He had another aim in view just then, too. This was to dispose of his three prisoners. He did not know how close the scrutiny of craft travelling up the river might be, and he realised how awkward it would be if he were searched by a patrol, and those three bound and gagged forms discovered. But he had in mind some one of the many muddy creeks which trickle into the lower basin of the great river, and when he had come close in to the northern shore, he sculled along steadily until he spotted the opening to one of them.

As far as he could see, there were few other craft about to observe him, so he took a chance on driving the wupan into the creek, sculling away steadily until he had rounded a bend which put him out of sight of anything passing on the main river. A little farther up he worked the wupan into the bank, holding it steady by jamming a pole into the mud.

Then, one by one he dragged his prisoners out and across the low freeboard on to the bank. When he had laid them out in a row, he returned for the knife, with which he severed their bonds. He left the gags as they were knowing that when they did recover consciousness they would soon tear them out. That job done, he returned to the wupan, removed the pole from the mud, and, swinging his craft round, urged the craft towards the mouth

All that morning Blake worked steadily at the stern sweep. It was about two in the afternoon that he saw Chinkiang again, this time just a confused mass far on the other side of the river, he kept on for another hour, until he came to a low bit of mud-bank, and there he tied up for a rest and some much-needed refreshment for himself. During the journey he had seen that Tinker took some stimulant and a little food several times.

He did not make another move until nearly nightfall. He

calculated that, by working leisurely, he could make Nanking any time during the night, and, figuring things over, he decided it would be wiser to reach it about dawn. Therefore, he continued by easy stages all through the night, with the exception of a snatched sleep about midnight. During that time Tinker kept watch, and, indeed, so much recovered was the lad that when they resumed he took one of the oars.

Blake's calculations proved exact enough. The grey dawn was just growing in the east when the vast stretch of Nanking came into view. For some time past the river had shown plenty of signs that they were approaching a large city, and by now, even at that hour, there were plenty of junks, sampans, wupans, and power boats of all sizes on the move.

Nanking is one of the largest and most important of the great cities of the Yangtse. Blake knew the water-front well, and in his mind was a jetty at the lower end, where he thought he could make a landing and abandon the wupan, if necessary, without rousing undue comment. Once it was seen that it was deserted it would not long lack an owner.

He was making for this mooring when they saw a good-sized river steamer coming up. Its yellow funnel told Blake that it was one of the Nanking River Fleet steamers, and, as it was coming, it would pass so close that they must receive a good deal of its wash. That did not worry Blake, however, and he felt secure in his present disguise to stand any scrutiny which might be directed from the steamer towards the wupan.

But when the side-wheeler was almost opposite them, an involuntary exclamation broke from his lips. The sound caused Tinker to jerk his head round sharply, and then, he, too, betrayed startled amaze.

Standing at the rail of the steamer, and gazing, it seemed, straight towards them, was a figure which, to Sexton Blake, was at that period a more sinister sight than aught else in all China —the figure of a monk in a black robe!

Fresh Disaster.

Nanking!

They were there among the vast medley of river craft —just a small unit in that tremendous stretch of activity. It seemed incredible, even now, that they had reached that first objective, and that, many miles behind them, was the tightly-drawn cordon which would certainly have picked them out of the yellow flood of humans bound up the Great River had they attempted to come that way. But they had won out against overwhelming odds. They had come through an underground maze that had swallowed them completely. And none knew they had got through.

None? There was one who knew! Blake could not forget the sudden and mysterious appearance of the Black Monk in the inner chamber of the caves of the People of the Pits. How he had got there —how he had sensed that the pair might endeavour to get through by that little-known way, was beyond Blake to explain. But it was proof sufficient that in the tall coolie and his youthful companion the Black Monk had seen something that ranked high as a danger to him and his superior, whoever that might be.

But Blake felt certain that not yet did the monk suspect he was other than pure Celestial. The interview in the cabin of the coffin junk would have revealed that, if there had been the slightest suspicion.

Yet the fact that he had been held alive and concealed in one of the empty coffins for transport up the river as far as Ichang and probably much higher was ample indication that he was looked upon as a most important capture. The Black Monk would never have gone to such trouble to secure the living person of, say, the Swatow serang. In some way he sensed that the tall coolie was a far more important individual than his dress and manner of living indicated; though how he had gained this idea was something that could only be explained as one of the numerous mysteries of China which has no beginning and no end.

Was that black-robed figure on the river steamer the same monk? He was too far distant for either Blake or Tinker to see his features clearly; but, certainly, his robe was of the same order. If it were the same, then how had he escaped from the inner chamber of the amphitheatre after Blake had blocked the exit by toppling over that gigantic statue of the Rat God?

And even if he had, how had he managed to do so and get to the surface in time to catch a river steamer from Shanghai for Nanking? Was it this same sinister being? And had he figured so correctly as to guess that Blake and Tinker might win through by way of that underground stream —that by some miracle they might pass unscathed among the leprous crocodiles which guarded that pool of horror?

If this were the case, he was, Blake realised, a unit in the scheme of things which must be considered as a major danger. Only a mentality of the highest order could have figured so truly as that, and could have allowed for all the pros and cons of the wild journey which the fugitives took when they dashed from the amphitheatre.

Whether it were the same or another, the fact remained that anyone who wore the black robe of that order was a danger to Blake and Tinker. It showed that the system of espionage which radiated from that mysterious monastery at Cheng-tu was extraordinarily efficient, and was in close contact with the whole basin of the Yangtse —yea, even the whole stretch of the China coast —for Blake could not believe that he had only become suspect after his arrival in Shanghai.

It began to look as if he had been expected to come, and if that were so, then he must have been under suspicion even in Hong Kong.

He was filled with a vague uneasiness as he worked the wupan in among the press of craft moored along the lower front of Nanking. His immediate object now was to get away from the wupan as quickly as possible, and to seek some hiding-place in the great city where he and the lad could lie low until he had time to plan the next move, which would take them another leg on their long journey to Cheng-tu.

And if he had been undecided before, Sexton Blake knew now that this great quest of his after the Golden Book of Buddha would take him into the very stronghold of the raven of Cheng-tu —if he survived!

It was on the outer fringe of a dense crush of small craft loading for upriver and down-river ports that Blake was forced to bring the voyage to a close. He found it impossible to work a way through to a jetty unless he was prepared to spend the entire day at the job. He knew there was a distinct element of danger in this, for there was no telling how soon the three prisoners he had left on the bank of the creek farther down the river might make their story known.

So, while he would rather have penetrated into the city after dark, Blake was forced to leave the wupan made fast to the outer line of craft and, with the lad stumbling along beside him, make across the massed boats to the shore.

(Another exciting instalment of this grand serial next Thursday! You mustn't miss a single instalment!)

Part 9.

First published in the Union Jack magazine, No. 1244, 20 Aug. 1927.

How this fine serial began.

ONE of China's most sacred possessions, "The Golden Book of Buddha," is stolen by the Black Abbot of Cheng-tu while on its way up the Yangtse from Canton to the Grand Lama of Tibet. Sexton Blake, having been implored to help trace it, is in China with Tinker, both disguised as coolies, for that purpose.

After many adventures, the pair barely escape with their lives from the underground kingdom of the People of the Pits.

They manage to capture a wupan and make their way up to Nanking. As they are steering their boat into the harbour, they are alarmed to see the figure of the Black Monk standing on the deck of a river-steamer. They had last seen this sinister figure in the passages of the underground kingdom. They are not recognised, but Blake and Tinker make haste to land and find a hiding-place for themselves.

The story continues:

FOR the last hour or so Sexton Blake had been shooting many an anxious glance at his assistant.

Up till the evening before, Tinker seemed to have made a fairly good recovery from the terrible privations he had undergone. But during the night he had become listless; and now Blake saw that his face was very white and drawn.

He had bathed the wound in the lad's temple, although the only water available had been the muddy liquid of the Yangtse. He had seen at the time that the blow had been a severe one, and when the lad stumbled again, Blake realised that he was feeling a far greater reaction than he would acknowledge.

For this reason alone it became imperative that they should find a hiding-place. Under ordinary circumstances it would have been a simple matter, for he had several influential acquaintances among the wealthy Chinese merchants of Nanking. But now even the most trustworthy must be tabu. His only way was to pick a hovel on chance, and lurk there until he could formulate a plan of some sort.

It was in this quandary that the detective shuffled along through one of the lowest of the native bazaars, one hand to assist him, although, for the sake of appearances. Blake made a pretence of dragging along an unwilling companion, adding to the impression now and then by breaking into vile abuse against his apathy. It was the only way in which to make such assistance appear among Chinese as a natural thing, for that race abandons to his fate the one who falls by the way-side.

As for Tinker himself, he was fighting hard against the burning fever and pain which racked him. Every part of his body seemed on fire, and the throbbing of his wounded temple was excruciating. He still retained sufficient understanding to know that, at any cost, he must not become a greater liability to Blake, and every ounce of gameness was summoned to keep going. Constantly he was reproaching himself for what he termed weakness, but he was in the grip of that which must become far worse before it could become better; he was in the throes of the first spasms of the violent Yangtse fever.

He was scarcely conscious of his surroundings. He had a vague idea that they were passing through a bazaar of sorts, and when Blake spoke harshly to him he knew that he was bluffing for the sake of appearances. But beyond that, and the determination which he kept before him to play up to Blake, he moved in a daze that was deepening each moment, and when —it seemed hours later —Blake thrust him through the low entrance of a vile hovel in a narrow alley of the bazaar, by the wide open door of which he was deserted, Tinker scarcely knew what was happening. No sooner did he pass into the gloom than he gave a lurch, and then became violently sick as the fever convulsed his stomach.

It was the unmistakable symptom which told Blake the truth. When the paroxysm passed, he eased the lad into a corner and knelt beside him in deep concern. He knew that, at any cost, he must get medicine and some sort of qualified attention for the lad. Blake knew the deep ravages that deadly fever could cause if let run; and, in view of the strain through which Tinker had been, it was a danger signal which he dare not ignore. It might pass swiftly in the galloping form, or it might drag on with intermittent attacks for days. But, which ever course it took, the lad's life was at stake while those deadly bacilli were coursing through his blood.

Tinker was lying back with closed eyes, apparently dead to his surroundings; but when Blake spoke in low, urgent tones, repeating the lad's name again and again, Tinker rallied and his heavy lids lifted.

"Yes, guv'nor," he whispered. "I —I'm sick."

"Listen, Tinker, try and understand what I say. Can you do so?"

The lad nodded.

"You are ill, young 'un —you may as well know the truth —you have a touch of Yangtse fever —that sickness is the sign —I must get out and get you some medicine and, if possible, secure a native doctor. I want you to try and realise that I shall not be a moment longer than I must. I shall return here as fast as I can, and while I am gone, you must remain just as you are. Keep in your mind that I am coming any moment. And do not go to the door. I shall close it when I go out. Can you understand all that?"

"Yes, guv'nor. Don't worry about me. I —I'll be —here."

"Good lad! You can take it that I shall not be more minutes than I can possibly help."

He gave Tinker's shoulder a reassuring touch, and, rising, made for the door. Before passing out he paused to look at the lad. His heart smote him sorely as he saw that bare, mud floor, not even a straw pallet on which the lad could lay his racking head. It was pillowed on his arm, and even in the gloom of that stinking interior, he looked woefully young and sorely ill.

Sexton Blake was very heavy of heart as he stole out and closed the door after him. That, he knew, would be indication that the hovel was occupied. It should be said here that the few rough boards which had formed the door being thrown open, had indicated to Blake that the place was unoccupied for the reason that, in China; a door must never be left swinging wide.

Should this occur, it gives entrance to some of the numerous evil spirits which play such an important part in Chinese superstition and, in that case, all sorts of noisy efforts must be made to eject them, or the place given up. It is for this reason that when a creditor uses all normal means to make a debtor pay and gets no result, his last —and usually effective threat is that he will remove the door from the debtor's house. As this is a calamity which the debtor dare not endure, he usually scrapes up sufficient money at most usurious rates of interest in order to avoid such a dreadful danger.

Up through the lane Blake made his way, turning twice before he came again to the central street of the bazaar where he would find a seller of drugs. He knew what he must have as normal treatment for the fever, and had there been fifty Black Monks observing him, he would still have run the gauntlet to secure what the lad needed.

It was not the Black Monk or one of his kind, however, that passed directly across the dirty street in front of Blake at the moment when he was making in a diagonal direction for a green-and-gilt sign, which told him that within he would find drugs.

It was a very different figure, and at sight of the burly, rough-clad Chinaman, who elbowed his way through the crowds as if they were dirt beneath his feet, Sexton Blake's eyes narrowed until they were as slit-like as those of any true Celestial. It was amazing that he should see this person in a low bazaar in Nanking.

A Friend in Sight.

DESPITE Tinker's dire need, Blake knew that he must have speech with this man who was passing, before he should vanish out of his life for ever. Once he were swallowed in the crowded bazaar it would be like searching for the needle in the proverbial haystack to find him again in China.

So, as the burly one swung down a side street, Blake turned from the entrance to the drug shop and followed. He did not approach him at once, although he was all impatience to establish contact. He did not forget that black-robed vision which he had seen on the river steamer; and he did not forget that if it were the Black Monk he had left in the amphitheatre then one who could get out of that prison and reach Nanking in such a brief space of time was quite capable of having already extended his espionage to every quarter of Nanking.

So it was with every inward caution and every outward semblance of stupidity that he shuffled along after the other, watching his chance to approach him. Each moment meant a longer delay in getting back to Tinker; each footstep in that direction meant added risk to discovery of the lad in the hovel. But there was nothing else Blake could do but watch for a favourable moment. To precipitate things might be to bring ruin on all that had gone before.

His opportunity came when his quarry turned into a small tea-shop. Blake followed, finding the other had entered a small open booth and was already squatting on the floor. He was giving his order to a boy and, after a swift look round, Blake entered a booth almost opposite. When the "boy" finished in the one he came to the other and, when he was gone, Blake seized upon a bit of crepe paper which dangled from the wall. Against one end of the booth was the inevitable small board, provided with a block of solid Chinese ink, a small dish of water, and a writing brush.

Swiftly Blake bent over it and, with the brush, painted a few characters on the paper. He did not fear that the attendant, if he did observe him, would be able to read what he had written, for very few of that class of Chinese understand the written language. He had finished, however, before the "boy" returned, and now, screwing the bit of paper into a small wad, he made a motion of his arm which attracted the attention of the man in the opposite booth.

That individual gazed at him with a frown, but when Blake sent the screw of paper skimming across to the other's feet, the man condescended to pick it up and spread it out.

Blake did not again look towards him. His tea was brought a few moments later and, after doling out several bits of "copper" cash in payment, he gulped it down as if very thirsty. Then he rose and shuffled out of the place. He had done all he could; the result was now on the knees of the gods.

Once in the street, Blake quickened his pace. His anxiety was keener than ever about Tinker and, entering the drug shop, he made purchase of several varieties of native cures which, for a poorly-clad coolie such as he was, caused the drug-seller to look at him in lazy wonder. But he took it evidently that Blake was but the messenger for some wealthy master, for he doled out the various articles promptly enough, and carefully counted the silver "bit" and odd "cash" with which Blake made payment.

Once inside the hovel again, Blake bent over the lad. By now the first course of the fever was in full swing, and he saw at once that the lad was delirious. He was not speaking distinctly, but he was muttering incessantly, and Blake knew that if the delirium increased it was quite probable that the lad would bawl out phrases in his mother tongue.

He set to work at once to administer some of the potent herbs which he had bought. A supply of clean fresh water would have been an asset just then, but that would have to wait. There was one powder which Blake knew was not only swift in its action, but would induce sound sleep in the patient if it were administered before the fever had risen to a certain height.

He had not dared to ask for a thermometer. Such an unheard of thing would have roused acute suspicion at once; so he had to do his best to gauge the lad's temperature by touch and taking his pulse at pure guess.

He risked a dose of the potent drug, then he applied a salve to the wound on Tinker's temple. Following that, he knew he must do something to get hold of some fresh water so, squatting on his heels just inside the door, he kept one eye on the patient while he listened for the high-pitched cry of a water seller.

It was some time before that distinctive call rose above the general din of the bazaar, but Blake recognised it quickly enough and, with a final look towards Tinker, who now seemed to be sleeping, he slid outside and closed the door. On his way to the main street he bought for a few cash a large earthenware pot, and then, overtaking the water-seller, bought a full measure of the precious liquid.

Again he returned to the hovel, and now he was able to mix another potion for the lad which, of his own experience in the past, he knew was more efficacious than any other medicine in the treatment of the deadly fever. He did not leave the lad again until nearly dusk. Although Tinker was still sleeping, his temperature seemed to Blake to have risen.

This might or might not be a normal phase of the course of the fever, but Blake knew that the thermometer, if he had one, would show somewhere round a hundred and four, and that was enough to increase his anxiety. Never did he seek rendezvous with as little heart as that evening, but he had to go. In that lay, so far as he could see, his only present hope of being able to get proper attention for Tinker and get both of them out of Nanking.

He was careful to close the door after him, breathing a fervent hope that Tinker would not wake during his absence. Then he shuffled out into the bazaar, making his way once more to the tea-house where he had followed his quarry earlier in the day. On entering he passed down the middle, so that he could see into the same booth which the other had occupied in the morning.

The man was there.

Blake entered quickly and, as if he were expected, bowed low in a respectful salaam. He did not attempt to sit down. The other was dressed in the ordinary garb of a river man, but his attire was that of one having the standing of a lao-pan or a tai-kung. Therefore, it would be the height of presumption for a dirty coolie, not better than a river "tracker," than which there is nothing lower, to sit in his presence.

Blake knew that everything depended on the other's first words. If he were suspicious of what had been written on that piece of crepe paper then he might kick the visitor out into the street. On the other hand, it was most unusual for one clad as Blake to be able to write at all, and for that reason he might look deeper before acting.

And that is exactly what the other did. His sloe-black eyes gazed at Blake with as little emotion as two marbles. His face was utterly blank, his hands were crossed across the "seat of wisdom" (the abdomen). Then he spoke.

"So, dog of a tracker, you have come!" he said at last, in perfectly level tones, "Is it that the junk must wait in Nanking for vermin like you?"

Blake whined.

"Honourable one, I was kept back by an accident. I have brought my vile and unworthy feet running to do the honourable one's bidding. I await thine honourable commands."

"Take thy miserable carcase into the road and wait!" snarled the other, bending once more to his cup of lemon-coloured tea.

Blake salaamed again, and shuffled out of the place. In the street he stood with bent head, slouching against the wall of the tea-house —a picture of abject misery.

That was such a common sight in any river port along the Yangtse, that not a single curious glance was cast his way as the throngs passed. It was nearly twenty minutes before the burly one emerged from the tea-house. As he saw Blake he bawled a curse at him and ordered him to follow.

As they proceeded through the bazaar, he kept up a stream of comments over his shoulder which were directed at the head of the unfortunate one whom everyone thought was a "tracker" —the term will be explained a little later —who was being haled back to his junk by the lao-pan, and which created mirth among those who heard them. The Chinese idea of humour is the least subtle, and the crudest thing among them.

Blake took it as only a tracker would. He shuffled along meekly until the bazaar was left behind, and they were in a region of big hongs and godowns close to the river. There, in the shadow of a huge hong, the man ahead drew up and as Blake neared him he shot out a hand, gripping the pseudo-tracker in a vice-like grip.

"Now then," he snapped, in the dialect of the upper Yangtse, "who are you, and what do you mean by that writing? If you are making play with me may Buddha protect your vile carcase, for it goes to the fishes."

Blake lifted his head and looked at him with level glance.

"Take your hand from my shoulder," he said curtly. "I am no dog of a tracker, but the honoured friend of your master."

The hand dropped as the other started back. He did not show amazement, but he was filled with that sensation. This dirty-looking river coolie to call himself friend of his illustrious master! This foul dog who could paint written characters and make use of them in a public tea-house! This scum of the river who had intrigued him by strange words so that he kept an appointment at the tea-house! Who, in Buddha's name, was he?

"My master! Dog —what meanest thou?"

"By the great toe of Buddha, I have spoken truth."

"Thou speakest truth! Then name my honourable master."

"Your master is the honourable river pirate, Kan-tse-wen"

And at the sound of that dread name the other shot out a hand and dragged him further into the shadow.

The Purple Crescent.

"KAN-TSE-WEN!"

The name escaped the lips of the other, despite his effort to suppress the effect it had had upon him. It was the last name he had expected to hear uttered by the ragged coolie who had made rendezvous with him in the tea-house.

It was the most potent name on the Yangtse between Nanking and Ichang. For years had the notorious pirate, Kan-tse-wen, harried the traffic of the Great River. In his lair of Changcha he lurked, impregnable. The Terror of the Yangtse, he was called, and even the river steamers of the foreign companies gave a wide berth to the junks of Kan-tse-wen when the word passed up or down the river that the pirate was abroad.

He was no celestial of North or South China; his name —the "Kan" part —stamped him as one of blood far beyond the western limits of China, and, indeed, he boasted that the blood of the marauding Tartar ran in his veins —the blood of the two dread conquerors of the Middle Ages who had marched across Asia and far into Europe —Kubla Khan and Genghis Khan.

So large was the fleet he controlled, so numerous the men who had flocked to his standard and fought like demons under him, so utterly ruthless was he, that he had been rightly called the Terror of the Yangtse. And not even a Chen had dared so far to beard him in his lair. On the contrary. Northerner and Southerner alike courted him for his friendship, for who had Kan-tse-wen with him, controlled the basin of the middle and lower Yangtse.

So this ragged, dirty coolie, who had the appearance of being a low-down coolie, used that dread name as if it had not burned his lips in the uttering. Slit eyes peered at him closely through the gathering darkness. Little did that burly lao-pan of Kan-tse-wen guess that the coolie who stood before him, had once been a guest of honour in the lair of the pirate; little did he think that this was the same man who, in one wild raid, had stood shoulder to shoulder with Kan-tse-wen while they had cleared the deck of nothing less than the State barge of the rich and powerful Manchu, Prince Wu Ling, from stem to stern. He wouldn't have believed it if Blake had made the claim.

But one who did speak so freely of his illustrious master must be dealt with forthwith. Drawing back a little, the lao-pan whipped out a short cutting sword that had severed many a head in its day. He laid this at the back of Blake's neck and snarled:

"Move on; I shall see who this is who uses the name of Kan-tse-wen."

Blake made no effort to resist. It was as much —or as little —as he had expected. And, besides, it would have been arrant folly to try to escape that blade. Had he done so, a single blow would have sent his head rolling in the dust. So, still bearing himself meekly, he began to shuffle along by the side of the hong, turning, when he came to the end of the building, as directed by the lao-pan who marched behind him with the blade of the sword cold against his neck.

Blake found himself descending some shallow steps which seemed to lead in under the pier on which the hong was built. Then he came to a sort of narrow platform, along which the lao-pan forced him to proceed until he came to the end. Just beneath him flowed the yellow water of the Yangtse. There he came to a stop, for another step would have precipitated him into the river.

Now the lao-pan's voice sounded again, lowered discreetly so that anyone who might be on the lower floor of the hong above would not overhear.

"Speak, dog, and say how you know the name of the honourable one of whom you have spoken. If your tongue is crooked, by the sacred toe of great Buddha, your head goes to the fishes and your vile body after it."

Blake did not even attempt to turn.

"Oh, one of mighty talk," he said slowly, "thou wilt lose more than thy head if thou but scrape the skin of the blood brother and friend of Kan-tse-wen. Lift up my shirt —look in the arm-pit on the left and thou wilt see proof of what I say!"

The lao-pan did not take the trouble to lift the shirt. With one swift stroke he had slit it from waist to shoulder and then, dragging the cotton aside, he bent down to look where Blake had directed. He saw a small tattooed crescent about half an inch long by an eighth of an inch broad in the widest part. It was of a peculiar purplish tint of ink which the initiated would recognise at a glance, and which could not be duplicated by the unauthorised for the reason that the ingredients were a close-looked secret in the inner council of the powerful Four Lakes Tong.

A faint whistling noise escaped the lips of the lao-pan as he saw that proof which could not be forged. The sword was lowered, and one hand swung Blake round so that they faced each other.

"Thou bearest the mark; who art thou?"

"I am of the inner circle of the Four Lakes; I am of the Silver Moon; I am of the Three Feathers! I am blood brother of Hsui-fsi, the Eagle of the North; I am blood brother of Hong-Lo-Soo, the Mighty One; I am blood brother of Kan-tse-wen, the Terror of the Yangtse!"

"Thou speakest with the tongue of knowledge! If thou art impostor thy head shall be severed this night! If thou speakest with a straight tongue, then name thyself! Who art thou!"

"I am called Sek-i-ton Bal-akee!"

"Aie!"

The age-old exclamation which covers so many different emotions in China burst from the lao-pan's lips with a whistling sound. He bent still closer, as if he would read Blake's soul.

"Sek-i-ton Bal-akee —the One of Fire! Art thou he?"

156

(Sek-i-ton Bal-akee was the Chinese rendering of Sexton Blake's name, by which he was known in the Four Lakes Tong and its subsidiary tongs, the Silver Moon and the Three Feathers.)

"I am he!"

"And thou knowest me?"

"Thou art called Fu-chen-pu; thou art lao-pan in the junk of Kan-wo, brother of the illustrious Kan-tse-wen! The honourable Kan-wo was with this unworthy one in the House of Wooden Lanterns in Canton!"

"By Great Buddha, but thou speakest with knowledge! Give me one proof, and the arm of Fu-chen-pu is thine!"

"Thou recallest the night when Kan-tse-wen swept down upon the State barge of the Manchu, Wu Ling?"

"It is in my mind."

"It was thou who led the attack over the stern?"

"Thou hast said it, honourable one! Take my sword, thou who art blood brother of the illustrious Kan-tse-wen, and sever the head of this foul dog who hast dared to speak with such words to thee!"

"Nay, Fu-chen-pu! It is not for Sek-i-ton Bal-akee to reduce the fighting numbers of the Terror of the Yangtse, but it is of the most pressing need that I seek the honourable Kan-tse-wen in Changcha! Thou art bound there?"

"Ho, hong, honourable one! The junk leaves with the dawn, when the river spirits are gone!"

"Aie. I would go with you."

"It is a command, honourable one!"

"I do not travel alone. I have with me one who is sick with a fever."

"Thy servants are as thyself, honourable one."

"He must receive that which I cannot give him. Hast thou in thy junk a man of medicine who understands the fever of the Yangtse?"

"Nay, brother of the illustrious Kan-tse-wen; but it can be arranged if it is thy wish!"

"It is more than my wish; it is my most urgent need. But I see not how it can be done."

"Honourable one, the men of the illustrious Kan-tse-wen take when they find need. We sail at dawn, for it has come to my unworthy ears that the boats of the southern dogs would interfere with the vessels of the honourable Terror when they ply alone. Therefore, we may see much spilling of blood before we sail into Changcha."

"The prospect is not unpleasant. But whence comes this daring to affront in such a manner the excellent Kan-tse-wen?"

"Honourable one, it is not understood by this unworthy creature. But it is said that the Black Monk of Cheng-tu roams abroad. And where the raven flies, the birds are restless."

Blake betrayed nothing of what those words conveyed to him. But his pulse quickened as he realised that he had been right in thinking that he had by no means finished with the Black Monk, yet it would take more than that threat to deter him in his purpose.

"Sometimes the raven falls," he countered. "I would go with thee, Fu."

"And the man of medicine shall come, too, honourable one."

"How wilt thou manage?"

"Where lieth the honourable one's servant?"

"In a hovel in the low bazaar."

"In an hour my men shall have him on board the junk. In two hours a man of medicine shall be there, and shall travel to the lair of Kan-tse-wen, whether he wills or not!"

"Aie! Those are good words, Fu-chen-pu."

"It is enough that I serve the honourable Sek-i-ton Bal-akee."

After further words on the subject they moved out from under the hong, and, a few minutes later, Blake found himself aboard an enormous junk that he knew, despite its innocent appearance, was one of the most formidable fighting craft in Kan-tse-wen's fleet. Then, accompanied by Fu-chen-pu and a score of pirates, he returned to the bazaar where, in that bare hovel, he had left Tinker.

The lad was in a high delirium when they entered, and a single touch told Blake that the fever was more fierce than ever.

There was no little risk in transferring him all that distance to the junk, but anything was better than the foul hole in which he lay, and so, in a chair which had been commandeered in the bazaar, the raving lad was taken at a slow trot to the junk, where he was placed in Fu's own bed.

Immediately the pirate started off on another mission, this time taking no less than two score of his men with him. Blake did not accompany them; he was needed too badly by Tinker. But when, an hour later, the party returned, they carried with them, slung from a bamboo-pole where he had been tied, Chinese fashion, by the wrists and ankles, a fat, smooth-faced Chinaman, who was dumped on to the deck with no more ceremony than if he had been a bale of cotton. It was the doctor who had been brought even as Fu-chen-pu had promised.

Promptly at dawn the big junk slid out of Nanking on her way up the river. Alongside Fu, as he stood with one arm thrown across the great stern steering-sweep, Blake gazed along the sharp dip of the deck and over the point of the stem to where the heavy mist was just lifting from the face of the water.

Somewhere there, he told himself, hovered the black shadow of the raven.

Who is the Black Abbot?

IT was dawn.

Over the low-hanging mist on the Yangtse River crept the gleam of coming day, finding out the corners and stealing through the three thousand and thirty narrow window-slits of the great Temple of Sublime Ways that reared its massive bulk upon the Hill of Peace which glooms above the city of Cheng-tu.

Yet no laggard did the stealing light find within those grey walls. Already in the cloisters were the black-robed monks, pacing up and down in profound meditation or busily telling their square-cut beads. In the great hall, where, on the long stone benches, the monks took their simple food, the lay brothers were busy preparing the wooden bowls for "first rice"; in the kitchens, hidden from sight in the deep cellars of the place, the lay cooks squatted before a hundred and twenty-nine fires, watching the brown, unhusked grain swelling in the cauldrons. Outside the walls the goat-boys were already astir with their flocks, driving them to fresh pasturage in the far-flung fields which were the property of the monastery —one of the richest in all China.

Even the presiding abbot was astir. In a long, narrow chapel, where the dawn found its own colour in the silver plates which lay overlapped from floor to ceiling, the abbot knelt at his devotions before a mighty statue of Great Buddha cast from pure gold, the inscrutable eyes glinting red through the facets of enormous rubies.

Kneeling some distance behind him was the resident abbot, and a little in his rear the three assistant-abbots of the monastery. The robes of the presiding abbot were of heavy, yellow brocade, the saffron hue which only he of Royal blood is permitted to wear even in new China. Those of the resident abbot were of morning blue, and those of the three assistant-abbots of grey. In the great monastery on an island in Tung Ting Lake one would have found equal ceremony at first devotions; and in the Temple of Eternal Purity, at Canton, the Chuen-to-yan exacted every formality, but in none was the full ritual more strict than in the Monastery of Sublime Ways, at Cheng-tu.

No religious order in the world was of greater antiquity. Not even the great monasteries of the Dalai Lama, at Tibet, had records which went further back into the mists of the past. This monastery at Cheng-tu was the chief stronghold of Buddhism in China—the point from which all religious, all spiritual control emanated over more than four hundred millions of people.

Until half a century before it had acknowledged the suzerainty of the Lama of Tibet; it had bowed to the edicts which the holy one there had seen fit to issue. For was he not the custodian of the sacred and never-to-be-equalled Golden Book of Great Buddha, in which, on golden plates, were inscribed the precepts which had fallen from his perfect lips?

Did not that book hold, upon one plate, the divine imprint of Great Buddha's thumb? And had not Buddha himself charged the Faithful that this and this only was his gift to the Chosen —that from that sacred source came all wisdom, all guidance, and every precept which man needed?

Therefore, while that sacred book was in the care of the holy one at Tibet he must be obeyed. But time had come when some blasphemous dog of the night had taken the book from its place of keeping. Despite the assurances which came from Tibet, it was known that the sacred book was no longer there.

Then over all China had swept greed and ambition born of the jealousy which had always lain between Canton and Tibet. Followed a whisper that the golden book was in China. Then came intrigue, so subtle, so deadly, so intricate in its incredible maze, that the mind of any but a Celestial would have been reduced to chaos to follow it.

What was afoot during those years? What devious ways did the monks of China tread in their search for the golden book? What depth of intrigue had its genesis in the Temple of Eternal Purity, by the Tiger's Gate, in Canton, as the ancient Chuen-to-yan plotted and schemed to discover the whereabouts of that sacred object, which, if he could but get it in his hands, would make him the spokesman for Great Buddha, would make him the supreme vicar upon earth for the divine one —would make Canton the directing power of all the Buddhist world, and would reduce Tibet to the position of a dependant upon Canton for the sacred crumbs which might fall from her table.

And at last out of the mists of the Great River the sacred book had been snatched. At the moment when those who believed in Tibet as the truly appointed spiritual home of Great Buddha were hastening to the west in order to restore the golden tome to its ancient ark, it had been snatched away on a crest of blood.

Where had it gone? Whence had come the shadowy hand that had stolen it from those who guarded its passage up the sacred river?

There were whispers —there are always whisperings and murmurings in China. But now the name which was spoken in hushed tones was persistent, and it never changed.

The Black Abbot of Cheng-tu!

Some had it the Raven of Cheng-tu. Who was he? Like the bird after which he had been named, he seemed to be here, there, and everywhere; or, if not, then his black-robed emissaries were ever to be glimpsed as they passed like shadows among the bazaars, along the river, over the hills, and even along the barren wastes.

The Black Abbot of Cheng-tu! It was a name —it was something to be spoken of with dread —it was that of one who wielded more power than even the great War-god, or the equally terrible divinity who rules the storm elements.

None could say with certainty that they had ever seen the Black Abbot. Perhaps he was one of those black-robed figures who had passed; perhaps he was so withdrawn from the world that he communed only with Great Buddha. But the whisper grew into a definite rumour that the golden book of the great one now reposed in China, and that the edicts of the Chuen-to-yan of the Temple of Eternal Purity, at Canton, were the truly inspired commands of Buddha; that Tibet had fallen into disfavour with the divine one; that all true believers must follow as Canton directed.

To those hundreds of millions whose lives were a complete cycle of superstition the effect of such rumours can be imagined. It meant that, did the Chuen-to-yan send forth a call to action of any extreme nature, those vast hordes would be roused to a pitch of uncontrollable frenzy; and the Chuen-to-yan hated the fan-kai-lo (foreigner) just a little less than he hated the holy one at Tibet —the gentle and good lama, whose life and teachings are as a mirror of purity.

It was said, however, that the Black Abbot of Cheng-tu was the master of the Chuen-to-yan at Canton; that it was his voice which spoke through the lips of the Chuen-to-yan. And, for once in a way, even Chinese rumour was right. The Black Abbot of Cheng-tu was the supreme power in Buddhist China. But not even the shrewdest among those millions of Celestials guessed within the millionth part of reality what lay at the back of the Black Abbot's mind.

Not even the resident abbot of the Monastery of Sublime Ways had seen his face! He came and went like a shadow. Although he wielded almost unlimited power, he appeared and departed with as much simplicity as the poorest lay brother. Only a single attendant did he have, and that stout, aged Celestial was as mute as a statue of Great Buddha. He, and he alone, was the confidant of the Black Abbot; he and none other in the monastery might gaze upon the exalted features of the great one.

So it was that, on this morning when great dawn found its way among the chinks and crannies of the Monastery of Sublime Ways, the presiding abbot knelt at his devotions. His head was bowed upon his breast, and his lips moved slightly as if he were invoking inspiration from the gilded statue which towered above him. Behind him the other four devotees moved not a muscle. They were rigid in their pose, their private worship dependant upon the mood of him who knelt closest to the god.

Presently his head lifted slowly, and then, had there been eyes to see, it would have been discovered that his hand went up swiftly to adjust over his features a mask of yellow silk.

Then, attended by the others, he rose and moved slowly along the full length of the chapel, until he came to a silver-covered door that fitted so closely into its frame as to be almost invisible. With one hand pressed against the metal, the Black Abbot paused and turned to the lesser abbot.

"Thou wilt take the morning devotions," he said, in low, penetrating tones.

The other bowed his head over hands flattened in a salaam.

"Ho hang, Holy One."

"And also the direction of the day; I would be left undisturbed in my meditations."

"With thy blessing it is done, Holy One."

"My blessing and that of Great Buddha go with you," answered the masked one.

Then he pressed on the silver door, and, a moment later, had vanished from their sight. For a full minute they stood with bowed heads, after which they moved in slow procession to the lower end of the chapel and out into the corridor which led to the great hall.

As for the Black Abbot, he found himself in a narrow passage when the door had closed behind him. This, like the chapel, was lined with beaten plates of pure silver, and, at the end, was another door clad in the white mail. Through this he passed into a small room, which was almost entirely lacking in equipment of any description. There was a stone slab on two stone pillars as a table, and beside it a narrow stone bench. On the table was an earthenware jar containing water, and in a wooden food-bowl a mess of cooked rice, steaming hot.

Here the Black Abbot seated himself, and clapping his hands, gazed towards a closed stone door directly opposite where he sat. It opened almost at once to admit a very stout Chinaman, whose face, though round and fat, showed signs of considerable age. He salaamed low to the abbot, then approached slowly to take up his stand behind the master.

Then and then only did the Black Abbot remove his mask, and as the growing light fell full upon his face, revealing thin, ascetic features, and the deep-set eyes of a super-intellectual, there were those in the world who would have recognised them as those of none other than the rich and powerful Manchu, Prince Wu Ling, master of nearly all China!

Seen From Afar.

THE Black Abbot was indeed Wu Ling.

There he sat clad in the heavy yellow brocade that, even as resident abbot of the Black Monks, he affected because it was the prerogative of his Royal Manchu blood. But now, before eating, he got to his feet, holding out his arms, while San, that faithful attendant who had been tutor to him in his youth and confidant in his manhood, his entire slave in body and soul, removed the rich garment, leaving the tall, spare figure standing in the plain black robe of the monks.

Then the faithful San disappeared, while Wu Ling attacked his frugal breakfast.

But no sooner had he finished the last few grains of rice and drank from the bottle than San re-entered, bearing a bowl of clear water and a towel. When his august master had cleansed his hands he turned to the servitor.

"Attend me in the inner apartment, San; there are matters of importance to discuss."

"At once, Illustrious One."

Wu Ling turned to still another stone panel, which formed a door behind where he had been sitting. Pushing this open, he stepped into a large apartment, lighted only by a skylight in the top that might have been the room of some scientist who had been born in the days of Galileo, and hard lived on through the centuries to the present day. The equipment consisted of a perfectly bewildering maze of scientific instruments, ranging from the crudest of early attempts to the finished, shining steel and brass complexities of the present day.

On one side was a perfectly arranged laboratory, that could not have been exceeded in efficiency in London or Paris. At one end was an enormous telescope, canted towards a sliding dome in the roof that was, at the moment, closed; and at the other end were piles upon piles of great, ancient-looking tomes —the treasured researches of Asiatic scientists through many centuries, containing secrets that had not yet been unlocked by the Western world. And, in the centre of the room, a great teakwood table, littered with books and papers and instruments.

It was towards this that Prince Wu Ling made his way. Seating himself in a heavy chair of the same wood, he bent over a pile of envelopes and documents which might have been lying on the blotting-pad of any business man of the West. And the speed with which he went through the pile would have done credit to any captain of industry. He was still rapidly scanning the contents of some of the letters when San entered, and, shuffling across to the centre of the room, took up his stand beside his master.

"The word has come at last," said Wu Ling, without looking round. "The man, Sexton Blake, is not in London."

"It was as your Excellency thought."

"Even so, San. He was cunning. But Hong-Lo-Soo has yet things to learn. It is said in London —Hong-Lo-Soo has seen to it that the papers have been fed with the gossip —that the dog Blake is in America on an important case.

"It is a lie, for here is a message from the head of the Brotherhood of the Yellow Beetle in New York, saying that after making the most careful inquiries in every part of America, he is certain that the unspeakable dog is not there. The same thing from Canada; the same thing from France. And he is not in England. Yet he disappeared from London several weeks ago. What has become of him?"

"Excellency, thou hast said that strange things have appeared upon the magic plate," murmured San.

Wu Ling's gaze left the desk and travelled diagonally along the room to where, against a part of the wall opposite was what might have been taken for a massive table of some sort of green stone. Above this was a shining drum of copper to which were attached several black handles, and from the drum led what seemed to be tubes of the same metal which disappeared into the wall. For a full minute Wu Ling sat pondering, while his eyes roamed over this strange contraption; then, with a sudden curt exclamation, he rose.

"Let me see what the plate reveals this morning, San."

He walked along and stood before the dark green slab that gave back a dim reflection of his head and shoulder in its dull sheen. It was polished to the smoothness of metal, and was, apparently, guiltless of even the tiniest speck of dust. But a gesture from Wu Ling caused San to take a large square of chamois leather and rub it very carefully until it was certain that nothing could be adhering to it.

Then Wu Ling lifted one hand, giving a slight twist to first one of the black handles and then another. As a low, humming sound broke out he uttered the one word, "Watch!" —at which San's eyes followed his in peering down at the gleaming surface of the green slab.

At first the face of the stone showed only a dulling, a clouding over that gradually began to come into movement as if the cloud was passing along the surface in the form of waves. Then slowly it began to clear, and as Wu Ling gave another slight turn of one of the black knobs overhead, it cleared still more, disclosing the pagoda-like roofs of a Chinese city.

The impression to one watching was almost as if he were passing overhead in an aeroplane, visualising the landscape as it unfolded beneath. Section after section of this great city was laid out in panorama before them, but only the upper parts of the larger buildings were disclosed to their gaze. Between the erections and entirely swallowing up the smaller buildings was a dense, whitish cloud that, to the uninitiated, would have been extremely puzzling. But it was understood well enough by Wu Ling and San, for the prince muttered:

"It is Nanking at this hour, San; the city sleeps; the mist still lies heavy on the river."

"It is even as your Excellency says," returned the servitor in an awed tone, for although he had witnessed many wonders under Wu Ling's hand, had never quite been able to grasp the magic of television —this unfolding before him on a polished plate life as it was actually proceeding hundreds, ay, even thousands of miles distant. Yet he had seen the proof of it over and over again.

Wu Ling reached up once more and again gave a half-turn to a black knob, one he had not touched so far. The immediate result of this was to cause the mist which had obscured the city to fade away as if wiped off a slate by some invisible hand. He had brought into action the smoke and fog penetration ray.

And now before them lay Nanking as Wu Ling had said—clear cut in hard tones as the morning sun tipped its myriad pagodas. Still the panorama kept unfolding on the surface of the stone, and now they were gazing down at the edge of the Great River —looking upon the Hundreds and thousands of river craft which lay moored along the banks which touched a dozen bazaars.

Slowly Wu Ling, with his fingers on one of the knobs, guided the course of the mysterious waves and rays so that they made a detailed tour, so to say, of the whole river front, and it was while they were watching this that Wu Ling's eyes suddenly narrowed until they were mere slits. It was the only expression of emotion that appeared on that mask-like countenance.

"Gaze well, San," he said, in level tones. "Look down upon that large junk that you can see just pulling out into the river."

"I see, Illustrious One," whispered San. "Excellency, it is like unto one of the junks of Kan-tse-wen who lurks in Changcha."

"Thine eyes still serve thee well, old friend," responded Wu Ling. "It is indeed one of the junks of the Terror; and there at the stern-steering sweep stands his chief lao-pan —Fu-chen-pu. Does your mind go back to the night when that dog of a pirate dared to lead his filthy hordes along the decks of my private houseboat, San?"

"Ho hang Illustrious One; it was a sacrilege for which the vermin should undergo the one hundred and thirty-six tortures."

"Ay, and they will, San! The day cometh when the rat they call the Terror of the Yangtse, shall squeal as no Chinese throat ever squealed. His Tartar blood shall run drop by drop as offering to the Great River. He shall see unto the last conscious moment, the eyes of the Black Abbot of Cheng-tu —the gaze of Wu Ling which shall see him into the barren wastes where he shall find no ancestors. But mark you further, San, and tell me what you see beside him."

San's eyes were already resting on the tall, ragged figure that stood beside the lao-pan on the high-pitched stern of the junk. He had recognised the figure as one he had seen on the face of that same stone more than once during the past few days.

"It is the —tall coolie, Excellency!"

"Aie! It is he! And where didst thou see him last?"

"Excellency, it was in a wupan lower down the river."

"You do not forget, San. And before that?"

"Among the People of the Pits, Excellency," whispered the fat Celestial.

"Aie!"

For some minutes longer, Wu Ling stood in silence watching that junk as she sailed out and out from the shore, watched her until the oarsmen were bending in mighty unison at the great oars, and then, as the huge mat sail was hoisted, he gave a twist of the black knob and the vision faded away.

Wu Ling turned to San, and, gazing at his master, the servitor knew that he was in the throes of one of the few rages he permitted to overwhelm him. As he lifted his hands they were grey and trembling, his face was ashy, his lips dry.

"That coolie!" he almost screamed, while San shrank back in terror. "That coolie! Dost take me for fool —dost think that Wu Ling is a babe of the West to be blinded by the tricks of children! That coolie! Was he not in Shanghai on the day when the monk caused riot at the Da-Tung Mun? Was he not taken aboard the coffin junk and placed in one of the spare coffins? Was it not my orders that he was allowed to live so that he should face Wu Ling before the end, and Wu Ling should read the truth?

"And then, in the night mist, was he not rescued by forces which came upon the junk in the costumes of river devils? Aie! Thinkest thou all this was done for a Canton coolie? Aie! Thinkest thou that the accursed Hsui-fsi who has crossed my path again and again would come out in person with his Mohammedan hounds for the sake of a coolie? Did I not see him by this means which the scientists of old gave us, as he roamed among the People of the Pits? And then he was lost until he again appeared in that wupan on the river, he escaped!

"Thinkest thou that a son of a pig could have found his way from the dens of the lost? Nay, by the sacred toe of Buddha, nay! What meanest these tidings we receive from London, from Paris, from New York? They mean that the accursed dog Sexton Blake has vanished from the sight of men. And with his disappearance there comes into China a —coolie!

"And this spawn who travels with him? Dost think the whelp does not follow the old hound even as in days gone by? It is he, San, it is he! The accursed Sexton Blake is in China. It is he who lurks beneath that outward cloak that even mine eyes cannot pierce as yet. But in my meditations understanding has come to me. It is he!

"This day we travel down the Great River. Give orders that my fastest wupan be got ready. Twenty rowers shall pull with the rush of the flood current to Chunkung. Send word by the private telegraph that a fresh company of rowers be in waiting. We shall pass through the gorges without pause, and word shall be sent to Ichang that my fastest power boat be in waiting.

"See to these commands, and have the word sent to the honourable Chon-Sun at Hankow that every available vessel must be in readiness to attack this carrion who calls himself the Terror of the Yangtse, Sun-Mo, the Black Monk, who travels up the river, already has his orders to use every means he thinks best. He may already have given the word to attack this single junk, that carries the Canton coolie up the river. But we shall make sure.

"Kan-tse-wen, the Terror of the Yangtse! And that dog of a Canton coolie who is Sexton Blake! The two are blood brothers in the renegade tong they call the Four Lakes; we shall show them that the Yellow Beetle can swim as well as bore. Blood brothers! Aie! Make haste, San! Wu Ling travels this night, and the blood of those rats shall mingle in the waters of the sacred river, drop by drop!

"The way is now clear; this time the accursed Sexton Blake remains to rot in the land he has sought so often, I, Wu Ling, have said it!"

Little did Sexton Blake guess that, as the big pirate junk swept out of Nanking, his figure and that of Fu-chen-pu were plainly visible to one who did no more than gaze down upon a polished green plate which was placed in the Monastery of Sublime Ways some two thousand miles away.

Once before, on a dangerous expedition to a mountain monastery in Turig Ting Lake, Blake had been permitted to see a demonstration of television as it had been developed by the scientists of old China. But he did not know that his old enemy, Wu Ling, was the mysterious Black Abbot of Cheng-tu, let alone that the great grey stone monastery which he had seen when passing through Cheng-tu was equipped with this same device.

Up to now the identity of the Black Abbot was a complete puzzle to him; nor, so far, had he come upon anything which might indicate that Wu Ling was involved in the mysterious affair of the Golden Book of Buddha, except that here and there he had noticed a perfection of organisation that reminded him of the sort of organisation Wu Ling controlled. But so far the Manchu had kept himself invisible.

If Blake had only known what was going on in the Monastery of Sublime Ways at that very moment, what was to follow would have been a very different tale. But, ignorant as he must be, he went on, being carried in that great junk up the Yangtse into such perils as would have made even him quail had he but foreseen them.

(Action, incident, danger —they follow thick and fast in this great Eastern adventure of Sexton Blake's, You already realise you must continue with this yarn; see to it, then —order in advance!)

Part 10

First published in the Union Jack magazine, new series, No. 1245.

How this fine serial began.

ONE of China's most sacred possessions, "The Golden Book of Buddha," is stolen by the Black Abbot of Cheng-tu while on its way up the Yangtse from Canton to the Grand Lama of Tibet. Sexton Blake, having been implored to help trace it, is in China with Tinker, both disguised as coolies, for that purpose.

After many adventures and hardships, Blake and Tinker barely escape with their lives from the underground kingdom of the People of the Pits, hounded by the Black Monk. They land at Nanking, where Tinker is seriously ill with fever. Blake, being friendly with Kan-tse-wen, the river pirate, meets one of his men, and with Tinker still ill, leaves the city in one of the pirate's junks. Unknown to him, however, the Black Monk, who is really Prince Wu Ling, the most powerful Manchu in China, discovers his whereabouts by means of television, and accordingly sends out orders for his capture.

The story continues:

SINCE that glimpse of the Black Monk on the river steamer early the previous morning, Sexton Blake had seen nothing more of the sinister figure. He thought he must still be in Nanking, and was no doubt actively searching for some traces of him if he suspected that he had escaped from the underground maze of the People of the Pits.

How he, too, had got out of the place in which he —and the People of the Pits —had been immured by the fallen rat god, Blake didn't know; nor did it matter now. The point was that the Black Monk was on his way up the river, and might have a suspicion that he had got clear.

Time alone would show that, for Blake had not a doubt that the Black Monk would show his hand quickly enough as soon as he became aware of the whereabouts of the tall coolie.

But it was not he who occupied Blake's mind the most; it was the puzzle of who was behind him —who was the man "higher up" whose brain was directing this uncanny and ruthless campaign. The knowledge that the Chuen-to-yan at Canton was participating actively was enough in itself to suggest Wu Ling, but if the Manchu was behind it all he was lying very low.

Blake was only on deck by fits and starts. Although the pirate had kept his promise to bring along a native doctor and had dumped that individual below deck with a promise to cut out his tongue and lop off his ears if he failed to assuage the fever which was racking Tinker, Blake did not feel that he dared trust the fellow alone too much with the helpless lad. He knew that, while curative medicines might be given with one hand, so to speak, a subtle poison whose effect would take some time to make itself evident might be administered with the other.

Tinker had stood the journey from the hovel through the bazaar to the junk better than Blake had expected. But no sooner was he placed in one of the primitive bunks below than his temperature had shot up in a most alarming manner and delirium seized him once more.

Therefore, although his Celestial countenance was placid enough to the observer, Blake, was inwardly deeply uneasy over the lad, and as soon as the junk was well away from Nanking, lumbering along under her huge mat sail, showing a considerable turn of speed despite her clumsy lines, Blake spoke a word to Fu-chen-pu and went below.

As he entered the "saloon" he caught sight of the native doctor squatting in one corner, apparently the prey to terror. Everywhere in China the mention of the pirates is sufficient to strike fear to the hearts of ordinary folk, for there are fearful tales of what happens to those who fall into their hands and cannot raise the ransom demanded.

This fat, flabby piece of yellow flesh was in about the worst state of funk in which Blake had ever seen a man. Perhaps, had his captors been of the white race, he would have revealed less agitation, for he knew that they did not use the torture. But to be a prisoner of the pirates was another matter, and to fall into the hands of the Terror of the Yangtse about the worst thing of all.

He was unaware of the entry of the tall coolie until Blake was standing over him. But when Blake's toe poked him on the thigh he jumped as if an electric shock had gone through him, and uttered a high-pitched squeal like a cornered rat. Then he got the worst shock of all as the ragged coolie produced an automatic pistol and poked the end of the barrel into his fat paunch, speaking not in Chinese but in cold, precise English.

"Get up!" came the command.

The Chink stopped chattering and looked up. He had already wondered at the apparent equality on which this dirty coolie was with the lao-pan and cheng-tu of the junk, but to see him standing with an automatic pistol in his hand (an article quite beyond the means of an ordinary coolie and only to be found in one's possession through being stolen) and to hear him speak in the accents of a cultured Englishman was too much for him.

He thought some strange phase of madness must be overcoming him, and a high-pitched howl was just forming in his throat when Blake choked it off with powerful hands, hauling the fat bundle to his feet as he did so.

The Chinese doctor, as Blake had heard from the men who had captured him, was not an ordinary native medico. He had studied both in America and London, and his medical training was more of the West than the East.

"Get up and listen to me," he went on. "You are here to do all in your power to cure the lad who is ill with river fever. You have heard what the lao-pan has promised you if you fail; what he will do to you will be nothing compared to what I shall do if you don't remain each moment beside the patient. Now get into that cabin and let me see you start to work."

Convinced now that this was no figment of his imagination, but that it was really the impossible —a flesh-and-blood coolie who spoke like an educated Englishman —the Chinaman waddled back into the cabin and, under Blake's urge, set to work once more. Blake bent anxiously over the lad.

For the moment the delirium had passed, and he lay there breathing stertorously, his face flushed and his skin hot and dry. Blake watched while the Chinaman produced an odd-looking five-sided thermometer and thrust it under Tinker's armpit. Then he bent over quickly to see the reading when it was withdrawn. The degree shown was in Chinese, but a quick translation into English revealed that it was above a hundred and five. There could be no doubt now that the lad was dangerously ill.

All that morning Blake remained beside the bunk. The doctor was working as if his life depended upon his skill, for those menacing, cold eyes of Blake's followed his every movement. Blake ate a little rice in the middle of the day, permitting the doctor to partake of a similar ration; then once more he bent over the bunk, and as the afternoon wore on he could see that a crisis was approaching.

Indeed, the Chinaman informed him about three o'clock that they would know the worst in another hour. Those sixty minutes seemed an eternity to Blake. Time and again he went out into the saloon to look at the cheap American clock that was on the wall. Half-past three came with maddening slowness; a quarter to four dragged into sight, and then even the professional instincts of the doctor were uppermost as he stood watching to see the effect of the medicine which he had administered in half-hour doses ever since morning.

Four o'clock came at last, and once more the thermometer was thrust under the lad's arm. Blake stood, trembling with real anxiety, while they waited. Then, as the Chinaman drew it out, he snatched it from his hand.

"A hundred and one!"

He showed it to the other, who nodded.

"He will live," he said. "Now he will sleep, and to-morrow the fever will be gone."

It was even as he said. But for another three hours Blake squatted beside the bunk, watching, watching until the lad's short, sharp breathing changed slowly but surely into long, measured respirations. Then he rose to go on deck. It was only then he noticed that it was almost dusk, and, keen to know now how much progress they had made, he started quickly through the saloon. Before he had got half-way across it, however, he heard a sudden hubbub on deck, then a quick rush of thudding steps as someone came tumbling down the crude companion. The next moment Fu-chen-pu burst into the saloon.

"They come!" he said as he pulled up just in time to avoid collision with Blake. "We shall need every man to defend."

"Who comes?" asked Blake quickly.

"A dozen craft or more —junks, sampans, wupans, and power boats. The Black Monk has done this; I saw him pass on a river steamer during the day."

And then from over the water came a medley of shrill yells.

Clearing for Action!

THERE was only a skylight in the little booth where Tinker's bunk was built, and it had been impossible to see anything distinctly through the oyster-shell windows of the saloon. Therefore Blake had had scarcely a glimpse of the river since he had descended early that morning.

He had been able to follow, to a certain extent, what they must have been passing. At times there was nothing to hear but the creak, creak, creaking of the mat sail and the bamboo cordage, with the accompaniment of the water slapping against the sides of the junk.

Then there would be intermittent periods of confused sounds which told Blake that they were passing other craft. Came times when a deep hum came over them —the voice of some teeming village or town, as they worked their way past it; and anon the chug-chug of power boats or the shrill hootings of river steamers.

It was the life of the Great River that never slept —the vast hive where more than eighty millions of yellow people lived and had their being.

But during the latter part of the afternoon few noises had seemed to come from across the water. Blake, who knew the Yangtse as intimately as any foreigner, and even better than some of the Chinese who lived on it, figured that, should they have kept the steady rate they had begun in the morning, they should be tacking by late afternoon along a somewhat dreary, deserted stretch which lies about midway between Nanking and Anking.

For a matter of a dozen miles or so there was no town or village —just bare mudbanks, and then the first settlement was on the southern side of the river, a long, straggling, uninteresting place called Taipung —a sort of second-rate market town for the district beyond. It was, Blake knew, practically without any foreign residents, except for a handful of missionaries, and, in addition, was reputed to be a hotbed of Cantonese activities. Its position alone made it worth while for the southerners to intrigue for its control, and on the previous occasion when he had passed up the river he knew that quite an exceptional number of craft had been gathered there. The whisper had been that the Cantonese were about to make a surprise descent upon Nanking, but as that rumour had been passing up and down the Yangtse for half a dozen years or more, Blake paid little attention to it.

But at Fu-chen-pu's startling news his mind immediately went to Taipung. The pirate said the river was swarming with all sorts of craft —junks, sampans, wupans, and power boats. If, as the pirate thought, their intentions were hostile to the junk, then it could only be, Blake figured, that they had come from Taipung, unless they had been lying waiting for some days, watching for the junk's return from Nanking.

The latter seemed unlikely. Not even a fleet like that would attack a solitary junk that bore the threat of Kan-tse-wen behind it. The Terror roamed down the river well past Taipung, and the sacking of such a place would be a matter of delight and ease to him if he gathered but the half of the vessels he could muster. Therefore, the people of Taipung would ponder deeply before setting upon one of his junks on its way up the river.

Then, if this fleet were hostile, what had inspired such a desperate hostility? Before leaving Nanking Fu-chen-pu had warned Blake that there was a danger of attack on the way up. He had mentioned the Black Monk, but whether those words would refer to the monk of which Blake had knowledge and whom he had seen on the deck of the river steamer just after dawn the morning before, Blake couldn't tell.

But now he said that he had seen the Black Monk pass on a steamer during the day. Taipung was a point of call for the side-wheelers of the different Chinese lines. Had the Black Monk got off there? Did he suspect that the tall coolie who bobbed up so persistently in his path was aboard the pirate junk? And did he want so badly to get him back into his power as to muster a fleet to attack that lone junk? If those things were so, this tatterdemalion collection of river craft could only have been got together after his arrival in Taipung, and have come forth to the attack because the Black Monk carried some very high authority which they dared not resist.

All this passed rapidly through his mind as he raced back to the deck on the heels of the lao-pan. The moment he reached the high stern he saw a sight that told him Fu-chen-pu had not exaggerated. Although dusk had almost closed in there was still enough grey light lying over the river for Blake to make out the collection of craft of all sizes that were unquestionably closing in on the junk.

At first, suspicious that this strange gathering had no friendly intentions, Fu-chen-pu had worked his vessel in towards the northern bank, for, some two miles up was, he knew, a small village, which was under the control of Kan-tse-wen. If he could but get close enough to that spot to send a man ashore or get a signal of some sort through he would be able to call upon reinforcements —several hundreds of men who would fight to the death for the Terror.

But while he was still a good quarter of a mile distant from the bank a portion of the fleet that was coming down fast on the current had swept round on that side, and from the moment their yells started they made no further pretence of their intentions.

From every craft a wild medley of yells and screams were rising. It was the typical Chinese way of working up into a passion until each man would run amok, and, as an accompaniment to the devilish racket there was the chug-chugging of the motor-boats, the snorting of small steam tugs, and the continuous explosions of fire crackers being set off to keep at bay the evil spirits.

It was a perfect pandemonium of barbaric sound that came sweeping down upon the lone junk, and, as far as odds were concerned, Fu-chen-pu's little force was outnumbered a score of times or more.

But the lao-pan had not risen to be chief of junks to the dread pirate, Kan-tse-wen, without proving his mettle in many a desperate foray on land and water. And now he stood with one arm lying across the great stern sweep, gazing with perfectly placid countenance at the down-rushing craft, while his lieutenant moved about among the fighting men, handing out swords and knives as if what was about to happen was an everyday occurrence.

Blake found himself possessed of a broad-bladed cutting-sword, such as the Chinese executioners wield. It was a heavy weapon, but well balanced, and he knew from experience what deadly work it could do at close quarters. He determined, however, to trust to his automatic while the magazine lasted, and, as a reserve, he had taken care to thrust a couple of spare clips in his pocket from the well equipped private arsenal which Fu-chen-pu carried.

"Forty beats of the oars and they will be alongside," remarked the lao-pan as he shot a quick look along the deck to see if the arming of the crew had been completed.

"How will you defend?" asked Blake.

"I shall let them touch, and then we shall sink some of them as a beginning, Sek-i-ton Bal-akee."

"You have explosives then?"

"Did I not tell you I had been in Nanking for supplies? Watch and you will see."

He gave vent to a low whistle, and immediately the cheng-tu

gave an answering whistle. Following that, the forward hatch was thrown off, and a dozen men jumped into the hold. There came on deck then a stream of cases which others of the crew prised open. And within an extraordinarily short space of time Blake saw a long string of short black sticks placed in the scuppers on each side.

"Dynamite!" he muttered in a low tone.

"Even so, Sek-i-ton Bal-akee. The honourable Kan-tse-wen fights with the weapons of the West when it is necessary. We shall send some of those dogs to their ancestors before twenty beats of the oars are passed. Look, Sek-i-ton Bal-akee! What did the unworthy Fu-chen-pu tell you? See you not the Black Monk on yon boat?"

Blake bent forward and peered through the dusk. Now the foremost of the sampans and yupans were closing in at a rapid rate, acting, Blake could see, on some general plan. The power boats were on the outside shepherding the others, so to speak, and, when necessary, giving them of their aid to offset the pull of the current. The junks —there were but four of them —were lumbering along by themselves, and the sidewheelers were in the midst of the smaller craft like ducks among ducklings. And it was on the deck of the nearest of these that, looking, Blake saw the sinister figure of a man clad in a long black robe.

"You are right, Fu," he muttered. "May your dynamite destroy the craft which bears that foul raven!"

"Aie! It may be that you will shoot him with your weapon," was the reply.

"I shall join you soon; I go below for a few moments."

A thought had come to Blake, and now he dived below. Swinging into the rough sort of booth where Tinker lay, he made straight for the native doctor. Out went his hand, gripping the other by his shoulder; then Blake's eyes bored into those of the Celestial, looking glitteringly cruel in the light of the single oil dip that had been lighted.

"There will be noise and much fighting!" he hissed. "You will remain here and watch over this lad. No matter what comes you will stick by your patient. Do you understand?"

He had discarded all pretence now, and his words were in English. The dominance of his tone impressed the Chinaman, so that the ragged coolie vanished and an Englishman stood before him.

"I—I understand." he stammered. "Who are you, sir?"

"One who can strike as far as the Terror!" snapped Blake. "Hark you well to my words. If you desert your charge I shall deal with you as I would a rat!"

Then he turned and raced up the ladder to the deck, for now he heard a roar that told him the attacking craft were sweeping in. Fu's twenty beats of the oars had timed them well.

Foes —and Fog!

BLAKE'S foot was just pressing on the deck at the head of the ladder, when a terrific explosion hurled him back so that he only saved himself from plunging into the saloon by clutching frantically at the wooden handrail. A great cloud of smoke arose on the port side of the junk, and while he raced for the stern, a mass of debris began to rain on to the deck.

He reached Fu-chen-pu as another terrific explosion came on the port side, and this caused the junk, big as she was, to heel over violently. Smoke and more debris followed, and then there came a surge of pandemonium from human throats that beggars description. Until then the shock of the two terrific upheavals had held the attacking party spellbound; now it sounded like an army of bandicoots gone crazy.

The hooters of the side-wheelers joined in the racket, and then a hail of bullets swept the junk as the raiders began to fire. In some way they had become equipped with weapons, despite the speed with which they had been mustered. Then came the first rush.

Dusk had settled into darkness. So far the river was free of mist, and, from the high stern of the junk, Blake could see the shadowy forms of the Celestials as they raced with extraordinary agility of balance across from the outer craft, using sampans and wupans as springboards, until they were in the lee of the bulwarks of the junk. Already those who had been in the inner mass of boats had begun to climb the sides, and now, for the first time, Fu made his voice heard above the din. It was a terrific bellow that rolled along the deck to where his fighting men were crouching in marvellous discipline of control waiting for the word. But that bellow did not release them. Instead, it caused a motion at only two points of the line on each side, and then in rapid succession there came four more upheavals as more dynamite was thrown out into the ranks of the attacking party.

The wreckage of boats filled the air; the destruction of human lives must have been an appalling percentage of those who had been crowding in upon the junk. Fu had chosen his moment well; he had struck to create as many casualties as possible among the enemy early in the fight, for he realised how greatly his forces were outnumbered, and none knew better than that hard-bitten pirate what would be their fate once they were overwhelmed. There would not be a single shred of men or junk left to mark the passing of that one lone craft of Kan-tse-wen's.

In this new shock the attacking party paused. Since the first glimpse of the Black Monk just as dusk was closing in, Blake had seen nothing of the sinister figure. But now, in the lull, there came through the darkness the same sort of cry he had heard days before by the Da-Tung Mun in Shanghai. And, as if it were some sort of mysterious inspiration, the enemy recovered and came on once more.

Even in the gloom they could see hundreds of figures leaping across from boat to boat to take the place of those who had been annihilated. Blake heard Fu muttering to himself, and turned his head.

"One more shot of dynamite," he heard the other muttering, "then it will be too dangerous for the junk. She must be smashed in many parts."

"It is a risk, but it clears them off," put in Blake. "As long as the junk remains afloat we shall hold her, Fu. Would you prefer that I descend to the deck and take charge of part of your men?"

"Sek-i-ton Bal-akee will fight where the battle rages hottest," answered the lao-pan, "but if the honourable friend of Kan-tse-wen will descend to the deck it will be a mighty aid."

Blake waited for no more. With a run he was down the sloping stern, and, a moment later, was among the crouching forms in the waist. They knew him, despite his ragged garb, to be an honoured friend of the valient Fu-chen-pu, and, indeed, it had been whispered from end to end of the junk that he was even as a brother to their master, Kan-tse-wen. More than that, there were some who knew of the man who had fought so terrifically once in the past by the side of their master, and there was a crowding towards him as he shifted his automatic to his left hand and gripped his cutting sword in the right.

Came the second wave of the attack, this time with a determination that carried the front ranks right up the low side of the junk and in amongst the defenders in the waist. It did not need Fu's bellow to set them into action. Out leaped Sexton Blake, shooting right and left with a precision that sent man after man crashing down.

All about him surged his men, cutting with their heavy swords and telling the sing-song battle-cry, with which the Terror's rabble always went into battle.

Up forward the cheng-tu was at it hammer and tongs with the portion of the crew under his charge, and, back on the high stern, was Fu, surrounded by a dozen or so of his veterans, hacking at every arm or head that protruded even for a moment above the rail.

Screams, yells, hoarse cries of agony —crazy whoops and barbaric battle-cries, made the evening hideous. Over the junk, the pall of the explosions hung in the still night air. The great mat sail was a motionless blur against the mast, and, up in the bows, at their oars, the rowers sat mute and watchful, not daring to leave their posts until the cheng-tu should give the order.

Again and again those climbing demons were driven back upon their fellows, or into the other battered boats that had taken the place of those destroyed. Here and there, among the attacking fleet, a lantern showed, and at one spot was a string of electric lights coming, Blake imagined, as he glimpsed them fleetingly, from one of the sidewheelers. He wondered if the Black Monk would be on the deck of that craft, well removed from the scene of battle.

Then all his attention was needed in a fresh rush, that came with even more determination than any of those that had preceded it. Over the low side they came in a steady wave that swept in upon the little band of defenders, each man of whom was fighting in a way that Blake had never seen equalled among the Chinese. It spoke mightily for the influence of Kan-tse-wen and Fu-chen-pu that the crew would stand up against such overwhelming odds.

Nor was there any more of a fighting demon than the tall, ragged coolie, who was ever where the struggle raged hardest. He was making no use of his automatic now. There had been no time to slip in a fresh clip when the other was emptied; it was all sword-work, and Sexton Blake was cutting, slashing, swinging in a way that would have horrified the orthodox school of sword-play.

But it was effective. Man after man went down before that scythe-like sweep and then, rallying his men with a great cry, Blake led an onslaught more furious than ever as a fresh wave showed over the side.

Some devil of battle seemed to surge among Blake and those who pressed about him. Their rush carried them through the attacking hordes until they were at the side, and then, as he caught a glimpse of a deck beneath him, Blake leaped.

He had not paused to weigh the terrific chances against a return. All that was in his mind just then was the rush of the combat and the knowledge that, by a sudden swoop, they might cut in through the enemy and divide their forces.

His men were not slow to follow. After him they went like so many fiends, yelling at the top of their lungs, and by the very fury of their descent cutting a swathe through the loosely-flung enemy.

It was a surprise move of such a daring nature that those in the surrounding craft had not guessed it would be attempted. They fell back under the swinging swords that swept among them, and before the first pause came Blake found he had leaped across three ranks of the crowded sampans and wupans, and was getting close to the nearest of the sidewheelers.

But that rush had not gone unseen by the eyes of the Black Monk.

Now, as the mass hesitated, uncertain what to do in the face of this furious assault, which had come as such a surprise, that high-pitched command rose once more, and, as if it were a physical spur, the hesitating mob burst into action.

From every side they came, leaping agilely from craft to craft, seeming to sense that it was the coolie whose head towered dimly above the others that they must reach. And then, while Blake and his men hurled themselves to meet the rush, there swept down upon them something which was as unlooked for by the attacking mob as by the defenders.

It was the river mist, rolling up with incredible speed, just as it unfolds in that swampy marsh country that lies in the region of Tung Ting Lake.

So amazingly swift did it come that, almost before he knew it was upon them, Blake found himself stumbling, bewildered against the curved mat shelter amidships of a sampan. As if by magic he had been separated from his men, although, to prove that some of the combatants still remained at grips, he could still hear the ring of steel, thuds, and groans, and scuffling all about him.

But for the moment he seemed to be alone. What had become of his most recent antagonist he did not know. Nor was the pandemonium as great. It seemed that even the Chinese must have been bewildered by the sudden lowering of the fog, and he knew that it was when the river mist hung low they believed the worst of the evil water spirits were abroad.

He had a general notion of the direction in which the junk lay, and now he started along, trying to feel his way from boat to boat in order to find it.

Now and then he would come upon others, also stumbling about in bewildered fashion, and he made more strenuous efforts than ever to reach the junk, for suddenly, high above the lessened noise, they heard the bellow of the lao-pan recalling his men. Whether he knew Blake was close or near the latter couldn't guess.

He swung to the right, for the voice seemed to come from that direction. He had covered some three or four boats, meeting only one other person, who slithered past him as if not anxious to discover whether he was friend or enemy, and then, all of a sudden, he saved himself just in time from pitching head foremost into the water. In some way he had reached a broken bit of the line of craft, or else he was at the outside.

He paused, listening. He knew what danger overhung him if he once got rattled. So he waited for the sound of the lao-pan's voice to come again, and a few moments later he heard it. But this time it seemed to come from far to the left.

The confusion of fog!

Many a time at sea Blake had experienced that sensation, which is the dread of every mariner. Before, the voice had seemed to be to the right, and he was certain he had been travelling towards it. Now it was much less distinct, and, apparently, away to the left.

He turned in that direction and listened again. Ever since the mist had settled over the scene the pandemonium had died away to what was but a murmur in comparison. But now, just as Blake once more heard the echoing bellow —was it an echo, he asked himself —for which his ears had been straining, there arose a renewed chorus of yells that drowned it utterly.

Acutely anxious to get back to the scene and his place on the junk, Blake began leaping from one dimly-seen sampan to another. He seemed to be approaching closer to the heart of the racket, and something told him this was a fresh attempt upon the junk. If the men who had followed him over the side had become lost, as had he, then he realised that Fu-chen-pu would be sorely put to it to keep the fiends at bay. That thought urged him to still greater efforts, and he was beginning to feel that he must be nearing the junk, for the cries seemed all about him now, when, without the slightest warning, he plunged full into the thick of a struggle.

It was enough for Blake. He still gripped his sword, and now he drove in, shouting the Kan-tse-wen battle-cry in order to try and distinguish friend from foe. He went through the press like a flying wedge, and, on the other side, turned to attack anew. But at that moment a flying figure appeared out of the mist, yelling like a lunatic. He caught Blake in full plunge as he landed on the craft where the detective stood, causing Blake to lurch to one side. So close to the edge of the craft had he been standing that he was forced to thrust out a foot to get purchase on the adjoining boat.

But there was no boat there —nothing but elusive mist, and before he could save himself Blake had plunged into the water.

He felt himself caught at once by the strong sweep of the current, but he figured he could grasp the side of another sampan as he swept on, for he was a strong swimmer. He had released his sword as he felt himself going, and now he used both hands in a frenzied effort to stem the tide-drag.

Yet fainter and fainter became the cries of the combatants, and then he knew that the current was too much for him —that he was being carried like a chip down through the mist beyond reach or call of his friends aboard the junk!

Cornered!

IT seemed to Sexton Blake that this vast river was a definite being, opposing him at each turn.

From the time he had left Shanghai he had been forced to fight it again and again. Even the comparatively small stream that had carried him and Tinker through the underground passages had at last precipitated them into the Yangtse. It was almost as if the spirit of the Black Abbot of Cheng-tu, who ruled that grim fortress far, far up the river had instilled itself in the rushing yellow waters of the great Thing that flowed east from the remote borders of Tibet to sink itself in the Yellow Sea. It was as if the mighty, passive soul of China had stirred, and was saying him nay.

He knew from the strength of the current that he had no hope now of winning back to the vicinity of the junk. Already the noise of the fighting was but a distant sound upon the still night air. Yet he hoped to keep from being swept by the full strength of the stream by swimming in a diagonal direction until he reached the slacker water near the shore. It was far more easy to tell how he was going by feeling the edge of the current than it had been when he had the sampans beneath his feet. And he was quickly sensitive to realise when the drag of the current was lessening.

Bit by bit he faced it more directly, so that, by the time he had covered a considerable distance, he guessed he must be within a couple of hundred yards or so of the shore, and was, he believed, now swimming about full against the downrush of water.

The mist still hung like a sodden blanket over everything, clinging even to the very surface of the river. But the night chill had not yet come, and while he kept in motion Blake felt no discomfort in the water. The danger would come, he knew, later, if he failed to find the boats from which he had swept. It mattered not now whether he found the enemy or the junk; all he was striving for was to get back in touch.

That old pirate junk, the vermin-ridden "saloon," Tinker, and rough old Fu-chen-pu —that was all he desired just then, and never before had he realised how fervently he would have sought them.

Now and then Blake would ease his swimming just enough to hold himself against the current, which was greatly diminished here from what it had been towards the centre of the river. He would listen for sounds from the group of vessels, and at times would think a distant murmur reached him; but he could not be sure.

So on he would struggle again, puzzled more and more that he did not pick them up, for if they were all loose on the current without any force sustaining them against its sweep, they, too, should be carried down.

But Blake did not know that very soon after he had taken that disastrous plunge into the rushing waters the junk had been overwhelmed by a final desperate attack, which had appeared from every side. Protected by the curtain of the mist, the assault had been carried at a dozen different points, and with such a big part of the defenders absent —lost, as Blake had been lost —Fu-chen-pu and the cheng-tu had been driven back and back until they and a few others were collected on the high stern in a last stand.

It was then that Fu-chen-pu thought of the helpless lad below. He knew by now that "Sek-i-ton Bal-akee " must be lost out there in the mist —was probably trying desperately to find his way back to the junk. But if he did not come now he would be too late, so Fu-chen-pu felt that the mantle of responsibility for Tinker descended upon him. At any cost he must cut his way through to the lad, and if he must die at the hands of these river rats, then it would be at the side of his charge.

He had been fighting a mechanical defence until this thought occurred to him. He had been vaguely aware that the drift of the junk had been halted, and now there reached him the swishing sound of water. He knew what that meant. In some way the sidewheelers had managed to work in near the junk, and ropes must have been fastened. Then the engines had been started, and now the whole fleet, with the sampans and wupans clinging on like flies, was on the move.

Fu-chen-pu had not been called "The Demon" without cause. With Kan-tse-wen, he was one of the most dreaded pirates on the whole stretch of the Yangtse, and now he proved that he had earned the name.

With a sudden great bellow he went completely berserk. Through the press that was crowding in on the high, sloping stern he cut a way with his sword. Nor could any stay him. It was a terrific feat of arm-and-blade play that left behind him a wide swathe where men lay huddled, with great gaping wounds or half-severed limbs.

Still the lao-pan drove on and on until he was close to the ladder which led below. Here was another press of men —mere shadowy figures in the mist —but Fu-chen-pu could smell them as the enemy. Like the very storm god himself, he went in among them, his sword acting as a flail of death. They scattered right and left before that whirlwind, and, with a cleared space before him, Fu dropped down the ladder.

In the "saloon" a single oil dip was burning; within the space where Tinker's bunk had been built was another dip, and here crouched the terrified native physician, thinking that death was his at last. But Fu merely kicked him aside, and, bending, managed to bring his voice to a minor pitch. He found Tinker's eyes wide open, staring at him in full sanity.

"You are free of the fever," was what Fu said, almost choking with the effort of his breathing.

"I am all right, but weak," whispered Tinker. "Where am I? Where is my master?"

"You are on the junk. Don't you remember? We have been boarded by river rats. Sek-i-ton Bal-akee is out there somewhere in the mist. They are too much for us. We have killed many, but still they come, like vermin. It is well that you should know, for the end is near. I, Fu-chen-pu, the leader of the fighters of the honourable Kan-tse-wen, am here to die by the side of his friend. And it shall be my sword that shall send you to your ancestors; the blade of a river rat shall not touch you."

The last words were enough to tell Tinker that some desperate turn had come to their position. He could hear the terrific racket overhead, and could guess what was going on.

Well, he thought desperately, weak as he was, he would meet the end in a way that would show the yellow men how a white man could die; and it were better that the stroke should come swiftly from Fu's blade than that he should go to the torture of those river rats.

But he never got a chance to put his thoughts into words, for now Fu was leaning towards the entrance, his body poised for action as a terrific clatter sounded outside the door of the saloon, which he had kicked to and bolted on his rush through. Then, all of a sudden, he bent down. Picking up Tinker, blankets and all, with the ease he would have snatched up a child, he dashed into the saloon as if he had chosen that as the place where he would make his last stand.

And Fate willed it that at this exact moment Sexton Blake, utterly pumped with his efforts to fight a way up against the current, was wading through mud and reeds along the river bank, far down from the scene of that last desperate conflict —wading until he could crawl up the soaking bank.

And there he fell prone, only half conscious that life was functioning within him.

(Look out for next week's stirring instalment —how Fu-chen-pu held the fort, and what happened to Sexton Blake.)

186

Part 11.

First published in the Union Jack magazine, new series, No. 1246

How this fine serial began.

ONE of China's most sacred possessions, "The Golden Book of Buddha," is stolen by the Black Abbot of Cheng-tu while on its way up the Yangtse from Canton to the Grand Lama of Tibet. Sexton Blake, having been implored to help trace it, is in China with Tinker, both disguised as coolies, for that purpose.

After being hounded by the Black Monk, Blake and Tinker are making their way up the Yangtse in a junk belonging to Kan-tse-wen, a very notorious river pirate, with whom Blake is friendly. While Tinker is just recovering from a bout of river fever, the boat is attacked by a fleet belonging to the Black Abbot, who is really Prince Wu Ling. He has discovered their whereabouts by television. During the fight, Blake gets lost in the mist, and while Fu-chen-pu, the captain of the junk, prepares to defend Tinker in a last stand, the detective, who has fallen into the water, and been caught by the current, is struggling ashore a long distance from the scene of the disaster, more dead than alive.

The Stand of Fu-Chen-Pu.

FU-CHEN-PU was a veteran in strategy as well as fighting.

His first care, therefore, was to provide a possible means of retreat before the hordes at the door should be upon him.

There was not, it is a fact, much prospect of ensuring such an avenue in that place, which communicated with the outside by only three means —the door at which the enemy was hammering and which they must have down within a few moments; the skylight above, which was beyond his reach unless he should mount the rough table, and succeed in smashing it; and the oyster-shell windows at the back of the cabin.

These latter were long and about a foot high, the "panes" of various sizes and shapes being fitted into bamboo strips that had been bent to follow their vagaries of curve and angle. Apparently, Fu-chen-pu fixed on this as the only way open to him, should he fail to stem the tide of the attack, which was coming by way of the ladder. For, when he had laid Tinker on the floor, he turned and, with a terrific sweep of his great cutting sword, using the back, he cleared the whole hotchpotch of oyster-shell panes and bamboo from their fittings.

Outside, on a sort of sill, were some narrow boxes in which, strange to say on that pirate junk, were some flowering narcissi, placed there by the little slender hands of Fu's tiny wife. A moment only the Chinaman hesitated as their purity became visible in that smoky hole.

Was he thinking of the Blossom of Morning who had planted them with such tender care? Was there room in that breast for such thoughts? Or did they represent just another impediment that must be cleared away? Who can read the mind or the heart of a Celestial? Whatever was in his thoughts the pirate lifted his foot and gave a couple of heavy kicks which loosened the boxes, precipitating them and the pale flowers into the yellow waters beneath. If he felt some compunction as he saw those tender blooms vanish through the mist he did not show it, for now, as the wooden panels of the door began to split he swung round, and, laying down his sword, took hold of the table.

It had been fastened to the floor with wooden pegs, but these presented no insuperable obstacle to Fu-chen-pu. With a mighty heave he tore the table free, heaving it over on its side as a sort of barricade to protect Tinker.

Let it not be thought that the Chinaman was doing this out of any personal regard for the lad. Tinker meant nothing to him except that he was a charge under his care, due to the friendship of himself and his master with his own honourable master, Kan-tse-wen. Therefore, as long as he could stand on his feet and wield a sword the lad, while helpless, must be his charge.

Scarcely had he placed the table than the wood of the door gave a great crack, and one of the strips of thick boarding dropped inwards. Now Fu could see the faces of those in the foremost of the attacking party, but these withdrew a moment later as a heavy log was brought down as a battering-ram.

Now Fu was standing, his sword once more gripped in his hand, waiting for the rush. He would not give up the junk of which he was captain until the last gasp, but he knew that the remaining defence depended solely on his own resource and strength. The rest of his men must have been cut down into submission long before this.

And then Fu caught sight of something that made his eyes narrow into such thin slits that the pupils were scarcely visible. Until this moment he had forgotten entirely about the native doctor.

He had left that individual chattering with terror in the place where Tinker had lain. But now he caught sight of a crawling figure, making, apparently for the door. The creature was jammed as close to the wall as his bulk would allow, and he had been sticking close to the shadow. Had Fu been engaged but a little longer in his toil the physician would have reached his objective and the door would have been flung open without more ado. The craven cur had realised that this solitary man was preparing to make a last stand in the cabin; he had thought to ingratiate himself with the conquerors by opening the way to them.

"Aie!"

That ubiquitous exclamation of the Chinese is capable of a vast deal of nuance of expression, depending on how the voice rises or falls as it is used. It may mean anything from simple agreement or even pleasure to a wail of mourning or, in extreme use, a terrific outburst of passion. It was this latter with Fu, although the sound was so low as scarcely to travel across the confined space of the cabin.

"Aie!"

A second time it came from his lips, even more softly, and now the fat physician was crouching back on his hams, his eyes dilated with terror. Fu-chen-pu moved slowly towards him. There was not the slightest vestige of hurry in his steps, even though the battering-ram was thudding at the door. Like one fascinated by a snake, the other watched him approach. Then, as Fu's sword rose, he gave vent to a high-pitched squeal that was so laden with terror that even the attack on the door was held in pause.

Like relentless fate Fu's arm went up and up until it was high over his head. Then:

Swish!

Down it came in a sort of sidewise sweep that caught the crouching Celestial clean. There was the force of a practised hand behind that blow; no executioner ever struck more true. One moment the craven crouched, a complete entity; the next, a headless body fell forward, and what had crowned it rolled in zig-zag fashion towards Fu's feet.

With one sweep Fu gathered up the gruesome object and, turning, hurled it with well-directed aim through the opening in the door. There came a chorus of yells from outside as the thing rolled among them; then another great crash as the battering-ram drove what remained of the door clean inwards. Fu had just time to leap in front of the table when the rush came.

The fight that followed in the cabin of that junk on the Yangtse was one which has come down as an epoch in the history of the river. All the way from Nanking to Ichang, the river folk tell about it at nights when they crouch over the coals, of the fire in wupan or sampan, or huddle beneath the mat shelters while the mist and the evil spirits of the water are abroad.

Fu-chen-pu, the fighting captain of the dread pirate, Kan-tse-wen had faced forty, fifty, sixty times his number while in defence of a worthless brat who was but a coolie who would not fetch ten cash at a sale, for he was already doomed to die. There were whispers that the lad was not that, but something very different, but there was no truth in the statement. It was fighting madness on the part of the mighty Fu —nothing else.

Fu-chen-pu had never heard of a country called Scotland, let alone any knowledge of the great two-handed broadswords that were once wielded by the rugged Highlanders during their forays among the lowlands and across the border into England. But, in meeting that rush, he gripped his heavy weapon in a manner strangely like those men of the North, and before him he kept a cleared space by sheer might of arm.

Once within the cabin there was no chance for the attacking party to spread out or retreat. Those behind came crowding on top of them, and, willy nilly, they were thrust in to meet the sweeping devastation of that terrible weapon.

Fu made no attempt to thrust; there was no refinement of that sort about his work. He set himself to cut and slash and sweep and even bludgeon with the heavy steel, holding his feet well apart and his thighs against the upturned table.

An arm, a neck, a head, a skull split clean open, a leg, a hip —all were food for Fu's blade. The place became a veritable shambles, in which blood flowed along the ancient teak, spilling into the gaping cracks until it overflowed and became a series of thin rivulets that broadened and lengthened until there was a patchwork of miniature canals. And still that slashing blade of Fu's fed them.

190

The native physician's was not the only head that rolled in grisly fashion about the floor; before the pirate was a steadily growing heap of maimed and bleeding creatures who whimpered or squealed as they tried to crawl away from that swishing death. Not once had a weapon got past that great blade; not one drop yet of Fu's blood had gone to swell the patchwork or darkling channels on the floor. It was a magnificent piece of offensive-defensive. It was an instance of co-ordination of man and sword that would have placed Fu-chen-pu high in the lists in the days when the sword was master of the fray.

And back of those confused hordes a sinister black shadow lurked, witnessing this unbelievably mighty work of execution —the Black Monk. Again and again his strange command rose above the sound of battle, and, again and again his men crowded in, only to fall beneath the scythe which was swinging within that cabin.

There was no way in which enough men could press into the place at one time to subdue this giant and his mighty flail. Some other means must be used, and the quick eye of Fu saw it when it came.

The black muzzle of a rifle suddenly appeared over the shoulders of those who were jammed in the frame of the door. It was held by a hand which protruded from beneath the watchful eye of the Black Monk. A moment for the aim and the leaden messenger of death would —

Crack!

The sound of the explosion came with terrific noise in that confined space. But on the instant when that finger had pulled the trigger Fu had thrown himself to one side. It was not enough to take him entirely outside the line of danger, for he felt a sudden hot sear along his shoulder as the bullet tore its way through his tunic. But it gave him a breathing space, and before a second bullet could come he had recovered. One step he took forward, then his arm went far back behind his shoulder; and the next moment the great sword was hurtling through the air, full at the man who stood behind the rifle.

Fu did not wait to see the effect of what followed. Even as the heavy steel found its mark he had swooped over the form of the lad who lay behind the table. He snatched him up and made for the window at the back. Without the slightest hesitation, he heaved the body through the opening, so that it went plunging down into the yellow waters. Then Fu, despite his bulk of frame, dived after, and the bullet that screamed after him passed harmlessly between his feet just at the moment when he disappeared from view.

He had taken the last desperate way.

Lost in a Lost Land.

CHILL grey dawn creeping through banks of swirling mist found a solitary, huddled figure on the barren, muddy bank of the Great River.

The attitude was one of utter exhaustion, arms folded loosely across the knees, and weary head resting upon them. It is an attitude only too common to be seen among the underfed, overworked coolies of the Yangtse, and, had any boat been passing or pedestrian moving along the narrow footpath a quarter of a mile back from the marshes on the river bank the sight of this lone picture of exhaustion would have aroused neither curiosity nor sympathy.

There is no thought in China for the human beast of burden who falls by the wayside; a broken creature is a potential carcase, and a carcase is a nuisance.

For several hours this ragged coolie had sat in that same position, scarcely moving. Indeed, to do so was a greater effort than he could muster, for his limbs were locked in a stiff chill, and his heart was beating low. His state of mind was one of suspension between the world of reality and that of fantasy; his mind was benumbed, his brain sodden with fatigue. His whole entity had reached the lowest point of bodily misery.

Not even dawn, for which he had been dimly waiting, served to bring movement to his huddled form. Not until the last wisp of fog had floated away and the long shafts of the warming sun found him out did he stir. Then his head lifted slowly, his bleared eyes gazed in half stupid manner out across the water. But not yet did his loosely clasped hands slip down his shins, nor his legs attempt to straighten out.

Little by little the blessed sun climbed up in the east. Warmer and more penetrating became the flood of light and heat which came from the great Ball of Life. Faintly but surely the feebleness within this bit of human wreckage himself responded to the primitive call, and slowly he got himself into a standing posture.

He lurched like one who has drunk deeply; his legs seemed to refuse to answer to the halting message which was sent out by the control in the brain; his arms hung like the hinged limbs of a puppet.

Yet all the time his bloodshot eyes searched, searched, searched across and up and down the yellow waste of water. For what?

Gradually, his will-power gained control, and some semblance of direction seemed to enter into the muscles of his limbs. Mechanically he began to stagger back and forth, his legs wobbling at first, and the swing of his arms drawing forth faint moans of agony as he forced them into a stronger swing that started the stagnant blood.

And all the time he moved in a restricted compass, so that his gaze did not leave the river. Once he saw, far across towards the other side, a small craft, at which he stared listlessly; then, again, a big junk came careering down on the current, with a slight following breeze behind her. His eager gaze searched her lines, but when she drew opposite him he turned away with a grimace of disappointment.

Where on that river was the object for which he gazed? A craft it was —could only be. Was she still locked in the midst of hostile boats as she had been in the blackness of the night? Was she even now standing upright in that inferno of noise that had raged up to the point where his brain had begun to numb, or was she dead flotsam on the current? Was her sturdy hulk lying at the bottom of the river, torn asunder by some terrific explosion, or eaten to a charred remnant by greedy flames?

From beneath his shirt the coolie who was Sexton Blake took a few bits of dried rice-cake and watermelon seeds. He munched these methodically, for he knew that a long and probably perilous day lay ahead of him. When he had finished the last crumbs he crouched over the bank and scooped some of the yellow, silt-laden water in his hands. It tasted gritty and brackish, but there was no other source near at hand, and his thirst raged violently. Then, staggering once more to his feet, he started off along the bank, keeping at a slight tangent away from it, in order to try and pick up a track, if there was one.

He did not know how far down the river he had been carried in the night. Judging as well as his numbed brain would allow him to calculate, he thought it might be anything between two and three miles. He had a rough idea of how long he had been in the water, of the rate at which the current ran at that part, and of about how much he would have been able to hold his own while swimming. But there were other factors to be considered, and anything but a vague guess was out of the question.

He had been hoping fervently that he would have seen some sign of the junk and the heterogeneous flotilla that had surrounded it. But not a single hull, large or small, was there to mark the spot where Hades had burst forth the night before.

He was by now acutely anxious about Tinker. It had been obvious, despite the heavy mist that at the moment when he had plunged into the river a renewal of the fight was in progress. Blake knew well enough that this last assault would be one of determination on the part of the combined enemy.

With the fog to cloak their movements they would be able to swarm over the surrounded junk from half a dozen different points, and, when he remembered that a goodly portion of Fu-chen-pu's fighting-men had been caught like himself among the sampans and wupans by the sudden rush of the mist, he knew that it would be a hopeless stand against overwhelming odds.

If, therefore, Fu had gone down, and the junk had fallen into the hands of the creatures who had come under the cloak of the Black Monk, then what had happened to Tinker?

Blake knew what the lad's eventual fate would be if he fell into the hands of the Black Monk. Instinct told him that, while his identity and that of Tinker might be unguessed at present, they would not long be a mystery once they came under the appraising eye of the Black Abbot at Cheng-tu. And there was no difficulty in imagining what that individual would do when the truth dawned on him.

Unless Tinker had been slaughtered in the final rush, Blake figured that there was just a chance the lad would have been taken prisoner. His sole aim now, therefore, was to discover what had befallen the junk, and, if she had vanished, to pick up the trail of the gang which had come out with the fall of dusk from Anking, and, through them, the sinister raven who had led them.

ON this side of the bank there was neither sign of town nor even village. Blake knew that for some distance along where the junk had been attacked there was, on the northern bank, a stretch of barren, marshy land, and it was somewhere here he knew he must have landed.

It was when he had been stumbling along for a matter of twenty minutes or so, the sun now uncomfortably hot on his back, but none the less welcome after the dank chill of the night, that he came to a rough zig-zag marking that formed a sort of track.

He kept to this, finding it led him in the direction he wished to go, and yet put him out of sight of any craft passing up or down the river. On the other hand, he wished he could move a little in that direction, and command a sweep of the water right across the dim line of the opposite shore.

Then came the sodden marsh country he had been expecting. It began with a few straggling clumps of reeds, which became steadily thicker and taller, until, when he had covered a matter of what he knew must be at least two miles, he found them well above his head. It was along about here that Blake thought he ought to get a glimpse of the pirate junk or the flotilla, if they still remained on the river.

He made his way through the reeds to the bank, and gazed out over the yellow expanse. He could see two river steamers, one going up, probably, Anking and Hankow, the other headed down in the direction of Nanking. There were half a dozen junks to be seen as well, and here and there was a dot which marked sampan or wupan.

But not the faintest sign of the pirate junk or the mob of craft which had surrounded her!

Blake pushed his way back to the ever-diminishing path. At long intervals it is possible it was made use of by some river "tracker." going up or down stream, but as a regular means of communication it was obvious it had lain forgotten for many years. In the past some effort had perhaps been made to keep back the spreading reeds, but now, as he continued to progress, Blake found them growing denser and denser, and, worst of all, patches of stinking bog moss began to appear.

But there was no other way he could go unless he retreated down river and tried to make Nanking. To go off at right angles inland would, he knew, bring him to some village or town, and that would be too dangerous. Everyone for miles around, on both sides of the river, would know what had taken place the night before, and he did not believe the influence of Kan-tse-fen would extend through this district to the extent that a fugitive from his junk would find protection.

The Black Monk had shown that he wielded a strange power among the people

Moreover, the farther Blake made his way inland the less likely was he to pick up any traces of Tinker, and, eventually, it was more than likely that he would be forced to find some means to get him across to Anking, if his search was to take him that far.

So, despite his growing weakness and the gnawing pangs of thirst and hunger, the lone white man struggled on until, some time after the sun had passed the zenith, he was driven to pause by the absolute refusal of his limbs to carry him longer.

Unmindful of the stinking ooze underfoot, he slumped down on to a little mossy mound, and there he sat as he had crouched during the night, completely worn out, his body and mind in a state of suspended animation.

No toil-broken coolie ever descended into greater depths of exhaustion than did Sexton Blake on that terrible pilgrimage of his through those reeds on the bank of the Yangtse. All he could feel was a dull hatred of the yellow river and everything it meant —a throbbing, dull anger that strove to rise but could not lift itself into action through that utter fatigue.

On that occasion there was burned into Sexton Blake's brain a memory that nothing would ever erase; to the day of his death the nightmare of the Great River would be with him in his waking and sleeping, his standing up and his lying down. It was one of those life experiences that goes to the centre of a man's soul.

By mid-afternoon he had forced himself to rise and stumble on once more. His strength was scarcely enough to carry him through the entangling reeds to the river bank; but at long last he succeeded once more in standing where he could gaze across the swirling, yellow waters. Something seemed to tell him that now he was looking at the spot where the fight had raged the night before; that it was out there his last thread with Tinker had been snapped. What had become of the junk? Where was the lad? And where was Fu-chen-pu?

Weary almost unto surrender, he fumbled back to the track which he had been following. For the next two hours he toiled on and on, seemingly through a purgatory of mephitic marsh that would be his portion for eternity. At times, when his mind soared into fantasy, he found himself wondering if he really did still live in the world of men, or if he had died in the night and this was his allotted progress to some Celestial destination. Then he would think of the junks and other craft he had seen pass, and he knew he still lived in the world of sorrows.

Night found him still fumbling along, almost entirely unconscious now of direction, and without having seen another human being. All that kept him on his feet was the indomitable urge of will. His teeth were clenched like those of a man in the convulsion of lockjaw; his eyes were staring from his head; his mouth was pinched, the lips white; his hands hung loosely from feebly swinging arms; he breathed like one whose lungs are fighting against an overpowering sedative.

Still he lurched and rolled through those giant reeds until darkness enfolded him and strange creatures splashed along to keep him company. No thought now of food or drink; there was no room in his mind for aught but that one supreme urge that he must keep on his feet, must keep going until he beat this forest of evil which was reaching out to drag him down.

But human being did not live who could survive what Blake had been through and then fight through that tangle. Once he went down and stayed down for many minutes; again he was on his feet, only to drop once more. And this time he did not rise.

With hands plunged into the ooze beneath him, he fought with all his remaining strength to get up, but could not. The agony of his effort caused a succession of feeble croaks to burst from his lips; then a great wave of despair swept over him as he hung on the brink of oblivion.

But that, too, departed as he fell forward into a world where was neither light nor sound.

In a Pirate's Keeping.

FU-CHEN-PU was born in a small sampan at the foot of the Tiger's Teeth Gorge at the beginning of the Upper Yangtse —that tortuous gorge which is the first in the perilous passage above Ichang. Almost before he could crawl little Fu could swim, and well it was for him that a callous father had begun by throwing his offspring into the deep, shadowy waters of the pool at the foot of the gorge; for, before he was ten, Fu was taking his part as a boy attending on the river "trackers," where more of his working day was spent half submerged in rushing torrents than on dry land.

The life cannot be equalled anywhere else on earth for its appalling hardships. Thousands upon thousands of coolies break under it at a comparatively early age, and are left to crawl away, maimed wrecks, to exist by begging, or to die where they have fallen, with no hand to lift them up.

Fu-chen-pu survived the life because even at that unformed age he was a fighter. By the time he was fourteen the great Boxer

Rebellion swept over China, and Fu left the river paths to take a hand in the game that promised much looting. It doesn't matter on which side he fought. Half the time he couldn't have told himself. One week he was to be found under the banner of this tuchun, and a little later under the banner of another.

Fu-chen-pu would not have understood if he had been asked the meaning of patriotism or "soul of country." It simply didn't exist for him, any more than for millions of his fellows. But a full belly and free opium were things that he could understand, and he didn't care two rice straws which tuchun was the winner, so long as the looting was good; they were all rogues, anyway, according to Fu's lights — and he was right.

Then he had drifted into the circle which surrounded Kan-tse-wen, who was just then becoming known as a scourge on the Yangtse. Before a year was past Fu was Kan's right-hand man, and in this service he found the ultimate conception of what life could mean to him.

Through all those years Fu had kept himself bodily fit, for on his quickness of eye and strength of arm his life hung every day, and sometimes many times a day. It was, therefore, part of his regular training to take a long swim whenever opportunity offered, and it was said further that every man of Fu's junk could swim, for the simple reason that when a new man joined he was taught the art through the simple process of being heaved overboard tied to the end of a bamboo rope and towed along in the wake of the junk until Fu took it into his head to cut the rope.

If the man had learned how to kick his legs and work his arms by then he survived and was picked up; if he had been too slow he was left to his fate. It was what might be called slightly crude education; but it had the merit of being extremely effective, with the result that one hundred per cent of Fu's crew could swim when occasion demanded.

And never in his life had Fu-chen-pu needed command of the water more than that misty night when he plunged through the smashed window in the poop of the junk and took a header after the helpless lad he had thrown with such apparent callousness into the Yangtse.

He came up some distance away from the spot where he "took water," and then, in a way that would have appeared uncanny to any

European, he began searching for the lad.

His hands gripped something that was struggling feebly so soon as to be amazing. Tinker, who could scarcely keep himself afloat, and was thinking that his last moments had come, yielded to the guttural command of the Celestial. He knew that Fu was doing what he could, and none could realise better than this lad trained by Sexton Blake how a struggling burden could handicap a man in deep water that was rushing with a strong current.

Then Fu-chen-pu set himself to fool any possible pursuers. By the sounds behind him he knew that there would be a-plenty, despite the mist. He could hear that cold, passionless voice of the Black Monk, seemingly very close, for it was held low by the heavy air.

But Fu's mind was working just one jump ahead of those who took the water in pursuit of him. He knew his own people, and he knew how they would come after him. Therefore he went in the opposite direction. They would think that he would give to the current and would struggle shorewards to the nearest bank, that being the northern shore of the river. Instead of this, Fu struck out with his burden towards the other shore, which was over a mile away, and which he had little chance of making under a couple of hours with the drag of the lad to hamper him.

But Fu wasn't intending to make that bank. He paddled along, keeping, as much as possible, breast to current, until he knew that his pursuers must have passed him. Then he turned abruptly and started back towards the northern bank. From time to time he could hear the splash of oars and voices startlingly close, proving that sampans and wupans were searching as well. But the wily Celestial threaded the danger, and, some time later, waded ashore, carrying his burden.

The night which followed was one of almost as much misery to Fu as to Sexton Blake, though the Chinaman was inured to the chills of his own river-cradle, so to say. As for Tinker, all the good that had been done seemed to pass away as fresh convulsions shook him and his temperature began to mount again.

If Fu had any doubts about the beheading of the treacherous physician it was only because he did not have him there then with some of his medicines. But in some miraculous way he managed to get a small fire going, round which he curled Tinker, refusing to take any of the warmth for himself, although the lad pleaded weakly that he should share it.

But his protests died as the fever grew more intense, and from then on Tinker knew nothing of the passage of time until he found Fu lifting his head to place a wooden bowl of appetising broth to his lips. It was chicken and rice!

Where, in the world of wonders, Fu had secured chicken and rice was beyond Tinker's powers to imagine. All he knew was that the sun was high in the sky and that he was lying on a grass bed in a reedy enclosure. He was weak, but the fever had died down and he knew now that while he tossed in delirium, Fu must have carried him to this spot, furnished him with this couch of grass, and then, leaving him, had gone off on some maurading expedition inland.

Nor would the Chinaman touch a morsel of the savoury stew until Tinker had had his fill. But then the pirate drank and chewed greedily, using fingers and lips with equal freedom. He was a big man, and hungry, and needed strengthening food for what the day might bring; but first he had attended to the needs of the honourable friend of Kan-tse-wen. Then Fu produced a gourd of sweet water, which was nectar to Tinker's parched lips.

"You have saved my life again and again, Fu," said the lad in a whisper as the Celestial lowered the gourd. "If I get through this I shall try to show what I mean."

Fu glanced at him as if his words were beyond his understanding. Someone, whether willingly or not, had supplied him with some opium to smoke, and without answering Tinker he applied himself diligently to this. But when the sun was just about overhead he grunted something which the lad could not catch, and, rising, pushed his way out of the screen. Tinker knew that he would have to contain himself in patience until Fu returned, and something told him it would serve no purpose to question the Celestial further about Blake. But he was frantically anxious about his master, and as early evening brought up his temperature he began to see fantastic pictures of Blake in the hands of the enemy, being tortured —pictures that looked so vivid as to bring low cries of pain from his hot, dry lips.

As for Fu, he had started on something which had been holding his mind all day. It was to search for Blake, but not until four o'clock had he dared to appear on the river bank. He knew that not for days would the enemy give up hope of finding him, and that during that time he would need all his ingenuity to avoid them.

But he could not move farther away from the danger zone until he had satisfied himself that the other honourable friend of Kan-tse-wen's was not within his reach. If he did, what answer would he be able to make when his illustrious master questioned him?

And so, while the shadows lengthened into evening, Fu-chen-pu cruised among those stinking marshes, back and forth, back and forth, going over every bit of ground which he thought might be in the certain area he had defined in his mind as covering the spot where Blake might have landed if he had succeeded in making the bank.

Darkness came, and still that shadow glided among the reeds. To him the gloom was no barrier. He had the "river eyes" and could find his way almost as well as in the light of day. Time and again he had touched the edge of the bank, and had caught glimpses of apparently harmless sampans and wupans; but Fu knew those craft were on the lookout for him, and at sight of them he would fade back into the cover of the reeds like a shadow.

Still he persisted, even when the mist came down, and he knew all hunting for him would be over for that night. But at last the realisation that his other charge would be needing him turned his footsteps towards where he had left Tinker.

He was pushing along cautiously where he knew that the morass broadened out into a very dangerous quagmire. And it was when he was sloshing through the worst of the ooze that suddenly he drew up as a succession of low sounds just ahead caught his ear. It sounded like nothing so much as the marsh harrier, except that the marsh harrier would not be abroad at that hour

Fu was not as superstitious as the average run of his countrymen, for he had exploded much of that nonsense to his own advantage time and again; but, nevertheless, he felt slight shivers course up and down his spine as he pushed on to investigate, for one never knew when some of the tales of old might prove true —and the marshes were evil haunts.

And then even his phlegmatic calm was jolted to the extent of a smothered exclamation as he stumbled headlong over something and came down full length. Then the obstacle, whatever it was, stirred under his prostrate form.

IT took Fu-chen-pu only a second or two to discover that the object which stirred beneath him was a human being; and then he knew that he had found "Sek-i-ton Bal-akee." The big Celestial did not find Blake as easy to pick up and shoulder as Tinker; and, despite his inurement to the life of the river and its extremes of climate and topography, he was feeding the effects of the great fight in the "cabin" of the junk and his long hours of caring for Tinker. That rice and chicken which had appeared so mysteriously in the primitive camp had necessitated a journey on foot for Fu-chen-pu of not less than some thirty miles, although Tinker did not know that. Then the long search through the terrible reed swamp for Blake had come on top of the first journey. Fu-chen-pu had taken it all in the way of what was due to his illustrious master, Kan-tse-wen, but his physique had had no such spirit of devotion.

He managed, however, to get the half-unconscious Blake over his shoulders, much as he would have portaged a bag of rice, and then he went stumbling along through the mire.

Some glimmering of what was afoot penetrated to Blake's numbed brain. At first the unsteady, swaying motion caused a feeling of even deeper lassitude to enfold him, but gradually the tiny spark of the determination that had been carrying him on, brightened to a flicker, and then, fanned by the renewed functioning of his will, burst into flame —feeble, it is true, but none the less sufficient for him to realise what was happening.

Blake's first thought was that he had been found by someone of the enemy, and that he was being carted along to a person in authority. That brought a recollection of the Black Monk, and with this he began to struggle. He caught Fu-chen-pu at a moment when the latter was wading through a knee-deep patch of slimy water, and the pair went down together. Blake squirmed free, getting feebly to his knees, prepared to battle desperately for his freedom. But a moment later he heard Fu spitting out mud and Chensi oaths.

The actual presence of Fu acted like a tonic on the detective. It seemed incredible that the pirate could be here with him in the midst of this almost impenetrable swamp; his still sodden senses told him it must be all a figment of some mad delirium into which he had plunged. But those Chensi oaths and the creeping chill of the swamp were too real. He knew it must be fact.

"It is you, Fu?" he gasped at last.

"It is the unworthy one, honourable Sek-i-ton Bal-akee. My honourable master will be angry with this dog of a person when he knows that his honourable friend was left to find a bed in the swamp. These unworthy arms would have carried the honourable one out if the devil of the swamp had not started the honourable one struggling."

Blake laughed from sheer weakness and relief.

"I was a fool not to ask first who you were, Fu. But no matter. What has become of the lad?"

"The honourable young one is safe."

"Thank Heaven for that!" breathed Blake, in English.

(Inactive in the swamp, and sought for by the minions of the Black Monk! Blake's quest for the Golden Book of Buddha is momentarily at a standstill, and it is imperative to push on! Forthcoming chapters will tell of the next startling move the detective, aided by Kan-tse-wen, the chieftain of the pirates, made in his great enterprise. Don't miss a single issue!)

Part 12

First published in the Union Jack magazine, new series, No. 1247; 10 September 1927.

How it all began.

ONE of China's most sacred possessions, "The Golden Bonk of Buddha," is stolen by the Black Abbot of Cheng-tu while on its way up the Yangtse from Canton to the Grand Lama of Tibet. Sexton Blake, having been implored to help trace it is in China with Tinker, both disguised as coolies, for that purpose.

After being hounded by the Black Monk, Blake and Tinker make their way up the Yangtse in a junk belonging to Kan-tse-wen, a notorious river pirate, with whom Blake is friendly. While Tinker is just recovering from a bout of river fever, the boat is attacked by a fleet belonging to the Black Abbot, who is really Prince Wu Ling. He has discovered their whereabouts by television. During the fight Blake falls overboard and is lost in the mist.

Fu-chen-pu, the captain, saves Tinker by leaping with him into the water. They reach the shore, where Fu hides the lad. The worthy Celestial then sets out to find Blake, who has also reached the shore, but has sunk to the ground exhausted. Fu stumbles on Blake, and the two set out to return to Tinker.

Reunion After Strife.

AT Fu-chen-pu's words, Sexton Blake was filled with a sense of relief such as he could hardly have expressed.

That the captain of the junk had been forced to leave his vessel and take to the shore was a providential thing for the detective; and no less providential for Tinker, whom he had managed to bring to safety, helpless as the lad had been.

The period of separation had been one of the acutest anxiety for Blake, and he forgot his own state of weakness and exhaustion in the news that his beloved assistant had emerged through that terrible inferno aboard the raided junk.

"The honourable young one is safe," repeated Fu-chen-pu in the silence that followed his first announcement.

"Near at hand?"

"The place is not far, honourable one, but the way is difficult. This accursed swamp is the playground of the river-devils."

"I can get along on my own legs now, Fu," said Blake, dragging himself stiffly to his feet. "And together we shall make it. I don't believe the swamp devils will worry you much, Fu."

The Celestial grunted.

In his heart of hearts he had very little belief in the devils which formed such a large part in the life of his ignorant countrymen. As has been said, he had often made use of that deep superstition to serve his own purposes. But just now, in this filthy swamp, with darkness and mud about them, his ingrained "feyness"[2] cropped out, and he would not have denied just then the existence of the devils, whatever he would have done in daylight.

But Blake was thinking altogether of Tinker.

"Has the fever left him, Fu?" he went on, as they started forward in single file. "And how have you come ashore? Where is the junk? What was the result of the fight? I got lost among the sampans, and before I knew it was over the side of one into the river. In the fog, I could not find my way back, but I could hear the fight renewed."

In his chirrupy gutturals, Fu-chen-pu related what had happened during the last desperate assault of the forces of the Black Monk on the junk. He told how he and his handful of men had made a last desperate stand on the poop, and that there the realisation of his duty to his illustrious master's friends had sent him below to make his last stroke by the side of the fever-stricken lad; told how he had planned to plunge his sword into Tinker's heart before the enemy should lay hands on him, and then kill himself at the last moment.

"But there was not the time," he said naively. "The accursed dog of a physician would have betrayed us. I saw him creeping to the door to admit the enemy. I used his head as a weapon." (He needed to be no more explicit for Blake to understand what he meant.) "And then I prepared a way of retreat, in case there should be a chance.

"I thought it better that the honourable young one should find death in the river than by the blade. Therefore, honourable Sek-i-ton Bal-akee, I cut the oyster-shell from the window, and upset the table as a shield to the honourable young one. They battered in the door;

---

[2] the quality of being mysterious and strange, or trying to appear like this: ie. With irritating feyness, Jack attributes mystic powers to the legend.

the sword of Fu-chen-pu made many bites before the last.

"Then came the Black Monk, and the unworthy Fu-chen-pu could not prevail. I gave them my blade to the last, and threw the honourable young one into the sacred river. I followed and found him. There was pursuit, but in the fog it was easy to evade them. And so we came to the shore, honourable one. The honourable lad has had another visit of the fever, but he will recover. It is a sorry tale for the unworthy Fu-chen-pu to take to his illustrious master; and he can but spill his blood for the loss of the junk. But until then the duty of Fu-chen-pu lies with the friends of the honourable Kan-tse-wen, so there is nothing more to be said."

Nothing more to be said!

Sexton Blake could read between the lines of this plain tale, which had been told with a complete lack of emotion. He could see Fu standing at bay in that stuffy cabin, keeping off the hordes who were crowding in upon him, while Tinker lay protected by the upturned table. He could see the great sword cutting and slashing as Fu, the mightiest of arm among all the Terror's men, fought his desperate stand.

Then he could visualise how he would secure a few precious moments by hurling his blade full into the faces of those who came at him —precious moments while he lifted his charge and dropped him into the mist-laden waters; could reconstruct from his own experience in the river how Fu must have searched for the helpless lad until he found him, and then, like the wily river-rat he was, had befooled his pursuers until he made the bank in safety.

It was an epic! And now the valiant fellow spoke as if he had utterly failed —as if the only thing left for him was to deliver his charges into the keeping of his master, and then, because he had failed and lost his junk, to take the yellow cord. In that moment Sexton Blake made up his mind that no such traditional end should be that of Fu-chen-pu. The man was a hero, and didn't know it.

The Celestial seemed to know just which way to turn in that heavy blackness that surrounded them. He was in the lead, with Blake keeping a hand grasped to the end of his tunic. On and on, seemingly for ever to Blake, they slumped and splashed their way until they came to firm ground. Then they struck a thick belt of tangled reeds, through which they needed all their combined weight to force a passage. But, at last, they came suddenly into a small open space where, through the mist, Blake could make out a small halo of radiance with a cloudy flame in the centre.

No need is there to dwell on the reunion between Sexton Blake and the lad who had shared so many perils with him. There was even more bond between those two than between elder brother and younger.

Ever since Blake had found the lad, a waif in the streets of London, and taken him under his personal care at Baker Street, so had the lad been growing into clean, fine manhood. Whoever Tinker's parents were they had bequeathed him a splendid legacy of inborn character which could have been developed under no better direction than that of Sexton Blake. Loyalty, affection, courage, complete honesty of word and deed, and an open, clean mind —what better equipment could any lad want on the road to full manhood.

Those qualities were Tinker's, and now, as Blake knelt beside the fever-racked lad, in the midst of that filthy swamp, with the heavy mist of the Yangtse soaking about them, he reproached himself again for having brought the lad into such hardship. Yet not once by word or sign had he shown any sign of flinching. And now he seemed to sense what Blake was thinking, for weakly his voice sounded as he murmured:

"Good old guv'nor! It's great to have you back. And you needn't worry about me; I'm feeling tophole. By the morning I'll be ready to move on."

And a great lump came into Blake's throat as he silently pressed the lad's hand; then, when he had control of himself, answered cheerfully:

"Of course you will, young 'un. You and I and our good friend Fu shall sleep in different surroundings to-morrow night."

His words were prophetic enough, but the conditions under which they were to spend the next night were not exactly as he would have Tinker understand.

The River and the Reeds.

WHILE Blake and Tinker were whispering together, Fu-chen-pu was preparing another savoury mess of the rice and chicken he had produced that morning in such mysterious fashion.

He made no explanation as to how he had come by it; nor did Blake question him. He knew the country well enough to make a pretty shrewd guess, and he was only wondering how far Fu had been forced to penetrate inland before he purloined the food or forced the owner to yield it up. Then, when the lad had fallen asleep again, free, Blake saw with intense relief, of the fever, he laid himself down beside him and sheer weariness of mind and body claimed him.

But not so Fu-chen-pu. For a long time the Celestial sat by the fire, devouring tiny doses of opium and staring with absolutely impassive gaze at the flames, which he had replenished from time to time. What was he thinking of? Were his thoughts of the loss of his precious junk —that big, lumbering craft, the command of which he had won by the sheer weight of his arm? Or was he thinking of his illustrious master, the ruthless pirate, Kan-tse-wen, and of what he would say and how he would look when Fu, his unworthy leader of fighting men, faced him with the confession that he had lost his ship?

To Fu there was only one end —the yellow cord. Until then he would care for the charges who were the friends of his honourable master, and then, when he had said his say, he would ask for brief leave. The honourable Kan-tse-wen would understand, and so would the tiny little creature with the almond eyes who awaited his return. It was she who had put the flowers outside the oyster-shell windows of the ugly junk, those tender blooms which he had sacrificed to the river when he had cut a way of retreat. Was it in that Celestial to feel any stray touch of sentiment? Who could say?

It was almost morning before he rose. He hadn't had a wink of sleep, but among his kind there was nothing very strange in that, for, when under stress, the Celestial can keep going for days without food or rest so long as he keeps stimulating his system with small, carefully graded doses of opium. The effect of the drug when taken in this way is much the same as that of the coca leaves which the native of South America chews to keep himself going over long periods without breaking down from fatigue.

Fu took one look at the sleeping pair; then he made his way through the reeds until he reached the bank of the great river. The mist still lay on the water and over the rice fields; the chill of night was harsh in the air. But through the fog from the east came the faintest suggestion of approaching dawn.

The eyes of the Celestial, accustomed as they were to every little sign of the river —to him a mighty living monster, who must be pandered to, placated —saw the sign. In an hour, he knew, the mist would be burned away and a hot sun would be sweeping up into the heavens. He had work to do before it should get too high.

Turning, he moved along the bank until he came to a small creek that was almost hidden among the reeds. Here he pushed his way among grass and reeds until he came upon a small sampan which he had purloined and hidden the previous day. It was not from Blake and Tinker he had hidden the craft, but from the searchers who would, he knew, still be prowling about.

He was just about to push it into the water, intending to go up the little stream after more food, when suddenly he paused and stared out across the mist-curtained water. From somewhere out there a loud, dull boom had reached his ears. Like a statue he stood, his head turned in that direction, his face like a mask, but for a tiny quivering of the nostrils. He was like a creature of the jungle that scented danger.

Boom!

Again it came, and at the sound, Fu-chen-pu gave vent to a most extraordinary sound. What escaped his lips was a sort of high treble squeal, the throat sound forming the inevitable "aie."

Boom!

For a third time, the sound reached him, and then hard on it came a somewhat lighter medley of sounds.

Fu-chen-pu turned back to the sampan. Gone now was his intention of paddling up the creek. That sound called him in some extraordinary way, and he was answering. Into the water slipped the sampan, and into the sampan sprang Fu-chen-pu; then the paddle was in his hands, and he shot out across the water, disappearing like a ghost into the mist.

THE slanting rays of the morning sun brought Sexton Blake into startled wakefulness. He came up into a sitting posture, his eyes searching wildly about him; for he had been dreaming that he and Tinker and Fu were being attacked by cave tigers. Then his eyes fell on the lad, who still slept quietly, and his face cleared.

Softly Blake got to his feet and looked about for Fu. There was no sign of the Celestial; so, thinking he had probably gone off to scout about, Blake began to push his way through the reeds towards where he knew the river lay. There he laved his face and hands, and, climbing back to the lip of the bank, sat down to see if Fu would come along. But at the end of ten minutes or so he concluded that the

Celestial must have gone in another direction; so, retracing his steps to the little enclosure, he replenished the fire.

Tinker woke while he was doing so, and, seeing Blake busy, sat up.

"Good morning, guv'nor!" he chirruped.

"Hallo, young 'un!" answered Blake, with a smile. "How do you feel this morning?"

"Absolutely all right, guv'nor! I know I haven't a speck of fever left. I guess I'll be a bit wobbly on my pins; but I feel fine —and darned hungry!"

Blake laughed.

"So do I," he confessed. "But since the gallant Fu secured the grub, I think we shall have to wait for his return. However, there is still a mixture in the pot, so I shall put it on against his return."

Tinker yawned.

"He's a good scout, guv'nor. I'll bet he's off now pinching some more grub."

Blake agreed and set himself to place the pot. They talked while Blake tidied up; but as time went on and the odour of the stew tormented their nostrils they both began to wonder what was keeping Fu. Twice Blake made his way to the river, and twice he encircled the enclosure. He saw no signs of Fu; but he did find the little creek, and there he observed the spoor which he thought might have been left by the Celestial.

At the end of an hour and a half they were so nearly famished that Blake doled out a portion each; and then, when they had eaten, he set out on another tour of their immediate surroundings.

But no sign of Fu could he find.

The morning wore on, and by midday Blake began to get anxious. He could only think that Fu had gone off, as on the previous day, to get some supplies, and that he must have run against some of the enemy. A fight may have ensued in which Fu had got the worst of it; or he might have taken to flight in order to lead his pursuers away from the place where his two charges were hidden.

Tinker was getting stronger every hour. By midday he would have got up to try his legs, but Blake would not permit it. They put in another anxious hour; then once more they ate sparingly of the fast diminishing mess of rice and chicken.

Slowly the afternoon wore on. Out in the open it was hot and steaming, and even here, among the reeds, the dank humidity brought on a heavy drowsiness. When Blake saw Tinker's lids growing heavy he made the lad lie back, and almost immediately Tinker had dropped off to sleep.

Blake fought off the lassitude that hung over him, too, and, pushing cautiously through the reeds, made one more trip to the river bank. He could see boats out on the water, but up and down there was no sight of Fu.

He returned to the enclosure and squatted down. The only thing to do was to wait.

If evening did not bring the Chinaman, then he and Tinker must put in another night in their hiding-place; and if Fu was still absent the next morning, then they would have to push on alone. Not for a moment did Blake think that Fu had deserted them. He knew that some prime factor had intervened to keep the Celestial away.

Sitting thus, he half dozed. His back was towards a thick bunch of reeds, which offered some sort of support, and he was facing where Tinker lay. So engrossed was he in his thoughts of Fu that for an hour or more he scarcely moved. During that time the different sounds that reached him from the swamp and the river became intertwined as a regular beat, so to say, with the life of the place. It was for this reason, therefore, that a new sound, very slight at first, impinged upon his senses and caused him to take note of it.

It came as a faint, crackling sound, not unlike flames eating at dry wood; then it would stop, and, after a few moments, begin again.

But if it had been some localised blaze it would have come from the same direction; but this sound moved about. Now it seemed directly behind him, now to the right, and again to the left. Also it grew more persistent, and distinctly nearer to where Blake sat.

He did not turn his head. His mind, however, was functioning acutely, and as each tiny noise came to him he shifted his wits, metaphorically speaking, towards that direction. His lids were lowered, and from under them he was peering as far as focus would allow him in every direction. No born Celestial could have gazed in greater sweep from slanted lids than did Blake just then.

All of a sudden every nerve in his body was on the alert.

A slight, but, to his strained hearing, startlingly-near noise had sounded almost immediately behind him. Still he did not move, but the hands that had been slipped up under the sleeves of his shirt began to come down so slowly that the action was hardly perceptible.

Far round to the right were the pupils of his eyes, peering out from beneath his slanting lids. And thus it was he saw a slight parting of the reeds not a yard from where he was sitting.

Into the long, narrow aperture came a yellow face, from which a pair of sloe-coloured eyes gazed at the one who sat with his back against the thick wall of reeds. Then the gaze went to the sleeping lad; and, at that, the face was withdrawn.

More faint crackling followed, and then a short silence. Still Blake sat motionless, waiting. How many persons might be crawling about the place he couldn't guess. But it was plain now that the enemy had found them out, and that in a few moments at most the rush would come.

Desperation and Renunciation.

SEXTON BLAKE did not move until that reedy clearing, which, until then, had seemed so safe and removed from all other humans, came into sudden howling pandemonium.

One minute the man who looked like a ragged coolie was squatting on his haunches, apparently drowsing, while the lad opposite him slept; the next half a dozen Chinese were rushing at him, swords or knives in their hands and the lust of murder in their eyes.

Blake met the rush barehanded. Before the first one could reach him with the short, thrusting sword, Blake was under the blade. Coming up, he drove in a terrific right that caught the fellow full in the solar plexus. He went down like an ox; and even before his body had hit the ground Blake had snatched the weapon from him and was turning to meet the others.

The clash of steel upon steel rang through space among the reeds. Blake had a small start in his desperate offensive, for the quick downfall of their fellow had held the others in sheer amazement. But as Blake's blade slithered along the side of a cutting sword, splitting the guard and carrying on until the point was two inches into the shoulder of another, the mob came into action once more.

The noise roused Tinker just in time to see Blake's desperate defence. One of the Celestials had already started for the lad, and at the moment when Tinker began to sit up, a long-bladed knife came whistling down. Without a moment's hesitation, Tinker flung himself to one side, his startled eyes widening as the blade plunged to the hilt in the reed ends which had formed his couch.

Before the other could drag the blade out Tinker was in at him. He was still too weak for any orthodox type of fighting, and he knew that if this fellow got a second chance at him he would not miss. Therefore he used the weapons which came handiest. Up came his foot, and in it went to the Chinaman's stomach; with all the power he could put behind it, which wasn't much, considering his weak state. But it served to send the fellow back with a grunt, and before he could recover the handle of the blade was in Tinker's grasp.

The Celestial gave a snarling cry and launched himself forward.

Tinker, backed up against the rattling reeds, threw himself on the defensive, and thrust upwards with the knife. Blade and body met in mid-rush, and the Celestial gave a queer, choking gasp as the impetus of his spring carried him on past the lad and down into the reeds. There he lay, choking.

Blake was being hard pressed. He had disposed of two of his assailants, but the other three had learnt a lesson from the fate of their fellows, and now they were circling round him cautiously, feinting when a chance came, and then leaping in to stab or cut. It was the type of attack which Blake could parry for a time, but he was being kept up to his utmost efforts of eye and arm and nerve, and they were making only intermittent efforts; in time, the strongest man must be worn down.

It was this which Tinker observed as he sprang over the beds of reeds and came towards Blake.

"Keep away!" called Blake, knowing that the lad was far from fit enough for such strenuous work; but Tinker paid no attention. Watching his chance, he rushed in just as one of the Chinks turned to see what was threatening. He kept on circling as Tinker rushed, and his cutting sword cleaved clean through the shoulder of the lad's shirt as it came down. By the veriest fraction of an inch Tinker avoided getting the full force of the blow on the bone. Half an inch, and his arm would have lain on the ground.

Something of all the pain and the danger and travail that he and Blake had gone through seized upon the lad, causing an intense wave of anger to sweep through him. For those few moments he possessed the strength of sheer desperation. His spirit had risen above all physical considerations. And out of the corner of his eye Blake saw with amazement that the lad had gone berserk.

With a snarl like that of a wild beast, Tinker crouched; then he launched himself full at the Celestial, who was even then on the point of recovering. Up came the lad's knife in a violent sweep, his forearm striking the Chink's arm in passing. But the urge behind that blow was such that the pause was scarcely perceptible. The Celestial's arm was knocked to one side, and then the blade went home. The fellow stood goggling at the lad in stupid amazement; then he whirled round and fell prone.

Blake, as if affected by the same fever of desperation, was attacking again with a fury that drove his antagonist back and back. They strove desperately to stem that whirlwind of arm and blade, but Blake gave them no pause. In and out and about them flickered the steel, so fast and with such vicious purpose that they could not follow it. Four of their number were already down, and, with the young one now coming at them in a fury that equalled that of the elder, it looked as if they would get the worst of it.

Some word must have passed from one to the other, for, in a sudden retreat, they turned to run. Blake followed close, for now it looked like a complete rout; and, if possible, he wanted to bag the lot before they should be able to get away and carry news of the hiding-place to him who had sent them.

But just then the two Celestials sprang back, and both Sexton Blake and Tinker followed suit as the reeds were once more thrust aside and fresh numbers burst upon the scene.

AND where was Fu-chen-pu during all that day? What had taken him out upon the fog-laden river? What message had that deep, booming sound brought to his ear?

To Fu-chen-pu it came as the voice of one whom he knew well. Waking or sleeping he would know that sound among all others. High up the river, or down in the lower reaches, he would recognise it as the roar of the master. Had he not fought to its bass music time and again? Had he not seen its fiery breath as it poured forth flame and destruction? From all other pieces of armament he would know it, for was it not the great master cannon which adorned the poop of Kan-tse-wen's own junk —the great piece that had once blazed in grim broadside from a British cruiser?

The pirate chief, Kan-tse-wen himself, was on the river! His own artillery was heralding his presence!

The sound had drifted slow and dull across the heavy air. But the

214

acute ears of Fu-chen-pu had guessed whence it came. Already had word of his lieutenant's defeat been carried to Kan-tse-wen. And now, without waiting for his coming, the Terror of the Yangtse was out on the trail of vengeance. That sound came from the direction of Anking, the nest from which the hordes of the Black Monk had come. At this very moment Kan-tse-wen might be razing the place to the ground. And while this was in progress, he, Fu-chen-pu —he who had lost his junk to those renegade rats, was idling on the other shore of the river.

Out into the mist went the sampan, as hard as Fu could drive her. If Kan-tse-wen were there, then he must find him quickly. He had a confession to make, but he could still take a hand before he sought his master and the yellow cord.

Never before did single-handed sampan cross the Great River at such a rate. Like a giant of fabulous tale did Fu ply his paddle until the yellow water rippled loudly against the sides. The splitting asunder of the morning mist found him approaching his objective. And then, as the last wisps floated away, he could see the water-front of Anking. And, standing out in what seemed to Fu stately fashion, was the great blue-painted fighting junk of Kan-tse-wen.

But no longer was the voice of Moloch breathing o'er the waters. There came to Fu's ears, it is true, the faint sounds of battle as they floated out across the water. But the main assault was over, and the fact that the red and black flag of the Terror flew at the masthead was enough to tell Fu that Kan-tse-wen was master of the situation. His lids lowered just a little as he thought of how the bloodthirsty hordes of the Terror would sweep through Anking. Well, "good hunting, and may they get the Black Monk!" would have been his words had his mind worked as that of an Occidental.

For Fu there would be no glory nor part in this. Now there was left only for him to go on board his illustrious master's junk and meet his fate. Nor did he flinch. Straight towards the great junk he drove the sampan, until he was close in under the high, over-hanging stern. Still he plied his paddle, until the sampan was alongside the low freeboard of the waist.

Then, as the eyes of those of the crew who still remained on board gazed in wonder at the sudden appearance of the man they had been told was dead, Fu put his foot to the sampan, and in one great shove sent it spinning away from the junk.

Thus went his way of retreat; thus did he renounce any will of his own; thus did he declare himself the vassal of his master.

Down the deck he strode until he came to the two guards who stood sentry over the teak stairs that led down to Kan-tse-wen's private quarters. There was not a flicker of their eyes as they gazed upon the mighty Fu, who had been reported dead —gone to the bottom of the river with his junk.

In silence they permitted him to pass. There would be no need to announce him to their august master. He had the entry at all times, and now they believed he was going straight to his doom.

Fu descended the steps without faltering. At the bottom a short passage led to a closed door, where two more guards stood. They permitted him to pass between them and knock, which he did in a way which Kan-tse-wen would recognise as his own.

A voice bade him enter.

Passing over the threshold, Fu-chen-pu stood at last in the presence of the pirate whose name was the Terror of the Yangtse.

Execution Postponed.

THE pirate chieftain, Kan-tse-wen gazed inscrutably at his chieftain, captain of junks.

Fu-chen-pu stood with head bent submissively and eyes on the floor waiting for his august master to speak. It was not for him to use voice until the Terror gave permission. All there remained for him was to make his report and then crave leave to possess himself of the "yellow cord."

The "yellow cord," it may be explained, is, in China, the resort of those who have been overcome by commercial or military disgrace. It is also used, to some extent, by debtors who are too sorely pressed by a creditor, in taking revenge by the simple means of self-strangulation with the cord at the threshold of the creditor's house. No greater disgrace could come upon one than to have a spirit pass out on one's threshold.

It applies in the military sense to the same urge which prompts a noble in Japan to commit hari-kari on the death of his emperor, so it can thus be understood what lay ahead of Fu-chen-pu for the disgrace of losing his junk to the enemy.

Kan-tse-wen was studying him closely. The Terror of the Yangtse was neither Chinaman nor Manchu. He had come from the far north-west, and the first syllable of his name indicated that he had

216

Tartar blood in his veins. As a matter of fact, the hawk-nosed, eagle-eyed pirate looked upon the Chinese and Manchus with supreme contempt. His own genealogy went back to the distant days when Kubla Khan and Genghis Khan rode out of Tartary and plundered half Asia and most of Europe. He could trace direct descent from the savage and all-conquering Genghis Khan, and, in the depths of his heart, he had an ambition to achieve in China some measure of leadership that would make him fit company, when he passed over, for his illustrious ancestor.

Until now, however, he had contented himself with ravaging the basin of the Yangtse in a perfectly impartial manner. All was grist that came to his pirate mill; it didn't matter two straws to him whether the ships he attacked were the property of Northerner, Southerner or foreigner. Kan-tse-wen was too shrewd to build his house on the shifting sands of present-day Chinese intrigue. He could have been "admiral" either in the fleet of Chan-tso-lin or that of Canton. Both sides courted his favour and sought his alliance.

Even the mysterious and mighty Prince Wu Ling, who, it was whispered, sat behind all the baffling maze of intrigue, moving the human pawns on the brown and yellow chessboard of China, did not treat Kan-tse-wen with the supreme disdain which he did to others.

The truth of the matter was that Kan-tse-wen was better equipped in junks and sampans, power boats and wupans, than any of the "official" forces on the Yangtse, and his fleet, together with his well-trained fighting-men, certainly held the balance of power, if he did not, in fact, control the far upper reaches and the lower estuary. Everywhere else he was supreme when he wished to make his power felt.

Therefore, when word was brought to him that a force had had the temerity to put from Anking and attack one of his junks that was proceeding alone up the river —that the attack had ended in the sinking of the junk and the death of his bravest captain, Fu-chen-pu, he had emerged in his anger from his own stronghold of Chancha and swept out across the waters of the sacred river.

Within a few hours the Terror was on the warpath. Anking had dared to do this thing, therefore Anking must be ravaged. A mysterious person called the Black Monk had had the audacity to lead the attacking party, therefore that fellow's head must roll at the feet of Kan-tse-wen.

Aie! But it must pay the price quickly! And the more so because it had been whispered in his ear that the Black Monk was acting on behalf of the Black Abbot of Cheng-tu.

And so Kan-tse-wen had swept down upon Anking while that place still made festival over the victory. There were a few wise souls who knew that a reckoning must come swiftly, and who, anticipating this, had closed their places of business, and with families and portable belongings, had moved out until the vengeance should be over.

The others remained, their belief in the Black Monk and awe of the mysterious power behind him causing them to forget, for the time being, the hawk who soared so close.

Kan-tse-wen swept down upon Anking with a fury that carried all before it. His men went through every obstacle with the Tartar's savage battle-cry, and even while Fu-chen-pu stood submissively before his master were the hordes sweeping through the place, ostensibly in search of the Black Monk —in reality taking toll of the heads for every one of their fellows who had been lost with the junk. It is the pleasant little way they have of doing things in China.

At last Kan-tse-wen spoke.

"I have been expecting you," he said in clipped gutturals that were very different in quality to the slurring tones of the Chinese. "It is not well that the fight should go forward without the presence of my captain of junks."

Fu-chen-pu made no gesture; nor did he lift his eyes.

"August master, thy unworthy servant is unfit to fight again under thy illustrious banner. Thou knowest his crime."

"It is true that your junk has been destroyed?"

"Master, I am guilty. I ask permission to take the yellow cord."

Kan-tse-wen paused and listened to the faint sounds of distant combat. Then he swept the other from head to toe with his gaze. To his experienced eyes it was plain that Fu-chen-pu had been through a good deal since the fight two nights before, and while he gave no hint of it he was curious on one or two points.

"They speak of a Black Monk," he said curtly.

"Aie! Honourable one, it was he!"

"What reason should he have for attacking one of my junks? It is understood that Kan-tse-wen is master of the basin. Hadst thou had a quarrel?"

"Illustrious one, it was on account of thy honourable friends who came under my care."

"Thou speakest in riddles, Fu-chen-pu. What honourable friends dost thou speak of?"

"The honourable Sek-i-ton Bal-akee and a young companion."

The pirate's eyes narrowed a little. This was the first he had heard of the presence on the Yangtse of Sexton Blake and Tinker.

"Thou still speakest in riddles. Tell me all."

Briefly Fu-chen-pu told how he had met Blake in Nanking, and how, when he knew that he sought his illustrious master, he placed his junk at his disposal. He spoke of hearing that, for some reason, there was an intention to attack Kan-tse-wen's junk if it proceeded up the river, and, later, how he knew from Blake that the Black Monk was making every effort to destroy him and Tinker.

Then came his description of the attack on the junk, how Blake had led a sally over the side, and became lost in the river mist which had swept down suddenly, how Blake's party had become separated, and many cut to pieces; of the disappearance of Sexton Blake.

Also, how he, Fu-chen-pu, had made a last stand on the poop and then had fought his way below to carry out the last duty of a host and kill the fever-stricken lad with his own blade rather than have him fall into the hands of the enemy.

Followed his story of his cutting out the oyster-shell window at the back of the cabin with a single stroke of his great sword, and how, at the very last, when the place was a shambles, he had hurled his blade into the foremost of the mob, and had thrown the lad bodily through the window, following himself, and, by luck, finding the lad in the mist before he sank.

Then an equally brief statement of how he had made camp among the reeds after reaching the shore, of how he had found a farm several li inland, where he had obtained food; and, lastly, how he had discovered the honourable Sek-i-ton Bal-akee lying exhausted in the swamp.

"It was while my unworthy feet took me again in search of food, honourable master, that I heard the voice of the gun of the great junk. I knew that thy illustrious face was turned this way and thy honourable anger was bursting over this rotten hole. Therefore, I came at once to make report, and crave permission to take the yellow cord."

(Another stirring instalment next week.)

Part 13

First published in the Union Jack magazine, new series, No. 1248.

How this fine serial began.

ONE of China's most sacred possessions —the Golden Book of Buddha —has been stolen while on its way up the Yangtse River to the Grand Lama of Tibet, and Sexton Blake and Tinker have been asked to go out to China to regain it.

Disguised as coolies they get on the track of the servants of the Black Abbot of Cheng-tu, who has instigated the robbery, and endeavour to discover who and where the Black Abbot is.

After infinite peril the pair succeed in penetrating the blockade of his spies, and eventually reach the Yangtse in an effort to go further up-river and discover the abbot's headquarters. They are aided by a river-pirate called Fu-chen-pu, but, unknown to Blake, the Black Abbot himself —who is in actuality his old enemy, Prince Wu Ling, and the most powerful Manchu in China —has located them by means of television and caused the pirate's junk to be attacked.

Blake and Tinker are aboard, but escape to shore, Tinker being rescued by Fu-chen-pu, who later leaves them in a reedy clearing on the river-bank while he returns to his master after the battle with news of their safety. Kan-tse-wen, the pirate chieftain, hears for the first time that it is his blood-brother, Sexton Blake, whom his junk captain has been befriending, and, though the latter thinks he has done badly in losing his vessel and asks permission to expiate his guilt by suicide by the yellow cord, Kan is privately of another opinion.

The Abbot's Messenger.

KAN-TSE-WEN had listened in silence. The Terror of the Yangtse was no fool; far from it. He was, with the possible exception of Wu Ling, the shrewdest and cunningest plotter along the whole course of the Sacred River. And he knew that he would go many a long day before he found the equal in fighting qualities and trustworthiness that were represented in Fu-chen-pu.

And, while he would not have said nay to any other of his men who demanded the yellow cord if it suited his purpose that they should have it, he knew that what he had heard was a plain tale of real heroism which more than wiped out the "disgrace" of the loss of the junk against overwhelming odds —that, above all, Fu-chen-pu had kept before him the duty he owed to the blood-brother of his illustrious master. And, as to the material loss represented by the junk, could he not hear, even now, the sounds which told him his men were exacting its price over and over again?

"Did my honourable friend, Sek-i-ton Bal-alkee, inform you why he was in China?"

"Nay, Illustrious One."

"How travels he?"

"As one of the lowest, master. I thought him a river tracker in Nanking."

"Then he travels on business of weight," muttered the pirate. "And there have been whispers about the Black Abbot of Cheng-tu — methinks my brother, Sek-i-ton Bal-akee, enters the cave of the tiger. Where hast thou left my honourable friends?"

"They lay asleep, master, when I came away."

"Are they safe?"

"There have been dogs of coolies searching, master, for two days, but this fighting will draw them away."

"Some rats will remain away while the blood flows. And this Black Monk will make his voice heard until his head rolls at my feet. Hark ye, Fu, take a well-armed sampan, and go at once to where my honourable friends are to be found. Bring them to me quickly. We shall speak of the yellow cord again."

When Fu-chen-pu returned to the deck of the great junk he gave no sign of what had passed in the cabin between him and his master. If there were any there who thought he would be disgraced for losing his junk they must have found cause for wonderment when they heard the hoarse bellow of Fu's voice demanding men to arm a sampan.

A score or more sprang to obey; and, with practised eye, Fu selected one of the fastest and longest fighting craft that lay against the side of the junk like a duckling close to the side of a duck.

Within a few minutes the sampan was shooting out across the Yangtse where the hot sun now shone brilliantly. Fu himself was at the steering sweep, directing it with unerring eye towards the little creek from which he had put out some hours before. When he could espy the muddy streak of water that marked its course, he pulled the sweep round a little and gave the sign to ease on the oars. Then the long sampan swept in with beautiful precision until it touched gently against the muddy bank just where Fu had walked that morning.

The pirate himself was the first ashore. Pushing on first by the bank of the main river, and then at right angles through the reeds, he made for the place where he had left Blake and Tinker, followed by the whole gang of men. Even before he came to the little clearing, however, the sounds of conflict reached him, and, with a low, guttural grunt, Fu broke into a lumbering trot.

Thus he plunged upon the scene at the moment when Sexton Blake and Tinker, after their desperate fight, had overcome the six who had crept so stealthily upon them.

One cry came from Fu's throat, and then the place was filled with his men, who made a short, and, to Blake and Tinker, decidedly unpleasant end to the enemy.

WHEN Fu-chen-pu departed from the great junk, the chieftain of the pirates, Kan-tse-wen, sat for a long time, quite motionless, his eyes almost closed, and the fingers of one hand working continuously at two polished walnuts which rested against the palm.

Had one been able to observe the workings of his mind one would have come upon a very complicated mental process.

The main factors which went to the making of these thoughts were Prince Wu Ling, the Black Abbot of Cheng-tu, Sexton Blake, Tinker, Fu-chen-pu, Hsui-fsi (Sir Gordon Saddler), and all the hotch-potch of events that had taken place since the attack on Fu's junk two nights before.

For some time past Kan-tse-wen had suspected —and rightly — that Wu Ling was the Black Abbot of Cheng-tu. For many months the regular sequence of mysterious events which had taken place along the Yangtse had made it plain to the shrewd, observing pirate that a very potent force was at work somewhere in the background.

When whispers of the Black Abbot had begun to fly about, Kan-tse-wen knew that the Resident Abbot of the Monastery of Sublime Ways at Cheng-tu could not be the power in question. It was not reasonable to think that this individual, after years of quiet, devout residence in the great monastery, would suddenly develop into an aggressive political and military schemer whose operations would embrace the whole of China.

Moreover, the cunning Kan-tse-wen knew that the sacred Golden Book of Buddha had disappeared in some mysterious fashion while being taken secretly up the Great River to Tibet.

His mouth had watered at the news of its capture by some unknown schemer; it would have been a wonderful prize to take into his stronghold of Changcha, although even Kan-tse-wen would have been a little careful in his handling of the Sacred Book. For, while he devoted little time to religions observance, he was, if anything, a Buddhist of the following of the Grand Lama at Tibet; and it was well known that if the Grand Lama could get the Golden Book of Buddha back into his possession he would once more assume supreme control of the Buddhists of Asia.

As it was, the ranks were split asunder and Kan-tse-wen had a shrewd idea that the Chuen-to-yan, or High Priest, of the Temple of Eternal Purity in Canton knew more than a little about the present whereabouts of the Golden Book. If he —the High Priest —could once get that priceless relic inside the walls of the temple by the Tiger's Gate in Canton, then Canton would at last become the Mecca and the Rome of all Buddhists, while the Dalai Lama would sink to a subordinate level. And if the Chen-to-yan of the Temple of Eternal Purity were associated with the present mysterious disappearance of the sacred book, then it wasn't hard for one possessing Kan-tse-wen's knowledge of the intrigue going on in China to realise that this individual meant Prince Wu Ling. And so the mysterious Black Abbot of Cheng-tu might be the Manchu himself.

This suspicion was strengthened in Kan-tse-wen's mind by the ubiquity of the Black Monk, of whom he had heard up and down the river for a long time past. This man —or men —must be an agent of the Black Abbot of Cheng-tu, and that meant of Wu Ling. This brought the pirate to the realisation that the attack on his second finest junk may have been instigated by Wu Ling; and, in attacking Anking, he was therefore making a direct stroke at the powerful Manchu himself.

Kan-tse-wen was about the only person in China who would not have been appalled at the prospect of seeking the open enmity of Wu Ling. But Kan-tse-wen had reached the point where he was prepared to pit himself, his ships, and his men against any one or any combination of the schemers along the Yangtse, for the day was fast approaching when he believed that greater power would be his.

But the sudden intrusion of Sexton Blake into this welter of intrigue was a new factor. He knew that Blake could by no conceivable possibility be working in conjunction with Wu Ling. Yet he felt almost certain that only a major problem like the recovery of the Golden Book of Buddha would bring Blake to China, and start him up the Great River in the disguise he had adopted.

Kan-tse-wen began to suspect that in some way Blake was the cause of the attack on his junk —that here again the mysterious Black Monk came into the picture, and that if Blake was bound higher up the river he (Kan-tse-wen) could look for another open move on Wu Ling's part before long. But before the Manchu could strike at him he would make him a present of the head of the Black Monk. That fellow, whoever he might be, should pay for his folly before Kan-tse-wen left Anking. And, as for Sexton Blake, his blood-brother in the Four Lakes Tong —he would deal with that phase of it when Fu-chen-pu brought him and the lad to the junk.

Fu-chen-pu should be allowed to think until then that the yellow cord was to be his portion, but Kan-tse-wen almost allowed his ruthless countenance to break into a smile as he thought how foolish it would be to allow Fu to do anything of the kind. He was his best man, and if he brought Sek-i-ton Bal-akee safely to the junk he should receive promotion —not death.

Thus did Kan-tse-wen settle things quite satisfactorily in his mind while he sat at the table in his cabin rolling and rolling the two walnuts in his hand —those polished walnuts which most of the educated Chinese use thus as an aid to calm reflection.

IT was at just about this point in his meditations that there came a knock at the door, and, in response to the pirate's guttural command, it opened to admit one of his lesser captains. Behind this individual was one of the fighting coolies, bearing a basket.

Kan-tse-wen sat immobile while the captain of junks stepped over the threshold and salaamed deeply. The coolie did not dare enter until he was bid.

"Thou comest with news?" inquired Kan-tse-wen curtly. "Is the work finished?"

"Ho hang, Excellency! It is finished even as thou didst command!"

"And he whose head I commanded thee to bring?"

"The unspeakable object is here, master."

"Bring it to me."

The lao-pan made a gesture to the coolie, who, with eyes lowered so that they should not affront the august face of his master, stepped in with his basket. The lao-pan took it from him, and advanced so that he stood close to Kan-tse-wen. Then he removed the cover, and, gazing down, the pirate saw a head lying inside.

He gave it a cursory glance, as if it were something of only slight interest to him; then he glanced at the lao-pan. "It is he?"

"It is the Black Monk, honourable master. His body is being brought for thee to cast thy honourable gaze upon it."

"The work is well done; place the basket here close to me."

The lao-pan obeyed, and then stood awaiting his master's pleasure.

"Recall the men to the junk," continued the pirate. "See that everything is in readiness to sail. I shall give my word at the moment."

"I go, Excellency."

With that, the Lao-pan and the coolie withdrew, leaving the basket on the floor close to where Kan-tse-wen was sitting. Only once did the pirate allow his gaze to stray towards it, and then his teeth showed in a cruel smile.

"We shall see what thou doest now, unspeakable Manchu," he muttered.

He picked up a brush, and, drawing a tablet towards him made ready to write; but before he could draw the first painting strokes with the brush there came another knock at the door. The lao-pan had returned, and, as soon as Kan-tse-wen gave him permission to speak, said:

"Honourable master, one has just come with a written message for thee."

"He comes from?"

"He names himself ambassador of the illustrious Manchu, Wu Ling."

"Aie!"

Kan-tse-wen's eyes rested on the writing tablet. He had written nothing; but, nevertheless, he pushed it away and carefully dried the brush before speaking again.

"Bring him to my presence," he said at last.

The lao-pan withdrew once more, and some minutes later a very stout Celestial was ushered in. He salaamed as equal to equal when he stood before the pirate; and, on his part, Kan-tse-wen knew the emissary as one San, the most intimate associate of Wu Ling. This confidant could only have come, then, on a matter of prime importance, for only on such an occasion would Wu Ling send him.

Kan-tse-wen rose, and, placing his hands across his "seat of wisdom" (the abdomen), the place in Chinese etiquette which showed highest respect, bowed.

San returned the salutation with due formality, then he strutted slowly forward as the pirate motioned him to a chair. Almost immediately there was another tap at the door, and Kan's personal steward came in, bearing a tray on which were tiny cups of clear, lemon-coloured Souchong tea, with a small pot beside them from which the cups could be replenished —a matter of Chinese custom which was essential to any interchange of conversation.

Not until each had refreshed himself with the beverage did Kan-tse-wen make courteous inquiry as to why the other had come, making offer at the same time of his junk and all his belongings, which, although they were unworthy beyond words, he hoped, his honourable visitor would accept.

It is curious to reflect what an unlooked-for result might have followed if San had accepted what was, of course, not meant to be accepted.

Then Kan-tse-wen waited to see what this emissary from the man had to say, who, he believed, was responsible for the attack on Fu's junk. It was rather curious that he should arrive just as he (Kan) had come to the conclusion that Wu Ling was, without doubt, the same person as the Black Abbot of Cheng-tu, and the very fact that San was here argued that Wu Ling was taking the initiative in some new move. It behoved Kan-tse-wen to carry himself carefully, and none knew it better than the wily pirate.

The fat San smiled benignly; then, with a preliminary opening of flowery compliments, he said:

"I have come from my illustrious master, the august Prince Wu Ling, to pay his honourable respects to the great and mighty Kan-tse-wen, and to communicate my honourable master's words to his honourable ear."

"My unworthy ears are open to receive the words of the incomparably great and honourable Wu Ling," murmured the pirate.

"It has come to the ears of my illustrious master that the great and mighty Kan-tse-wen has suffered the loss of a junk," pursued San. "His Excellency Prince Wu Ling, has knowledge of the vast possessions and wealth of the honourable Kan-tse-wen, but it has reached his ears that unworthy tongues use his august name when speaking of the honourable's Kan-tse-wen's junk.

"Therefore, I, the unworthy San, have been sent by my illustrious master to make an offer to the honourable Kan-tse-wen on his honourable behalf. It is by grace of Buddha that the unworthy San shall speak so that his words may not offend the honourable ears of the illustrious Kan-tse-wen."

When the pirate indicated his willingness to listen, the fat San came, in a roundabout way, to the point.

Boiled down, the gist of what he had come to offer was: A sum of one million silver dollars; five new junks, to be built at Ichang to Kan-tse-wen's plans; fifty new sampans and fifty new wupans, with arms amounting to five hundred modern rifles, ten thousand rounds of ammunition to go with them; and two thousand cutting swords, as a mark of friendship, in return for which he desired very little.

As the catalogue of this munificent offer was unrolled Kan-tse-wen remained as impassive as ever. But he knew that the gifts were fit for an emperor, and he knew that there was something far deeper behind it all than just a desire on Wu Ling's part that he should not believe him guilty of having had any participation in the attack on the junk.

Gradually the two arch-plotters got nearer and nearer the point — Kan-tse-wen being perfectly courteous all the time, and neither accepting nor declining the offer. It took a full hour before the last word came from San; but when it did the pirate knew at last just why he had come.

The statement that it was on account of the junk and as a gesture of friendship was, as he knew, all bunkum. What Wu Ling wanted in return, however, was put by San so slyly that it did not sound much.

He wanted handed over to him the Black Monk who, it was understood, had fallen into Kan's hands. Then there were two coolies in Kan's power who were also desired by Wu Ling.

It was at this point Kan-tse-wen reached down and dragged the basket towards him. With his hand resting on the cover he glanced at San.

"It will give me deep honour to meet the wishes of your illustrious master." he said evenly. "Is the never-to-be-forgotten face of the honourable Black Monk known to your honourable eyes?"

"Aie!"

"Then it is the unworthy gift of Kan-tse-wen!" With that, he flipped off the lid of the basket.

And there, grinning up at him, San saw the head of the Black Monk!

"Sold —at a price!"

IF San was shocked at the sight of the head of the man he had come to rescue he gave no sign.

One look told him that it was indeed that of the Black Monk, and, inwardly, he quailed at Wu Ling's anger when he knew the truth.

Privily, San had been amazed that even the Terror of the Yangtse should have dared to flout Wu Ling as he had been flouting him for some time past, and it was not on his advice that the Manchu had sent such a munificent offer to the pirate.

If San had had his way a vast force would have been sent into Changcha to wipe out the lair of the pirate. But now he realised that Wu Ling had been wiser —that this man in whose presence he sat was not one to be intimidated by a display of force. Shrewd as he was, San had underestimated the power of Kan-tse-wen though Wu Ling had not made that mistake. And now San knew that the other was mocking him, although his regrets that the head was no longer attached to its body were the quintessence of politeness.

San shrugged fatly.

"It is a matter of no moment," he said, in tones that matched the evenness of the pirate's. "The offer of my illustrious master is yet open for the acceptance of the honourable Kan-tse-wen."

The pirate dropped the cover back on the basket, and reached for a handful of watermelon seeds. He munched a few of these meditatively for some minutes. Then, with an oblique glance at San, he said:

"The illustrious Wu Ling asks additionally for the persons of two coolies. Such vermin can be of no interest to one so high. It is true that I have among my men two coolies who might be those desired by his honourable Excellency. It is said that, sometimes, the fan-kai-lo — the foreign devils —find it possible to pass as those of our own distinguished race."

San leaned forward until his stomach pressed against the edge of the table.

The masks were off now; Kan-tse-wen himself had just hinted that he had in his charge two Europeans who were passing as coolies, and it was those two who, above everything else, San had come to buy if he could.

San knew as well as Wu Ling that, on one or two occasions in the past, Sexton Blake and Kan-tse-wen had been in alliance, and that Wu Ling had realised perfectly well before he sent him that Kan-tse-wen might resist an offer of any number of millions to betray Blake.

On the other hand, bribery was a powerful weapon in China — the most powerful generals and governors were susceptible to it, as Wu Ling knew. Then why not Kan-tse-wen?

In the Monastery of Sublime Ways, when, by means of the system of television which had been perfected by early Chinese scientists, Wu Ling had glimpsed Sexton Blake and Tinker, and knew that Kan-tse-wen was extending his protection to them, he had sworn to tear the hearts from both of them. Nor had he altered his oath. But, for the time being, the pirate could wait. He would bribe him, if possible, in order to make quick work of Sexton Blake and his young assistant, but later on he would have a settlement with the pirate himself, and in the finish he would get back far more than the money and ships he was offering now as a bribe.

Thus figured Wu Ling, and against this subtle scheming the agile mind of Kan-tse-wen was working with equal speed and cunning. He had given the hint it was now up to San to lay his cards on the table.

"It is known to his Excellency that there are among those who are gathered about the honourable Kan-tse-wen two such persons," said San cautiously. "For possession of those two persons, alive, his Excellency is still prepared to offer the money, ships, and arms as a token of his honourable friendship. And he bids my unworthy tongue to add that it is his honourable hope that the illustrious Kan-tse-wen will make common cause with him along the whole of the Yangtse — as brother and brother."

Truly a tempting offer —to share equally with Wu Ling the power and loot of the whole Yangtse!

"How would one know which two persons were meant?" asked the pirate after a short pause.

"They will be known to the honourable Kan-tse-wen; there can be no mistake. They have been known in the past as the friends of the honourable Kan-tse-wen."

"There are, known to me, two of the fan-kai-lo who sometimes appear as Chinese coolies," responded the pirate, as if reluctant to make the admission. "I shall meet the words of the illustrious Wu Ling as a brother. Beneath the stain and change in appearance are the two who were once my friends. But they are no longer in the mind of Kan-tse-wen."

San's eyes narrowed the veriest trifle. Was the other referring to Sexton Blake and Tinker? And if so, was he telling the truth when he hinted that he no longer felt friendship for them —that, in effect, he was not disinclined to sell them to Wu Ling at a price? It needed wary treading here, and San knew it.

"The name of the one is Sek-i-ton Bal-akee," he said at last.

Kan-tse-wen smiled innocently.

"The illustrious Wu Ling sees with the eye that loses nothing," he said courteously. "There are indeed two such of the fan-kai-lo in my power. But it is through them that I have lost one of my junks. Through them my most trusted lao-pan was betrayed, and many men went to their death. Therefore has the channel of Kan-tse-wen's friendship been closed. It is well that all the fan-kai-lo should be swept into the sea."

A long silence fell between them.

If Kan-tse-wen could be believed, San realised his mission was promising to be far more successful than he had dared hope. But he would soon know if the pirate were trying to fool him.

"Then the proposals of my honourable master are to receive thy honourable consideration?" he hazarded at last.

"The Black Monk —there is no difference between us if his mouth shall not speak again?"

"None; I can speak for the illustrious Wu Ling. He would have fared the same had he returned. My illustrious master will thank you for saving him the trouble."

"And for these two of the fan-kai-lo who are in my power —your illustrious master will enter into bond to pay me as thou hast said?"

"Even so —I pledge the honourable word of my illustrious master on the great toe and sacred ear of Buddha."

That was an oath that dared not be broken.

"One million silver dollars?" said Kan slowly.

"Aie."

"Five new junks to be built at Ichang?"

"Aie."

"Fifty new sampans and fifty new wupans!"

"Aie."

"Five hundred rifles and ten thousand rounds of ammunition?"

"Aie."

"Two thousand cutting swords?"

"Aie."

"It is an honourable offer, and my unworthy lips would frame an acceptance. But there is one thing more."

"Thou hast but to speak it."

"Two thousand automatic pistols in addition, with ammunition to go with them."

"I answer for the illustrious Wu Ling; they shall be added unto the rest."

"When wilt thou deliver them?"

"The money, the arms, the ammunition, the swords, the sampans, and wupans within ten days; the junks as soon as they can be built."

"Then I accept the generous offer of the illustrious Wu Ling. On one condition."

"My unworthy ears attend."

"It is that these two of the fan-kai-lo should be held for the torture until the unworthy Kan-tse-wen arrives to witness the entertainment. There are reasons why the unworthy Kan-tse-wen would witness the sufferings of the dog Sek-i-ton Bal-akee."

"The condition will be accepted."

"On the oath that cannot be broken?"

"On the oath that cannot be broken."

"Then it remains but to arrange the moment."

And thus it was that San received Kan-tse-wen's promise that in return for the long list of money, ships, arms, swords, and ammunition which he would give, Sexton Blake and Tinker should be handed over to Wu Ling; the only condition made by Kan-tse-wen being that he should witness the torture on the occasion of his visit to Ichang to receive the gifts which had been promised.

The fat San was jubilant for, at last, Wu Ling would have Sexton Blake and Tinker at his entire mercy.

And just when this unholy pact was being concluded, Blake and Tinker, all unaware, of what was happening, were on their way across the river in Fu-chen-pu's sampan.

The Shock of Betrayal.

ALL unsuspecting of the amazing contretemps that was awaiting him and Tinker at Anking, Sexton Blake squatted in the stern of the sampan, gazing ahead towards the water-front of the place which had paid so dearly for its temerity in fathering an attack upon the pirate chieftain, Kan-tse-wen.

Tinker, far fitter in health and spirit than he had been for several days (the scrap among the reeds seemed to have put new life into the youngster), was on his hams beside Blake, listening to the occasional remarks which his master let fall as they swept along under the efficient steering of Fu-chen-pu.

The thought of the next step was in both their minds, and Blake felt that he had some reason for believing that as soon as he got into direct touch with Kan-tse-wen (which was only a matter of minutes now) the pirate, who was his friend as well as his blood brother in the Four Lakes tong, would be of considerable assistance to him in getting him and Tinker past Hankow.

Blake had no intention of asking anything of the pirate which would embroil him openly with any of those who might be watching a chance to catch him napping. Nor would he accept any lavish escort of men or boats in order to get him farther on the perilous journey towards Cheng-tu, which place, he now knew, was their ultimate goal.

Whether they would find the sacred Golden Book of Buddha there when they arrived was a different matter, but the attack on the junk had cleared up many puzzling questions which until now he had not had sufficient time to analyse.

He was hopeful, though, that once he was past Hankow and therefore through the ring of watchers spread across the Yangtse, he would be able to find further means to continue on the journey. A good deal lay with what Kan-tse-wen could do for them, and, certainly, it seemed a big asset just then that they possessed such a powerful friend in the thick of the dangers that surrounded them. It never occurred to Blake for a single moment to doubt that Kan-tse-wen would give them aid and protection. And it was this belief that coloured his words as Tinker questioned him.

"We shall know soon," he was saying in answer to the lad's inquiry as to what he intended doing after Anking. "Kan-tse-wen is there in person; from what Fu-chen-pu has told me I take it the 'Terror' has put his heel very heavily on Anking for daring to destroy one of his junks. Also, Fu intimated that Kan had given orders for the Black Monk to be sought out and his head brought to him as a trophy.

"There is no doubt in my mind now that the Black Monk has been the direct agent of the Black Abbot of Cheng-tu, and something tells me, young 'un, that the Black Abbot of Cheng-tu is our old enemy, Wu Ling. I have gone over in my mind every possible figure who could wield such power in this country, and none answers to the requirements like Wu Ling.

"Sir Gordon Saddler and I suspected in Shanghai that Wu Ling must have had a hand in the raid that carried off the Golden Book of Buddha, and we know that the Chuen-to-yan in Canton is under Wu Ling's control. Moreover, I don't believe that the Black Monk would have dared lead that raid on one of Kan-tse-wen's junks unless he had had the weight of Wu Ling behind him.

"Not even the tuchuns of the surrounding provinces would have dared incur Kan-tse-wen's enmity in that way. And I believe Kan-tse-wen must know that Wu Ling is the power behind it all.

"It shows how far the 'Terror' is prepared to go that he loses no time in raiding Anking and destroying those who attacked him. He must be even more powerful along the Yangtse than when we were here before. I am hopeful, therefore, as I said, that we may benefit materially from our friendship with him. If we had not his aid in view my heart should almost fail me in contemplating how we were to get past Hankow and on to Ichang.

"Even then, there are the mighty gorges to ascend. It is one of the stiffest problems we have ever tackled, young 'un, and the end is still far distant. But we shall go on as long as our strength will carry us."

"Hear, hear, guv'nor," said the lad in low but eager tones. "That's the stuff to give 'em. I've quite a lot of my own to get back before I finish with these Chinks. My aunt! If we could only wipe up that yellow sphinx Wu Ling at the same time, I'd call it the prize case of all."

How little those two —now so hopeful after all they had gone through that this day was to bring them surcease from those terrible privations —dreamed how differently was that day to die from what

234

they thought!

Blake was almost as visibly eager as the lad to get his feet on to the deck of Kan-tse-wen's great junk when the long sampan slid in against the low freeboard. It was Blake's light touch on the lad's arm that held Tinker back, for Blake knew full etiquette must he observed in approaching Kan-tse-wen, despite the fact that they were blood-brothers.

As soon as Fu-chen-pu came over the side he spoke a guttural word to Blake requesting him to wait; then he strode along the deck and disappeared below. Within a few moments, however, he was back again, but in his oblique eyes was no hint of the surprise he had got at finding the fat emissary of Wu Ling sitting in apparent friendliness with his master. He had received orders to bring the two "coolies" to Kan's presence, and he lost no time in doing so.

Then suddenly, as a door was swung open, Sexton Blake and Tinker found themselves facing the notorious pirate. Blake's eyes sought him tranquilly, Tinker's eagerly.

He seemed not a whit altered in appearance since last they had fought shoulder to shoulder with him. The same cold Tartar eyes looked out on the world, the same hawk-like nose gave a predatory expression to the face, which was accentuated by the hard, pointed chin, an unusual facial feature among Celestials. There was a new scar, still red, along his right cheek which hinted at some desperate combat in which it was safe to say his antagonist had paid with his life. But altogether he was the same, and had it not been for the need of etiquette, Sexton Blake would have started forward, hand outstretched in European fashion.

Then, all at once, Blake felt something chill in the level glance which Kan was giving him. He was puzzled. There was no hint of the friendliness he had looked for. Instead, there was menace in it, and its force seemed to tell him to turn his head. He did so at the moment that Tinker must have felt the same urge, for an almost inaudible gasp came from the lad as he saw San sitting in one corner.

San the trusted confidant of Wu Ling! San here after the sacking of Anking! What did it mean?

Slowly Blake's gaze came back to Kan-tse-wen. He had given no hint of recognition as his gaze fell on San, but there was something in the eyes of the other that told him his disguise and Tinker's were no masks to San.

Blake felt the stir of something here that caused him to hold every nerve on the stretch. He dared not give Tinker a sign, but the youngster felt something electric in the atmosphere, and that was enough to warn him.

Kan-tse-wen did not keep them long in doubt. When he spoke it was in the northern dialect of Peking, out of deference, apparently, to San, who was "of the north."

"It has been told to me by my captain of junks, Fu-chen-pu, that thou art the fan-kai-lo known as Sek-i-ton Bal-akee," he said in emotionless tones.

"Aie."

The acknowledgment in the ubiquitous word was all that Blake vouchsafed. If Kan-tse-wen chose to treat him as one who was a stranger to him —chose to forget all the close association of the past, then Sexton Blake would not remind him. But inwardly Blake was sorely puzzled, and a great weight had descended upon his spirit. Instead of finding relief from constant danger and privations they had, seemingly, walked into something that promised even worse. Never before in all his career had Blake been more utterly dumbfounded.

"It has been told to me that in Nanking thou didst seek the aid of my lao-pan, Fu-chen-pu, as due from Kan-tse-wen to Sek-i-ton Bal-akee."

"Aie,"

"Thou didst claim this at a time when, as now, thou art in the appearance and dress of one of this country; thou didst this at a time when powerful persons sought thee."

"Aie."

"In doing so thou didst bring upon my lao-pan the anger of these powerful persons to such an extent that one of my largest junks and many of my fighting men were lost."

"Aie."

"If any relationship in the past made claim between me and thee, art thou satisfied that I have already paid well?"

"Aie."

"And that I am justified in extending it no longer?"

"Aie, if so be thy mood."

"It is the mood that is in my mind."

"Then thou must proceed. Had I known that thou wouldst regard the past in this light I should have sought other means at Nanking. It is well that there should be no falsity. Thou hast named me; this one who sits with thee is well known to me and I to him. He is the trusted one of the Manchu. Why does he sit here?"

"Dost see that basket?"

"Aie."

"Remove the cover."

With a face as impassive as the countenances of the two Celestials, Blake took a step to one side and, bending down, jerked off the lid of the basket. Nor did the slightest change of expression cross his face as he saw the head of the Black Monk grinning with back-drawn lips in the stare of death. He stood aside a little so that Tinker could see also, and then dropped the lid. Here was proof that Kan-tse-wen had kept his word; the head of the Black Monk had paid for his temerity.

"I have seen," he said briefly.

"Thou dost recognise it?"

"Aie."

"Knowest thou that his Excellency Prince Wu Ling didst send this one down the river?" The pirate, gestured towards San.

"It was in my mind."

"For what he did I, Kan-tse-wen, exacted payment. Had the honourable San come in time it would not have been done. But as emissary of the great and honourable Wu Ling he is generous. The matter has been arranged. I have taken the head of one of the honourable Wu Ling's men; I shall pay by giving him two heads."

Blake did not pretend to misunderstand him. It was he and Tinker who were to be offered up in appeasement of Wu Ling's anger in this new and amazing alliance that had been formed between him and Kan-tse-wen. China had given Sexton Blake a good many surprises in the past, but none more shocking than this.

Instinctively he stepped back, and then swiftly he recovered his poise. Confident in the thought that they would find nothing but welcome on Kan-tse-wen's junk, the two had left their weapons in the sampan. Besides, what would they avail here? If they were to be handed over to the mercies of San, to be taken to Wu Ling, they would stand not a chance in a million of getting clear. Before they could get ten yards, even if they did succeed in reaching the deck, they would be overwhelmed. But, even so, they would commit as much damage with their bare hands as lay in them.

Thus, with his mind surging in hurt and amaze and anger, Sexton Blake stood gazing at his professed "friend" — his blood brother. How could one who was this do what Kan-tse-wen was doing? How could he sponsor such betrayal unless he had betrayed his tong and broken the sacred oaths he had taken in it?

It seemed incredible to Blake that he could have heard aright — that these words had come from the lips of Kan-tse-wen, on whom he would have "banked" as surely as on Hong-Lo-Soo in London. He would have believed, had it been possible, that this was all some mad dream born of the mental and physical sufferings through which he and Tinker had passed. But the actual presence of fat, smug San was proof that it was no chimera.

It was true!

"It is then that we are to be handed over to this fat rat?" he said curtly, not attempting to tone down the insult.

"It is the agreement."

"For what you do to me I shall not offer opposition. I had counted on the friendship which I believed to exist. I was a fool to believe in anything in this country. It was the strain of thy Tartar blood that I believed made thee different. But that is past. I ask only that thou shalt spare this lad who followed me, out of love and loyalty. Do unto me what thou wilt —extend the torture which I know must be my portion, but for the sake of the days when my arm didst wield the sword in thy behalf, touch not the lad."

"Thy words are useless. The bargain is made; two heads shall be given for one. But thou art to have a fighting chance. Thou wilt be given a sampan and some portion of food and drink. While the drops of the water-clock may measure a hundred moments, thou and the lad may seek freedom. At the end of that time my men shall start in pursuit; thus do I clear all demands of the past. If thou canst win free, none shall harm thee."

"And this wondrous generosity of thine is to be exhibited — when?"

"Now."

The word was spoken at last.

A Hundred Drips.

FOR one brief moment Sexton Blake was tempted to risk all on a wild, desperate throw. Then he remembered that, were he and Tinker giants, they could not prevail against the overwhelming odds which beset them here.

Kan-tse-wen had said that they were to be given a chance. A gust of savage laughter shook him inwardly. A chance! What would it be —what could it be but the hopeless race of a quarry that was already marked against an encircling foe?

Well, they would take even that sop. In some way a miracle might happen, so that Tinker at least could get clear. For himself it was finished. Here, among these yellow hordes, he had come to the end of his run.

Blake stood with a calm dignity that held San in check. When he had referred to him as a rat the fat Celestial had half risen from his seat; but this was no place for his fat wheezings, as he now realised. Let it stand as the end of his master's old enemy.

Thus, while Kan-tse-wen sent for his ancient water-clock —a most cumbersome piece of primitive workmanship that, incidentally, would have fetched an enormous figure in Bond Street, Tinker had moved a little closer to Blake, and the latter, disregarding the presence of others, had turned his head to whisper a few words of encouragement. Tinker had gathered all that was said; he knew as well as Blake that they were in the cage, and that no matter which way they moved, the wheel would only keep on turning with them, leaving them always in the same spot.

He had heard, too, how Blake had pleaded that he should go free, but never would he have availed himself of the chance had it been given. He had pinned his life to Sexton Blake; he was content to keep on or to pass out with his master, neither sooner nor later. But there was no need now for concealment, so in a savage voice, with his eyes fixed on San, Tinker exclaimed, in English:

"I'd like just one chance to plant my feet in that fat paunch, guv'nor. Then I don't think I should mind so much."

And just because Blake knew nothing worse than Wu Ling had already planned could happen to them, he grunted a consent.

"If you feel like it —go to it, young 'un!"

Neither Kan-tse-wen nor San were aware of this by-play, although both of them spoke a considerable amount of English and understood more. They did not realise, therefore, what was happening until suddenly Tinker made a wild leap across the cabin. Straight towards San he came, and then, while the fat Celestial goggled in surprise at his coming, Tinker left the floor in a jump that had all his young strength behind it.

With beautiful precision he landed with both heels full in San's enormous paunch. His heels, although bare, went in deep, enfolded by heavy creases of flesh. An amazed and indignant grunt was forced from San's lips, and then a terrific crash followed as Celestial and chair went over.

Came a rush of feet as the door was flung open at the noise, and guards made to rescue the pirate's illustrious visitor.

Kan-tse-wen hadn't batted an eye. Through it all he sat, his face utterly emotionless; while Tinker, quite beserk now, did a fandango on San's stomach. Groans and squeals of agony came from the Chinaman, which only ceased when Tinker was forcibly dragged away and back to where Blake stood.

The latter, like Kan-tse-wen, had not moved. He had watched the display knowing full well that nothing of material benefit could be achieved by it, except the depth of satisfaction which Tinker would get from the pain and indignity he was inflicting on that fat, placid schemer.

Then, without more ado, they were hauled out on to the deck, where Fu-chen-pu stood at his side, his eyes fixed astern of the junk as if he would not, or could not, gaze upon this startling treatment being meted out to the mighty Sek-i-ton Bal-akee who had fought so gallantly at his and his master's side in the past.

Into a small sampan which floated alongside the two were thrust. After them was thrown a bag of rice and a keg of water. Following this, Kan himself appeared on deck, followed by two men who carried the ancient water-clock. After him waddled San, both hands pressed against the "seat of wisdom" upon which Tinker had danced.

Advancing to the side, Kan-tse-wen gazed briefly at the bag of rice and the keg of water. Then he gave a sign for the sampan to be pushed off.

"A hundred drips of the water-clock dost thou get," he said so all could hear; "then after thee goes the pursuit in charge of the honourable one who comes from the illustrious Wu Ling."

That was all. The next instant they shot violently out from the side of the junk, and, with a quick word to Tinker, Blake seized one of the sweeps.

It was almost incredible.

An hour before they had rested, momentarily secure in the thought that at last they were coming to a temporary haven; now the two of them were afloat again on the Yangtse in a tiny sampan with less than one hundred drips of the water-clock between them and the howling pursuit of those hordes who but hung on the sign.

Whither could they go? In what direction might they seek safety? Up the river was the wide-flung barrier of the millions who moved at the will of Wu Ling. Behind them and in front was the area over which Kan-tse-wen was supreme. Down the river lay Nanking and Shanghai, the latter a place of safety if they could have reached it. But what hope had they with that yellow net hanging between them and it, already poised to snare them?

There seemed nothing but to go on and on until pursuit overtook them, and then to die as befitted their race and breed.

Tinker was using a smallish sweep on the starboard side as a pull against the drag of the current, while Blake was standing in the stern, sculling and steering at the same time with the long stern-sweep. Thus they shot out from Anking water-front and into the full thrust of the river.

Now the atmosphere was as clear as crystal. Up river and down and across they could see every detail for a great distance. There was no mist which might have given them friendly cover. There was just the blazing stretch of interior China, cut athwart the vast yellow stream.

From the moment of starting Blake had been keeping mechanical count with the swing of his oar. With ominous rapidity the strokes mounted until he found himself passing the ninety mark. Nor did he turn his head until he had measured the hundred. But then his eyes sought the waterfront, and a muttered imprecation escaped him as he saw a full score of fast sampans become detached from the maze of craft along the bund and dart out towards the centre of the river.

The hunt was on!

(Betrayed by his blood-brother, and with a mockery of a chance for freedom! Blake and Tinker cannot —and do not —win clear, but what happens when they are handed over to Wu Ling you shall see next week. The most dramatic and thrilling part of this fine serial is yet to come —so get your copy regularly from now on!)

Part 14.

First published serially in the Union Jack magazine. This part, '14' in issue 1249.

How this fine serial began.

ONE of China's most sacred, possessions —the Golden Book of Buddha —has been stolen while on its way up the Yangtse River to the Grand Lama of Tibet, and Sexton Blake and Tinker have been asked to go out to China to regain it.

Disguised as coolies they get on the track of the servants of the Black Abbot of Cheng-tu, who has instigated the robbery, and endeavour to discover who and where the Black Abbot is.

After infinite peril, the pair succeed in penetrating the blockade of his spies, and eventually reach the Yangtse in an effort to go further up-river and discover the abbot's headquarters. They are aided by a river-pirate called Fu-chen-pu, but, unknown to Blake, the Black Abbot himself —who is in actuality his old enemy, Prince Wu Ling, and the most powerful Manchu in China —has located them by means of television and caused the pirate's junk to be attacked.

Blake falls into the water and reaches the river bank separately from Tinker who is rescued by Fu-chen-pu, who hides him ashore while he searches for Blake. The pair are once more re-united, and heralded by Fu, make their way to Kan-tse-wen's (Fu's pirate chief and Blake's friend) junk. On confronting his "friend," however, Blake and Tinker are dismayed to find that Kan has betrayed them to one San, an emissary of Wu Ling's, for gifts of ships and arms. They are to be given a "sporting chance," and are sent off alone in a small sampan to be hunted by San and his yellow hordes.

Blake's Fighting Stand.

"STEADY on, young 'un!"

The words came quietly enough from Blake as he dragged in the long sweep and stepped into the body of the sampan.

Tinker who, up to now, had not gazed behind, turned his head a little and looked at the fleet racing after them. He grinned savagely.

"The rats smell the cheese, guv'nor," he said, as he continued to pull slowly. "What shall we do —hang here or keep on?"

"Hold her steady against the current, my lad; I shall get together these small oars —there isn't anything else that looks like a weapon. Then we shall wait for them."

"Right you are, guv'nor!"

Sexton Blake's eyes grew suddenly very sombre as he looked down upon the lad's bowed head.

What he was thinking of Tinker he would never be able to put into words and, even at the last, there would be nothing more pass between them than a hand-clasp and a few unemotional words. But in his heart Blake was suffering acutely that the lad should have come to this ending with him. For himself he had known years ago, when he first took up the profession that had called him, some such finish might be his fate. In every part of the world there were enemies among criminals and schemers who would have gone to any lengths to encompass the death of the man who had hunted them down. But he had never counted on the lad being a part of such annihilation.

Tinker's courage was sublime. Not a single whimper had come from him, even unconsciously when the fever racked him. He had taken it all with a grin as part of the day's work. And now, with yellow death but a stone's throw away, he could grin, too.

Blake gathered together the few shafts of wood that lay in the bottom of the sampan. He placed these so that they were ready to the hand. Then, bending down, he put his hand on the lad's shoulder.

"That's enough, young 'un! Let her ride as she is. Give me your hand."

Tinker pulled in his oar and laid it ready; then he stood up, and his eyes were perfectly clear and steady as he put out his hand and gripped Blake's.

"It —looks —like —the—finish," Blake said slowly. "I'm sorry, young un!"

"I'd rather be here than anywhere, guv'nor —honest!" jerked the lad. "And if we've got to meet our finish in this way I'll guarantee we smash a few skulls before they get us. I've had one good chance at that fat porpoise, San; I'd like just one hefty crack at Kan-tse-wen — the darned old traitor, to sell us out!"

"I don't understand him, Tinker. I would have staked everything on Kan-tse-wen. Even now it is difficult for me to believe that he has done this thing —but here comes the evidence. Now to your weapon, my lad; you keep just where you are —I'll take the stern."

Each grabbed his oar firmly and took stance. By now the foremost of the sampans were within twenty yards, and, standing up in one of them was San the corpulent. Instead of coming straight on, the boats swept round in a closing circle, and, when he knew they must hear each word, San called out.

"It is impossible for you to escape," he stuttered in English, "We must overcome your efforts. It will be well for you to surrender now; it will be remembered in your favour."

"If you intend to take us you had better get started," answered Blake curtly. "We shall defend ourselves to the last. That is my last word."

San attempted to parley further, but Blake was mute, so at last the signal was given. Then, with one accord, the sampans came racing in towards the craft that floated idly on the current.

There was no definite plan of attack.

It seemed sheer confusion of effort in one mad scramble to reach the sampan. Blake and Tinker stood motionless, waiting. Each knew that a blow wasted would be one of which there would be no second chance. Neither had even a faint hope that they could prevail against such overwhelming odds. But man and youth were determined to keep on his feet until the last.

It was Blake who got in the first blow. One of the sampans had swept in close to them, and, unaware that the two on the defence were other than two stray fan-kai-los whom Kan-tse-wen had set adrift for the sole purpose of providing a "hunt" for his quest, the fellow thought they would be "easy meat."

His self-confidence cost him a cracked skull as Blake's oar came round, swiftly catching him just over the ear. The impact was audible even above the rush of water and voices. And the force of the blow sent the Chink plunging into the river.

None paid him any attention. What was a mere coolie more or less? Like rats whose appetites have been whetted by a taste of what is to come, the gang surged in upon the two defenders.

Tinker got in second blow with a heavy downward sweep of his oar that sent a man prone into the bottom of a junk. And then a human wave came at them from every side.

The pandemonium was of the sort that accompanies every effort among the Chinese. Squeals and yells, grunts and groans —every bestial voice was clamant.

The two who formed the centre of the maelstrom fought like madmen. To right and left and up and down their oars went crashing, finding a human head or limb almost every time.

By sheer force of desperation and precision of effort, they kept a circle cleared about them until San, who had remained discreetly in the background, grew frantically impatient.

Above the melee his voice could be heard offering ten thousand "cash" to the man who should bring down the big fan-kai-lo —foreign devil —and another five thousand cash to him who should subdue the lesser.

All this time, Blake had been wondering why no swords or knives had been displayed. The attacking party had come upon them with only long bamboo fighting staves —the sort of "*lathis*" that are used in India. One of those staves was quite enough to split a man's skull, but if it had been intended to butcher them out of hand, as Blake had thought might be the intention, then swords would have been shown. But now, as he heard San's voice above the tumult, he realised that it was not their severed heads that were to be presented to Wu Ling, but their living bodies so that the Manchu might work his will in the torture.

Better to die then and there, than to go to the torturers. Compared to the Chinese system of exquisite torture, the methods of the ever notorious Inquisition of old Spain were insipid.

It was this that turned Sexton Blake into a sudden human bomb. Up to then he had been fighting with the determination born of despair —the will to hold off death until he had added up the cost to those who assailed him. But now he was seeking death —a very, different thing.

The amazing change in him was such that those who immediately surrounded him fell back in amaze. Like some legendary superman, Blake fell upon them, using his oar as those Celestials had never dreamed such an unwieldy thing could be wielded.

Nor did Blake know that, on the high poop of his great fighting junk, Kan-tse-wen watched the progress of the battle through a pair of very modern prism glasses. He saw this sudden upheaval of the mob just when it had appeared to him that the two central figures were going down; his oblique eyes would have shown an odd gleam if one could have seen them just then.

But Blake and Tinker were, of course, ignorant of that keen

regard as they battled in the midst of that yellow surge. The first break came when the lad was driven down by a combined onslaught of seven of the brutes, who came over each low side of the sampan. Blake, in the stern, saw the danger and made a desperate effort to reach the lad's side. But another press shut him off, and he gave a groan as he saw the lad go down, his oar wrenched from his grasp, but hands and feet going as the mob of Celestials bore him under.

Blake charged. He drove the gang ahead of him until he was in the midst of a confusion which seemed to have no end and no beginning. It was a scramble in which a maze of arms and wooden staves sought Blake from every side. He was lifted, literally, from his feet and carried back and forth like a chip on the stream.

Then a jabbing "lathi" caught him a violent thrust in the ribs just under the heart. He staggered. This first sign of weakness was seen at once by San, who broke into a fresh torrent of screams to egg his men on. They responded with answering squeals, and Blake, almost fainting from the violence of the blow, could do nothing but hold his stave on guard in an attempt to keep them away until he could come into action again.

He had lost sight of Tinker. The gang amidships seemed to be crawling about like frenzied eels in a dish. Somewhere at the bottom was the lad, and, with swimming senses, Blake made one more desperate effort to reach him.

The flash of his gathered strength carried him through once more, and there he stood, beating with his oar upon the heads of those who hid the lad from him. Again and again that stave descended, taking its toll each time until, from the outside of the ring that surrounded him, a heavy lathi reached its mark.

From somewhere it descended, the round shaft of wood catching Blake full on the crown of the skull. He rocked on his feet like a tree that has been hewn through the trunk, then he toppled over.

The next second his body was blotted from view as the yellow men poured over him.

A Visit in State.

ICHANG was clad in full gala dress.

Not since last New Year's festival, which had lasted for three days, had Ichang been decked out in such flaunting colours as now; nor would she exceed this even at the coming New Year, which was

246

due again in a little over two months.

The occasion was one which called for no settling of debts, as must accompany the end of the Chinese year. Rather was it a "free show," in which every man and woman and child in all Ichang could demand what he would of food and drink in any of the bazaars without need of payment.

Among the lower castes it was not exactly understood why this bounty had descended upon them. There were rumours that it had come from the inexhaustible coffers of the illustrious Prince Wu Ling, and that the great Manchu himself was to be present on a certain day. It was said, too, that the dread pirate, Kan-tse-wen, the "Terror of the Yangtse," would also be on the scene, and that a vast concourse of craft of all kinds would be in attendance.

Somehow or other, the Black Abbot of Cheng-tu was spoken of also, and it was whispered that a new and powerful alliance was to be proclaimed between Wu Ling and Kan-tse-wen. At any rate, this was the word that came down from the mandarins, and from them, too, came the thousands of strings of "cash" which were distributed among the bazaar dealers so that the people might eat and drink without stint. And no one in all the long period of China's history had ever heard of a mandarin or tuchun providing actual money for the entertainment of the common people. A tuchun might give a feast on first assuming office, and prisoners might be released, but this widespread scattering of actual copper "cash" was a thing unheard of.

News of the coming gala spread like wildfire throughout the countryside. From every quarter people began to pour in —from the rice and poppy fields to the north; from across the river to the south; and even down through the chain of tortuous gorges above Ichang they came in their thousands.

But it mattered not that the population of Ichang was doubled and even trebled. The strings of "cash" kept coming from the mandarins as if there were an inexhaustible store. The whole place was a-tremble with crimson paper streamers on which were emblazoned verses and good-luck slogans in gilt letters. The whole place, even on the river front, seemed alive with colour and movement. During every minute of the day and night there sounded on every side the explosion of firecrackers to keep away the hostile spirits and encourage the presence of the spirits of beneficent mood.

Then, as the day approached nearer, certain things that had been mere rumours crystallised into definite statements, which found their way on to great red posters that were placarded outside the large hongs. It was stated, said those who could read, that the illustrious Prince Wu Ling, who, although of the Manchu blood royal, was the one who would eventually drive the hated fan-kai-lo (foreigner) out of China, was coming to Ichang on such and such a day, that every omen was favourable, and that the dread pirate, Kan-tse-wen, would also be there.

So the gossip was true!

It was said further in the posters that Kan-tse-wen would arrive with such a flotilla as had never before been seen on the Yangtse, and that after the ceremonies a formal declaration of alliance between Wu Ling and Kan-tse-wen would be made, that the "Terror of the Yangtse" would then depart down the river with Wu Ling's flag beside his own, and that he would sweep the whole of the Sacred River clear of the fan-kai-lo. It was to be the beginning of a vast military, naval, and religious upheaval, of which Ichang had been chosen as the centre.

During those days of gala, food and drink, and all that one desired, would be free. No coolies would need to toil; only the shops in the bazaars would be open, where every person could demand and would receive.

Nor was that all. During the festivities there would be gambling, and famous masked play-actors would perform; there would be combats and races; and, it was whispered, a great thrill was to come in the torturing of two of the hated fan-kai-lo, who were being brought specially for the purpose of entertainment.

This was to be no common mob violence. It was to be much different. It came from the mandarins themselves that the victims would be submitted for one hour by the water-clock to each of the one hundred and thirty-six different forms of torture in the first category —an hundred and thirty-six hours without cessation of exquisite torture —and at the end they were to be immersed in ground-nut oil, which was to be heated slowly to the boiling point.

What more, as a perfect climax to such a prodigal festival, could any Celestial want?

Excitement grew apace as the day approached. Gradually the water-front became a veritable throng of sampans and wupans and junks. All traffic up the gorges ceased. Everything bound up the river halted at Ichang. No lao-pan could get his men to proceed past that point until the gala was over. And every craft coming down found ample excuse to tarry at Ichang on the same pretence.

In this instance Dame Rumour was no lying jade. On the contrary, gossip did not do justice by half to the great sight which greeted the thousands upon thousands on a clear afternoon when Prince Wu Ling arrived off the waterfront in his great blue-and-white State barge.

As an escort there were a score of junks, gaily bedecked with flags and crimson paper streamers, power boats, river steamers, sampans, and wupans. It was one of the most impressive spectacles Ichang had ever gazed upon, and further excitement was created when a vast array of new sampans and wupans came sweeping up, in perfect formation. These, it was announced, were to be Wu Ling's gift, among other wonderful things, to his friend and ally, Kan-tse-wen.

Scarcely had the excitement run the length of the water-front when an even more imposing spectacle came into view. It was the arrival of Kan-tse-wen —the "Terror of the Yangtse" —and many a Celestial felt a shiver course down his spine as he saw the mighty array of the ruthless pirate who ruled the middle and lower river.

He came in a state that was greater by far than that displayed by the powerful Manchu; but the latter had deliberately arranged that this should be so, in compliment to his new ally.

In the very centre of the array that came up slowly against the westering sun was Kan-tse-wen's great fighting junk, pennants and crimson streamers flying from every point. About her, moving in stately fashion, were fifty-nine lesser-junks, in similar gala dress, but each one a complete fighting unit. Then came small, narrow power craft, and such an array of armed sampans and wupans that the eye was dazzled. If Wu Ling had come with a fleet, Kan-tse-wen had appeared in an armada!

Cannons boomed, rifles spat on every side, and prolonged huzzahs swept over Ichang again and again. All sorts of wild rumours were afloat. These combined fleets, it was said, were to sweep down the Yangtse, even to Shanghai, and without more ado the hated fan-kai-lo were to be swept into the Yellow Sea. Among those ignorant masses, it seemed that all the other nations of the world could never assemble such a powerful display, and in the fever of the moment hysteria seized upon the great mass.

Not for them was participation in the formal visit paid by Wu Ling to Kan-tse-wen, and the return courtesy an hour later of Kan-tse-wen. Ashore the white rice spirit was flowing freely, the temples were in gala dress, the beggars were reaping an harvest, and the bazaars buzzed with an excited murmur that rose slowly to a crescendo, which was to be sustained until the affair was over. Three days had been named as the duration of the gala; but if it were true that two of the hated fan-kai-lo were to be given the whole catalogue of one hundred and thirty-six varieties of torture, it surely must last longer.

As for Kan-tse-wen, he had kept his rendezvous to the minute. Back at Anking, before San departed up the river with his two prisoners, it had been arranged that on a certain day and at a certain hour, Kan-tse-wen would arrive at Ichang to meet Wu Ling, and confirm with him there a treaty of alliance. The terms hinted at by San had been received with every sign of favour by Kan-tse-wen, and from that moment Changcha, the pirate stronghold, had buzzed like a beehive in preparation for the event.

Never before, not even on his greatest raiding expedition, had Kan-tse-wen travelled in such display of magnificence and force. He had sent a gaily-decorated power-boat on ahead, with a letter to Wu Ling, worded in flowery phrases and deprecating the state in which he was coming. He begged the illustrious prince to overlook the unworthy assembly of craft which was all his poor resources would allow him to gather about him, but it was his humble and unworthy desire to meet with the august approval of the prince, if such be his pleasure.

What Wu Ling thought of this "poor and unworthy" assembly as the mighty armada of armed craft came in slowly was not known even to San. The Manchu, clad in full regalia of saffron silk tunic and purple trousers, the great clasp of yellow topaz, which was the mark of his rank in the Brotherhood of the Yellow Beetle, fastening his tunic, was gazing at the approaching armada from the private saloon in the stern of his State barge.

If he had ever wondered just what display of force Kan-tse-wen could produce at a pinch he knew now, for not even he could have placed such a fleet on the Yangtse at such short notice. He realised that San's diplomacy had indeed been a good thing, if it had such a powerful ally as Kan-tse-wen in the cause which he dominated.

For all that, Wu Ling had been puzzled at the entire success with which San had carried out his mission.

Ever since his return from Anking, Wu Ling had been trying to probe the mystery that lay behind Kan-tse-wen's surrender of Sexton Blake and Tinker. The fact that, immediately before San arrived on the scene, Kan-tse-wen had flouted him —Wu Ling —openly, he had sacked Anking and had taken the head of the Black Monk, who was Wu Ling's creature.

The Manchu did not doubt for a moment that the pirate had been fully aware of this before he struck, and then he had accepted the offer which San had made.

Was he, after all, susceptible to bribery? Was it just that, and did he feel the anger he professed towards Sexton Blake for having been the cause of one of his lao-pans losing a junk?

Try as he would, Wu Ling could find no flaw in the tactics of Kan-tse-wen. He had carried out his agreement to the letter. He had given Sexton Blake and Tinker a brief respite, which was natural in Chinese etiquette, since, technically, they were his guests. But he had not allowed them to get so far that he could not overtake them easily, and then his men, in fact, had overwhelmed them.

Followed their surrender to San, and during the next three days they would undergo such tortures as they had never visualised in their wildest dreams.

There would be for Ichang a spectacle that would be remembered for three generations to come. The name of Wu Ling would be whispered over the whole vast extent of China in even greater dread than before, and this pirate, Kan-tse-wen, should be his ally on the river for as long as he behaved himself. For the present, therefore, he, Wu Ling, would extend to Kan-tse-wen every possible courtesy which one of his exalted rank would show to an equal.

Thus mused Wu Ling, while Kan-tse-wen, clad in full fighting dress, stood on the high poop of the "flag" junk, watching the medley of craft keeping pace with his vessel as the whole fleet sailed slowly in to the anchorage.

And down in a vile black hole in Wu Ling's state barge were two haggard wretches, chained at wrists and ankles, sacrifices to be offered on the altar of Wu Ling's savage hatred, those two who were, in fact, the centre round which this whole barbaric display was centred.

The Feast and the Fan-kai-los.

WHILE the common rag-tag and bobtail of Ichang might feast and drink throughout the bazaars, the great event of that first evening of the festivities, from the point of view of the mandarins and other high officials, was the grand banquet which was to be given by Kan-tse-wen on his great fighting junk in honour of Prince Wu Ling. There were few of them who had ever laid eyes on either the Manchu or the "Terror," although each one had, at some time or other, felt the weight of their power. As a third factor, which had made itself felt with persistence, there was the mysterious Black Abbot of Cheng-tu, about whom so many strange things had been whispered; but during that day the rumour spread through the bazaars with a speed that hinted at an inspired force that Wu Ling was none other than the Black Abbot.

If that were so, then it meant that all power which mattered on the Yangtse was gathered there that day, and for once Ichang felt that it was indeed blessed and safe.

Ordinarily, Kan-tse-wen's fighting junk would not have accommodated all the notables who were to sit at the board that night. But before sailing up the Yangtse the pirate had had several bulkheads removed, so that now, from his private saloon, the whole interior of the junk was opened up right along forward, giving ample room for seating a full hundred and thirty-six guests.

Strange that Kan-tse-wen should fix on the same number to meet at his board as there were variations of torture in the first-class —the number which was the magic word in Ichang just then. It may have been pure chance, or it may have been a subtle compliment to Wu Ling. But who might read the workings of a mind that was part Tartar and part Celestial?

Not even Wu Ling's great state barge was more brilliantly illuminated and decorated than the fighting junk. It seemed that Kan-tse-wen must have had a rare collection of silks and tapestries at Changcha, or else he must have combed a score of bazaars between that place and Nanking to produce such a wondrous display. The junk's interior was literally swathed in the finest silks that the many silk-producing centres of China could loom; and the lanterns on deck, hand painted on thin silks of every conceivable colour except white, made the scene one of fairyland as the glow was reflected from the water.

Nor was this lavish display confined to the "flag" junk. Every other craft that had accompanied Kan-tse-wen made a brave show, too, even to the tiniest sampans and wupans, and, from the shore, it was a scene that could only be produced in the heart of China.

In deference to his host of the evening, Wu Ling's fleet showed only a few yellow and red lights. His illumination would come the following night, when he returned the compliment and gave another great banquet. But his dress for the evening was the full regalia of a Manchu royal prince, and his private launch was awninged with nothing but flowers twined in profusion about a thin bamboo frame that had been erected over the body of the launch. He was accompanied by only one intimate, San, who had carried out his ambassadorial mission with such distinction and success.

And thus, with the crew of the launch in full state livery, was Wu Ling borne across the waters of the Sacred River to the blaze of coloured lights which marked the spot where Kan-tse-wen waited to welcome him.

Wu Ling was received with the most complete Chinese formality as he stepped on to the deck. Kan-tse-wen did not wear the royal saffron, but he was dressed in deep crimson brocade edged with gold and green and kingfisher blue that all but covered the loose grey silk trousers that ballooned to his richly-embroidered slippers. From under his tunic hung a short cutting sword —a mere toy it looked, although the pirate could have told that blade was three hundred years old, and of the finest steel that could be forged. The hilt was a mass of great diamonds, rubies, sapphires, and pearls that would have brought a fortune even in the values of the West, had he cared to dig them out and sell them.

It was, in effect, a formal Chinese scene such as has become rare indeed since the downfall of the imperial family at Peking. Each of the leading figures had plenty of wealth to indulge his taste for pomp and display, and it is little wonder that the people at Ichang buzzed long and loud over the affair, which seemed to indicate that the old days of plenty had returned.

Let it not be thought that the general run of the Chinese welcome the ravaging of the country which has been indulged in during these last fifteen years or so; on the contrary, they would give much to return to the "sad old, bad old days of the Dowager Empress."

Hard on Wu Ling's heels came the mandarins. Their boats and barges had been waiting off in the shadow, until the guest of honour should choose to take his august presence to the junk; then they came on, one at a time, in strict order of precedence —a matter that had been settled through hours of polite and complimentary wrangling over the past few days.

To each the dread pirate gave the exact meed of courtesy which his position demanded. And, one by one, they were ushered along the deck and down to the saloon by Fu-chen-pu, who was now magnificent as Chief Lao-pan in blue and purple. He wore, too, the cap of a mandarin of the purple button, for upon Fu-chen-pu would fall the duty of conversing with those who ranked lower than the chief guest of the evening. Once Kan-tse-wen and Wu Ling took their seats, the pirate must confine his whole attention to the prince.

At last Kan-tse-wen and Wu Ling entered in solemn procession. There followed a general rising and deep obeisances while the two powerful Celestials moved to the head of the great table, where two big teakwood arm-chairs had been placed on a low dais. It was not meant that they should sit on the same level with ordinary mandarins.

Then began one of those forty-course Chinese banquets which are the amaze and despair of the Westerner. It was all there —chop suey and sen-ke, rice and chillies and birds' nests, bamboo shoots and watermelon seeds, fish, chicken, and eggs in a dozen different forms, cakes and sticky soya nougat, pork and something that might have been well-fed vermin —and heaven knows what else. And strong, white rice liquor that was drunk like water.

It was something that could only be in China, and for three solid hours those fat mandarins would sit and guzzle food and drink until one would think their skins must burst.

So it went through, course after course —if it could be said that there was any such actual divisions in the service. Not even Wu Ling could lay a more lavish spread than that. Nor was it confined to the one hundred and thirty-six guests on the flag junk. Throughout the whole fleet there was feasting and drinking without stint; and from a purely money point of view, it must have cost Kan-tse-wen a good many thousands of silver dollars.

It was not until the end of the meal had come at last, and the guests were munching watermelon seeds and drinking heavily of the white rice spirit, that Kan-tse-wen broached a subject that had some bearing on his visit to Ichang. This was the two fan-kai-los —foreign devils —whom he had handed over to San at Anking, and whose torture was to be such a prominent feature of the festivities. They had been kept, in fact, as agreed, so that the pirate might have the pleasure of witnessing the spectacle. And it was just because Wu Ling had also been waiting for this moment to come, that he had made but one visit to the prisoners during the days they had been in his power.

That visit had been brief. The Manchu had stood before Sexton Blake and Tinker, his cold eyes gazing at them as if they were nothing but interesting specimens of insects. But his words, though brief, had revealed what was filling his mind and heart.

"At last, Sexton Blake, at last!" was all he said.

Then he had left them, and from that moment Blake and Tinker had known nothing but the foul den into which they had been thrown. Had seen no one but the man who came each day with a small portion of rice and water. Had felt no couch but the hard boards over which the rats coursed in hundreds. Had felt the ease of no pillow but the links of the chains which manacled them.

And now, when every guest was replete, did Kan-tse-wen speak of the prisoners. He prefaced his remarks with many flowery phrases and deeply-expressed regrets that the Black Monk had lost his head. Then he made polite inquiry as to when the torture would begin.

"It is my poor wish that thou shalt set the time, honourable friend and ally," responded Wu Ling. "The victims are kept safely on my barge; no hand has been laid on them. It is for thee that the spectacle waits."

"Aie. It is long since mine eyes have gazed upon the writhings of a fan-kai-lo," responded Kan-tse-wen. "If the illustrious one would condescend to such an unworthy plea, my poor gaze would once more fall upon those vile devils. It is my unworthy thought that some measure of amusement might follow if the dogs were produced before us. Then let the torture begin. They are tough, Excellency; they may last a long time."

"Even so, honourable friend. It shall be as thou desirest. But first, my mind, which is poor and works slowly, would know why thou has turned with such hatred upon the dogs who once sought thy honourable hospitality. "

Kan-tse-wen was gazing down the table at Fu-chen-pu as he listened to the words. They were casual and polite, but they told the pirate that Wu Ling was curious to know why he had abandoned Sexton Blake, who was his blood-brother in the Four Lakes Tong.

Such a thing either placed Blake, through some great crime, outside the pale of the tong, or else it meant that Kan-tse-wen held his tong oaths and the sacred ceremony of blood transference as nothing at all.

The "Terror" moved his lean shoulders just a trifle, and his hawk-like eyes were veiled above the bony, predatory nose as he made answer.

"Was it not enough that I did what hospitality demanded, honourable one?" he asked gutturally. "Was it not a price to pay that, through him, I lost one of my best junks and many men? Did he not lead me to sack Anking, and to behead one who was out of thine own household? Behold! The Celestial tie is stronger than all else. The fan-kai-lo has no claims, because he is a fan-kai-lo. Aie."

Wu Ling nodded slowly. He had his answer and it was fair. It was right that no oath should bind a Celestial to a fan-kai-lo; and yet he had regarded Kan-tse-wen's associations with Sexton Blake —who was one of the few foreigners who had ever been admitted to the inner circle of any tong —as different.

There was, too, that rich and powerful Chinese merchant in London, Hong-Lo-Soo, who was also powerful in the Four Lakes Tong. Nothing would ever cause him to desert Sexton Blake, and just how Kan-tse-wen was to explain matters to Hong-Lo-Soo was not quite clear, unless, as it seemed, he intended to cut entirely adrift from the Four Lakes and come into the fold of the Yellow Beetle. If that could be accomplished this night, then indeed had he —Wu Ling — moved in the paths of wisdom!

"It shall be as thou desirest; honourable friend and ally," he said slowly. "The dogs shall be paraded for thy inspection, and within the hour shall the torture begin. Later, honourable friend, it would bring great joy to this humble one if thou wouldst permit his hand to place upon thee the inner bond of the Brotherhood of the Yellow Beetle."

"Aie! Thou offerest this unworthy one great honour, illustrious prince," murmured Kan-tse-wen. "My lao-pan, Fu-chen-pu, shall take a small barge and bring the two dogs before us."

"As thou desirest. It will be necessary that I should send a sign which will release the guard."

With that Wu Ling took from one of his fingers a small seal ring, which he laid before the pirate.

"If the lao-pan presents that poor bauble it will serve," he said slowly.

Kan-tse-wen's fingers closed over the ring, and then he made a sign to Fu-chen-pu. The big lao-pan rose at once, and, passing up the table, made deep salaam to Wu Ling and his master. Then Kan-tse-wen spoke a few words.

"Thou wilt take the ring of the illustrious Wu Ling and show it to the guards on the State barge," he said. "The two fan-kai-los who are prisoners will be handed over to thy care. See that their chains are removed before they affront the honourable presence of the illustrious Wu Ling. We would have them before us for our amusement."

"Ho hang, honourable master; it is done."

With that Fu-chen-pu took the ring; and thrust it inside his gorgeous tunic. Then he salaamed again before straightening up, to pass, with firm stride, from the great saloon to the deck. Nor, till his broad back had vanished from view, did Kan-tse-wen's eyes turn once more to his illustrious guest.

(Betrayed into the hands of his most implacable enemy by the man he thought his friend —his own blood-brother of the Four Lakes Tong —Sexton Blake is in a really desperate position. Never has his outlook been so hopeless, nor has it been embittered with the thought of such unnerving treachery. The future is dark, indeed, both for him and Tinker, but things are going to take a turn in a way that astonishes them both. How and why you will see next week. Is your copy on order?)

Part 15.

First published in the Union Jack magazine, number 1250.

How this fine serial began.

ONE of China's most sacred possessions —the Golden Book of Buddha —has been stolen while on its way up the Yangtse River to the Grand Lama of Tibet, and Sexton Blake and Tinker have been asked to go out to China to regain it.

Disguised as coolies they get on the track of the servants of the Black Abbot of Cheng-tu, who has instigated the robbery, and endeavour to discover who and where the Black Abbot is.

After infinite peril the pair succeed in penetrating the blockade of his spies, and eventually reach the Yangtse in an effort to go farther up-river and discover the abbot's headquarters. They are aided by a river-pirate called Fu-chen-pu, but unknown to Blake, the Black Abbot himself —who is in actuality his old enemy, Prince Wu Ling, and the most powerful Manchu in China —has located them by means of television and caused the pirate's junk to be attacked.

Blake and Tinker, after being separated in the fight, are rescued and reunited by Fu-chen-pu, and are brought to the junk of Kan-tse-wen (Fu's chief and Blake's friend). On confronting his "friend," however, Blake and Tinker are dismayed to find that Kan has betrayed them to one San, an emissary of Wu Ling's, for gifts of ships and arms.

Accompanied by a huge fleet, Kan-tse-wen ceremoniously meets Wu Ling at Ichang, where there is great revelry. It is announced that the two fan-kai-los are to be tortured publicly, but during a great feast given by Kan, the pirate sends for the two captives, who are imprisoned on Wu Ling's state barge.

A New Hope.

"WHAT is it, guv'nor?"

Through the pitch blackness of a foul hole a whisper crept. There was a clinking of metal as someone moved, and then the scamper of rats disturbed in their prowling.

"Did you hear, young 'un?"

The voice was low and hoarse, full of utter fatigue and lassitude.

"I thought it sounded like someone outside."

"It can't be time yet for the rice and water, unless I have slept. But I do not think I've been so lucky."

There was a further clinking of chains as Tinker crawled across until he could feel Blake's limbs. Then he sat close to him.

"I haven't been asleep, guv'nor. I've got a fierce headache. It is this vile hole. I wish they would get busy and do something. Anything would be better than this. I wonder where we are?"

"I don't know, Tinker," answered Blake as he put out a thin, bony hand and laid it on the lad's arm in a poor effort to comfort him. "I have almost lost count of time. But we have been moving for the last few days, and now we are at anchor. We are probably lying off some river port. It might be Ichang, if Wu Ling keeps the rendezvous which was arranged between him and Kan-tse-wen."

"That dog betrayed us, guv'nor," remarked Tinker wearily. "I wonder what Sir Gordon Saddler and Hong-Lo-Soo would say if they knew?"

"Hush, young 'un! There is someone outside."

They sat close together now, listening to scraping sounds which came from outside the door. Then suddenly the panel, which they had never yet been able to touch, slid aside, and a light shone upon them. Some blurred figures stepped in, and the light was swung nearer. Then, even in his weakness, Sexton Blake stiffened as he saw the lao-pan, Fu-chen-pu, gorgeously clad as he had never seen him before.

The lao-pan seemed to be in charge of the proceedings, for it was at his orders that the manacles which held the prisoners' wrists and ankles were struck off. Not once did he glance towards Blake or Tinker, but when they were free, gave curt, guttural orders for them to be dragged to their feet.

Neither Blake nor the lad resisted. Each knew it would have been useless. What must come must come. They were entirely surrounded by Chinese a thousand miles up the Yangtse, and no puny effort of theirs could bridge that vast gap.

They were dragged and prodded out of the filthy hole and along through a passage to some steps. Up these they were hauled until they were flung on deck, and then their wondering eyes gazed upon the myriad lights which were reflected in the dark waters.

But they were given little time to wonder over this. A dozen or more men hustled them along and over the side of the barge into a large sampan which was waiting below. There others seized upon them, forcing them in under the curved bamboo matting shelter which covered the waist of the sampan. Their hands and feet were seized by unseen guards, and then they had a fleeting vision of the light shining on Fu-chen-pu's gorgeousness as he passed before the opening of the shelter and took up his position in the stern.

Followed the rippling of water against the side as the sampan was pushed off. Low voices, speaking in the Szechuan dialect, followed them, and Blake could make out that someone was wishing those in the sampan a pleasant feast and amusing spectacle. It was enough to tell him that Wu Ling was bringing his devilry to a head, and that soon he and Tinker stood a good chance of tasting the torture which had been promised them.

He lay quiet. His heart was heavy, for he was fretting over the lad. Ever since he and Tinker had been overwhelmed in their last desperate struggle, his spirit had been like a leaden ball. He had explored every way to try and find a means of ensuring the lad's safety. He had even gone to the lengths of sending a pleading message to Wu Ling, offering him to stand double any torture he cared to inflict if he would give the lad safe conduct out of China. But Wu Ling had not even deigned to answer.

And now, amidst all this riot of light and colour, they were being taken to some place where the Manchu would inflict his evil will upon them. Blake groaned aloud as the thought of such a fate coming upon Tinker in all his splendid youth smote him, but a heavy hand struck him into silence again.

How long a period of time passed before the pace of the sampan grew less and less, until it finally came almost to a stop, Blake did not know. But a few moments later he recognised Fu-chen-pu's voice, speaking in command, and then they were hauled out on to the open. Suddenly they were thrust over the side, to find themselves in a tiny sampan, scarce large enough for three persons.

Their guards released them, and in one wild urge Blake was turning to the lad to take him with him in one last, desperate dive for freedom or death, when Fu-chen-pu caught him and thrust something into his hand. Then the amazed Blake caught the acrid odour of opium, as the Celestial put his lips close to his ears.

"The sampan is for thee, Sek-i-ton Bal-akee. Take this paper. It is from my honourable master, Kan-tse-wen. Go up the river, and not down. He has said his honourable word on this paper. Beneath the mat thou wilt find supplies and other articles. Go with all speed, for he holds Wu Ling and all his fleet this night whilst thou dost flee."

Then, while the astounded and stupefied Blake still stood grasping the paper which Fu-chen-pu had thrust into his hand, the big Celestial had leaped back into the larger sampan, and it shot off with extraordinary speed.

"Wh-what is it, guv'nor?" gasped Tinker, who had only heard a few murmurs while Fu-chen-pu was speaking.

"I don't know, young 'un," answered Blake, with a new hope in his tones. "But it looks to me as if Kan-tse-wen has not betrayed us, after all!

"Unless this is some ghastly joke —some subtle form of torture —we have been given a chance to escape while Kan-tse-wen holds Wu Ling and all his boats in his power. There is either some extraordinary Chinese subtlety in what is going on about us, or the refinement of cruelty is being employed.

"But the oars are here, young 'un. Get to work; we shall do as we have been told. Up the river! If this is Ichang, then the gorges are not far distant. We shall follow instructions, and when we are out of sight of those lights I shall read the paper. We shall believe that Kan-tse-wen is still my loyal blood-brother, and not the foul traitor he has seemed."

With that, Sexton Blake grabbed up a long sweep and jumped to the stern; while Tinker, galvanised into action at Blake's words, snatched an oar and flung the shaft into the hole. Then the tiny sampan got under way, heading out across the black waters where only the faint reflection of the distant coloured lights reached them.

The Fulfilment of the Feast.

THE first indication that Wu Ling felt of movement in the great fighting junk was when the long table canted, ever so slightly. Until that moment not the faintest suspicion crossed his mind that they were not lying at anchor in the midst of the hundreds of illuminated craft along the Ichang waterfront.

His mind had been busy, pondering over the conversation he and Kan-tse-wen had held about the latter's severance of his relations with the Four Lakes Tong, and in waiting for the two prisoners, Sexton Blake and Tinker, to be brought before them in the great saloon.

The one hundred and thirty-four mandarins and high officials who made up the rest of the banqueting party had noticed nothing; nor, even if they had, would one of them have dared to raise his voice to either Wu Ling or Kan-tse-wen. They were in guttural conversation among themselves, doing lip-service as the occasion demanded, but each scheming mind was occupied with the two powerful chieftains who sat at the upper end of the table.

There were the men who ruled the whole basin of the Yangtse; they sat in amicable conversation, so it must be true that the rich and powerful Wu Ling had bestowed the mantle of his friendship upon the dread pirate, Kan-tse-wen. Here was opportunity to "make face" and "save face." Through those two were many channels leading to wealth and power, if one could but get favourable eye and ear.

Aie! It was good to be of the favoured number who had been invited there that night! Let the common ragtag and bobtail huzzah and guzzle to their hearts' content; they were but pawns of whichever tuchun ruled Ichang.

But the subtle brain of Wu Ling was now as acutely on the alert.

There was something wrong!

He did not turn his head. His eyes, heavy lidded, mere slits, were fixed on the long table. Had it been imagination? Was the focus of his eyes affected by the potent spirit he had drunk? No; it would have taken much more than that to upset the equilibrium of the cold control of that nervous machine, which always functioned at concert pitch.

Again there was that almost imperceptible slanting of the table.

The junk was moving! Whither? Why?

Slowly, ever so slowly, Wu Ling's head came round until his oblique eyes could look at Kan-tse-wen. The pirate was sitting back in a relaxed attitude, apparently waiting only on the pleasure of his illustrious guest to speak further. As the sloe-black orbs of the Manchu sought his, Kan-tse-wen gave a slight movement of his body.

Only the upper part was visible to Wu Ling, and therefore he did not know that the pirate's slippered foot had slid into a large loop that hung under the table. But he did see one hand drop to the jewelled hilt of the short sword which, with the richly chased scabbard pulled round, was now lying across Kan-tse-wen's knees, the handle within an inch of his relaxed fingers.

For his own part, Wu Ling's hands had sought each the loose billow of the opposite sleeve —a quite usual manner of sitting among high-caste Chinese gentlemen, for in one sleeve was carried the fan, while in another the silken handkerchief.

But Kan-tse-wen knew that other things were sometimes concealed in the capacious pockets which one had inside one's sleeves.

Thus the two sat looking at each other, their faces utterly impassive, and not by the slightest sign giving any hint to the others who stretched away on two long lines that a chill abyss had suddenly opened between them.

Then suddenly Kan-tse-wen smiled in such bland fashion that a child would have given him its confidence.

Not so Wu Ling —for now the Manchu knew.

There was a further slight movement of Wu Ling's hands in his sleeves, and, in the same moment, Kan-tse-wen's foot pressed down upon the loop which hung beneath the table.

Outside somewhere clattered the brazen sound of a gong. Immediately two sets of heavy silken curtains at the far end of the great saloon were thrust aside, and two files of armed men marched in. At the head of one double column was a stout lao-pan who was one of the Terror's most trusted captain of junks; at the head of the other his chief lao-pan, Fu-chen-pu!

But this was no guard of the two fan-kai-los who were to be brought before the assembly for their amusement. Not the slightest sign was there of them. And still Kan-tse-wen smiled blandly into the slits which all but covered Wu Ling's sloe-black orbs.

Round moon faces, thin, lined countenances, heads of old, young, and middle-aged, turned from the strange array of armed men towards the head of the table. Those who had obeyed the impulse quickly were just in time to witness a most incredible thing. Up from his chair sprang Kan-tse-wen, and under the myriad lights in the great saloon flashed the blade of his jewel hilted sword as it flew from its scabbard and rested in a thin, glistening line against Wu Ling's throat.

"Aie!"

A long-drawn-out wave of voices rose from one hundred and thirty-four throats at the amazing sight which met the eyes of those astounded mandarins and upper officials. Could they believe their eyes? Was this a sword which the Terror was holding against the throat of the august Wu Ling?

Some of them who held preferment through Wu Ling's favour

made effort to rise, despite the ominous presence of the armed men at their backs, but, to their astonishment, their legs refused to do their bidding. One and all they were paralysed from the waist down. And then those who had made use of the potent drug "kan-ti" knew that this had been their portion at some time during the banquet. Kan-tse-wen, the Terror —Kan-tse-wen, the arch-fiend, had drugged each and every one of them, with the sole exception of Wu Ling.

Now, hard on the pirate's action, the guards drew their cutting swords, one flat bit of steel being laid over the right shoulder of each guest. Thus the whole company remained for a few moments of dramatic tableau. Then Kan-tse-wen spoke, though his voice was meant only for Wu Ling's ears.

"It is a matter of deep regret to the unworthy Kan-tse-wen that he must thus restrain his illustrious guest," he murmured smoothly, "but there are reasons which are binding upon Kan-tse-wen. The august one was foolish to believe that Kan-tse-wen, whose descent is as noble as his own, would thrust aside the oaths and obligations of the illustrious Four Lakes Tong in order to gain the favour of even the honourable Wu Ling. It was a mistake to think that Kan-tse-wen would abandon his blood-brother, the most excellent and to-be-loved Sek-i-ton Bal-akee, to the tortures of the tong of the Yellow Beetle.

"It was not known to Kan-tse-wen that his honourable brother, Sek-i-ton Bal-akee, was journeying up the Sacred River, nor for what purpose he came. It was enough that he sought his aid. Kan-tse-wen was sore troubled how he could help his honourable brother when the way was beset by the people of the illustrious Wu Ling and the powerful Black Abbot of Cheng-tu. But when Kan-tse-wen decided that they were one and the same he knew he must deal with the august Wu Ling alone. Thus came his honourable ambassador San to make specious promises and to offer great bribery.

"It was pleasant to Kan-tse-wen to know that the honourable and great Wu Ling should condescend to seek him out and offer him friendship which, it was known to Kan-tse-wen, would last so long as it pleased the illustrious Wu Ling to continue it. And then the unworthy Kan-tse-wen would be a loser of his head just as the Black Monk.

"Aie! Did the honourable Wu Ling think he was dealing with a child? Did he think the unworthy Kan-tse-wen was blind and deaf and dumb? Was it in the honourable Wu Ling's mind that Kan-tse-wen had gained his name and power through the ways of infants or through the ways of men? Aie! The unworthy Kan-tse-wen loves so much the honourable Wu Ling, and is so deeply conscious of the honour of his coming, that he goes down the Yangtse for a few days. The honourable Wu Ling and all these who sit here accompany him in this poor junk. There will be many of my men and many of my poor craft to act as escort, and at Ichang the ships and men of the honourable Wu Ling will be well cared for by my fighting junks. Even now this junk is beyond sight of Ichang, and it is known throughout the bazaar that the honourable Wu Ling and his friend Kan-tse-wen go for a cruise in order that they may discuss at leisure many matters of moment.

"Aie! Wilt the honourable Wu Ling continue at the table, or would he desire to take his illustrious presence to the state cabin which has been prepared for his honourable repose?"

Through all this Wu Ling had sat motionless. Not the vestige of expression showed on his countenance or in his sloe-black eyes. But inwardly the man who counted himself the super-brain in all China — who regarded all others as but pawns to be moved as he listed —was realising at last that he had been outmatched and outplayed by this pirate Kan-tse-wen.

It seemed incredible that this outlaw, this rat of the river, should claim equality of descent with a Manchu of the blood royal; it seemed all a mad dream that he, the illustrious Wu Ling, should have walked open-eyed into such a childish trap as this.

It was unbelievable that anyone could plan so complex a means of assisting another, even though he be blood-brother in the same tong, as Kan-tse-wen had taken to give aid to Sexton Blake.

No Celestial ever breathed who would not risk his all on a gamble, but this grand throwing of the dice against all the chances of Fate was something not even Wu Ling had ever known. Kan-tse-wen had played a subtle game that, despite the present situation, gained him a greater respect from Wu Ling than the prince had given to any other man, with the exception of Sexton Blake and Sir Gordon Saddler.

He knew now that he had underestimated the pirate very badly. San had been played with as an infant, and San was one of the cunningest plotters in China.

The pirate had made his cast so daringly that he had actually handed over the persons of Blake and Tinker into Wu Ling's keeping. For ten days they had been at his mercy; he could have put them to the torture and death a hundred times. And now he needed no telling that they were free again, liberated by his own command; while he, Wu Ling, was a prisoner, with a hundred and thirty-four of the most powerful mandarins and officials of Ichang as hostages.

And so completely had Kan-tse-wen sprung his trap, than there was no way, until he willed, that the truth could be spread in Ichang. His fleet, too, was helpless in the power of the pirate's greater armada. It was a complete coup —a fait accompli —and for the moment Wu Ling could do nothing. There was one chance only, and he would make the effort; if he failed, then a day would come, and may Great Buddha help the pirate when he, Wu Ling, should be free to act.

That chance —what was it that was in Wu Ling's mind?

When Kan-tse-wen finished he stood over the Manchu, waiting for his answer. His heavy-lidded eyes were watching closely, for he could not have sprung this trap had he been prone to miss even the little things. And he knew the very moment when Wu Ling's fingers began stealthily to fumble within one of the pockets of his capacious sleeves.

"Aie!"

Softly the imprecation came from Kan-tse-wen's throat, and gently, ever so gently the sharp edge of the sword slid along Wu Ling's throat.

"It would be unwise for the illustrious one to carry out his intention." he said pleasantly. "The unworthy Kan-tse-wen would see both the hands of the honourable Wu Ling placed on the table. The fingers of Kan-tse-wen grow beyond his control. It were unfortunate if they drew this blade tighter against the illustrious Wu Ling's throat."

Wu Ling knew when he was beaten. Slowly his hands came into sight and he laid them on the table. Then Kan-tse-wen flashed a look at Fu-chen-pu, who came close. At a word from his master he thrust his hand into the pocket of the left sleeve of Wu Ling's yellow silk tunic, and a moment later laid on the table a small glass phial and tiny, polished metal box.

Again did Kan-tse-wen smile that bland smile. Well he knew that in the metal box was one of the deadly yellow beetles, the active and living symbol of the brotherhood of which Wu Ling was the supreme head. And in that tiny phial was the pungent liquid which acted on the beetle like a magnet on a needle.

One smear of that on a human throat, and when the beetle was released it would go to the spot like a well-aimed bullet. Kan-tse-wen guessed what had been in Wu Ling's mind when his fingers began slily to fumble within his sleeve. But Kan-tse-wen was not yet ready to have that inch-long proboscis of the deadly beetle plunged into his throat.

Still smiling, he directed Fu-chen-pu to throw the articles through the open window into the river, and then, while the amazed company, who still sat literally paralysed from the waist down, gazed at the drama which was being played out before them, Kan-tse-wen lowered his blade and once more gave courteous invitation to his illustrious guest to rise.

And this time Wu Ling obeyed.

The Word of Kan-tse-wen.

SEXTON BLAKE and Tinker worked desperately at the sweeps until the myriad lights behind them were out of sight.

Then they rested, allowing the sampan to drift on the current until once more they saw the first of the coloured illumination.

"This won't do, young 'un," remarked Blake, who was still leaning on his oar. "We shall have to do as Fu-chen-pu said, and keep on. It isn't safe enough yet, though Heaven knows we are in poor fettle just now for this sort of game."

It was the first word of any kind that had been spoken since they had seen the large sampan sweep away from them. Each had been too utterly fagged to do more than hang over his oar. The past days of imprisonment in the foul hole in Wu Ling's barge had taken heavy toll of both body and spirit. But this unhoped-for chance of freedom —a real fighting chance —had acted on each like a heady stimulant at first; and now, with the rest, Tinker was ready again.

"I'm all right now, guv'nor," came his answer through the gloom. "But I can't believe yet that we are clear. What was it Fu gave you? And what does it all mean?"

"It means, young 'un, that we have been doing Kan-tse-wen an injustice. I don't quite understand yet just what game he has been playing, but I am beginning dimly to guess. If it is what I think, then he has outplayed any Chinese subtlety I have ever come across. It must have been a masterpiece of farsighted cunning to fool Wu Ling. What Fu gave me was a paper, but we dare not look at that now. Let us continue until we are another few miles higher up; then we shall make for the bank and try and get a light by which I can see what is written. I think we should be wiser to make across the river."

"What place was that where the lights were?" asked Tinker, as he grunted over his oar.

"I believe it was Ichang, but, with the confusion of lights, I could not make out any points that I should recognise. At any rate, it is in full gala, which means that the surrounding country will be empty, and if it is Ichang then it means that, through Kan-tse-wen's cunning, Wu Ling himself has carried us a good four hundred miles up the Yangtse, through some of the parts which we would have found most difficult to pass. It should mean that Hankow, a point which would have caused us great difficulty even if we had succeeded in getting through, has been left far behind us,"

"And we go on, guv'nor?"

Out of the gloom came Blake's voice, calm and purposeful.

"We go on, young 'un, to the point which has been our objective ever since we read that verse on the crimson paper streamer in the temple by the Si-Mun in the native city of Shanghai. And that point is Cheng-tu, another several hundred miles —if this is Ichang."

"You think the —what we are seeking is there?"

"I'm almost sure of it now, Tinker. But enough —keep all your strength for the work."

For the next two hours they toiled steadily, Blake steering as well as possible at an angle which he reckoned would bring them to the southern bank of the river higher up from the place they had left. There was no mist here, and while they were still travelling a moon showed from behind a bank of heavy cloud. In the sudden way which it has in those parts, the sky cleared completely, and where it had been a night of gloom it became an impressive scene, with the dim bulk of mountains off to right and left.

Blake's gaze rested on these heights as he sculled along. There was something familiar about them which he was trying to place. He knew, from the fact that there were mountains, that they must be somewhere above the middle Yangtse, and if it had been day he would have been able to orient himself at once. But in the moonlight it was confusing until, suddenly, a big rounded peak came into view. And that told him.

What he was looking at was the eastern spur of the far-flung and mighty Baian Kara Mountains, which wound from there through the whole of Szechwan province, and on into Tibet. It was this which told him it was indeed Ichang where they had been given their chance of freedom that night.

Therefore, less than a dozen miles from where they were must be the first of the gorges which cut a great gash through the mountains, beginning with the tortuous Tiger Teeth Gorge, whose jagged pinnacle of rock had taken toll of many a stout junk.

More than ever now Blake was anxious to see what Kan-tse-wen had written, and it was with a grunt of relief that he heard Tinker call back in a low tone that he could see the dim line of the bank ahead. Ten minutes later they had drawn the tiny sampan up on a narrow, gravelly beach and were squatting in under the mat shelter while Blake made search to see what had been sent along with them.

There seemed a great variety of articles, but what pleased him most just then was the feel of a long tube which could only be an electric torch —an object delightful to see and handle after their long absence from the conveniences and inventions of the West. His fingers sought the switch, bringing an exclamation from the lad as the bright circle of light fell upon him.

With this being held by the lad, Blake took the paper from under his shirt, and, squatting down, tore it open. It was of thin but opaque bamboo pulp parchment, and was covered with finely painted characters in the Szechwan dialect. As he scanned it Blake read aloud in a low voice, making a rendering into English as he proceeded, and this is, roughly, what it said:

"HONOURABLE and much-loved Brother, —It has grieved me sorely that it was beyond my power to give thee direct aid as thou didst need. The cunning and much-to-be-hated Wu Ling had his men at every point. It might have been within the power of the unworthy Kan-tse-wen to force a passage through the ranks —and this indeed, was his intention until the coming of the fat pig San gave him guile and inspiration. What he had done has been with the thought of helping his Brother. It is known to him that he must suffer during imprisonment, but he builds on the bargain he made with San.

"He will appear at the gala at Ichang, and he has planned that Wu

Ling and many notables shall fall into his power. If Buddha looks with favour upon the unworthy Kan-tse-wen, then, at an hour on the first evening, his brother and the young one will find themselves free. The worthy Fu shall go and release them; a small sampan, provided with articles of immediate need, will be provided; there will be food and clothing and two fighting knives.

"The spirits tell Kan-tse-wen that his brother will not seek refuge in flight down the river, but will continue on to his goal, no matter what dangers beset him. Therefore, it is the wish of Kan-tse-wen to help.

"If the honourable Sek-i-ton Bal-akee gets safely away from Ichang he must make up the river and cross to the other shore. Let him look for the road of red stone which he will find three li below the entrance to the Tiger Teeth Gorge. He must travel along that road for seven li until he sees before him a small hut, at the outside of which will be three prayer wheels.

"In that hut lives a holy man who is the honourable friend of the unworthy Kan-tse-wen, and he will give his honourable advice as to how it will be best for thee to travel through the gorges. If thou dost get through thou wilt find that which thou seekest in the Monastery of Sublime Ways at Cheng-tu.

"It had come to Kan-tse-wen's knowledge that a thing of great value has been taken there, and it is also known now to Kan-tse-wen that the degraded pig Wu Ling is he who travels abroad as the sacred Black Abbot of Cheng-tu.

"Seek the aid of the hermit in the hut of the three prayer wheels; then, when thou hast passed through the gorges and are on the upper river, go thou to Cheng-tu.

"In the bazaar of the Five Pagodas in Cheng-tu thou wilt find one who is called Fenghi-an-kani —a dealer in grain. He is kinsman to Kan-tse-wen, and with this letter thou wilt find a paper which thou must give him. He will do all in his honourable power to aid thee.

"And if thou dost return thou wilt find his aid useful to bring thee to Chinking above the gorges. However thou comest there, watch for the power boat which will have a blue-and-yellow pennon at its head. That boat is the property of the unworthy Kan-tse-wen; it will await thee for seven moons; it is thine to bring thee back through the gorges, and if thou dost reach Changcha, then none may harm thee, for the unworthy Kan-tse-wen will enfold thee with his protection and see thee safely on thy road. If thou dost not return, then will the heart of Kan-tse-wen grieve for his brother. May Great Buddha guard thee."

THAT was the letter of instructions which the wily pirate had sent, and as he finished reading it Blake's hand trembled a little. To think that he had ever entertained doubts against Kan-tse-wen! He had gone to lengths to aid him which must have cost him thousands upon thousands in money and brought into action every man and boat he could control.

He had done all this for his blood-brother, and, as far as lay in his power, had shown him the best road to travel. If it wasn't his Chinese blood that prompted this, it must be the Tartar strain that was so strong in his veins.

Blake put the letter away carefully, and, after a brief scrutiny of the paper which had been given him to hand to Kan-tse-wen's kinsman at Cheng-tu —if he ever reached that place —he turned to the lad.

"Well, what do you think of Kan-tse-wen now, young 'un?"

Tinker shook his head; he could not speak just then.

Blake smiled gently. His own heart was very full.

"He is solid gold," he said quietly. "We shall hope that the day may come when we can tell him so, my lad. And now let us forage among these packages. I fancy we are going to find the first decent bit of food we have seen for many a day. After, we shall get some sleep, for at the first sign of dawn we must find the 'road of red stone' and travel it until we come to the hut of the three prayer wheels."

The House of the Prayer Wheels.

THE two worn travellers slept until the first faint streaks of day came stealing up the mighty river. Sharp on the moment Blake woke, and, reaching across, laid his hand on the lad's shoulder. Tinker, who had been dreaming of the ghastly hole from which they had just escaped, came up sitting with a cry on his lips, but Blake smothered the sound with a quick hand, reassuring him in a low voice.

Then they ate sparingly of the pressed chicken which was part of the supplies which Kan-tse-wen had sent in the sampan. When this had been washed down with water, they crawled out from under the shelter and sought a place where they could conceal the sampan in their absence. They found a spot in under an out-jutting bank which offered moderate concealment providing no one came too close from the riverside, and now Blake thought this was unlikely, for, since reading Kan-tse-wen's letter, he knew that the whole countryside would be at Ichang.

Then they set forth on foot, the towering landmarks being familiar enough to Blake in the morning light. They could see, a few miles ahead of them, the two peaks which form the "gateposts" to the gorge of the Tiger's Teeth. Somewhere between them and those gigantic pillars was the "road of red stone."

As they went along they saw bits of outcropping here and there which had a reddish tinge, and when they had covered a couple of miles or so the soil in the fields took on a distinct tinge of terra cotta, much as the naked fallow of Devon would look. Now and then they would pass narrow, stony tracks, but none was sufficiently indicative in colour to fit the directions Kan-tse-wen had given them.

But then, when the two mountains at the entrance to the Tiger Teeth Gorge loomed —seemingly within touch, although they were still half a dozen miles distant —they came to a narrow, rough track which showed a deep brownish red.

Blake paused and studied it. The track wound away to the south from the bank of the river, and was, he considered, sufficiently distinctive to fit the directions they had received. He decided, at any rate, to try it. The hut they were seeking lay, according to Kan-tse-wen, only a matter of seven li —which would be between four and five miles —so, even if they were wrong, they would not lose much time by investigating.

So they turned off and started along the stony path which, to judge from its appearance, was little used either by man or beast.

As they proceeded the way became, if possible, more scattered with lumps of reddish quartz, making it painful work for their naked feet. But that was a mild discomfort compared to what they had been through, and now, with the light of renewed hope before them, they plodded on doggedly.

A matter of seven li Kan-tse-wen had said the hut of the three prayer wheels was situated. A Chinese li is materially less than a mile, and they had covered what Blake figured must be a couple of miles, or in the vicinity of five li, when he began to search anxiously for some signs of a hut in the distance.

Three prayer wheels was the mark which would indicate if they were right. A Buddhist prayer wheel is nothing more than a cylinder of wood or stone of baked clay, on which are a multitude of prayers and invocations to the Buddha. One may read a prayer wheel in endless turning much as one of the West may say one's beads. In a way, it all serves the same purpose, and away back in the interior of China a holy house will usually have the prayer wheels in some prominent place, such as outside the door or window-frame, or easily accessible for any devout person who may be passing.

It was Tinker who first descried what he took to be a small place of human abode some distance off to the right. When he had called Blake's attention to it the latter mounted the track to the side of the path and peered towards it.

"You are right, young 'un," he announced; "it is a hut of sorts. We shall soon know if it is the abode of the holy man. It is too far distant to see if there are prayer wheels outside."

They pushed on again, and at length found the track wound round in such manner that the tiny hut appeared near the edge. It was little larger than a good-sized dog kennel, built of the same reddish soil which surrounded it, and roofed with bamboo. There seemed to be no windows of any sort, and for a door there was a low opening not more than four feet in height by some eighteen inches across. Of human presence they saw not a sign.

Pausing before the hut, they looked for the three prayer wheels. Neither in front nor at either side was there one to be seen; but at the back, in a kind of wooden rack, they came upon three cylinders which had been baked from red clay and the surfaces of which were covered with finely cut characters.

It was the hut of the three prayer wheels.

They returned to the front, and, bending down, Blake put his head in the opening. As he did so he spoke, using the dialect of Szechwan.

"A pilgrim seeks the holy hermit," he said slowly. "Art within, honourable one?"

Out of the darkness came a quivering voice.

"One who communes with Great Buddha is within. Who art thou to disturb this holy solitude?"

"One who has travelled far and brings word from another who has knowledge of thee, holy man."

"Aie! There are many. By what name is this great one known?"

"The honourable Kan-tse-wen."

"Aie! Art come from him?"

"Even so, holy one. I have word for thy holy ear."

"What number hast thou brought with thee?"

"One other only, holy one —a lad who travels on the same pilgrimage."

"Then enter."

Blake crawled with some difficulty through the opening, and was followed by the lad. So little light came through the opening that all they could see of the occupant of the hut was a small, huddled heap against one wall. But as their eyes became more accustomed to the gloom they could make out a long, white beard framing a sunken, yellow face, out of which a pair of burning eyes stared fixedly. This ancient creature was undoubtedly an ascetic, and, Blake thought, probably an adept.

Then the voice came again.

"Thou sayest thou come from him who is known as Kan-tse-wen. It is long years since my solitude has been disturbed. The last one to come was this same Kan-tse-wen. Only a matter of urgency would cause him to send to me in this manner. Why hast thou come?"

Blake hesitated. Kan-tse-wen had given him no hint of what he should say to the hermit. All he had done was to direct him to the holy man, leaving it to him apparently to be guided by what he found. And in the absence of anything more, Blake decided to speak openly but briefly of who he was, why he had come to China, what had beset him and Tinker on their way up the Yangtse, and whither he was bound. Well was it for him that he came to this decision, for before he had entered the hut the highly attuned nervous system of the hermit had been humming with the contact of a strange aura, and he knew without asking that this stranger was no Celestial.

So, in the gloom of that tiny hut of baked mud, Sexton Blake began, and related the story that had been built up about him and the lad since they had left Shanghai. The hermit listened in silence. Only when Blake had come to a finish did he speak.

"Thou hast spoken with a straight tongue, stranger, and thou sayest thou wouldst go to Cheng-tu. What seekest thou there?"

"Something of great value —a sacred treasure which lies in hands which should not hold it."

"Thou must name this thing."

Again Blake hesitated; then he took the plunge.

"The Golden Book of Buddha."

"Aie!"

That one word came, then a long silence endured. For nearly half an hour Blake and the lad sat waiting. It seemed that the hermit must have forgotten them entirely, for he was sitting with closed eyes. But all of a sudden the lids opened, and his burning orbs fixed Blake's gaze.

"The holy resting-place of the Sacred Book is not Cheng-tu. What wouldst thou do with the celestial treasure?"

"I would return it to the place from which it was taken —the ark in which Great Buddha has decreed it should lie —the holy of holies at Tibet."

"Thou, an unbeliever and fan-kai-lo, would do this?"

"Aie —by my own faith!"

"Then, stranger, thou hast been well sent by Kan-tse-wen. The aid of the hermit of Chianting is thine."

The 'Trackers' of the Great River.

THROUGHOUT the whole world, neither within the range of history nor past when incredibly violent subterranean upheavals threw vast mountain ranges heavenwards and cut great chasms through solid rock, has Nature duplicated the extraordinary formation of tortuous gorges which lie above Ichang, near the borders of Szechwan in interior China, and through which the mighty Yangtse finds its way on its long course from the mountains of Tibet to the China Sea.

In the Grand Canyon of Colorado there are, it is true, deep and mighty gorges, the walls of which are painted in colours which flame with the magic of Nature's brush. Down in Death Valley, in the Mohave Desert, one may find great ranges of cliff which show where, in the long ago when earth was slowly solidifying, vast areas of lava were laid down in folds which, as the terrific hardening process came, gave them a wealth of colour which is repeated nowhere else.

Other great valleys, dry and river-coursed, reveal, too, many tortuous chasms in their journey, but the gloomy gorges above Ichang on the Yangtse were born in the midst of some special upheaval, when all that part of the hemisphere split asunder from the eastern Himalayas through the Baian Karas, and right across China to the boiling spot where Japan was flung above the surface.

They begin and end suddenly, as if the cosmic giant who had been making a mud-pie of the earth had pushed and prodded fitfully, and then, tiring of his play, had thrown the globe down carelessly, leaving the dried surface to split from mountains to sea.

For miles they extend above Ichang, beginning with the lofty and gloomy Tiger Teeth Gorge, and coursing through Ichang Gorge to find an outlet higher up in the gigantic and marvellous Mitan Gorge, like which there is nothing on earth.

It is little wonder that among a people who have been cradled in uncountable millions in the valley of the Yangtse, and whose whole course of existence is impregnated with superstition, there should have grown up about those mighty chasms many a weird tale of spirits and of doings which could never be attributed to the powers of man.

They form, as it were, a barrier between eastern China and the far west, and the passage up from Ichang, until one reaches the comparatively calm waters at Chungking, is a thing separate and distinct from all other navigation on the Yangtse.

The "attack" on the Tiger Teeth Gorge is a matter of careful preparation, which is only relaxed when one comes to the less violent stretch of water that lies before the Ichang Gorge opens up. Then another brief spell before tackling the worst of all, the mighty Mitan Gorge, through which the waters flow at a rate that is appalling.

A quick passage up may be accomplished in a matter of three weeks; a slow journey may take months. One slip, and the journey ends in a crashing debacle on the greedy rocks round which the foaming torrent boils incessantly.

It can be understood, therefore, that there has grown up about the traffic through the chain of gorges a quite individual caste of people, who live entirely from the terrible labour attendant upon the hauling of the junks and wupans through the rush of water and the maze of rocks which lie scattered throughout their length.

Of all the various phases of life to which the multitude of conditions in China have given rise, there is none lower in the human scale than that which subsists along the gorges from Ichang up to Chungking. These people are born into an existence that for poverty, squalor, filth, and disease cannot be equalled. From earliest years they are thrown into the toil of the cauldrons of the Great River, and even while years sit few upon them they are bent and broken —decrepit wrecks which, if they falter by the way, are left without succour to die where they fall.

The river "trackers" of the Yangtse!

Hundreds and thousands of them drag out a ghastly existence from one year's end to another, living in encampments close to the edge of the water when the river is low —shifting to higher ground when the floods sweep down.

At the foot of each gorge may be seen at all times a collection of junks, wupans, and sampans waiting to go up. On the bank are the rough shelters of the trackers —men and boys, and a collection of ducks which live with them —thrown-up heaps of rough branches and bamboo for the most part, inside which every form of human debauchery is rife.

Words can never describe the utter wretchedness and evil of the existence led by these half-beasts, and it is little wonder that their untutored, unopened minds are ripe fields for the preaching of any crazy doctrine that comes along. Their food is what they can scrape together; clothing consists of a few filthy rags; payment is a few "cash" here and there, amounting in a full year to no more than a few shillings. Their amusement is the evil debauchery which runs riot among them —that and "watered, twice-smoked" opium when they can beg or steal it, and the annual celebrations at the Chinese New Year early in February, when they drink their fill. A terrible existence which is a natural outcome of conditions in the interior of China where the tuchuns rule supreme.

Whereas the ordinary junk may have a complement of men for the normal sailing of the river, numbering anything from forty to seventy, the passage up the gorges demands the taking on of an additional hundred or so, whose sole duty is to seize upon the long bamboo cable which is fastened to the bow of the junk, and drag it along a worn, rocky path along the edge of the gorge; scores and scores of them stumbling and sweating in a terrific struggle against the wild rush of the water through the gorges, which may keep them for hours on end planted in the one spot.

Inch by inch and foot by foot they battle against the drag, the lao-pan and the tai-kung on the junk watching like hawks for the first sign of weakening. The head tracker does not content himself with shouting curses but wields a heavy stave, and woe betide him who falters when that cruel gaze searches him out.

In many instances, after hours and hours of this heart-breaking toil, a cable may snap where it had chafed against a stone ledge, or where there is some flaw which is only discovered in the terrific strain to which it has been subjected. Then the whole line of men go sprawling on their faces, while the junk, now freed of the restraint, is caught by the down-rushing torrent and hurled back through the boiling gorge among the rocks which lie ever in wait. A terrific crash, and all is over. What was a moment before a sturdy craft is now but a mass of tossing planks and timbers, dissipated along the river with incredible speed. A few bodies toss here and there —a red-painted patrol boat puts out in vain effort to rescue the wretches, but the percentage that ever regains the bank after such a crash is woefully small.

It is over and forgotten at once. Another junk is drawn in and once more the long line of beast-humans grabs a bamboo cable and starts on the toilsome journey up the gorge. If they reach the top in safety there is a spell in the calmer waters before the next is tackled; and if they make the passage of all three, then the trackers cast about for a return job down —rushing through the torrent with the junk running under the control of only the lao-pan, at a rate that would appal one who was unaccustomed to it.

Down, down, down, seeming to be dashed to pieces each moment on one of those pinnacle-like rocks; and then with a terrific rush of white foam to swerve into the seething pit of water at the bottom. The journey up may take weeks; the rush down a matter of hours.

And with no other means of reaching the vast rich territory beyond, the traffic of the Yangtse through the gorges will continue in this same way, paying toll of thousands of lives and hundreds of junks each year, until another means is found.

It was about a week after the sensational and unexpected gala at Ichang, that the first signs of activity at the foot of the gorges could be seen. From the camps on the bank and from the junks lying in the pools at the bottom of the Tiger Teeth and Ichang Gorges, as well as from the surrounding country for a full seventy li back from the banks, every, man, woman, and child had gone to Ichang.

During the celebrations the gorges were wrapped once more in the wild and undisturbed grandeur which had been theirs when the world was young. Only an old crone here and a decrepit coolie there had been left in all that stretch of roaring waters. Junks and sampans and every other form of craft lay deserted. There was no fear of stealing, for there were no thieves to steal. Even they had trudged into Ichang, where the promise of pickings was good.

But at the end of the week the trackers and junk coolies had begun drifting back. The boats once more showed life on them, and the banks again resounded to the "aie-han-aie" of the trackers as they resumed their toil beneath the dead, sagging weight of the massive, bamboo towing cable.

It was some days later before the junks at the foot of Ichang Gorge revealed a like resumption of life, and, being the second one along, it was but natural that the full quota of trackers who had left it had not returned. Some had remained in Ichang to wind up heaven only knows where; others had got jobs aboard junks on their way down to Anking and Hankow; still more had got as far as the foot of the Tiger Teeth Gorge, and were waiting to go up with one of the junks from there. Thus, even up to Mitan Gorge, the longest and (in population of river trackers) the greatest of them all, there was scarcity of labour, and would be for some days to come.

In order to meet the shortage every crock of a human was drafted into service. Even women were pushed under the cables, for every arm that could pull was an additional ounce against the terrible water devil whose greed had to be fought. It was natural, therefore, that any stray coolies who drifted along would be snapped up by the head trackers, and so it happened, on a certain evening, that two individuals who came to the bottom of Ichang Gorge on foot, arriving from somewhere to the south —one an elderly coolie with a prominent hump on his back, but with a strong frame that the head tracker of one of the contract gangs regarded with approval, the other a sturdy but evil-looking youngster who soon made it evident that he was deaf and dumb —no unusual form of affliction in that country where the breeding has degenerated to such levels.

They came into camp slowly, truculently. For some time they stood on the boulder-strewn bank, close to the edge of the pool at the bottom of Ichang Gorge, watching a gang of trackers at work preparing the bamboo cable for an attack on the rapids the next morning.

Later on they were seen squatted over a small fire, cooking some rice for their evening meal, and once, when a curious tracker paused by them, the deaf and dumb lad flew at him with such a fury of guttural snarling that the tracker fled precipitately.

They approached none and, after that rebuff none approached them, until at dawn the following morning a burly head tracker appeared beside where they lay. The deaf and dumb lad, who seemed to be almost beastlike in his snarling rage, would have flown at the man again had not the humpbacked one restrained him. Then the head tracker, holding off from reach of the lad despite their great difference in size, approached the man on the question of labour.

The humpbacked traveller was indifferent. He and the lad were travelling up the river, but he was prepared to pay his way, for he had some silver coins. The head tracker, on the other hand, was anxious to press every possible human being into service, and at the end of some twenty minutes wrangling it was agreed that for thirty-five "cash" per day the humpbacked one and the deaf and dumb lad should join the trackers as far as the upper end of Mitan Gorge.

No further questions were asked. The two new arrivals joined the party, and within an hour were bending to the weight of one of the giant bamboo cables, toiling along the worn stone path at the edge of the gorge —just an insect in an army of ants, and now completed absorbed in the life of the gorges.

But before another night had passed they were to discover that even here whispers could reach that told of two fan-kai-los, disguised as Chinese, who were the focal point of a most mysterious affair that was still puzzling Ichang.

They reached the top of Tiger Teeth Gorge that evening. Not once since early morning had the line of trackers been permitted to pause.

Now and then the tortures of thirst drove an occasional wretch from the line to plunge into the torrent and suck eagerly at the cooling water; more often than that a broken figure would fall to the ground and roll to one side, there to remain until he recovered or died. There was none to tend him and none to care; every other unit in that creeping line of humans thought only of reaching the end —if they had any thoughts at all.

The position of the humpbacked coolie and his deaf and dumb companion was near the front of the line. The former had chosen this at the beginning, knowing that the greatest strain would come upon those who were nearer to the other end of the bamboo cable. But even here it was a gruelling strain.

The path ran along the solid rock cliff at the side of the gorge, and was worn in some places as deeply as two feet from the surface, from the press and scrape of the myriad feet that had dragged over it through countless centuries. Sometimes it would mount high to the very top of the cliff, a good hundred feet above the torrent, from which point the junks beneath would look like toy ships tossing in a miniature cauldron; then it would dip and wind down again, always as close to the edge as human ingenuity could effect a passage, until it would bring the trackers down within a few feet of the river.

(Another fine instalment next week.)

Part 16

First published in the Union Jack magazine, number 1251.

How this fine serial began.

ONE of China's most sacred possessions —the Golden Book of Buddha —has been stolen while on its way up the Yangtse River to the Grand Lama of Tibet, and Sexton Blake and Tinker have been asked to go out to China to regain it.

Disguised as coolies, they make their way up the Yangtse, meeting many perils. They fall into the hands of the Black Abbot, who is in reality Wu Ling, the Manchu Prince, but are rescued at Ichang by the pirate chief, Kan-tse-wen, Blake's blood-brother in the Four Lakes Tong. Following his instructions, they seek the aid of a hermit, and eventually reach the bottom of the Ichang Gorge, where they start on their perilous journey through the gorges in the guise of river-trackers. Blake disguised as a humpback, and Tinker as a deaf-mute, they reach the Tiger Teeth Gorge, toiling with the other trackers at the tow-rope of the big junk which they are hauling up the river.

Servants of the Black Monk.

AS Blake and Tinker toiled at their rope, the detective gazed with a feeling of repulsion at the inhuman wretches before and behind them, gasping and groaning, muttering and cursing as they strained at the bamboo rope of the heavy junk.

Now another line of trackers would appear, moving more quickly as they dragged the lighter burden of a large sampan, string of sampans, or a medium-sized sampan up the gorge. In some of those instances the trackers would be wading through the water near the boulder-strewn edge, and would effect a passage by crawling in under the greater cable attached to the junk, working the smaller craft in between the larger and the bank.

Then would follow an entangling of ropes, and even above the roar of the rushing waters would be heard the chorus of screams and oaths as one gang reviled another. It was all, seemingly, without method of direction; and yet steadily the moving craft crept upwards through those waters of death, winding as the cliffs wound, staggering and buffeted through the long day until late afternoon brought into view the twin pillars at the head of the gorge.

Came one interlude which passed with appalling swiftness. It was just when the head of the gorge came in sight, and even the gasping trackers gave audible grunts of relief, in anticipation of the rest to come, when some distance above them the cable of another great junk snapped where it had been chafing against the edge of the rock.

Immediately the whole line of trackers who had been bearing on it were pitched forward on to their faces, and half a dozen or so who had been close to the edge of the path went headlong over the side into the torrent.

Down came the unrestrained junk with a rush, twisting and turning like a cork as the wild, sportive waters seized upon her.

She cannoned into the other junk with a terrific crash, hung a few tense moments, while the head trackers raved in profane screeches at the line of men who still hung on to the sound cable grimly. For a full ten seconds that seemed an eternity, it was touch and go whether the second junk joined the first. Then, in the savage instinct of self-preservation, those on board the second junk swarmed to the side with every bit of wood that came to hand, and, heedless of the cries of the men on the other craft, pushed it off into the torrent.

A great wail rose from a hundred throats as the junk was swept once more into the midst of the jagged pinnacles of stone. Bumping and twisting in a way to sicken the onlooker, it was carried down and down at terrific speed, and then two of the toilers in the line turned to watch as it struck a mass of rock at the bottom of the gorge.

There was the sight of great timbers in a smother of spouting foam being shattered to splinters, of a mass of wreckage being hurled into the air, of men appearing and disappearing in the spray which rose mast high —and then it was all over.

A red-painted patrol boat put out into the pool, but of all those who had been aboard when the junk struck not a score were saved.

It was just one of the incidents of the passage, and a stinging whiplash reminded the two who had turned to look that there was nought for them to watch.

In the late afternoon, when the goal was almost within their grasp, the line of trackers pulling the second junk were halted by a terrific shouting from the boat. They dared not turn round to see what was threatening; all they could do was to hang on, bent so low that their shoulders were but a foot or so from the path. Thus they hung, knowing that something momentous was going on behind them —that any moment might see them pitched forward on to the stone or into the torrent, while the junk went tearing down through the gorge after the other.

It was, in fact, a fraying of the cable which had been discovered by the tai-kung. Ten minutes more, and the great twist of bamboo would have snapped. As it was, the line was compelled to hold in that position, without a move to ease the strain, for a solid half an hour while a fresh length of cable was bent over the weak spot. Then, on again until they staggered round the pillar at the top and on to a rocky beach, from which they could see the filthy shelters which would house them before they set to once more to tackle the Mitan Gorge, the longest and worst of all, if one excepts the terrible Hsin-tan rapids.

Like animals, the trackers herded into the shelters, which were mere stacks of logs and bamboo and stone left open on one side. Here they squatted, a dozen or so to a circle, and wolfed the cold ration of food which was thrown to them. Those who had a few grains of opium settled down to a few hours of forgetfulness; those who had not huddled together and shivered in the cold. Blankets they had none, nor anything else to use as a cover.

Gradually, however, they warmed a little, and with the warming came talk —gossip of the great festival at Ichang. The humpbacked one and the deaf-mute lad sat together in one corner listening, but taking no part in the general gathering. They heard much, however, of what had passed at Ichang —a dozen different tales of the gala, none of which was correct, for each was based on that small portion the teller had seen in whatever spot he had been in at the time.

But along in the evening there was an occasional reference to certain mysterious happenings, and it came out, piecemeal, that many mandarins had accompanied the dread pirate, Kan-tse-wen and the equally dread Manchu, Wu Ling, down the river in the former's great fighting junk. There were wild hazards that the whole fleet was on its way to Shanghai, and that the hated fan-kai-lo was at last to be driven into the sea.

Others, however, had heard whispers which had arisen from uneasiness, and from this it could be gathered that there was something sinister in the gossip which was growing out of what had followed after the great banquet given by Kan-tse-wen to Wu Ling.

Bit by bit the talk died away as one after another lay back to try and sleep. A single fire burned in the centre of the shelter, and this was but a glow of coals when a dark figure appeared. A voice broke in harsh gutturals, and at the sound every tracker lifted himself up, for it was the head tracker. Then they saw that another was with him —a tall, black-robed person, whose face was almost hidden under the cowl of his religious order. It was one of the black monks from the Monastery of Sublime Ways in Cheng-tu.

How he had come to that camp at the foot of Mitan Gorge, none knew or guessed. But the sight of a black monk was sufficient to cause uneasiness among them all, and at a further word from the head tracker several crawled up to put fresh wood on the fire. As the flames mounted, the black monk and the head tracker came closer, the former peering closely at each man as he passed. It seemed as if he sought some particular person, from the care with which he scrutinised every countenance.

Up to now, the humpbacked coolie and the deaf mutes lad had remained seated, but as the black monk approached they were forced to rise, and stand so that the light from the fire fell on their faces.

Then the figure was in front of them, studying them with cruel, sloe-coloured eyes, and missing no single detail of their appearance. He seemed to pause before them longer than at any other, but at last he passed on, and a few moments later both he and the head tracker passed on to the next shelter.

A buzz of conversation broke out immediately after, and in some way it became whispered that the black monk had come up from Ichang in a small, fast sampan, that he had but arrived at the head of Ichang Gorge, and that he was in search of two coolies who had escaped from Ichang —the same two coolies of whom there had been mysterious gossip some days before.

But just who these two coolies were none seemed to know; nor, for the moment, was any eye of suspicion cast upon the humpbacked one and the deaf mute.

Little did those trackers guess how tensely the pair had stood while the eyes of the black monk had examined them. Then, when they were once more settling down, a further interruption came. The head tracker and the black monk re-entered the shelter, pausing just inside the opening. Next the head tracker spoke harshly, demanding volunteers to take the black monk's small sampan up through Milan Gorge that night.

Now, it should be explained that no tracker is expected to pass through the gorges at night. It is believed that, during the hours of darkness, the gorges are the haunt of the evil spirits of the river; that at that time they hold revel unchecked, and that it is during these hours the devils give birth to other devils of their kind. No matter what terrible poverty a tracker may suffer, not all the gold in China will persuade one to make that journey at night, unless he be some drifter from beyond the borders of China, or some "lost soul" already cut off from any hope of joining his ancestors when death overtakes him.

Probably a hundred years would pass without such volunteers being asked for, and it would serve no purpose that, as in the present instance, the black monk should not only offer the unheard-of sum of twenty silver dollars to each volunteer, but a definite promise that the abbot of the Monastery of Sublime Ways at Cheng-tu would spread his protection over any man who went. It seemed that certain of those who had brought the black monk up through Ichang Gorge were prepared to go on during the night —men who came from the monastery and were immune to harm from the devils. But more were needed, and must be found.

But not one man stepped forward. Twenty silver dollars meant a fortune to each wretch there —more than he would see in ten whole years. But not even that would lure him out among the river devils when they held carnival. Nor dared the head tracker drag them to it — his own soul would be imperiled did he do so.

But suddenly the humpbacked coolie stepped forward, dragging the deaf-mute lad with him. In the guttural tongue of far Sotan, he offered to go, and to bring the lad. The head tracker motioned him outside, while fearful eyes followed them. To the rest it meant that he was undoubtedly going to end as a meal to the devils before the night was over. But the humpbacked one seemed immune to that fear, for he trudged stolidly across the boulder-strewn beach to the edge of the water, where a small sampan had been pulled up.

And ten minutes later, when the other trackers had been lined up, they started, following a wavering lantern that was carried by the black monk himself at the head of the procession.

Exposure!

THE passage up Mitan Gorge was a very different thing from the gruelling contest of the day. The sampan which had brought the mysterious black monk was only of moderate size, and with only the lao-pan and tai-kung on board, the dozen or so trackers found it no great task to drag the craft along. The chief difficulty lay in avoiding the sudden whirlpools which marked wicked, jagged rocks, and to keep to the path, which in places sloped sheer away to the water.

Just who the black monk might be, and why he was travelling in such earnest fashion, was something that puzzled the humpbacked tracker a good deal. In this guise he looked very different from the coolie who had arrived at the Hut of the Three Prayer Wheels; and the deaf-mute who accompanied him bore little resemblance to the lad who had marched along the road of red stone.

But beneath those outer masks which had been devised by the wise old hermit to whom Kan-tse-wen had sent them, were Sexton Blake and Tinker, and it can be understood that neither of them missed a single word of the gossip that had been going on back in the shelter at the top of Ichang Gorge.

It was plain to Blake now that considerable mystery was abroad concerning the departure of Kan-tse-wen with his guests down the river; that, despite the report which Kan-tse-wen had caused to be bruited abroad, there was a feeling of uneasiness in Ichang. Blake felt almost certain that the sudden coming of the black monk had some bearing on the affair.

He had begun to look now for sinister doings whenever he saw one of those sombre robes. And the fact that this one had made close examination of all the trackers in the shelters, pointed to confirmation of the rumour that the two fan-kai-los who had been disguised as coolies, and who had been the centre of such sensational reports in Ichang, had escaped.

Was this black monk an agent of Wu Ling? Was he acting on instructions from the Manchu? And did it mean that, despite Wu Ling's imprisonment on board Kan-tse-wen's junk, those instructions had reached him in some way? Or, alternatively, was he acting on the initiative of the abbot at the Monastery of Sublime Ways at Cheng-tu, or perhaps on his own? If his journey up the river had some connection with the escape of the two fan-kai-los at Ichang, it seemed to Blake a reasonable guess that he was travelling up at top speed to spread word of this, and have a close scrutiny kept on every traveller.

Whatever the motive, it had provided Blake and Tinker with a chance to continue up the Yangtse towards their goal without waiting for the slower movements of the junks, and Blake had seized it, for he realised that his sole remaining chance of success lay in reaching the Monastery of Sublime Ways at Cheng-tu before anything definite should be known there.

It all lay, for the moment, in whether the black monk had any suspicions of him and Tinker. If he had felt any doubts back in the shelter, why hadn't he proclaimed them. He had done nothing, and Blake was hoping that at the top of Mitan Gorge they would find some means of continuing on to Chungking, and thence to Cheng-tu with no great delay.

These thoughts were passing continually in his mind during the long haul up the gorge. He was scarcely conscious of fatigue or the passage of time, so intently was his brain concentrated on the problem. It seemed all a dream what had gone before; it seemed that, in reality, it could not be he and Tinker who were toiling along that stony path as river trackers. Existence seemed to have passed from the realm of real things to a fantasy, since their visit to the hermit in the Hut of the Three Prayer Wheels.

He had assuredly been the refuge which Kan-tse-wen had promised. Out of the depths of his great age had come cunning to meet the test they must pass. When they once more emerged into the world, it had been as the humpbacked coolie and the deaf-mute lad; through the instructions received from the ascetic, they had been able to travel by a little-known path to a point on the river above the Tiger Teeth Gorge, thus lessening the risk of too close an inspection by those fresh back from Ichang. Blake had figured that, if any suspicion were abroad that the two coolies who had escaped were travelling up the river, it would be at the foot of the first gorge that the search would be keenest; and he was right.

Thus his thoughts as the night wore on and on, and at last the first grey streaks of dawn appeared behind them. But not even then were they permitted to pause. Not until they had covered another three miles, the most gruelling of the whole night's journey, did they drag the sampan into comparatively calm water, where they moored it against a narrow ledge of stone, the footway of which ran some dozen feet or so above the torrent.

Just then neither Blake nor Tinker was capable of any strength of mental functioning. All each wanted was to rest, for they had been at it for a full twenty-four hours now —a full span of the turn of the earth at the most heartbreaking work a human being can stand up under —with the exception of the two hours or so lay-off in the shelter at the head of Ichang Gorge.

Therefore, as soon as the sampan was moored, they staggered off towards the nearest shelter; nor was either aware, until they got inside it, that none of the other trackers had followed.

Instantly Sexton Blake was on the *qui vive*. He felt an inrush of premonition that there was something sinister hanging about them, and, a few moments later, when he saw the black monk approaching, closely followed by the others, he knew his mental warning was right.

"Something going to happen, young 'un," he whispered quickly. "Keep your fingers near your weapon, and if it comes to a show-down, leave the monk to me. There is certainly going to be trouble."

They stood, apparently unnoticing, while the group drew nearer, but each had his hand ready to snatch out the long-bladed fighting knives which Kan-tse-wen's thoughtfulness had provided in the boat in which they had escaped.

The black monk did not stop until he was within a yard of them; then he signed with a downward thrust, for them to step out into the growing light.

Blake obeyed, the lad followed. Then they stood dejectedly while the sloe-coloured eyes of the monk once more scrutinised them. Suddenly he spoke.

"Whence comest thou?" he asked abruptly.

Blake peered up out of eyes that he made bleary, and waved a hand vaguely towards the south.

"From beyond the gorges, honourable one of the black robe," he answered.

"Thou wert not in Ichang during the gala; thou and the other came to the gorges as strangers?"

"It is true; we travelled far."

"And goest thou whither?"

"To one who awaits us up the river."

"Why didst thou offer to draw on the rope through the night? Didst not thou fear the spirits of the gorges?"

"What fear need there be, when the honourable one of the black robe is here?"

"Thou liest. Ever since leaving Ichang have I been seeking two fan-kai-los who move in the disguise of coolies. At the shelter above Ichang Gorge I demanded that some should offer to come through the gorge at night, because I knew if those two I sought were among the trackers they would step forth. I was right; thou art no fellow of the hump. Thou art the fan-kai-lo who escaped at Ichang! And now dost thou return with me until the illustrious one, who speaks over all, shall give his august word as to what shall be done with thee?"

Both Blake and Tinker knew it would be futile to bluff further. This monk before them had had an inspiration, and had acted swiftly. Of all those at Ichang he alone had figured what might have happened, and slinking to gain deep favour with Wu Ling, he had started out to test his theory. He had been right, and did he take the two back to Ichang he would indeed secure Wu Ling's favour.

But Sexton Blake was determined that this gang should not subdue them without a struggle, so, knowing that the offensive is very often the best form of defensive, he spoke to Tinker in English, and then, leaping forward, drove his clenched fist in under the black monk's arm, to land with a dull thud just over his heart.

As the monk staggered back, the whole gang of Celestials set up shrill howls, and, jerking out their knives, rushed in with a fury of attack that drove Blake and Tinker back into the shelter.

In the Grip of the Black Monk!

IF the black monk thought his discovery of Blake's race had come as a surprise to the latter, he was labouring under a great mistake.

Ever since the call for volunteers the evening before at the shelter, Blake had suspected something to lie beneath the incident. The particular scrutiny to which he and the lad had been subjected had been enough to give colour to this idea.

But he had accepted the subtle challenge for the reason that he was at a point where he knew he must take any risks in order to get up the river without any more delay than was absolutely necessary. Now, with things having been brought to a head by Kan-tse-wen at Ichang, time was the essence of everything. If he failed to reach Cheng-tu and to devise some means there for gaining entry to the Monastery of Sublime Ways before Wu Ling should be free to communicate with the abbot, then all he and Tinker had gone through would stand as nought.

Moreover, it was plain to Blake now that, even if Wu Ling were not at liberty, he had still plenty of reliable agents who possessed sufficient intelligence and initiative to move without actual direction from him. It would serve little purpose, even if he and Tinker did get clear of this new complication, if the black monk were left at liberty to warn the abbot at Cheng-tu.

But first he and the lad must gain the upper hand, if possible, and later settle the problem as it appeared then. Any chance that they might be overpowered and dragged once more at the wheels of Wu Ling's chariot, so to say, was not allowed to enter Blake's thoughts. He had cast all on this last desperate throw to get up the Yangtse, and he went into the fight with a savage determination that was edged with the acuteness of his need.

Something of this communicated itself to Tinker, who, with his knife out, was standing against the first shock of the assault. Like his fellow whose head had rolled from his body at Anking, this monk stood off to allow his men to do the butchery. It is, of course, a tenet of the Buddhist faith that a monk of any Buddhist order must not resort to violence, but it seemed there was no objection to them directing such, both vocally and mentally, if one were to judge from the numerous attacks which Blake and Tinker had been subjected to since leaving Shanghai.

The gang of a dozen or so came on confidently. This humpbacked coolie and the deaf-mute lad seemed a simple matter to those ruffians. It was difficult for them to believe that they could be fan-kai-los as the black monk said, their disguises were perfection, and in speech the elder had given no hint that he was not of the country, so perfect had been his diction of the dialect he had used.

Therefore, they rushed in recklessly, being almost within touch of the two victims-to-be when Blake came into action. His knife play was a marvel of speed which was dazzling, and Tinker, who had acquired several new tricks with that weapon, was not slow to follow Blake's lead.

It could be no time for restraint. Unless they drove off these assassins, they would be sliced to ribbons in that miserable shelter. Not even Wu Ling would have their living bodies to torture if one of those cutting swords reached them. But the nearest fellow to Blake reeled back suddenly with a gaping wound in his side, and at the same moment Tinker plunged his long-bladed knife almost to the hilt in the shoulder of another, who had brought his weapon up in a way that would have disembowelled the lad had the point touched him.

Then utter confusion swept over the fight. In the half-gloom it was difficult to see what was happening. The black monk moved from one point to another, speaking now and then, cautioning his men to wound but not to kill. He was seeking to drag the two fugitives back living; to his bloodthirsty master, counting his reward the greater if he succeeded in doing so. But it was not so easy to control those flashing blades as he had imagined it would be, and, with two of the attacking party down already, the rest were hot for the blood of the two who still remained untouched.

Then suddenly Sexton Blake spoke in English.

"Stick close, young 'un! Make for the boat!"

"Say when!" gasped Tinker.

"Now!"

On the word they both hurled themselves forward with a recklessness of the blades that jabbed at them from every direction which was amazing. The unexpectedness of the rush, the fury of their attack, and the precision of their knife play, cut them a way through until they were on the other side. The black monk gave a cry, and hurled himself forward. By sheer weight of tongue, he got his bullies together again, and, turning, they rushed after the two, who were now running at top speed towards the sampan.

But half-way there, Blake and Tinker had to pull up and face the steel behind them. There the gang once more surrounded them, and with a free sweep to his arm, Sexton Blake revealed a capacity for knife play which could not have been equalled outside Mexico, where the most finished blade handlers are to be found.

He was in and out and from one side to another with a speed and accuracy that baffled the Chinks entirely. Not once did his knife plunge down or up or sweep from side to side but it drew blood. Not a single fatal stab had he given, but slowly and methodically he was cutting to ribbons those who came within range of the steel. Nor was Tinker far behind him. Urged on by Blake's example, the lad threw himself into the fight with a recklessness that was amazing. Time and again he slid in under the flashing blade of a short-cutting sword, and, delivering his blow, was out again while the steel swept futilely over his head or down past his arm.

Five of their opponents had been accounted for, and another two were barely able to stagger about, leaving only four more unscathed when the black monk saw that the case was getting desperate. Better it were to strike these fan-kai-los down mortally than to take them alive, now that some spirit of their own devils seemed to guard them.

He flew into a perfect frenzy of rage, driving his men on with epithets which called upon them all the wrath of Buddha. They rallied, and, with desperation in their eyes, rushed in once more.

But Blake and Tinker were ready for them now. At a word from Blake, the lad jumped clean out of the circle and, racing round to the back, charged from that direction while Blake kept the four busy in front.

In a few moments the Celestials were in utter confusion. They knew not which way to turn with Blake's knife stabbing at them from the front, and the lad's steel biting at them from behind.

Here the black monk threw off all restraint. One hand went under his robe, and then the dull blued-steel of an automatic pistol showed as his hand emerged. No knife could stand against that spitting death.

Sexton Blake was too far away to jump in and knock up the monk's arm before the trigger could be pulled. Tinker did not see the action. And Blake knew that, if he were to save himself and the lad, he had a matter of two seconds or so in which to act.

His arm was on the backward swing even as the heavy German-made pistol came level with his heart; then his arm shot forward, every atom of strength of his shoulder being added to the force which sent the knife flashing across the space straight towards the arm that held the weapon. On the same instant, seemingly, the pistol crashed out, but in Blake's action there was just that fraction of a second which counted.

The bullet zipped past his side, and as the automatic fell to the ground a wave of crimson spread over the monk's hand. Blake's blade, hurled in the Mexican "twist," had severed the other's thumb clean.

But the monk was by no means finished. Despite the terrible wound, he rushed in towards Blake. The latter was nothing loth, and plunged in to meet the rush. They met with a terrific crash close to the edge of the ledge where the sampan lay moored.

The touch of body to body roused in Sexton Blake all the savage rage which had been smouldering against these sinister devils in black who had harassed him from the moment he and Tinker had landed in

Shanghai —had dogged their every footstep like sinister ravens waiting for a chance to pluck out their eyes. And in the straining of the monk there was a fury of hatred of the fan-kai-lo which rose above all physical pain.

Forgotten by both was the combat that still raged a few yards away. Those two epitomised East and West, and all the lurking antipathy of the yellow for the white. In that moment the black monk was the stirring of the dragon, savage, hateful, unreasoning.

Back and forth they swayed and struggled, each quick to seize the slightest advantage. For all his black robe of priestly order, the monk had learned to use his great frame and muscles, and within a few moments of the contact, Blake knew he was faced with no mean adversary. Again and again he strove to get a subtle arm-lock about Blake's neck which, the latter knew, was one of the most deadly holds in Chinese wrestling.

Well was it for Blake in those moments that he, too, was an adept at the art, for his counter came up time after time just at the critical moment.

Blake's endeavour was to employ his own methods of fighting, and in order to do so, he must break free of that hold. But the monk seemed to sense this, hanging on all the more tenaciously while continuing that upward push of the arms.

At last, however, he weakened the barest trifle. Blake was quick to sense the slackening, and with lightning-like speed he relaxed his hold, allowing the other to think that he, too, was fagging.

As he had anticipated, the monk threw himself into a fresh effort. And then Blake came up, every muscle and tendon taut.

The shock to the other's hold was terrific. It tore his arms apart, and sent him reeling back with a gasp of agony. Blake jumped in to catch him again, and there followed a wild heaving of the two as the monk strove once more. He did succeed in giving Blake a terrific knee jab in the groin which sent the detective bending with a groan of sudden agony. The monk plunged in to finish his work and Blake, knowing that he was helpless at the moment, managed to throw himself aside just as the long arms sought to enfold him.

The fury of the monk's drive carried him clean over Blake's prostrate form, and then there came a wild cry of baffled rage and fear as he tottered like a crazy marionette trying to regain his balance, and then he disappeared from view into the raging torrent that raced down through Mitan Gorge.

TINKER had been so hotly engaged with the remaining Celestials that he had not been able to follow the progress of the fight between Blake and the black monk.

He had heard the crash of the pistol as the first indication that the monk was taking an active part in the fight, and he had turned his head in time to see the flash of the knife which Blake had hurled. But then he had needed his full attention for the task in hand, and the next he knew of how things were going with Blake was when the three Celestials who now remained broke away suddenly and took to their heels.

Then, panting heavily and with a deep gash in one arm which was bleeding profusely, Tinker turned to find his master.

One hand clutching at his arm, he staggered forward, his eyes wide with wonder at seeing no sign of the monk. But Blake, who was only now finding it possible to straighten up, waved an expressive hand towards the gorge. He did not need to speak. Nor did Tinker need to be told what fate lay in wait for anyone who plunged into that torrent. Now he knew why the remaining Celestials had taken to their heels.

Blake would say or do nothing until he had examined the lad's arm. He bathed it at the edge of the river after they had found a tortuous way down from the ledge, and, after binding it with a strip torn from his garment, motioned the lad into the sampan.

"We'll get away at once, young 'un. The monk is gone, and these others are settled for the time being. But there are other shelters at the main camping ground half a mile higher up, and we want to get past there before any of the coolies reach it with the tale. Above there we stand a chance, but not below."

Tinker obeyed, and when the sampan was released took over an oar with his sound hand, despite Blake's protestations. Blake was in the stern with the large sweep, both sculling and steering. Not even the lao-pan had remained on board. Every man-jack had joined the rush at the word of the black monk, and now, as things turned out, Blake was glad that the whole gang had joined in.

They worked steadily until, on rounding the bend, they saw the lines of shelters in the main camp. There were plenty of trackers about this spot, and as they drew near Blake kept a sharp eye out for any signs that the approaching sampan was under suspicion. But beyond a casual look at the craft no particular curiosity seemed to be shown.

There was nothing strange in a lone sampan passing. At that hour of the day and above the gorge the conclusion would be that it had come up through Mitan the previous day —which was exactly what Blake was hoping would be thought until they were in the wider, freer river higher up.

They sculled past the camp slowly, but each moment they were on the look-out for sight of a figure running towards the shelters with news of what had happened half a mile down. Nothing occurred, however, and it was with almost a sigh of relief that Blake rounded another bend which shut the encampment from view.

(This exciting yarn is now reaching its most thrilling chapters. Don't forget to read the final chapters, now imminent.)

Part 17.

First published in the Union Jack magazine, number 1252.

How this fine serial began.

ONE of China's most sacred possessions —the Golden Book of Buddha —has been stolen while on its way up the Yangtse River to the Grand Lama of Tibet, and Sexton Blake and been asked to go out to China to regain it.

Disguised as coolies, they make their way up the Yangtse, meeting many perils. They fall into the hands of the Black Abbot, who is in reality Wu Ling, the Manchu Prince, but are rescued at Ichang by the pirate chief, Kan-tse-wen, Blake's blood-brother in the Four Lakes Tong. Following his instructions, seek the aid of a hermit, and make their way through the gorges, disguised as river-trackers, helping to haul a heavy junk through the dangerous waters. At the head of the Mitan Gorge they are exposed by one of the Black Monks of Cheng-tu, but after a stern fight, the two capture a sampan and continue on to their ultimate goal —Cheng-tu.

The Goal in Sight.

WITH Blake at the sweep, and Tinker working an oar, the sampan glided up the river, away from the trackers' camp and the danger of pursuit.

From that moment it seemed that the perverse fate which had pursued them for so long had stayed its hand. Steadily all that day, with only short stops for food, Blake sculled, while Tinker aided him to some extent with his sound arm. Even the gash in the other seemed to close up with extraordinary rapidity, leaving little soreness and no sign of fever.

For some days this luck held until on an evening they sighted the big city of Kiukiang.

Blake would have preferred to pass this place in the dark, for he knew not what had happened in connection with Wu Ling and Kan-tse-wen. For all he knew, the Manchu might now be freed, and, were that the case, it was a dead certainty that every town and village on the Upper Yangtse would be watching for the two fugitives. On the other hand, if Kan-tse-wen, still held him prisoner, then there was still a chance that they could pass unmolested, for Blake had little fear of the monk surviving to furnish a clue. The jagged rocks in the gorge would see to that.

But they must have food. Their supplies had run down to a few crumbs of rice, and they could not go on the last long lap to Cheng-tu on that. So circumstances forced them in among the maze of craft which hung off the Kiukiang waterfront, and each was on the alert to watch for the slightest sign of suspicion being shown. But they were unmolested.

While Tinker remained on guard, Blake, as soon as dusk had fallen, made his way up into one of the bazaars and purchased the necessary supplies. He found everything in order when he returned, with Tinker lying out of sight under the shelter. They remained under cover during the night, and at the first sign of dawn pushed off once more.

The sampan was larger than they could have wished, but in their position they could not be choosers, and certainly a sound craft with freedom to take it whither they listed, was better than lying manacled in that foul hole at the bottom of Wu Ling's barge.

More days passed, during which they progressed steadily. Now and then they hitched on with other sampans to a junk that was sailing free, and in this way covered several miles without fatigue. But mostly it was solid pulling against the current, and, with Tinker's arm healing more and more every day, it was not long before the lad could bear his full share.

The character of the river had changed now. No longer were they among the mighty gorges and overhanging rocky crags; the banks were low and green, and by contrast it was pleasant indeed. Nature, as well as Fate, seemed to have turned towards them the smile of her favour.

Blake's objective, Cheng-tu, lay to the north, and when they arrived at Sui-fu they left the waters of the Great River, Yang-tse, and directed their craft into the tributary stream of the Fu that entered it on its northern bank Here sandbanks and matted growth of a peculiar sort of sword-grass were their chief troubles, but even those difficulties were pleasures compared with the dangers they had already endured.

There came an evening at last, when the sun was sinking over the green rice fields —the sight of which reminded them of the words in the doggerel verse which had been on the crimson paper streamer in the temple by the Si-mun in Shanghai —they saw the gilded minarets of a great city far ahead on their left. A little later they came into view of the pinnacled roof of a vast, great stone building which lay on a low hill overlooking the city.

And Blake knew that, at last, they were gazing upon the goal of all their struggles —The Monastery of Sublime Ways. Behind those grey walls that appeared so impregnable was the Golden Book of Buddha.

How were they to take it from its resting place, where it was guarded night and day, and how, even did they succeed in doing so, were they to carry it away from that place —the heart of the China that is Chinese? Those two bedraggled creatures in the lone sampan seemed so pitifully inadequate for such a task.

On the Threshold.

AT one end of the Street of the Seven Bridges in the bazaar of the Five Pagodas at Cheng-tu, is the large and prosperous establishment of the rich mandarin, Fenghi-an-kani, dealer in rice and other grains.

Fenghi-an-kani was the head of one of the oldest and most influential Mahommedan families of Cheng-tu, for his forefathers had come across the far western border of Szechwan many centuries before, and although during the long descent which had produced Fenghi-an-kani, none had embraced the Buddhist faith, this did not deter the shrewd line of traders from piling up an immense fortune and acquiring wide lands and power.

Fenghi-an-kani was no politician. He had no ambitions that way; nor did he aspire to any part in the military hotchpotch of China. He was a devout Mahommedan of the orthodox school, believing in the literal interpretation of the writings of the Prophet, that all sacredness on this earth lay in Mecca, and that one must pray at the stated times five periods each day.

His establishment was a large one, his family consisting of the first, or orthodox, wife, and three others which the Prophet permitted —all of whom, strange to say, were on highly amicable terms with one another. His retinue of servants and hangers-on was enormous, even for a wealthy mandarin. Upwards of three hundred people received rice each day in Fenghi-an-kani's house, and instead of begrudging it the mandarin smiled complacently when they flocked about, for it was right that one of wealth and power should give, even as the Prophet charged one to give.

Nor were his public charities any less in comparison. All about the Cheng-tu plains are the vast fields of rice, which are the richest in China. These have come to be such through the beneficent work of him who was known as the "blessed tuchun," who ruled all that part of China more than a thousand years ago.

This goodly and godly man laid out vast sums in harnessing the mighty Yangtse, and so well did he build —so nobly did his son carry on after he was gone —that those gigantic works stand to-day exactly as he left them. Towards the upkeep of these, which is a first charge on the people who live on the bounty of the Cheng-tu plains, Fenghi-an-kani contributed deeply from his purse. Through the rice and grains which were harvested there had his family garnered its wealth; therefore it was meet that a large percentage of that wealth should be returned to the fields. So would Allah bless the seed of Fenghi-an-kani.

Although he and all his forbears had been of strictly conservative mould, and none of them men of arms or violence, there was in Fenghi-an-kani the strain of the mighty Tartar warriors of long ago. And, in a collateral branch of the family, this flow had revealed itself in certain of the mandarin's kinsmen, the most prominent and famous of whom was the dread pirate of the Yangtse, Kan-tse-wen.

It might be thought that Fenghi-an-kani would have nothing in common with such a kinsman as the "Terror of the Yangtse," for deeds of violence seemed far indeed from the nature of this peaceful merchant. Moreover, there had been times when shipments from Fenghi-an-kani had fallen prey to the looting of the pirate, which was surely cause for some measure of anger on the part of Fenghi-an-kani.

But if, on his visible life, Fenghi-an-kani was no man of feats of arms, he yet retained a mighty reverence for his famous ancestors, the terrible Kubla Khan, and the conqueror of Europe, Genghis Khan; and in his leisure moments his reading was very often spent in the perusal of records telling of such doings.

It was this spirit of adventure which had never found outward expression, that caused him to have what an Englishman would call a sneaking admiration for his daredevil cousin, and, to tell the truth, Fenghi-an-kani rubbed his smooth hands with inward enjoyment every time some new tale of Kan-tse-wen's deviltry came up the river.

From this it will be seen that the conservative merchant had within him some of the red corpuscles which had caused his forbears to ride at the head of charging hosts, and with the warmth of his feeling for his cousin, it was not unnatural that he should look with some degree of favour upon anyone who came from Kan-tse-wen.

Thus it was that on a certain evening when the bazaar of the Five Pagodas buzzed with the traffic of a late market, Fenghi-an-kani took his ease in his pleasant gardens, which were enclosed on three sides by his great godowns and hongs (for he did no business after six o'clock, being above bazaar dickering) and bounded on the fourth by the river.

It was whilst he was thus meditatively engaged, that his ear was attentive to a servant, who informed him that visitors from far down the Yangtse waited in the outer courtyard.

"They are of the honourable mandarin caste?" inquired the merchant of the Sitang boy, who was clad in the green livery of his master.

"Nay, honourable master; they are but two deformed beggars who have been driven from the place many times during the evening. Even now this unworthy one would not offend the honourable ear of the honourable master were it not that one of them has caught two of thine people within his arms, and threatens to crack their unworthy skulls if word is not sent to thine honourable ear."

"Aie! Two deformed beggars, sayest thou? And they seize upon the persons of my household in violent fashion! Aie! Strange beggars indeed are these. Goest thou, and bring them before me."

The Sitang boy salaamed and withdrew. When he was gone Fenghi-an-kani lighted a yellow cigarette which had come from far Manila, and, walking slowly along a shrub-lined path by the river, mused on what he had just heard. He was still pondering mildly upon the mystery when the Sitang boy once more appeared, followed by two human scarecrows —one being a stooped coolie with a prominent hump on his back, and the other a dirty-looking, low-browed lad, who seemed as if he might be capable of any villainy.

The mandarin paused and surveyed them as they stood before him. He was not at all pleasantly impressed by their appearance, but he was still curious to know why two such creatures had dared enter his establishment and demand, in such violent manner, to speak to him. It was not that any beggars in Cheng-tu could have cause for seeking alms at his house; his benefactions were so large that he should be spared anything of that nature. But these fellows came from far down the river —whence and why had they sought him in far Cheng-tu?

He put the question curtly, and, instead of answering by speech the elder of the two thrust a hand inside his shirt, taking out a piece of folded paper. This he passed to the mandarin. Fenghi-an-kani took it, waving the Sitang boy away. Beggars who came with written paper were even stranger than beggars who came with violence.

There was no change of expression on Fenghi-an-kani's calm visage as he opened the paper and read what was written; but in the quick look which he flashed the elder beggar there was a swift question which he could not restrain.

If he were to believe what had been written on that paper by his kinsman, Kan-tse-wen, then, instead of these two creatures being dirty beggars from another province, they were two fan-kai-los of a sort who should be the honoured guests of the highest.

It was incredible, and entirely outside any of the experience which had befallen Fenghi-an-kani. Were it not for the feeling he entertained towards his kinsman, it is likely he would have ordered them to be driven from the place. But now, instead of that, he dismissed the Sitang boy, and led the way along several scented paths until he came to a secluded summer-house.

With a courtesy strange to see exhibited towards two such scarecrows, he invited them to be seated, and then, assuming his own lacquered chair by a teakwood table, he swung in through an open window a wooden arm from which hung one of the scores of painted lanterns that made the gardens a perfect fairyland at night. Then under the soft light of this he gazed at the humpbacked beggar.

"Thou hast brought me a strange paper," he said evenly. "It is difficult for me to believe that thou art the person of whom the honourable writer of the paper speaks."

The other made a somewhat weary gesture.

"Thou hast read the truth, honourable mandarin," he said, deliberately using the cultured tongue of Peking, which no beggar would know. "I know not what my honourable friend Kan-tse-wen has said, but I have his honourable word that thou, his kinsman, will give us at least shelter while we are in Cheng-tu."

"Thou speakest with the tongue of the intellectual," responded the mandarin. "Art thou indeed fan-kai-lo?"

"Aie! I am of the English. Hast the honourable Kan-tse-wen spoken aught else of me?

"He says the note will be brought by one who is fan-kai-lo and his blood-brother in the Four Lakes."

"Aie! I am he who is known as Sek-i-ton Bal-akee, and, am in truth blood-brother to Kan-tse-wen."

"Then thou must take from thee those rags, and receive of the best which my miserable abode will provide," exclaimed Fenghi-an-kani. "I, too, am one of the illustrious Four Lakes tong."

"Then thou art no believer in the Yellow Beetle?"

"Aie! The curse of Allah rest upon them!"

"I would accept thy offer for myself and the lad who travels with me, but before doing so, I must tell thee why I have come to Cheng-tu."

"Thou speakest as thou wilt."

"Thou must know the truth, for there is great danger to those who have dealings with me. I come to take away something of great value which lies in the Monastery of Sublime Ways."

"Aie. Thou goest at the will of the abbot?"

"I go as one who would be tortured unto death were my errand suspected. I go to take from the inner holy of holies a thing which the Black Abbot of Cheng-tu has placed there. At this moment the Black Abbot may be the unwilling guest of the honourable Kan-tse-wen or he may be free. I know not; but thou mayest have it in thy mind that the Black Abbot is none other than Wu Ling, supreme head of the Yellow Beetle?"

The mandarin gazed at Blake in silence for some minutes. For a long time past he had heard many strange whispers about the Black Abbot of the Monastery of Sublime Ways, but not even in Cheng-tu was anything definite known of that mysterious individual. All that had come to the ears of the mandarin was cautious gossip of the abrupt arrival of the Black Abbot, or his equally sudden departure, though he had suspected for a long time past that the Black Abbot was playing a deep game in the turmoil which prevailed throughout the length and breadth of China.

"Thou speakest as one of knowledge," he said at last. "It was not known to me that the Black Abbot is the same as he of the Yellow

Beetle. I am no Buddhist, but were I of that breed, then should I say that poor work cometh from the Monastery of Sublime Ways in the turning of the house of Buddha into a place of intrigue.

"But if thou art he whom thou sayest, then what wilt thou? Thou mayest command me to the extent of my poor resources. Thou wilt take up thy abode in this poor house, and what the miserable and unworthy Fenghi-an-kani may do will be done."

"Our wants are simple, honourable one," answered Blake. "We crave a little food and lodging for but a night and a day. Then, if thou canst provide us with means to reach Chinking, which, as thou knowest, lies far down the river above the Mitan Gorge. This only shall I ask of thee if I return from the Monastery of Sublime Ways. If aught happens to keep me within those grey walls, then do I crave the same boon for this lad."

"Thou askest little, honourable stranger. More than that shall I do for the blood-brother of my honourable kinsman. But thou dost not mean that thou wilt enter the Monastery of Sublime Ways? Those great walls are not to be pierced by the curious."

"Nevertheless, I shall go. I need garments which I do not possess, and for these I beg your honourable aid."

"What dost thou desire?"

"A black robe such as is worn by the Black Abbot."

"Aie! Dost know if it is the same as that which the raven monks wear abroad, for never hath mine eyes rested on the Black Abbot?"

"It is the same."

"Then of my poor resources thou shalt have what thou desirest, and as soon as it can be procured. Dost thou wish it this night?"

"If the honourable mandarin wouldst condescend."

"It shall be done. And when thou hast it?"

"I go to the monastery."

"Alone? Knowest thou the danger?"

"This lad accompanies me to the gates to await my return. If I come not by the dawn, then will he seek thee once more, and crave thy assistance. At Chinking there will be means for getting down the river to Changcha where the honourable Kan-tse-wen will be waiting."

"Thou art possessed of an honourable madness," said the mandarin slowly. "Thou wilt never penetrate to the inner parts of the Monastery of Sublime Ways."

"I have heard it said that the Black Abbot of Cheng-tu moves abroad in a mask," murmured Blake.

"Aie. By the beard of the prophet, but thou hast pricked my dull wits. Thou goest as he?"

"Aie."

"Thou doest that which hath one chance in many millions of succeeding. A black robe and a mask, and thou knocketh at the gates as the Black Abbot?"

"Even so."

"Then indeed art thou worthy to be the honourable blood-brother of my honourable kinsman, and this unworthy man of no action giveth thee that for which thou hast asked. The unworthy Fenghi-an-kani would sit in happy contemplation until the call of the Prophet could he but know that the accursed Black Abbot, whom thou sayest is he of the foul Yellow Beetle, had been outwitted."

"I go this night to do so, or to remain for ever within those grey walls." was the low reply.

And it came about, even as Blake had said, that a few minutes before midnight that same night a black-robed figure travelled a short distance up the river in a closed sampan which departed from the bank alongside the garden of the merchant Fenghi-an-kani until it drew in beneath the heavy shadows of the grey walls of the Monastery of Sublime Ways.

Then, as it rested, two figures came forth —one, he of the black robe, and the other a lad dressed as a lay brother of a religious order. Together they mounted the long, shallow steps that wound up to the massive gates of the Monastery of Sublime Ways; and, as a great bronze gong clattered the hour of midnight, so did the black-robed figure thrust out an arm and raise the ancient stone knocker which had hung on the great gates for many centuries.

At last Sexton Blake stood on the threshold of the goal he had sought through so many perils.

The Shrine of the Golden Book.

ALTHOUGH Fenghi-an-kani had never seen the Black Abbot abroad in the streets of Cheng-tu, he had heard, as he had told Blake, many rumours about that mysterious individual, and it was known to him, therefore, that the abbot always wore a black mask to conceal his features.

Blake had heard this same thing before, but he would not have dared to make use of that addition to his disguise, had it not been confirmed by the mandarin.

It was this addition to the black robe, in fact, which he counted of greatest value in his daring attempt that night to enter the monastery, and, when he sounded the great stone knocker at the gates, he affixed the piece of black silk in position

After a long wait he heard sounds within, and then the clanking of chains as a small, individual wicket set in the larger gate was opened. By the light of a primitive flare which was held at eye-level, Blake could make out the flat features of a man in the dress of a lay brother, who was peering at him closely. Blake did not speak; he was waiting to see if a silent pose would achieve his purpose. And, after a few moments, the man spoke.

"Is it thou, Illustrious One?"

"Aie! Why dost thou bar the way?"

"Forgive, Illustrious One, it is the caution, as thou knowest, and didst of thine own words command."

As he spoke the lay brother drew back, and without hesitation Blake stepped over the threshold. Then followed a muffled clang as the portal closed, cutting him off completely from all contact with the outside world.

And, in the shadow of the great stone walls, the watching Tinker felt a sudden weight descend upon his spirit.

Blake's instructions had been that he was to wait until dawn, and then, if he did not return, he, Tinker, was to make his way back to Fenghi-an-kani's house and, through the mandarin, try to get back down the river to civilisation once again.

But at the sound of that closing gate, Tinker's jaw set grimly, and he vowed silently that if Blake did not appear before dawn he would attack the gates himself, single-handed. If his beloved master remained in the Monastery of Sublime Ways, then he would share his incarceration.

Although Sexton Blake had seen the Monastery of Sublime Ways on two other occasions, he had never before stepped within its gates. Therefore he had no knowledge of how one must proceed to enter. Yet he knew that he must not betray the slightest hesitation in choosing the way, for, of course, it would be familiar to the Black Abbot.

His objective was the apartments which would be given over to the use of that dignitary. In the ordinary course of things, Blake would have had some doubt on the matter, but knowing Wu Ling as he did, he figured that the Manchu would not share accommodation even with the Resident Abbot, but would have his own private quarters. Wu Ling was not one to permit his solitude to be intruded upon, and it was plain to Blake that, in the great monastery, he would find an ideal retreat for the planning of his many schemes.

And it was in Blake's mind further that, if the Golden Book of Buddha did rest within the walls of the Monastery of Sublime Ways, no place was more likely than in the depths of Wu Ling's apartments, for never in all his long career of intriguing had the Manchu seized a greater prize than that.

Blake paused for a moment within the gates as if waiting to assure himself that the lay brother had chained them safely; then he faltered suddenly as he made to move forward, recovering himself with a faint groan and putting one hand against the wall for support. The lay brother was deep concern in a moment.

"Thou art in pain, Illustrious One?" he stammered, approaching.

"Aie! It will pass, but do thou give me thy arm."

The lay brother was only too ready to do anything which would bring him under the favourable notice of one such as the Black Abbot, who was even more powerful than the Resident Abbot, so he quickly placed himself so that Blake's arm could lie across his shoulder. And in this fashion did Sexton Blake succeed in traversing the various courtyards through which one must pass to reach the great inner hall of the monastery.

There he paused, noting that there was only one other lay brother in sight. He did not know how many would be on night duty, but he had chosen this hour as being the safest, and one which would not be so likely to bring him into contact with the Resident Abbot or his assistants, unless they felt in duty bound to rise and extend personal welcome to the Black Abbot. It was this he was trying to avoid as he leant against the long, stone table, breathing shortly as if finding it difficult to get his breath.

"Thou wilt remain with me," he gasped. "My attendant is not with me to-night. I have left a lay brother without, but thou wilt accompany me to my apartments."

"Aie, Illustrious One. Dost desire that the Resident Abbot shall be warned of thy coming? Or that the lay brother of medicine should attend upon thee?"

"I require nothing; my own potions will ease the pain. Let us go."

They moved on again, and through the eye-slits of his mask, Blake noted every item of his surroundings with such care, that should he ever get the chance to return, he would be able to find his way even were it dark. The illumination was only from a couple of large stone basins filled with oil which hung from the beams above, and out of which dangled a few cotton dips, but it was enough to drive the shadows back into the corners, and be sure Sexton Blake was tensely on the qui vive when the lay brother murmured something and bent forward towards what looked like an oblong of burnished silver plates in the wall.

But when he slid the great panel back Blake saw a passage stretching before him. A further journey along this brought them to another silver door, and then something struck to the depths of Sexton Blake's heart as he stepped over the threshold into a bare chamber.

A TORCH burned in a stone socket beneath a narrow opening which served as a window; a stone table and bench stood almost in the centre; a wooden food bowl and stone carafe were on the table. That was all. It was the cell of an ascetic; it was the cell of the Black Abbot. Sexton Blake knew that, at last after months of weariness and danger and suffering, he was within the walls which would render up that which he sought —or would form his tomb.

He sank on to the stone bench and placed his elbows on the table, resting his head on his hands as if in great fatigue. The lay brother begged to know if he could be of some further service, but Blake made a gesture of dismissal.

"I wish nothing now," he said hoarsely. "I desire to be left alone. I would meditate. After the dawn I shall be moving. Go thou now, and see that his holiness is not disturbed this night."

"Ho, hang. Illustrious One. Thy servant obeys."

With that the lay brother went out, sliding the door after him. At last Blake was alone, but not even when he knew that the other must have reached the great hall did he move. Nor even when a full quarter of an hour had gone by had he changed his position. He was waiting to make sure that the Residential Abbot had not been roused. What he had to do now needed complete freedom from interference.

But at the end of that time Blake stirred. Lifting his head, he rose and stole to the panel by which the lay brother had passed out. He bent his head close and listened. Not a sound reached him, but while he still stood thus he heard a distant gong clang brazenly. It must be the half-hour after midnight being struck somewhere within the monastery.

Then he straightened up and began a tour of the cell. He soon discovered there were two more doors, one exactly opposite the stone table and the other on the right. He managed to open the former, finding that it revealed a flight of stone steps which led down. He closed the panel and made for the other. The first might lead to the inner place he was seeking, but he would see first what the second revealed.

And then, as he slid back the great panel and gazed into a vast apartment which was lighted from three filigree lamps, Sexton Blake knew that, at long last, he was gazing upon the innermost lair of the Black Abbot of Cheng-tu —of Prince Wu Ling, the mighty Manchu, and his inveterate enemy.

If the Golden Book of Buddha rested within the walls of the Monastery of Sublime Ways, then here it would it be found.

Blake stepped cautiously over the threshold and stood gazing in careful, methodical fashion at the amazing array of laboratory equipment, scientific instruments both ancient and modern, great piles of ancient tomes which had never before been seen by Western eyes, and the rest of the paraphernalia which filled the place.

It was one of the most wonderful retreats he had ever gazed upon, and gradually as he passed round the room, identifying first this and then that item of the equipment, he realised that here indeed did Wu Ling have a place fit for his mental activities.

Once before in a monastery on an island in Tung Ting Lake, which lies south of the Yangtse some distance above Hankow, Blake had seen in operation the amazing system of television as perfected many centuries ago by Chinese scientists. Therefore, he quickly recognised the use of the green slab which stood at one side of the room, and now he had the answer to the riddle of the persistency with which he and Tinker had been trailed up the river by the black monk who had succeeded in following them as far as Anking, and almost destroying them at that point.

Wu Ling had been keeping track of their movements through this self-same instrument.

Had he dared to spend the time, Blake would have put the mechanism into operation now, but every moment was as a precious jewel just then. His objective was still to be found, and then came the greater problem of getting out of the monastery.

He continued his tour until he came to a great lacquered stand which stood behind some saffron silk curtains in one corner of the apartment. Drawing aside the curtains so as to admit further light, Blake started forward with a suppressed cry as he saw, reposing on a thick cushion of yellow silk brocade, a beautifully lacquered box or ark.

With a hand that trembled despite his efforts to control his nerves, he lifted the lid of the ark, and then his breath exhaled in one deep contraction of the lungs and violent leap of the heart as he saw under his eyes the object of all his strivings since entering China — the sacred Golden Book of Buddha!

THERE it lay before him in all its wonderful sheen.

In actual weight of pure gold metal it would not be more than thirty pounds; but as a relic of Great Buddha who had walked the earth many centuries ago, it was certainly the most priceless relic in existence.

There lay the symbol of all power in the Buddhist world; there was that which held the inscribed writings of Buddha dictated, it is said, while he still lived among men.

With a reverence that could not have been exceeded by the Grand Lama himself, Blake stepped closer and put out both hands until they rested on the metal which, strangely enough, seemed warm against the flesh. Then he lifted it out and carefully raised the upper cover of the "book" —the first of his race and creed to do so, and, with the exception of Sir Gordon Saddler and Tinker, the last. Within, he found the "pages" to be wondrously thin sheets of beaten metal, inscribed in ancient characters which seemed as clear-cut as they must have been when first written there.

With infinite care Blake turned page after page, revelling as only the true antiquarian can over such a treasure. Then he closed it, and replaced it within its lacquered ark. Not now was he to revel in all the thrills which that ancient tome could give; ahead of him lay a dangerous journey, and no time must be lost.

But, standing there beside that ark, Sexton Blake vowed that he would pass beyond those stone walls with the Golden Book, or die in the attempt.

The ark was a weighty burden to carry, but he dared not discard it for fear of damage to the priceless book. So, bearing it in his arms, he took one last look round this hidden lair of Wu Ling's, wondering as he did so when he and the Black Abbot would again come face to face. Then he stole towards the door through which he had entered.

Passing through, he set the casket on the stone table, and was just in the act of closing the panel which communicated with the great inner room when a sudden sound came from behind.

Turning sharply, Blake saw a movement of the panel through which he had entered with the lay brother, and now the same man reappeared.

By the expression of his face, Blake knew that something had happened in the interval. The man was nervous and ill at ease, and at sight of the masked figure faltered in his step. But then he stammered:

"Your pardon. Illustrious One, but the honourable Abbot wishes audience of thee. A message has come by the speaking wires which puzzles the honourable one's thoughts."

In a flash Blake knew what had happened.

Even though this great monastery was a relic of the distant past, it possessed, probably for Wu Ling's convenience, a private telegraph wire. It was this the brother meant when he mentioned the "speaking wires," and intuitively, Blake felt that some warning had reached the Resident Abbot. It was now or never.

He did not answer, but, stepping forward quickly, hurled himself upon the lay brother. That astonished individual went down without opposition under the attack, and Blake made short work of reducing him to a semi-conscious state.

Next he dragged him into the inner apartment, where he securely bound and gagged him.

Leaving him on the floor he reentered the cell, gathered up the ark, and opening the other panel, stepped into the corridor. He strode swiftly along this until he came to the second panel, which gave admittance to the great hall.

Here he knew was his next great danger. If the Resident Abbot had had his suspicions aroused, he would by now have alarmed the other monks and lay brothers. On the other hand, if he had had some word warning him in vague terms, he might wait to speak to the one who, from what the lay brother had told him, he could only think must be the Black Abbot himself.

Sliding open the panel, he stepped into the great hall, finding himself at the end opposite the archway which led to the first courtyard. At first he could see no sign of anyone, but as he made his way towards the archway, keeping close to the wall, he espied a second lay brother moving towards him.

Blake did not pause in his stride. He kept on steadily until he knew from the manner of the other that he was gazing at him in amazement. Blake did not give him time to think.

In one swift movement he laid the ark on the stone floor and leaped. He landed close beside the other, and while that individual still goggled at him, Blake's fist caught him clean on the point of the jaw.

(Don't miss the closing instalments —now imminent.)

Part 18.

The closing phases of our popular Sexton Blake-in-China serial.

Backs Turned on Cheng-tu.

THE man went down with a crash, rolled partially over, and lay as he had fallen. He would take no further interest in the proceedings for another twenty minutes at least.

Snatching up the ark, Blake broke into a run. He reached the archway and entered the courtyard beyond. Next came another courtyard, a short passage through a more massive archway, and then he was in the third and outer courtyard.

On the other side were the great gates which still stood between him and freedom —and possible safety.

Still running, staggering somewhat from the hampering weight of the ark, Blake was almost across the outer courtyard when suddenly the night was shattered by the harsh clanging of a great bell somewhere in the massive dome of the monastery. It was like the alarm bell of a prison when a convict has scaled the walls and is fleeing for his life. But in Blake's case the outer wall still stood as a barrier.

Blake reached the gates and set down his burden. Then he began frantically to fumble at the chains, not knowing just how they were secured. One went down with a clatter, and then a stiff iron bar gave him considerable difficulty. From outside he heard Tinker's voice raised in English.

"Is it you —is it you, guv'nor?"

He answered the anxious call with a reckless shout; then he tore at the bars until they fell with a metallic clatter, one after the other, on to the stone. Over his shoulder he could see a crowd of robed figures coming with an array of torches.

They still did not seem to realise the truth yet, but when they saw the lone figure by the gates they guessed that something serious was afoot. With one accord they broke into a run.

It was at this point that Blake, dragging from inside, and Tinker pushing with all his weight from outside, managed to get one of the big gates open a few inches. Still they strained at it until there was a space of some inches. Blake caught up the ark once more, and pushed it through to the lad.

"Take it —quick!" he charged him, "Make for the sampan —if I don't follow on your heels, keep on —you know what to do. Go!"

SEXTON BLAKE bent, and, catching up one of the iron bars, hurled it with all his force towards the oncoming crowd of monks and lay brothers. The bar crashed into the front ranks, evoking cries of pain. The whole mass paused in amazement, and seizing his chance, Blake sent a second and third bar into them.

Under this savage attack the peaceful monks retreated a little, but just then there appeared three other figures coming rapidly through the archway. The Resident Abbot and two assistant abbots were on the scene, and even above the clanging of the great alarm bell, Blake could hear the stern voice of the Resident Abbot whipping the monks into action.

Blake seized a fourth bar which he sent crashing into their ranks with unerring aim. He could have squeezed through the opening before this, but he was fighting a rearguard action so that Tinker would be given full chance to reach the sampan.

Now, however, as the furious and alarmed Resident Abbot fell upon his monks, Blake struggled through the opening, and without waiting to try and close the gate, set off at a run for the steps.

He took these three at a time, reckless in the darkness whether he went headlong or not. But some guardian spirit seemed to be with him in that great effort, for he reached the bottom in safety and a few moments later was over the side of the sampan, which Tinker was holding ready for him.

Scarcely had Blake's foot come over the side than the lad pushed off, sculling frantically in the direction of Fenghi-an-kani's garden bank, Blake snatched up an oar and joined him, but already the city was being roused by the continued clanging of the alarm bell at the monastery.

The sampan struck the garden bank so furiously that the nose of the craft buried itself in the mud. Tinker leapt ashore with the precious ark, and as Blake landed beside him, the bulky figure of Fenghi-an-kani loomed up in the gloom.

Now only three or four of the coloured paper lanterns made effort at illumination, but it was enough for them to see the features of the mandarin.

"Thou hast returned," he gasped. "Thou hast succeeded?"

"Aie! But the whole pack is in full cry," answered Blake.

"This mad thing has been done," cried the merchant.

314

With that he led them to where a small but very modern motor-boat lay moored.

"Take it, and go quickly," he said. "Thou wilt find provisions, water, arms, and money. It is all that Fenghi-an-kani can do. Go quickly, and may Allah guard thee on the way. If thou ever dost lay thine honourable eyes on my kinsman, thou wilt tell him?"

"Aie! He shall know that thou art indeed worthy to be kinsman of the Terror of the Yangtse."

The mandarin sighed.

In that moment he would have given much to be of the life which could do these things. But they were not for the staid merchant mandarin of Cheng-tu.

So he stood and watched while Blake and Tinker leaped into the motor-boat, which appeared to them as nothing less than a miraculous godsend.

Tinker, who was an expert on internal combustion engines, found to his relief that he had the familiar stroke of a Kelvin to deal with. He started the engine up, and as it spluttered, Blake jumped for the tiller, and they shot out into the river.

A last dim sight of Fenghi-an-kani they had then, while the great alarm bell at the monastery filled the night with harsh sound, they went racing down on the full sweep of the current which they had toiled and fought against for a thousand miles since Shanghai, but which now, in their desperate need, was going to give them the friendly aid of its mighty thrust.

PROBABLY never before had any craft covered the five hundred miles from Cheng-tu to Chungking in the record time which Tinker set up in that motor-boat.

From the moment he first jumped into the cockpit until they came in sight of Chungking he did not once leave the engine, even taking his food in the cloud of oily spray which was flung about him, and snatching his spell of sleep on the bottom boards.

In addition to the regular sweep of the current of the great river, they were riding on the advance crest of the great annual floods which had just come tumbling down the sides of the Baian Karas —they were a mere chip on the seething torrent which was racing eastwards and, in addition to their need to leave Cheng-tu far behind, they were striving to make the gorges before those terrible canyons should be filled with this new flood, even now racing down on them from astern.

Fenghi-an-kani had done nobly by them. Down in the small shelter forward they found food and warm clothing, arms, and a variety of other useful articles, and there the precious lacquered ark containing the Golden Book of Buddha reposed, until they came in sight of Chungking.

Here, if Kan-tse-wen had kept his word, they should find waiting another power boat to take them through the gorges. Blake was anxious to pick up this craft, for he knew that the pirate would have been certain to send with it a trustworthy pilot to run them through the gorges —a passage which would have to be made at terrific speed among the myriad pinnacles of rocks which jutted throughout the stone canyons.

Nor did Kan-tse-wen fail them.

On an evening when they sighted the waterfront of Chungking they saw a small power-boat coming upstream in their direction. As it drew nearer it cut across their course and flung over the side in full view the blue and white colours of the "Terror of the Yangtse." That was enough for Blake and Tinker. At a word from Blake the lad slowed down the engine, and in a few moments the other craft was alongside. For ten days, they learned, had this agent of Kan-tse-wen been watching every craft that came down the river, and now he was at their service.

Blake did not hesitate about the transfer. While the two boats floated side by side on the current, he and Tinker threw in the few things they wished to take along, including, of course, the ark of the Golden Book, then Blake fixed the tiller of the smaller boat, while Tinker dragged out the throttle to full speed ahead.

It seemed a pity to send such a noble little craft to destruction, but it was the only way, and as they flung themselves clear it shot away, heading towards the opposite bank at ever-gathering speed.

Soon it would dash itself to pieces against the rocks above Chungking, and if the remains were found there was just a chance that it would be believed the two fugitives from Cheng-tu had perished with it.

Then they were off once more, and the following morning began the rush down through Mitan Gorge.

Neither Blake nor Tinker can ever forget the journey from the top of Mitan Gorge to the bottom, on through rapids and lesser gorges, until at last they reached the Ichang Gorge, and then the mad race through the rocks of Tiger's Teeth Gorge.

As they rushed past the trackers camps at each point, startled eyes watched them plunge into and out of view; down through the roaring cataracts, they shot past junks which were being dragged painfully up, with a speed that was terrific.

Yet not once did that hand of their pilot falter on the tiller. It seemed miracle after miracle that they could plunge through and in and about those jagged points of rock without being impaled upon them.

Yet they slid through in safety, and leaving Ichang of evil memory on their left, kept on down the river.

Not until they eventually made Changcha, several more hundreds of miles east, did Sexton Blake learn the full truth of what had happened at Ichang.

There he found Kan-tse-wen watching for their arrival. Few words were said between Blake and the pirate, but sufficient passed in glance and handclasp to cement more strongly than ever the deep bond between them.

To Kan-tse-wen, Blake owed as much as to any living being. The pirate had resolutely faced and taken prisoner the strongest man in China for the sake of his blood-brother; and at Changcha Wu Ling still remained, for Kan-tse-wen had sworn that if his blood-brother, Sek-i-ton Bal-akee, did not return from the upper river, then never again should Wu Ling walk the world in freedom.

The conclusion of this story appears next week.

Kelvin engined boat circ 1920s /drf

Part 19.

Concluding Instalment.

Homeward Bound.

BLAKE did not seek an interview with Wu Ling during the few days he and Tinker spent at Changcha. His sole desire was to continued down the Yangtse to Shanghai, and make some arrangements for getting his precious cargo out of China.

Wu Ling might be individually helpless for the time being, but after their daring raid on the Monastery of Sublime Ways at Cheng-tu, and their escape, he knew that a flood of black-robed ravens would be hurrying down the river to use any and every means to intercept them.

Now that they had accomplished so much after all the dangers and terrible privations they had survived it would have been heart-breaking to lose the prize they had won. Not until he knew that priceless book was safely on its way to the Dalai Lama at Tibet would Sexton Blake breathe easier, and certainly not until the coast of the Empire of the Dragon was far behind him and Tinker would either of them sleep at night.

But Kan-tse-wen had not finished providing Blake with surprises.

He did not reveal his latest effort until the detective and his assistant had rested at Changcha for a full three days. But on the fourth morning he took them to a wide plain outside the city which was his stronghold; and there, under cover of a great canvas tent, he showed them an object which was part of recent loot.

It was nothing less than a pile of many great cases containing the parts of a military aeroplane.

"Thou hast talked in the past of many flights, O my brother," he said, after telling of its capture. "It came to me that thou couldst make use of it for speedy passage to Shanghai. Men —as many as thou desirest —are at thy service, if thou shouldst wish to use it."

The thing was a godsend, and forthwith Blake and Tinker with a score of men set to work to assemble the plane.

In a week they made a trial flight, and the day after that they bade farewell to Kan-tse-wen, circling thrice round the city of Changcha in compliment to the bloodthirsty pirate who was, at the same time, their warm friend and in his heart of hearts a friend of their race.

Anking nor Nanking possessed no terrors for them now. Those

teeming centres were left far beneath them as they raced east in the light bomber which had originally been intended for the Chinese Nationalist forces.

It was about ten o'clock in the morning when they hopped off at Changcha, and just after four that same afternoon when they landed easily on the Shanghai racecourse.

Half an hour later they were on their way to the residence of Hsui-fsi, and that elderly gentleman was just being served his afternoon tray of Suchong when his two visitors arrived. As they stepped out on to the upper verandah where he sat, he came to his feet, gazing at them as if they were ghosts.

"You —it is you!" he stammered. "I —I thought you were both dead!"

"Not yet, Sir Gordon," answered Blake, with a smile, as they shook hands. "But between ourselves Wu Ling nearly succeeded in accomplishing just that. But I need something urgently, Sir Gordon." went on Blake in a low tone. "I have got it, and I want it placed in the vaults of the Hong Kong and Shanghai Bank without delay."

For the first time Sir Gordon took note of the wooden box which Tinker had placed just inside the door. He stared at it in silence for some moments. Then his old wise eyes sought Blake's.

"Do you mean —in that box —you have —it?"

"I mean it," answered Blake quietly. "We went into the Monastery of Sublime Ways at Cheng-tu to bring out the Golden Book of Buddha, and we have done so. But if you will dine us at the club to-night I shall tell you all about it. I think I would almost brave Cheng-tu again for a civilised meal."

It seemed impossible for Hsui-fsi to grasp that the Golden Book of Buddha actually reposed inside that plain wooden box, but a little later —after he had sent word to the manager of the Hong Kong and Shanghai Bank asking him to make a special appointment at the bank, in spite of the fact that it was past the officially closing hour —when the little group stood in the manager's private room he saw that Blake had spoken nothing but fact.

For the first and last time in his life Hsui-fsi gazed upon that sacred tome, the existence of which many believed to be but a myth. Not even the manager looked upon its sacred sheen, for, at the moment when Blake opened the ark, he was in the vaults preparing a place for its reception.

When it had been safely locked away, Blake and Tinker returned with Sir Gordon to his house, where they would remain until the following, day.

As soon as he ascertained that he could catch a Jardine-Matheson boat down to Hong Kong and connect with a British India steamer there for Colombo, Blake decided that he and the lad and the precious ark should go that way.

They were glad enough to rest until evening, but that night at the Shanghai Club, clad once more in the formal whites that the Briton wears out East, he and the lad took turns in giving the old baronet a description of all that had befallen them since they had left him in Shanghai and had plunged down into the bowels of the earth among the People of the Pits.

Old as he was in intrigue, and many as had been the experiences of that long, eventful life of his, Sir Gordon had never listened to such a tale.

It was an epic of the race in the inmost maze of the realm of the yellow dragon, and, when Blake had finished his modestly-told tale, Sir Gordon knew that while he himself might have done this thing in his younger days, Sexton Blake was then the only man who was capable of carrying through such a terrible task.

Nor was Sir Gordon forgetting for a moment the gallant part Tinker had played in the long battle against odds.

His voice quavered a little with emotion as he lifted his glass, and pledged them each in the finest bottled sunshine the club cellars could produce.

THE following day the two weary adventurers got away on the Kwai Sang, taking their precious charge with them. It had been arranged that Sir Gordon was to get in touch by cable with the Grand Lama at Tibet, and by the time Blake and Tinker reached Hong Kong he hoped to be able to advise them how the ark would be taken charge of.

They did hear at Hong Kong, being advised that a strong personal mission was being sent to Colombo by the Dalai Lama to receive the ark from Blake, and at that port the precious casket and golden book were handed over.

And it was with a deep sigh of relief that they saw at last the Golden Book of Buddha in the hands of those in whose charge it rightfully should be. Their eyes held a look of quiet content as they faced the westering sun which shone across the Indian Ocean, for there was Home —and never before had either yearned more for a sight of it.

Yet each knew that in the famous "Index" at Baker Street this case must go down to record as probably the greatest Blake had ever tackled. Certainly, Tinker felt it was the riskiest thing in which he had ever had a share.

NOT until nearly a year later did Sexton Blake find it possible to obey the summons of the Grand Lama to proceed to Tibet. But business in India some time after the long affair in China made it possible for him and the lad to obey the "command."

There was no difficulty about permission from the Indian Government, in the face of that direct invitation, so it came about that on a certain day some weeks later, when the mighty snow-clad peaks of the Himalayas were gleaming under a brilliant sun, the two stood in the great audience chamber of the Grand Lama's palace at Tibet.

Then it was that the Diamond Cross of the Inner Shrine was hung about Blake's neck by the Grand Lama himself; and on Tinker's finger was placed the Sapphire Ring of the Sacred Fleece —the possession of which the lad is proudest above all others.

Thus was there fitting end to the last journey of the sacred Golden Book of Great Buddha.

THE END.
[129,300 WORDS]

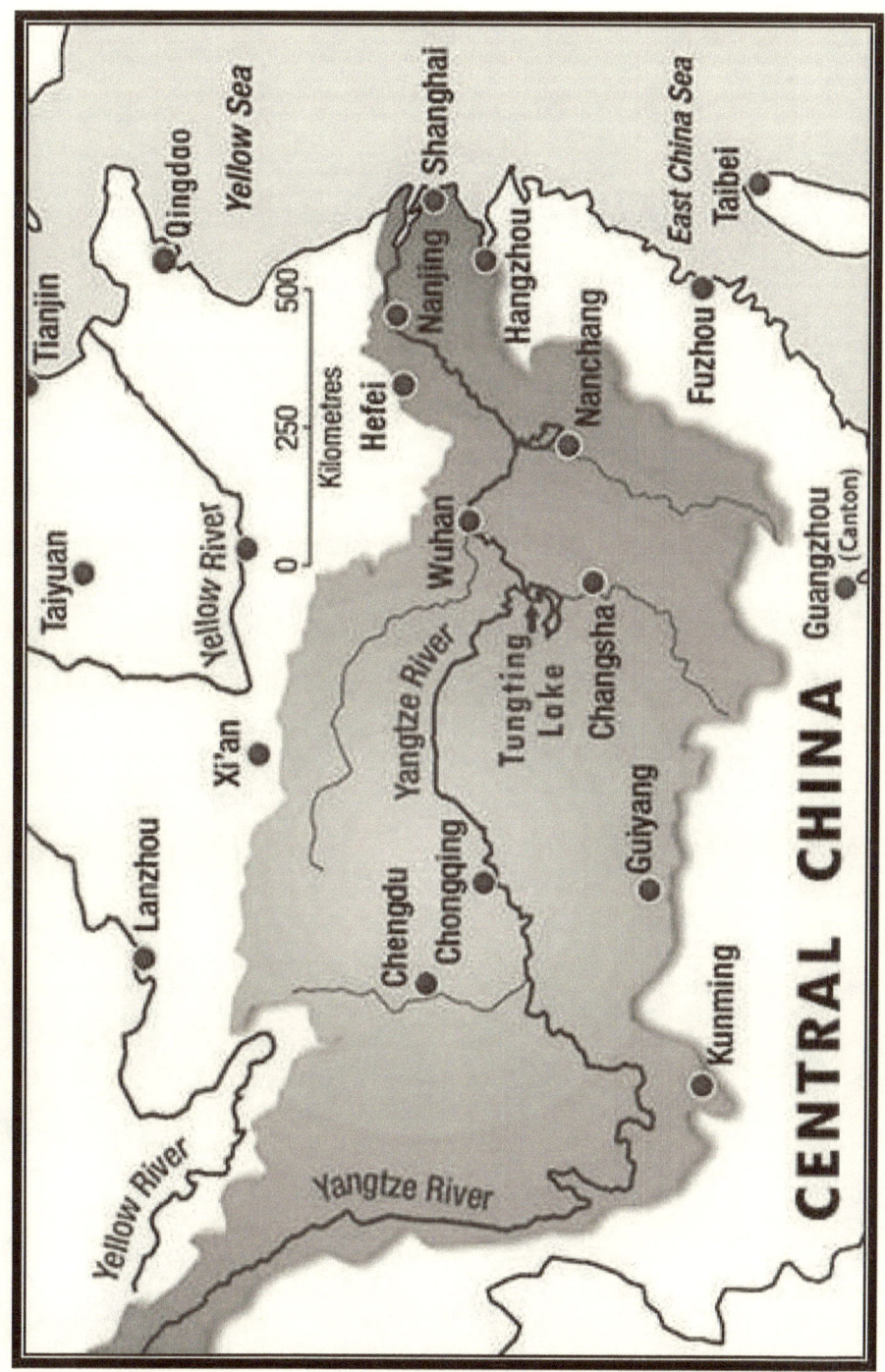

Tianjin

Qingdao

Yellow Sea

Shanghai

Nanjing

Hangzhou

East China Sea

Taibei

Taiyuan

500

250

Kilometres

Hefei

Nanchang

Fuzhou

0

Yellow River

Wuhan

Guangzhou
(Canton)

Xi'an

Yangtze River

Tungting
Lake

Changsha

Lanzhou

Chengdu

Chongqing

Guiyang

CENTRAL CHINA

Kunming

Yellow River

Yangtze River

www.ingramcontent.com/pod-product-compliance
Lightning Source LLC
Chambersburg PA
CBHW060422030726
47495CB00003B/695